rules are there to be broken

BASQUE

LOVE STORIES

HJ FURL *HJfurl*

First Published in Great Britain 2021 by Mirador Publishing

First edition: 2021

A copy of this work is available through the British Library.

ISBN: 978-1-913833-86-2

Mirador Publishing
10 Greenbrook Terrace
Taunton
Somerset
UK
TA1 1UT

BASQUE

LOVE STORIES

HJ FURL

For my true friends

CONTENTS

Heathen

That I can live my life with you, is all that I can pray.
That I can learn to love you more every passing day,
That you will find fulfilment in all the things we do,
That we enjoy the happiness which lives in love so true,
That when you go to heaven, I'm waiting there for you.

Wednesday 7th December 1644: daybreak.

THE PEASANT UTTERED AN EAR-piercing howl, a wounded animal, slumping on a wooden seat. His bloodied mouth kissed his bare chest. Both of his wrists were securely tied to the arms of the chair, palms down. Wright let go of the finger on the right hand, which stood proud: broken at the knuckle, pointing at the thatched roof, as the young man raised his head and cried,

'I know not where she is!'

Rogers stepped forward to embrace him, holding his wailing head to his chest, stroking his wet hair until he had calmed. He gripped the boy's bleeding chin, forcing back his head.

The farmhouse was a timber-frame barn without windows. A fire burned in its hearth, fending out the winter chill. There was a sturdy oak table, a few chairs, an unmade bed in the corner, raggedy bedding strewn on the floor: where the young girl slept.

'Where is she, lad?'

There was no answer. Rogers glanced at Wilding standing at the open door surveying the yard. The heathen eked out a meagre life. A few hens and geese ran free in the toft, a small drove of pigs grazed their muddy croft at the rear. They owned a horse which grazed a strip of grass beyond the toft. There was a dovecote. And a stable with a haybarn that opened out onto the yard. From where Wilding perched, it was impossible for the girl to escape without being seen. It would take the men minutes to find her, but his bloodthirsty accomplices had to have their evil way. He sighed reluctantly, then nodded.

Rogers grasped the scruff of the peasant's hair and tugged at his head, baring his face to Wright, who landed a haymaker punch on the lad's nose, shattering the bones in the bridge in an instant, sending thick plumes of blood gushing out of his nostrils. He convulsed, fitting with the pain.

The young girl hid under the bed trembling, shuddering, weeping in fear, her mouth covered to stifle her cries, horrified at the boy's torment.

Wright took a finger and prised it upwards, enjoying the crack of knuckle, his deafening wail,

'I know not where she is!'

Soon, he ran out of patience, 'Damn you, boy! Shall I break all the bones in your body?'

Wilding stepped in, seeing him falter, dragged Wright off the brat, pushed Rogers aside, and held the lad's hysterical face in his hands,

'In the name of God! Where is she?'

'She is hiding, in our barn…'

The heathen was dragged kicking and screaming from the barn, her teeth chattering with cold.

Rogers, seizing her crudely from behind, clamped his large, hairy hand over her small mouth,

'Be quiet, child, or I'll cut out your tongue.'

He felt her wriggles subside, felt her calm, save for her shivering. She quivered as, holding her tight, he ran his hand down her thigh, drew up her skirt, and felt her soft, bare skin. He saw her blue feet. The girl was barefoot. On such a cold and drizzly day. Rogers felt for her,

'Take you to a warm inn, eh?'

She nodded. He removed his hand. His fingertips were wet. She was crying. It started to rain.

'Best we be going, eh, girl?' Wilding smiled.

They forced her arms behind her back and bound her wrists with twine. Rain washed over her, drenching her, matting her hair, trickling down her face, her neck. She stared into the cloudy heavens, praying to herself:

That I can live my life with you, is all that I can pray.

The men slipped a hand under her armholes, appreciating her warmth, and walked her across the puddled yard. She cocked her head. No sound came from the farmhouse. They hoisted her onto the back of a cart like a sack of swede, then sat by her side. Wright untethered his shire horse, took the reins, and they made off down the muddy rutted track. The heathen took a last longing look at her home, pining for the boy, praying for the girl, bowing her sad head, fearful for her life.

They reached the outskirts of Alting. It was market day, but the filthy, puddled, pot-holed road was empty. She felt the villagers' eyes studying her from behind their gloomy panes. Felt their intense hatred of her. Wright pulled sharply on the reins and the cart drew up in front of the Red Lion Inn, a timber-beamed haunt with double-width leaded windows either side of a wide black door. There was a square transom window over the door.

Rogers and Wilding manhandled the bedraggled girl off her seat, dragging her through a sludge of stinking human excrement that constituted a gutter, hauling her to the doorway. One of them clamped a hand over her mouth,

'Not a sound, child, do you hear?'

She nodded. Wilding lifted a wrought iron latch, shoving the heavy oak door open, and stepped inside. Being over six-feet tall he bowed his head to avoid the duck and grouse beam, inscribed with the year 1539, on the way in. Rogers followed with her. Both men took it in turn to stamp their boots and shake the rain off their capes. Majestically, they swept off their broad-brimmed hats.

The common room was a mishmash of boards to sit at and forms (benches, three-legged stools) to sit upon. At the centre of the room was a roaring hearth. By the fireside was a high-backed settle. Sitting on the settle, nursing his frothy mug of ale while wolfing down chunks of bread and cheese, was the sternest, most imposing character the girl had ever seen. A florid bear of a man with long greasy black hair (his own, not a wig), plain black coat, waistcoat, short trousers, stockings, square-toed court shoes with dumpy heels. He watched Rogers and Wilding lead the heathen past him, the closed door to the kitchen, the stone steps leading to the beer cellar, then disappear up a narrow, winding staircase. Other than the Puritan, the place was empty.

By now the girl was petrified. The short stairs led to a cramped landing with an uneven wooden floor. There were three doors, each of a different shape and size. Rogers pushed at the smallest door and pulled her inside. The room had a low, slanting ceiling. Wilding stooped. The heathen recognized the small, leaded transom window. There was a neatly made bed, a welcome fire burned in the hearth. Rogers kindly untied her wrists so that she could kneel by the flames and warm herself. She felt the heat on her rosy cheeks, smelled the smoke, loved the crackling sound of the little fire, feeling herself relax. Exhausted, Julia Pettitt slumped on the bare wood floor and drifted off to sleep.

* * * * *

ALICE, A PRETTY LITTLE THING with frizzy red hair, freckles, and holes pierced in her tongue, left it till she was sure the rogues had departed before she slid out from under the bed. He was sliding off the chair, slumped, unconscious, his head resting on his bloody chest. The girl let out a tiny scream when she saw his bent fingers,

'Oh Seth, what've they done to you?'

There was no immediate reply. She smiled and spoke to herself. Alice always spoke to herself, her make-believe friends, her gods, whenever she played their strange, pagan games in the toft,

'Soon be right as rain!'

She giggled, skipped outside to the yard, fetching a pail of water from the wishing well, walked up to the wretched boy, and threw the lot over his head. He stirred with a jump and a start. The girl laughed, her mischievous eyes filled with play, and merriment, sweet, childish innocence,

'There! Woke you, didn't I!'

The lad lifted his broken head, drawing gasps from Alice when she saw his misshapen nose. He went to speak. She pressed her soft little fingers to his lips. Then, very gently, the girl placed her hands over his face, making him wince with pain, and held them there. Alice stared at the ceiling, then she started to chant,

> *Bless this boy with all my heart,*
> *Bless him till the clouds do part,*
> *Sun, shine on you through the rain,*
> *Heal your wounds and end your pain.*

She lifted her hand and spread her arms upwards. Rays of sunlight poured through the open window, warming, healing the boy, soothing his tortured soul. At first, he was frightened. But what happened next was beyond his comprehension. He felt the shattered bones in his nose mend, shaping his new bridge without pain. Felt his knuckles mend. His upturned fingers bent, bowed, and stretched. Alice ran out to the well and returned with more ice-cold water, some dirty rags. She rubbed him clean: his face, bloodied chest, and stomach; she dried him with her cloths. He closed his eyes and fell into a deep slumber. Seth found peace at last. Not poor Alice though… she went off and sat on the bed, covering her face with her hands, and wept for Julia.

I don't like it here. Something evil, terrible, will happen to her here, near the dark forest, in his alehouse, in the pond, by the old oak tree.

* * * * *

'WAKE UP, GIRL!'

'Wake up, child!'

They woke her at sunset. Julia saw her captors, joined by the squat, muscly man who drove the horse and cart - and the Puritan. The huge man announced himself grandly as Gareth Hopkins, then introduced his three assistants, Callum Rogers, Royston Wilding, Matthew Wright. When he informed Julia that she was to be investigated and discovered, her heart sank into her belly. She began to cry. All hope was lost.

As the sun set, Julia heard a commotion in the common room beneath her feet: mobs of rowdy, beer-swigging men, shrieking barmaids granting them favours. Her stomach rumbled. She was famished, thirsty, hadn't eaten or drunk since daybreak. There was an empty bucket beside the bed, filthy rags to rub herself with. She squatted over the bucket, lifted up her skirt, and soiled the pail as the coarse men stared. Rain strummed on the glass panes. Her life was misery itself.

Hopkins left shortly afterwards, leaving the men in black to taunt her. They subjected Julia to sleep deprivation that night, prodding, nudging, cajoling her as she lay, fully dressed, on the bed, in the hope that they might extract confessions from her lips,

'Confess to us, girl!'

Julia could not confess. She was starved hungry, her throat was parched, she could not ask for food and water.

Hopkins returned at sunrise. Exhausted, Julia perched on the edge of the bed while Rogers cut her left arm with a blunt knife. She did not bleed. Rogers pulled her off the bed, forcing her to stand in front of Hopkins,

'You won't bleed. Confess to me, child,' he demanded.

Her mind filled with dread at the thought of the ordeal that lay ahead of her. Julia longed to lie with Seth, to play strange games in the toft with Alice. Defiant, she stared Hopkins in the eye.

'Take off your clothes, girl.'

She shook her head.

'Do what he says, child!' Wilding hissed.

'Take off your clothes,' Hopkins repeated, pointing at Rogers, 'Or he will!'

Julia turned her head and saw the dirty leer spread over his face. She recalled how he held her. How he ran his hand up her thigh, drew up her skirt, felt her soft, bare skin. She felt sick in her belly. Julia quivered, trembling, shaking with cold fear.

The heathen was wearing a thick, warm, dull red linen bodice with a skirt she made herself. Slowly, she untied the spiral-bound laces holding her bodice together, pulled the garment open, slipping it off her shoulders, tugging her arms out of the sleeves, letting it drop to the floor. The fire blazed and crackled in the hearth, but Julia felt no warmth, only shame. Julia was wearing a shift, a light linen slip, under her bodice. Her eyes met her captor's. She looked into his icy stare imploringly. Calm, unsmiling, obsessed by his perverse quest for purity, goodness.

Julia untucked the shift from under her skirt, then pulled the garment off over her head, baring her ample breasts. Her nipples protruded like shiny bronzed buttons, stiffened hard by her fear.

'Now there *is* a pretty sight,' Wright observed wryly.

'Quiet!'

Hopkins moved in close to her, so close she could smell the stale ale and cheese on his breath,

'I have to discover your mark.'

The mark which all witches were said to possess, a mark that was said to be dead to all feeling: a mole, a birthmark, an extra nipple. Julia cupped her breasts, showing him her nipples, the soft undersides, then she held them apart, so that he could feel her crease. He traced an index finger down her chest. Rogers and Wright moved intimately close to watch him examine her. But her skin was free of moles, spots, and pimples. Her nipples were perfectly formed, evenly coloured,

She looked at the four men hopefully.

'I have to find your mark,' Hopkins insisted, without the slightest trace of emotion.

She finally wilted.

Today was going to be a beautiful winter's day, on the outside. Harsh sunlight streamed through the glass casting shards of light, unseasonal radiant warmth, on Julia's skin. Her interrogators made her stand in the sunbeam so that the witchfinder could appreciate her beautiful body.

He made her bow her head. She rested her chin on her chest. Then he inspected her scalp. Hopkins parted her fine, blonde hair inch-by-inch, meticulously searching her pale scalp for a sign: 666, to no avail. Julia felt his fingers: smooth, soft, and warm, behind her ears, brushing the hair from her eyes. She had lice. Her ears were filled with dirt. But he wasn't disgusted.

The Heathen were notorious for their lice, fleas, disgusting intestinal worms, their pestilence,

'Put your hands on your head.'

Julia obeyed him, clasping her hands behind her head, staring him in the eye as he lifted her chin with one finger, inspecting her blackened nostrils. Her eyes were clear, red, sore from lack of sleep, but clear. She opened her mouth for him, parting her dry, cracked lips in order that he could inspect her gums. He made stick out her tongue, she did: her perfectly normal tongue.

He fluffed up the hair at the nape of her neck. There was not a boil, bite, or pimple to be found. Her chest and breasts were perfect with no lesions or sores. Her armholes were flush with bushy fair hair, stinking to high heaven. The soft skin on her stomach, her midriff, her belly were free of blemishes. He inspected her navel: she hid not so much as a freckle. She turned to face the window while he felt her shoulders, back, small of her back, backs of her arms, her hands. Julia had a perfect complexion. There was no sign of the mark. The witchfinder eyed Wilding who shrugged his shoulders. Rogers leered at the girl. Wright looked embarrassed. He gazed at her, admiring her beauty, her resilience. She had not confessed, not yet. But she soon would. They all did in the end. She bathed in the warm sunlight, watching Hopkins's smile, hoping above all hope that she might be set free.

'Take off your skirt and lie on the bed,' he ordered.

Her hopes dashed, she undid her skirt and let it fall to the floor. She was naked, with no panties. Her feet were daubed in dried filth and excrement. Her slender calves were spattered with mud. Wright handed her some rags so she could rub herself clean. His face bore a strange expression, the look of pity. Julia regarded him with a sense of renewed hope. Perhaps, he would make the others see reason. Tell them she was not a witch. Her spirits sank when he shook his head and turned away.

The men pinned her arms and legs to the bed while Hopkins examined her unmentionables for the mark. Tears of humiliation streaked down her cheeks when she felt his fingers inside her. He ordered his witch-pricker, Wilding, to shave Julia's body of all her hair. She squirmed as he plucked the hairs out of her armholes. He made her hurt, like the dickens. Rogers and Wright held her legs apart while he shaved her with a razor-sharp knife. Hopkins examined her shaven pudenda, the cleft between her buttocks, her thighs, calves, feet, toes. But Julia's complexion was unblemished. The witchfinder had failed to find her Devil's mark.

Shortly after sunset, Wilding discovered a third nipple in the crease between her breasts, cutting a circular wound in her flesh with the tip of his knife. As she lay bleeding, they subjected her to further sleep deprivation, in the hope that they might extract confessions from her. Julia knew she was innocent. She was so terrified that she couldn't speak, her dumb pleas for mercy.

Friday 9th December 1644: mid-morning

The embers in the fire's hearth glowed then faded, like Julia's hopes of survival. She stared out of the square window and saw that it was sleeting. Her mouth was parched. She was starving, cold, weak, mindless: she had no mind left of her own. No will. The men dressed her in her bodice and skirt, not the shift. They led her outside onto the muddy road, now known as Simmel Street, strapped her to the seat of Wright's cart, then paraded her, bare headed, through Alting.

The sleet turned to snow. Freezing cold, feverish, shivering, Julia clasped her hands together, closed her eyes, and prayed. Even as she was subjected to the baying mob. Who lined the road in their warm winter cloaks, coats, dresses, hats, and boots, who defiled and mocked her, crying,

'She is a Witch! She is the Witch! Kill her! Kill her! Kill the Witch! Kill the evil Witch!'

Julia prayed, silently, to herself, her gods – the sun, the moon, the sky, the soil, the rain.

'She is the Witch! She is the horrid Witch! Kill her! Kill the Witch! Kill the evil Witch!'

She was carried as far as the village pond, followed by a cruel, merciless crowd. There she was unbound, then dragged kicking and screaming, to the ducking stool: a chair fastened to the end of a pole which the witchfinder used to plunge offenders into the ice-cold pond as punishment. Hopkins waited by the stool. He crouched beside her. As Rogers tied her to the chair, shaking, trembling in the bitter north-east wind, blinking snow from her eyes.

'Confess to me, girl,' he said.

She shook her head.

Hopkins turned to face the angry mob, lying to them,

'She did *not* bleed. She will *not* confess. She has *not* bled. What say all you good people?'

'Guilty! Guilty! Guilty! Guilty!' came their reply.

The Witchfinder General nodded at Wilding, Rogers, and Wright, who clung to the other end of the pole bearing the heathen's full weight. They edged the ducking stool forward, until she was hanging suspended, insane with trepidation, in mid-air above the murky pond, then waited.

'Confess to me, child!' Hopkins thundered.

The young woman shook her head.

'Then go down!'

They lowered her into the icy cold water until she was fully submerged, ducking her for twenty seconds. Hopkins then ordered that the heathen be ducked for periods of forty, fifty, even sixty seconds at a time, till she either confessed, or was drowned.

The crowd thrilled to the spectacle, jeering at Julia, 'Ah, see the poor, little blue girl, dying?'

Each time she emerged from the pond, choking, wheezing, coughing stagnant water, Julia took a deep breath and gazed up at the white vellum sky, as if pleading her innocence. After she had been ducked seven times, to the astonishment of the men in black she suddenly found her voice,

'Father!' she gasped, flailing her white arms, kicking her dripping, wet legs, to gain attention.

Hopkins stared at her wide-eyed, in utter disbelief, 'What is it, child?'

'Bless you, Father!' she wailed, hysterically, 'For you have sinned!'

A murmur of dismay rippled through the crowd, 'Sinned? He sinned? With her? With a Witch?'

'He sinned! With me!' she croaked, 'The Sins of the Flesh! My flesh!'

Hopkins recovered quickly, 'Damn you, lying wench!'

She was dunked again, for her sins, then left to drown. A fading froth of bubbles appeared on the surface of the pond as her lungs filled with water. Once the Puritans were satisfied that the heathen was dead, her body was raised out of the pond, and taken to an old oak tree, where she was hung by the neck, an example to the villagers of the punishment meted out to women who dared to indulge in the occult.

Friday 9th December 1644: nightfall

Julia, an uncommon name in those times, meaning youthful, or love's child, derived from the soft, downy, facial hair that appears on the face of an adolescent girl. Pettitt, from the French *petit*, hung dead for a full eleven hours. It was the peasant, Seth, who cut her off the noose. Her mystical lover, the child-witch Alice, truthful, of noble birth, who breathed fresh life into her:

that she might live to haunt you all

Myrtlesham Halt

Suffolk, 1946:

IT WAS SNOWING WHEN THE train pulled into Myrtlesham Halt. The station was deserted. As the steam lifted, a young man with a large black metal army trunk alighted from the end carriage. He skidded on the icy platform as far as the ticket hall, then slumped on the bench, exhausted. Once he had caught his breath, the man resumed his solitary trek, slipping and sliding his way up the icy hill to the isolated cottage.

* * * * *

SHE MADE UP A FRESH bed, then lit a roaring fire in the hearth. For the first time since her teens, she prettied herself: putting on make-up, curling her grey-streaked hair, dressing in her best floral dress. It had been years since she last entertained a visitor, let alone had a lodger to stay at her picture postcard home.

The modest, pargeted, half-timbered lodge, with its 'duck and grouse' beamed ceilings and creaking floorboards, lay on the outskirts of the charming village of Myrtlesham. She looked out of the kitchen window at the rolling landscape: mud-furrowed potato fields daubed in snow, an 18th century post-mill, the spire of the Church of St Andrew. And, on the horizon, the control tower at the US airbase, a constant reminder of war.

I should think myself lucky, living in such a lovely place. I hope he enjoys his new life here. I get lonely living here by myself.

A delicious scent of home baking filled the kitchen. She prodded a sultana rock cake made with powdered egg and a pinch of fruit to test that it was cooked, permitting herself a treat - and burnt her mouth.

'I generally avoid temptation...unless I can't resist it!' she laughed, justifying her vanity.

She licked her fingers clean and served two cakes onto a china dish decorated with pink roses. The cups, saucers and milk jug were stacked in the kitchen dresser. She couldn't find the teapot or sugar bowl. Her mundane existence was this colourless carnival of such trivia, devoid of excitement.

Since the rumours spread about her husband's death, she seldom went to the village, preferring the life of the hermit. Then the letter arrived out of the blue, from the respectable, hard-working, bandsman in search of board and lodgings – together with a faded photograph.

She shook her head and pulled herself together. Found a coffee pot for the tea and a Chinese finger bowl embossed with jasmine flowers for the sugar. The grandfather clock in the hall chimed three times. She dashed to the larder, fetched her red tea caddy, and blew off the dust. Unscrewed the lid and inhaled the stale aroma of a classic blend of selected teas she bought at Fortnum's - after dragging herself out of the gutter in the only way she knew.

She stared at the painting on the caddy: The Garden Bench by Jacques Tissot, an idyllic summer scene: a mother reclining on a garden bench with her three adorable children. She had married at the age of nineteen, before the outbreak of war. There were no children.

* * * * *

Whitechapel, September 1914:

JIM AND HELEN SHARED A filthy, dark, airless slum with another family. The deprivation they suffered was degrading. They lived from hand-to-mouth in a tiny room with a squalid outside toilet. Street urchins gathered out in the cobbled street, huddles of human hopelessness, vacant faces. Slums were horrible places in which to live, black labyrinths which reeked and swarmed with vermin. No-one dared leave their house after dark; the alleyways crawled with criminals.

The most destitute men like Jim stood shame-faced in the shadows, beyond salvation. Helen Cade was a simple, lively lass who doted on her idle husband. Every day she watched the wretched world go by from behind her grimy window.

When she wasn't cooking, washing, sewing, or mending their clothes she stood under the porch with Jim, waiting for the better times that never came. By contrast, he was an unassuming man who couldn't read or write. He had held a variety of jobs: chopping wood, rag and bone man, coalman. Recently, he hadn't done so much as a hand's turn.

The night before he went off to fight for King and Country, Jim stood in the street, fists clenched, thrilled at his forthcoming adventure. The rain teemed down in silver strands, glistening in the lamplight. He stared at the heavens, soaked to the skin, exhilarated yet afraid. He heard her calling him:

'Come in out of the rain before you catch your death.'

Helen knelt by the bed in her nightie, willing her man to return from the fighting,

'Lord, let my sunny Jim come home safely,' she prayed.

Silently he crept into the room, dripping with rain, listening to her with a heavy heart.

'What was all that about?' Jim said, rocking his wife in his arms.

She felt soft and warm. How he would miss her tenderness.

Helen sobbed, 'I'm scared you won't come back.'

He cradled her head against his chest,

'Course I'll come back. I love you.'

'Dance with me.'

Jim was startled, 'Dance? I can't dance to save my life!'

'I'll show you how. Come here!'

Helen laid her hand on her man's shoulder and pulled his arm sharply round her waist,

'Now just you sing me a luverly song, like you used to Jim.'

He sang her the song men would sing as they languished in the trenches:
They Didn't Believe Me.

They danced into the night until she felt he was ready to love, ready to fight, ready to die for her.

* * * * *

Passchendaele, October 1917:

JIM'S CRIME WAS TO BE found asleep on sentry duty, lying in the sodden mud at the head of the trench. Most of the soldiers endured chronic insomnia and anxiety attacks. The endless death, torrential rain, seeping damp, filth, blood, rat-infested mud, and bloated corpses were enough to drive anyone mad. But Jim was different. He suffered from shellshock. A condition that wasn't recognized at the time. A condition that was overlooked by the army medical officers.

Jim was granted the right of legal representation at the court martial hearing. He declined. There seemed little point. He was denied right of appeal. The Field Marshall's decision was absolute. The hearing lasted twenty minutes. Jim Cade was found guilty of falling asleep on duty. The private was duly court-martialled and sentenced to death.

He was held for two weeks in one of two cells in the grounds of the nearby town hall. On the day of his execution Jim was taken out into the courtyard. There they hooked him up on the execution post, tied him securely and left him to hang like dead meat in a butcher's shop. His eyes were bandaged. The medical officer came forward and pinned a piece of white cloth over the man's heart. A priest said a few words of blessing for Jim's short life.

He cried out for the love of his life,

'Helen! I love you, Helen!'

The officer called the battalion to attention. There were twelve soldiers in the firing squad. One rifle was loaded with a blank so that no one soldier could be sure that he had fired the fatal bullet. A nervous volley of shots rang out.

There was a brief pause as the medical officer examined the victim. He raised his eyebrows in surprise, looked up at the officer and gave an awful sign. The cloth was dyed scarlet but Jim was still alive. His arms outstretched in prayer.

Even the most hardened men in the firing squad were moved to tears.

Without a moment's hesitation, the subaltern strode forward and despatched Jim with a single shot to his temple. The victim's life finally extinct, the detachment marched back to a hearty breakfast while his company picked up shovels and paid their last tribute at his graveside.

* * * * *

HER HEART FLUTTERED WHEN SHE heard the heavy rap of the iron door knocker.

Ah, that will be him!

She ran out to the hall and threw open the front door. He stood before her: freezing cold and shivering, his head and coat, covered in snow. Her young man! Unscathed! Jim's double.

'Mrs Cade?'

'Helen, please, call me Helen,' she insisted. 'Now, just you come in out of the cold before you catch your death.'

It was snowing when the train pulled into Myrtlesham Halt.

They tell me a snow year's a good year, filled with the love of the dead, who lie so deep.

Pretty, Still

July 1969:

MICHAEL FLOSSED, SLOOSHED, CLEANED HIS teeth, rinsed his face, then went to his room. His dapper, crease-resistant, charcoal three-piece suit awaited him on a hangar, along with his grey y-fronts, navy socks, black garters, blue birds-eye shirt, and tartan tie. He dressed expediently, slipping on a pair of tan punched-wing brogues, collected his leather satchel, and flew out of the house.

He checked his wristwatch as he ran: Mr Humford's assembly was due to start in five minutes! Byfield Comprehensive School was a four-minute jog up Shipleigh Road, past a bland row of council houses.

He spotted her running ahead of him in her school uniform: blazer, blouse, amber house tie, an outrageously short grey woollen skirt, white ankle socks, scuffed sandals.

Pretty, still…catchable. He put on pace and raced up to her side. Together, thigh by thigh, calf by calf, they rounded the acute curve of the road to knowing glances from the insidiously knit network of gossips that frequented those impoverished parts. Slums that were confounded by gleaming new motorcycles standing on turd-ridden forecourts, sourced on tic, the new credit regime perpetrated by the blood-sucking bourgeoisie of the City.

Speed's their creed, those hot rodders, swingers come to their hot rod hullabaloo! The jet-age crowd – they're with it, but they barely earn enough to pay the rent. Ha!

His thoughts turned to her, puffing, and panting next to him, as the chainmail fence of Byfield's tarmac playgrounds appeared on the overcast horizon. A window was open in one of the squalid flats. He recognized the music immediately, the censored record cover, the teaser:

Censored! Censored! We wanted to illustrate 'Je T'aime...Moi Non Plus!' the sexational single (on Fontana TF1042). But they wouldn't let us. Listen to it - and you'll see why.

He stared at her as they slowed on the final approach, listening to the screams of the children, bustling through the school gates. Her perfect spoilt-brat face. Her impossibly deep grey eyes. Her freckled nose. Her thin pink lips, and gappy teeth.

Linda Newman, the future glitterball queen of Byfield.

Michael looked ahead and saw *him* waiting for her at the gate. Her bloody saviour. Daniel, the high school drop-out, *always there*, waiting.

Why couldn't he get a job? Get out of his way. The boy was bloody old enough. Layabout! Ha!

He barked at Linda as she slowed to a walk, narrowly avoiding colliding with an old dear out walking her sausage dog towards the girl's rounders pitch.

'Good Morning, Linda!' he said effervescently, for the girl brightened his every waking hour.

'Morning, Mr Dunster!' she smiled cheekily, adding, 'Sir! How is Mrs Dunster feeling?'

Michael's voice shook. He struggled to control his trembling hands, gripping his satchel tightly.

'Thank you for asking. Mrs Dunster is feeling a little better this morning. She took breakfast.'

Linda grasped his right wrist in her left hand,

'Oh, I am pleased for you, Sir. You must love her very much to care for her so. I want you to know I understand. I hope she gets well soon.'

Daniel stood at the school gate watching teacher's pet fawn over boring old Dunster, clenching, and unclenching his fists, staring at the storm clouds gathering overhead. He loved Lin dearly, but hated the way she teased him. The games she played for personal gain. Still, she had had a hard life. Her dad, a night security guard, passed away last year, and her chain-smoking mum had gone to pieces. Linda was *entitled* to have fun in her tragic life. Not with her chemistry teacher, though, with *him*. He exchanged glances with Dunster, who blushed and mumbled at the girl,

'Linda, I think you should let go of my hand.'

Her grip on his hand tightened,

'Why? I like holding your hand.'

'If you don't let go of my hand this very instant, young lady, I won't tell you the exciting news.'

July 20th, 1969, yesterday: Neil Armstrong and Buzz Aldrin became the first men to set foot on the moon. Michael's news was little more than a titbit compared to their epic achievement. He looked at her expectant face. This morning, she would take pride of place on the hallowed front bench at double Chemistry, after assembly. He trembled with excitement at the prospect of his announcement to the whole of form 3D1.

'Yesterday,' he would say, 'two men walked on the surface of the moon. Today, I am delighted to announce that…'

School term ended on Wednesday at lunchtime. He wouldn't see Linda again until September. His heart bled at the thought of her and her bloody lazy sweetheart, playing tennis on the school courts. The strange haunt she alluded to, through the hidey-hole in the hedge. What did she call it? Her secret place? He dreaded to think of the games she played with her so-called boyfriend there but was powerless to intervene. He hoped she liked the news. Perhaps she would think better of him.

She let go of his right hand.

'Well, Michael? What have you got to tell me that's so exciting?'

They neared the school gate.

Daniel smiled at them, 'See you after school, Lin.'

She waved.

He walked straight past the teacher and his star pupil without so much as a 'How do you do?'

Michael drew breath, clenching his sweating hands,

'I have proposed that you receive the Academic Award for Third Year Pupils at Byfield in recognition of your excellent work this year. I am delighted to say that School has agreed.'

They were late for assembly. The playground was empty. Michael took the teenager in his arms and hugged her. She didn't resist. Would that she might kiss him on the lips...

The prefabricated Science Block at Byfield overlooked two chainmail-fenced compounds, and beyond those: The Junior School, girls' rounders pitch, tennis courts, and the boys' soccer pitch from where it was possible for truants to escape to the overgrown Mudhills and go home, on one side. The other side of S Block faced the school quadrangle, a threadbare patchwork quilt of grassy tufts and hard-baked mud wedged between S, M&W, H and ML Blocks.

Mr Gunn taught metalwork to the smattering of boys who could afford an apron, while Mr Scruton spent most of woodwork bragging to his young carpenters about his holiday flat on the Isle of Wight. The voluptuous young François Renault struggled to retain control of the modern linguists: French and Spanish, occasionally German after school, if there was sufficient interest.

H Block contained Ena Smyth, the formidable School Secretary, an interrogation, and corporal punishment room (the cane for the boys, a verbal slap on the wrist for the girls), the reading room and the Head's Study. After assembly, Mr Humford, a taciturn Settle & Carlisle man of modest means and furry whiskers, would sit at his desk, dunking stale digestives in his mug of milky tea, surveying the barren wasteland as he contemplated retirement. In the sure knowledge that Smyth would bat away any stray balls from his shuttered back door. A man at peace with himself.

Viewed from Smoker's Corner, behind the school gates, the Chemistry lab was first of three, followed by Physics (Mr Butcher, glass right eye, roving left), and Biology (Dr Goodman, married with kids). The prep room was located between Chemistry and Physics.

Pretty, still, at 35, Mrs Josephine Bunsen, devoted wife of Ernest, mother to twins Hilary and Richard, 3T1: lime-green ties, worked part-time as a laboratory technician at Byfield. Her hours of work, 8am to 330pm with breaks for coffee, lunch in the canteen, tea, and fags, suited her to the ground. She invariably enjoyed the company of her loving children on the short walks between school and their modest council flat in Shipleigh Road. She thought of Ernest, her proud man of German descent, sweeping Trusper Road, heading for Byfield Avenue, merrily pushing along his little barrow-full of dusty brooms, dusky daydreams…

Josephine snapped out of her reverie and glanced up at the white prep room clock. The atomic clock old Cyril called it. The clock that would stop at one minute to midnight when the human race teetered on the brink of nuclear war, as it did over Cuba, and surely would again. She felt for the old grammar school boffin. Not much fun him telling the naughty boy off on the front bench when his eye was fixed on a blonde girl at the back. That was Josie all over, the matriarch of the scientific fraternity, the woman who *really* cared for Dr Goodman, Cyril, and Michael.

She took a sip of her lukewarm cup of tea, set it down, looked in the prep room mirror, and tied her dark brown hair back in a neat ponytail. Her bald patch, the pronounced widow's peak, had got quite bad, quite bared. Still, he seemed to like it, kissed her there. Josie slipped her spotless white lab coat over her crisp blouse and skirt, then applied a thick slap of rouge to her lips, to match her unusual red-rimmed, tinted glasses.

That'll do nicely, she smiled.

The clock: the big hand was coming up to ten, the little hand next to nine.

Best get a move on!

Josephine had grown fond of Michael, listening patiently to him in the prep room at teatime as he poured his heart out. His wife's condition had deteriorated rapidly since the third, crushing, seizure. Esme had changed from a beautifully mature woman of 35, a keen swimmer and tennis player, into a floppy, slobbering, bed-ridden zombie. Josie had listened to him confide in her. Every aspect of his tormented private life, like a confessor to a priestess, taken him in her arms. And consoled him. Truth be told she had fallen in love with him.

Until today…

Her hands were shaking. She marched angrily as far as the Chemistry lab door and peered thru the reinforced glass panel.

Reinforced, why? In case there was an explosion?

The place was empty. Josie strode inside and surveyed the benches. There were twelve in all: six on either side of the gangway, each equipped with four gas taps and four three-legged stools. Some of the older girls had complained to Smyth that they found the stools uncomfortable. The old bag rebuffed them: saying they should be thankful they could sit down. Tough old crow!

She looked up at the brown stains on the girdered ceiling, a dichromate oxidation reaction that had gone horribly wrong. Then mounted the plinth, his plinth, and stood before the bench, his altar, her slender back flush to his scrubbed-out blackboard. The benches were polished, the sinks on each side of the lab spotless, stools straight. Even his fume cupboard was clean. Not that he ever used it. She saw to all that before her second cigarette.

Josephine Bunsen saw to everything for Mr Dunster.

The apparatus was on the bench in pieces. She began to assemble his apparatus, beginning with his round-bottomed flask. She grasped the flask by its neck and poured a quarter of a beaker of rock salt into the bottom…

She'd seen it all from the dark recess of Smoker's Corner, as she drew on her second cigarette.

Josephine Bunsen saw everything.

Assembly had begun. The playground was empty. Hilary, Richard, and the other children had gone inside, thank goodness.

Very carefully, Bunsen inserted the soda glass tubes: the straight one and the bent one, into the rubber bung. She cut her hand doing this once. Cut her hand and had to go to hospital to have the ball of her thumb stitched, Josie still bore the scar…

Dunster had taken the girl in his arms and hugged her. She hadn't resisted. On the contrary, the little madam had stood on tiptoes, reached up for him, and thrown her arms around his neck.

Bunsen carefully attached a round pipette to the straight tube, checking that the ground glass stopcock was in the closed position. Then she grasped the flask around the neck and clamped his apparatus in position, over her Bunsen burner, using his retort stand…

Would that she might kiss him on the lips. The little slut had grasped her man around his neck, clamped her lips in position, pressed her round breasts to his chest, his fiercely pounding heart. His Bunsen burner. Held him still, as if she were his retort stand, washing his slobbering mouth out with her mouth, eating him alive…

Bunsen fitted the rubber bung with the pipette and tubes loosely into the neck of the flask.

Nice and loosely does it! Wouldn't want it to get jammed Mister Dunster would we now?

She had watched in horror as he slid his fingers under her skirt, inside her pants, and over her round bottom…

With the round-bottomed flask rigidly mounted, but loosely fitted, Bunsen slid the bent tube into the hole in a round cardboard cover, before slipping it inside his gas cylinder…

He had seen her watching him. Let go of her. Eased her hot, flushed, body to the ground. His eyes had burned with anger, his face suffused with rage. Her head had turned like a revolving head in a horror film. Horrors! The film! Ernest had taken Josie to the movies for popcorn seven years ago to watch the professor obsess over his schoolgirl, his little Lolita… his Linda!

Bunsen returned to the prep room, took off her red-rimmed readers, donned a thick pair of goggles and rubber gloves, then took the large smoked-glass bottle down from the shelf. She placed the bottle on the draining board by the prep room sink and carefully unscrewed the cap. Imagining the screwed-up look on Humford's spent face when Dunster and his girl appeared at the back of the hall. His caustic sarcasm in front of the whole School:

'Ah, Mister Dunster! We were just about to say prayers. Do come in and take a pew. And you, young lady. Newman, isn't it? Don't be frightened. Come and join us. That's right! Let us pray.'

Bunsen carefully poured the concentrated Sulphuric Acid into a sturdy 500ml conical flask and stoppered it with a bung.

Nice and loose! Wouldn't want it to get stuck, Dunster, would you?

Then, she re-sealed the quart bottle, took the phial of Oil of Vitriol outside and set it on his sacred altar.

The school bell rang. The door flew open. Mr Dunster appeared, his face dripping with sweat, his whole body, trembling like a Potassium Dichromate volcano about to explode.

'Ah, Bunty!' he cried in a jocular tone, 'Are we ready yet!'

'Almost ready, Mr Dunster,' his technician mumbled sheepishly, 'Almost ready…'

Dunster began to undress in front of Mrs Bunsen! There was a line of coat hooks on the wall by the doorway, and Dunster began to undress by it. Not that Michael hadn't undressed in front of Josie before, but that had been in her bedroom when they'd had sex, while Ernest was busy sweeping Warren Drive.

Bunsen removed her glasses, polishing them furiously, desperately trying to contemplate Dunster's next move. Only half an hour ago this animal had molested Linda Newman, 14, thirty years his junior. Now he was going to molest her. She reached for the sturdy conical flask of concentrated Sulphuric Acid on the demonstration bench and carefully removed the bung.

Dunster looked as if he hadn't shaved for a week. He had huge, dark bags and weals under his bloodshot eyes. He took off his jacket and hung it on the hook, not once taking his beady eyes off quivering Bunsen.

He must be ill. Why else would he grope an impressionable young schoolgirl who didn't know her own mind in front of School?

Josie thought of Esme, lying in her vegetative state. How Michael had offered to introduce her. How she had politely declined. She felt sorry for him, wanting to reach out and hold him in her loving arms. But he wasn't all there. Michael's mind was elsewhere: brooding, stressed-out. She noticed that his hands were shaking. He hung up his waistcoat. She held up her acid,

'Would you like me to fill the pipette with the Sulphuric Acid for you, Mr Dunster?'

His whole body visibly sagged, the relief. She knew it was the relief, she'd felt it before in him.

'Would you please, Bunty?'

Why did he insist on calling her that dreadful name? She hated that! Bunty, the girl's comic! Carefully, she poured the highly corrosive contents of the conical flask into the round pipette. He unknotted his tartan tie and hung it up on the hook, then unbuttoned the first two buttons of his shirt. Josephine shuddered. Dunster had never undressed thus far at School.

She thought of the children. The children would arrive for double Chemistry at any minute! She had to protect the children! Dunster rolled up his sleeves like a strangler, blocking her way out. He moved towards Mrs Bunsen. She in turn edged towards the prep room door. If, and it was a big if given Dunster's demented state, she could make it as far as the prep room, sidle past Butcher's Physics set in the dark (they *were* shining box lights through prisms to create rainbows), and find Dr Goodman teaching *taenia solium*, the so-called pork tapeworm to her Zoology elite. *Then* she could raise the alarm and report Mr Dunster to the Head of Science for assaulting a minor. Her ordeal wasn't over yet. He was closing in, rubbing his sweaty hands with glee. She heard a babble of schoolchildren approaching the laboratory…

'Bunty!' he shouted, spitting in her face, 'Did you watch the moon landing yesterday?'

'Of course, Mr Dunster,' she cried honestly, feeling her way off the plinth, 'Didn't we all?'

He followed her, climbing down from the plinth, the minty fragrance of his toothpaste stinging her nostrils,

'And…?!'

She backed away, nearly reached the prep room door, not far now,

'And what, Mr Dunster?'

He scraped his fingernails down the blackboard, making a shrill, squeaking noise,

'What did you make of the… moon landing…eh… Bunty?!'

She reached the door, felt her bottom swing the wood inwards, to safety,

'I thought it was nice.'

'Nice?!' he roared, 'That historic moment: that small moment for man, giant leap for mankind will be remembered for generations to come, and all you have to say is that it was nice?'

Mrs Bunsen fell into the prep room just as the laboratory door burst open. Linda appeared, took off her blazer, hung it over Dunster's clothes, put on her white lab coat, ran to him, took his trembling hands in hers, and kissed him on both cheeks, gazing up into his red eyes, and said:

'What are we making today, Mr Dunster?'

'Hydrogen Chloride.'

His heavy heart pounded with stress. More than that: guilt. Weighing down his soul. Heavier than it had ever weighed before. He thought of Esme:

waiting for his return in her catatonic state. Josie, dear Josie, who was always there for him, his shoulder to cry on. The fear in her eyes when she backed off and slid into the prep room. The look of hate, her disrespect for him, when he lost control, and made himself look such a fool.

If she went to Rita Goodman and made a formal complaint about his behaviour, he would be shamed. Dr Goodman, despite her overt affection for Michael, would be forced to act, to take the matter to Mr Humford, who would enact his immediate suspension, pending a full, if not lurid, investigation into his act of sexual assault on a 14-year-old girl. The game was up for Dunster. *If* Benson reached Goodman.

He tried to wrest himself from Linda, but she refused to let go of his hands.

'What is it, Michael?' she asked, seeing the tension in his face, his right eye rolling wildly, as it tended to do when his restless mind was in a turmoil, 'Why are you upset with me?'

He looked down at her sad face. There were tears in her eyes, shiny tears. His first reaction was to hold her tight. There wasn't time. The whole of 3D1 would burst into the lab at any moment. Instead, he brushed her straggly blonde hair, her soft cheeks, with the back of his trembling hand. He'd initiated the act by holding her body against him. He thought of her being grilled by her form tutor, Gina Bracewell, on the facts of life, of love, in the aftermath of his summary dismissal. Linda, his reason to live. He didn't have the heart to tell her that they'd been caught, red-handed, en flagrante, by Mrs Benson. Instead, he apologized to her,

'I'm sorry,' he stumbled, 'I should never have touched you down there. I got carried away.'

Linda sniffed, and wiped her runny nose on his shirt,

'It doesn't matter, I like it when you touch me, it feels... nice.

The disturbing innocence behind her words stung his heart like the shock of a stingray thrusting its tail inside his chest. Emotionally shattered by his guilt, his heartstrings torn apart, feelings imploding then exploding recklessly, he uttered the dreadful, uncaring words of the desperate:

'Newman, this childhood fantasy of yours, this obsession you have with me, has to stop, do you understand?'

Devastated by his cruel, heartless barb, she clawed him, clutching at love-straws, burying her weeping head against his chest,

'But I love you, Michael. Can't you see that? You're my world?'

'You can't love me! I'm old enough to be your father!'

They shared a ruinous silence as she remembered her dead father, Leonard. Her ever-loving, proud dad. Who bought her a chemistry set for Christmas when she was twelve years old. Who took her on the green train to Victoria, the number 38 bus across London, on his day off work. To buy her hazardous chemicals from the odd back-room chemists in Stoke Newington. Who would never see his beloved daughter receive the coveted Academic Award for Third Year Pupils...

The fractious tension between the broken hearts ended abruptly as the sneering hordes of 3D1 piled into the laboratory, with a vengeance,

'Good Morning Mr Dunster! Sorry, were we interrupting you? Like us to wait outside, while you...?'

'Hello Linda! Fancy meeting you here! Having a nice kiss and cuddle with Dunster were you?'

'Morning, Mr Dunster, Linda! Well, look at you two!'

The children changed into their lab coats. There was a screeching of stool legs as they all took their places at a bench. Miserably, Linda joined David Miller, Cara Stephens, and Gary Hassler, at the front. The gibbering wreck that was once Mr Dunster took up position on his plinth. And double Chemistry began...

The children sat in stony silence staring at Dunster's guilt-ridden face as he attempted to control his frayed emotions. His whole body shook violently like a prefab in an earthquake. His shirt, string vest, and y-fronts were saturated. Perspiration ran in rivulets down his strained face. He strutted about the laboratory clenching and unclenching his fists like a fallen prince with a guilty secret. Dunster looked to Linda for encouragement, but she just smiled and turned away, relishing his torment after the callous way that he'd dismissed her love for him.

The condemned man returned to his makeshift cell, the plinth behind the demo bench, and gazed at the sea of young, innocent, yet accusatory faces, raining contempt down on his pathetic attempts to exert authority. At that precise moment, Dunster's nervous system went into full breakdown mode. He lost control,

'Yesterday,' he began, 'two men walked on the surface of the moon. Today, I will, I will, will.'

The room fell silent. The children exchanged worried glances. Linda shut her eyes and saw the look of panic on Michael's face, when he reached out to her for comfort. She thought of Esme.

'Today, I will, I will, will...'

He was crying, falling apart in front of class. He needed help. Where was Mrs Bunsen? Linda stood up, scraping her stool with a loud squeal that shook the other children out of their stupor, scurrying to the prep room. Bunsen wasn't there! Dr Goodman, she had to find Dr Goodman! She felt a steely grip pull at her elbow, dragging her onto the plinth for all the class to laugh at.

'Linda has some important news for you all, don't you Newman?' Dunster trilled, 'About us?'

'Stop it! Stop it!' the girl cried, her face all flustered, bloodied with embarrassment, teary-eyed.

'Leave her alone, you bully!' a small voice, Angela Smith, 13, squeaked from the back benches.

'Silence!' roared Dunster, 'Newman, you will return to your stool immediately!'

Fearing for their safety, everyone shut their mouths and watched their shaken classmate slump down on her stool. The pervading atmosphere of resignation amongst his pupils galvanized Mr Dunster into action. He took a stick of white chalk and started scribbling across the blackboard, talking as he chalked.

'Today, I will prepare Hydrogen Chloride.'

He glanced over his shoulder,

'What is Hydrogen Chloride... Gary?'

'A gas, Sir!'

'Ha! Yes, it is a gas. But what happens when it dissolves in water... Helen?'

'It forms a solution, Sir!'

'What kind of solution?'

'An acid, Sir!'

'Which acid?'

'Hydrochloric Acid, Sir!'

'Very good, well done!'

The children relaxed a little. Mr Dunster was back on top form or seemed to be. He looked at Linda, regretting his crazy outburst. She knew the truth about Esme. She was only trying to help.

'Yesterday,' he said proudly, 'two men walked on the surface of the moon. Today, I am delighted to announce that Linda Newman will receive the Academic Award for Third Year Pupils at Byfield in recognition of her excellent work this year. If you would like to come up and receive your award, Linda?'

'There will be a formal presentation by the new Head of School with parents invited in September,' he added.

There was a polite smattering of applause and a fair few calls of 'Well done, Lin!' as she went up to the plinth to accept the academic prize. Mr Dunster gently shook the girl's right hand and presented her with a thin orange-and-white booklet. He flicked the front page open so that she could admire the sticky-back label with the oak tree crest:

Byfield School

Linda Newman

Academic Award for Third Year Pupils

Dated: 14th July 1969

Signed: DJ Humford, Headmaster.

'Revision Notes for Ordinary Level Chemistry!' cried Lin, 'Thank you! Thank you so much!'

'Now Linda,' Michael said happily, 'If you would like to turn to page thirty-two and read out what it says under section 3.5 to Class, I thought you might like to help me prepare Hydrogen Chloride. Would you like that?'

She beamed from ear-to-ear, 'Would I? Yes, please!'

Michael switched on the gas tap and lit the Bunsen burner with a wax taper. The gas burned with a blue flame tinged with yellow, a flame that grew stronger when he opened the collar around the base of the burner to let in more oxygen. Linda moved closer to him and started to read. The other children looked on, transfixed:

'Hydrogen Chloride, HCl, is a colourless gas with an irritating smell.'

There was a chorus of laughter from the benches as the children conjured up irritating smells, wrinkling their noses in disgust.

A delighted Mr Dunster joined in the fun, 'Ha! Ha! Carry on!'

'The gas is very soluble in water,' continued Lin, 'and heavier than air. Hydrochloric Acid is a colourless solution. Concentrated hydrochloric acid contains about 35% Hydrogen Chloride. The acid turns blue litmus red.'

'Very good, Linda,' remarked Michael, 'I think I should prepare the gas now, don't you?'

'I think you should, Sir!' she laughed, loving her moment of stardom, stage centre, 'Hydrogen Chloride is prepared by the action of concentrated Sulphuric Acid on Sodium Chloride.'

Mr Dunster carefully turned the ground glass stopcock, releasing the oil of vitriol over the rock salt in the round-bottomed flask. The round-bottomed flask, mounted, yet loosely fitted. Nothing happened.

'And the chemical equation?' he asked her, positioning the Bunsen burner under the flask.

'NaCl +H2SO4 > NaHSO4 + HCl,' she recited.

The acid in the flask began to bubble ferociously as the rock salt dissolved. Linda shut the book and moved in to watch. Colourless gas poured off the boiling liquid, passing through the bent tube from the flask and collecting in the gas cylinder. She was several inches shorter than her Chemistry teacher. She noticed the irritating smell and coughed. Dunster turned to face the class:

'Because Hydrogen Chloride is heavier than air,' he explained, 'the gas can be safely collected in the covered gas cylinder.'

The experiment was over. He went to turn off the gas tap. The rubber bung on the flask worked loose. Hydrogen Chloride gas poured out of the open flask. Linda coughed and sputtered, felt the gas dissolving in her watery eyes, the acid tears streaming down her cheeks. Her eyes hurt. She rubbed her eyes, couldn't see. She went to scream, couldn't. The acid etched her mouth. Her nostrils bled. She fell into his arms, collapsed into his arms. Children screamed. Michael wailed. Goodman appeared at the doorway, with Gunn and Scruton.

Linda lay pretty, still, barely breathing in Michael's arms. Esme was dead. Esme died last week. He couldn't let Lin go, wouldn't let her go, carried her to the first aid room with Dr Goodman. Ena Smyth called for an ambulance, then called the Police. Bunsen was nowhere to be found.

And all the children cried…

Strange Taste

Foretaste:

HE DIDN'T KNOW WHAT TO do with her at first. Her behaviour was erratic and daring. Her love, the tactile touch, their passion, intoxicated him. Then, when she came to him, he smelt the animal scent on her, she savoured his strange taste, and they lost all self-control.

July 1972:

HE ARRIVED AT THE END-of-terrace house dressed in a smooth velvet jacket, shirt, and cords, carrying a litre of Malibu. The stained-glass door was open, the opening riffs of *Schools Out* could be heard in the street. He checked the house next door. Its curtains were drawn. The lights were out.

When he went inside, he found himself in a small hallway with a door on the left, stairs on the right, and a narrow corridor. The atmosphere was thick with smoke. He choked on the acrid fumes: cigarettes mixed with a rich aroma of cigars, burning josticks, candles, other, less familiar smells. There were couples huddled on the Indian rug, sprawled over the stairs: eating, drinking, smoking, talking, kissing, embracing. Careful not to tread on them, he entered the living room to find the party in full swing. The place was heaving with strangers, their arms wrapped around each other's necks, pretending to slow dance.

The girl stood at the heart of the throng swaying her child-bearing hips to the music. She twisted her head to the left, noticing him in the doorway. He assessed her. She was short, stocky, with long blonde hair, blushing cheeks, and a bronze suntan. Finding her sexually attractive, he moved in closer to her.

The lights went out. She went into a dancing fit. Her breasts flopped out of her flimsy summer dress. She made no attempt to cover herself. He'd never forget the wild, glazed, drug-crazed look in her eyes. The girl was high, flailing her arms about clumsily in front of him. The other dancers formed a protective ring around her. Intrigued, fascinated by her distorted state of mind, her distending body, he joined in, keeping an ever-watchful eye on her. She implored him, stoned out of her tiny mind, seeking his permission to continue,

'Shall I?'

'If you want to.'

He watched beguiled as she pulled off her dress. She whirled, a spinning drunken dervish, colliding into friends. They pushed her, shoving her, egging her on, roaring their approval. She slumped against him. He felt her soft, supple body, her breasts, squashed against his chest. The girl was sweating, clearly in distress. He held her. Then, he freed her to dance. The rock anthem reached a crescendo. All her inhibitions lost, she peeled off her panties and danced naked for her appreciative audience, who joined in, tearing at each other's clothing in an orgy of unspent lust.

Somebody changed the record. The music slowed to *Without You*. And he left the room.

There was no sign of Janis, the other twin. She was identical to Lindsey in every respect, apart from her hair which she wore cupric red. He assumed she was upstairs, making love to a boy. Either that, or she was in the kitchen. The tension gnawed at his stomach. He felt hungry. Clambering over the scattered human debris, he made his way to the scullery.

He eased his way past humps of entwined teenagers as far as the sturdy oak kitchen table. Half the table was taken up with Party Sevens, spirits, open lager cans, full foil ashtrays. The other was allocated to food: decadent displays of fatty cocktail sausages, pineapple-and-cheese on sticks, chicken vol-au-vents, sausage rolls, mini pork pies, salted peanuts, and crisps. Famished, he grabbed a plate and helped himself.

She was standing by the bar pouring herself a glass of 'the real thing', gorgeous in a plain white t-shirt, drainpipe jeans. His heart leapt in his chest at the sight of her pale angular face, tinted wispy hair, slim, petite, scant figure, her fake drop-pearl earrings. She cried, happily, above the din,

'Hello! Come here often?'

She was Australian. He stopped eating. Didn't know what to say. He gave her his bottle. She unscrewed the top. Poured herself a large shot. Mixed it with Coke. Drank a swig,

'Ah, thanks! Needed that. Gets boring when you don't know anyone, doesn't it?'

He didn't answer. She topped up her glass, found a clean glass, half-filled it with Malibu, and offered it to him,

'Fancy a drink?'

She was tipsy. He started to sweat. His hands shook. She made him apprehensive. His mouth was parched. Desperate for a drink, he took the glass from her, downing it in one.

He struck her as the silent type, vulnerable to her charms, pleasantly shy. She wanted him, badly, wanted to push her hand through his wavy hair, stroke his face, kiss his split lips, and feel his slim-toned body. He excited her. She needed to touch him,

'Feeling lonely?'

The drink went to his head, 'Yes, very.'

'My name's Georgie,' she disclosed, 'Shall we go outside and play in the garden?'

She took hold of his hand and led him through the outhouse to the garden. It was getting dark. He made out the stars appearing in the young night sky, a half crescent moon. The mossy lawn was surrounded by shrubs, bushes, overhanging trees, creating a feeling of privacy, peace, quiet. They were alone. Georgie took a deep breath, relishing the fresh evening air, reached up for him, drew him to her, and kissed him. She was wearing scent.

He responded: parting his lips, opening his mouth. She explored his palate, savouring his strange taste, coating her flickering tongue in his saliva. He crushed her in his arms. When they eventually came up for air, she was panting, breathless, clamouring for him, gasping,

'Think we should go and play on the swing now, don't you?'

Georgie took off her t-shirt. She wasn't wearing a bra. Her back was dripping with sweat. She took his breath away. He couldn't speak. There was a child's swing in the corner of the garden. She led him there.

The twins must have played here once, as little girls, he thought, feeling a sickening rush of guilt over the wretched state he'd left the girl in. *Now Georgie wants to play with me.*

She forced him to perch on the seat while she unbuttoned his shirt, undid the stud on his cords, unzipped his fly, and slid her hand inside his pants. He groaned as she played with him, on the swing. Georgie ran her tongue down his neck. Her langue explored his torso, licking his stiff nipples, tasting the salty tang of sweat in his navel. Tenderly, she caressed his proud, velvety, flesh with her soft hand, gently squeezing his taut sac until he felt fit to burst,

'How does that feel, good?'

He didn't know how to answer her. Georgie knelt in the grass, grasping him, staring into his flushed face, she asked him,

'Would you like to make love to me?'

'Yes.'

She spoke to him, as if he were her child,

'Shall we go inside then, see if we can't find a bed?'

'I don't have a sheath.'

Georgie felt inside her back pocket, and took out a thin silver foil pouch,

'It's alright,' she intimated, 'I've got one. Come with me.'

Quickly, she tucked him away inside his pants, put on her t-shirt, held his clammy hand - and led him to the scullery door.

Save for a few scattered cans, empty bottles, and overflowing ashtrays, the table was bare. The food had been devoured. The gaggle of teenagers had dispersed. Gripping his hand, Georgie negotiated the animalistic lair of bodies writhing on the floor. They reached the stairs. There was a queue stretching from the hall to the landing for the upstairs toilet. She felt him tense. He turned to her and confessed,

'I've never made love to a girl before.'

Georgie smiled at him, lovingly, 'Don't worry, I'll take care of you.'

Her love, her care, her warmth towards him, infected him. He loved her smile, wanted to make her happy, always. Eager for her to take the lead, he followed her upstairs, his eyes fixed firmly on her rear, avoiding the knowing glances from a handful of sober voyeurs.

They arrived at the landing which was decorated in flock wallpaper. There was a solitary picture of a few snowdrops growing out of a bed of dead leaves, which Georgie took as symbolizing new life out of death. Other than the loo, on her right, there were three doors off the landing. Two of them were shut. She wondered if they all locked from the inside.

The sensual thrill waves permeated her body. Trembling with anticipation, she brought her lover to the threshold. They ventured to the open door and peeked inside. The bedside lamps were switched on, casting gloomy shadows.

He hesitated.

How Can I Be Sure? was playing in the background.

Georgie kissed him fully on the lips, rubbing his crotch, stimulating him, hardening him, murmuring,

'Shall we go inside?'

* * * * *

SHE COULDN'T BELIEVE HER LUCK. The main en suite bedroom was free. Georgie entered first, followed by him. His chest felt tight with expectation. She shut the door, blinding prying eyes, turned the key in its lock, and slid all three bolts in place. The ballad: *Alone Again, Naturally*, faded into the background. The bathroom was at the far end of the room, beyond the giant-sized bed. He felt her squeeze his hand,

'I have to go to the toilet to prepare myself. Will you wait for me?'

She'd looked at him so seriously. Was she that worried he might stray?

He felt an enormous surge of relief flush through him. A sensational burst of happiness, feeling so protective of her. A strong sense of caring he had never felt before. He adored her. She gave him hope. For the first time, he smiled,

'Of course, I'll wait for you. I love you.'

He made her blush. She let go of his hand, pecking him on both cheeks, his lovebird. No-one ever uttered those words to her. Her soul sank at the thought of their parting, the morning after. She *needed* him, she wanted to reciprocate his feelings, but couldn't bring herself to say the beautiful words, for fear of breaking his heart.

Georgie struggled to control her emotions, stinging inside with guilt. Tonight, she would give of herself to him. Heartbroken, she told him to switch off the light, take off his clothes, lie on the bed, and wait for her to make love to him.

Elated, euphoric, he watched her close the pure-white door. He looked around the room. There was a pine dressing table, a turquoise stool, to one side of the bed, cluttered with lady's make-up: lipsticks, combs, a clutch of old photos: a woman on her wedding day, sunbathing on a white sandy beach in her scarlet bikini, suckling her babies, holding them over the font, as they were anointed.

Strange, no photos of her husband?

He decided: this should be Georgie's side of the bed.

The twins were conceived here. She wants to make love to me, here, on their parent's bed.

He switched off her light. There was a royal blue armchair on his side of the bed. He soon undressed, folding his jacket, shirt, and cords, placing them in a neat pile on the chair. He pulled off his socks and pants, throwing them in soft balls at the chair. Switching off his light, he stretched out on the bed, shut his eyes, and waited, as innocently as a new-born baby – for her.

* * * * *

GEORGIE CREPT INTO THE BEDROOM and took off her t-shirt, jeans, and panties, strewing them over the carpet. Then, as naked as the day she was born, she climbed on the bed, to kneel - beside him.

Their intense mood was interrupted by loud banging on the door, a boy and a girl's slurred, drunken voices,

'Let us in!'

'Come on! You've had your five minutes!'

He froze.

Georgie gently stroked his belly, gliding her soft hand downwards, into his hairy groin,

'Ignore them,' she soothed, 'They'll soon go away.'

The din outside ceased.

He groaned as she sheathed him,

'There,' she whispered, 'Now keep still. Forget the world. Think about me.'

She straddled him. He felt the soft insides of her thighs rubbing against his hips. Her fine hair, brushing his hair. Her belly, resting, lightly, on his abdomen, as she fed him inside her. He loved her tenderness. She was tactile for him: relishing her impalement, fully aroused, holding his hands to her breasts, her nipples, stiffened by his firm caress. Her heart pounded. His chest heaved. He cried out for her,

'I love you, Georgie! I love you, Georgie!'

She shuddered as his spasms subsided.

It was over.

His mind was riddled with guilt, 'I'm sorry, I couldn't hold on any longer.'

She comforted him, brushing his cheek with her hand, 'You felt good! You were great!'

Masking her disappointment, she dismounted him carefully, grasping the root of his shrivelled stalk to ensure that his sheath didn't slip off inside her. He felt her climb off the bed, watching her intently as she padded off to the bathroom.

Shattered, frustrated by his inability to satisfy her, he rolled onto one side and fell asleep.

* * * * *

EVEN AS SHE WENT TO open the bathroom door Georgie felt her guilt, mixed with a sense of shame at how she behaved. It didn't help her that she was tired out, emotionally drained by the intense effort of seducing and making love to the virgin - or that she was still left wanting him. She turned a handle with her clean hand and stepped inside, quietly closing the door, so as not to wake him, sleeping.

Christ! What's his name? I don't even know his name!

Georgie pulled the light switch cord, the immensity of what she'd just done weighing on her mind. She'd played with him intimately on a garden swing, even though she knew the others were watching her through the kitchen window. She'd borne her breasts for him, exposing herself to the sultry, summer evening air. Then, she had caressed him, tenderly, lovingly, leading him to believe she might love him. She thought of him, crying for her as he squirmed and wriggled under her on the twin's parent's bed.

Bizarre notions teased her confused mind. She thought of the black and yellow book her mother gave her when she was eleven: Peter and Pamela Grow Up, imagining that she was Pamela and he was Peter.

Pamela Becomes a Young Lady she reminded herself, wistfully.

How careful was she? Could he have made her pregnant? How would she explain a baby to her mother in Oz? She squatted over the toilet and peed. Her mother was a devout who believed in the sanctity of marriage. What was it she told her, before Georgie left home to see the world?

'When you fall in love with a man, find your husband and marry him, it's only natural that you will want to kiss and embrace each other. You will want to come together in the closest possible contact.'

She'd smiled naughtily to herself, *Come together?*

'Thanks so much for explaining that to me, Mummy,' Georgie said, interrupting her.

Her mother continued, 'Oh, and darling.'

'Yes?'

'This act of loving union between a husband and wife is commonly referred to as sexual intercourse.'

Another knowing smile, *Really?*

'Commonly, Mummy?'

'Yes, commonly.'

That was how she felt: common, soiled. The hand basin was porcelain white with original brass taps. One of the taps, the hottest one, was still running from her previous visit, when she prepared herself for him. Georgie picked up the bar of Cussons Imperial Leather and scrubbed her hands, ridding herself of him. There was a strange taste in her mouth - his taste. She shook her head despondently, daring herself to pluck the used pink toothbrush out of the mouldy beige tooth mug, applied a splodge of Colgate, then brushed her teeth.

The idea of her having a pen friend in England had been her mother's. Ironically, Georgie started writing to Lyndsey when she reached eleven: the same age she became acquainted with Peter and Pam. As they grew older the teenagers became distant friends, confidantes, alluding to each other about the changes occurring in their bodies. Then, on her eighteenth birthday, she had embarked on her backpacking Tour of Europe starting in Italy, visiting Monaco, the South of France, Spain, Portugal, ending in London from where she called Lyndsey – and heard about the party.

She rinsed the toothbrush clean, drying it on a pink face flannel, and returned it to its mug. There were four *'his and her'* towels hanging by the handbasin. Georgie felt them all. The pink ones were sopping wet. She recoiled. She would have to use a navy-blue men's towel after her shower. The shower head was unscaled. It protruded over a spotless four-legged bath. She turned on the twin brass taps, mixing the water to steamy hot, lifted the shower knob, and drew the curtain, ensuring it hung inside the bath. Then she climbed in, thrilling to the invigorating sensation of water cascading down her body, feeling all tingly inside. As she soaped her breasts, her belly, and crotch, the lure of him, lying naked on the bed, returned to haunt her.

The delicious surge of arousal spread through her body. Just as the red light of anticipation lit her up mind. She had tried to use the young man lying on the bed next door for her personal gratification and failed. He was at best inept, an awkward lover, but he held a fascination, a mystique, she found intriguing. His v-shaped torso, muscular physique, the smoothness of his skin, his warm hair, demanded her caress. There was no doubt: she'd lost control of herself, taking an incredible risk when she made love to him. But deep inside her heart, she felt an inner compulsion to be with him. Georgie wondered if this was what *real* love felt like.

She shampooed her hair with Silvikrin and tried to bring the intensity of her feelings under control, to rationalise her thoughts.

Tonight, she would tell him how much she loved sharing her precious moments with him, bid him a tearful farewell, kiss, embrace, and say goodbye. Tomorrow, if she managed to get out of bed, she would spend the day sightseeing in London.

Except, the time for rational thinking was over.

She rinsed her hair, turned off the shower, drew the curtain, and climbed out of the bath. Some of her hairs were stuck in the plughole.

'Always leave the toilet, sink and bath as clean as you'd expect to find them,' her finicky mother said.

Georgie bent down, plucked out her hairball, and threw it in the toilet. Dabbing her eyes, she took in the array of lady's cosmetics crammed onto the vanity shelf. There was a Mum rollette deodorant. She rubbed it on her hairy armpits.

The mirror had steamed up. She opened the window and stared out at the starry night sky, feeling ridiculously small and lonely. On the shelf was a phial of perfume. Georgie took the atomiser and sprayed scent on the back of her hand: the heady aroma of roses. Feeling ashamed for using the mature woman's fragrance, she quickly sprayed her fingers, dabbed the love potion behind each ear, fluffed her hair, wrapped the towel around her waist, and padded back into the bedroom. The music had stopped playing in the lover's discotheque.

He was lying on his back, sound asleep, making stertorous nasal noises. Georgie sealed his mouth with hers, dangling her tongue inside his, teasing him delicately, savouring his strange taste, kissing him awake with a start. He smelt her fragrance. His head span. Their lips parted. She whispered,

'I have to go now. Come and say goodbye to me.'

She switched on the light. He blinked in utter astonishment. Georgie looked sensational. They stood on the plush crimson deep-pile carpet embracing. He ran his fingers through her damp hair, down her neck, over her knobbly spine, as far the small of her back. She felt him stir against her belly through the towel. She wanted to know his name.

He mumbled incoherently, smothering his face in her clean, fresh hair, nuzzling her neck, behind her ears, loving the scent of her, kissing her soft earlobes.

Georgie sighed contentedly: *so, this is the love, the tenderness, the intimacy I need.*

She felt him tear off her towel. His hands grasped her fleshy buttocks, drawing her to him. His rigid flesh stood proudly for her, pressing insistently into the slight round of her belly,

'Want to *please* you, Georgie.'

She started to cry, venting her frustration, 'You can't! I don't have any protection left.'

'Wait!' she added, after a brief silence, 'I have an idea. Give me your hand.'

* * * * *

AFTER GEORGIE HAD FINISHED, HE watched her squat beside the bed, wiping her sweaty body. He cherished her like this, recovering, her nipples stiff burnt caramel, her breasts heaving, her soft, hairy mound glistening with intimate dew, her protruding scarlet lips. She smiled fondly at him, reclining lazily on the bed, hands behind his head, his puddle of grey messing the manly growth of hair on his belly, testament to her hand's tender caress. She sighed,

'That was really lovely. Thank you.'

'Did you come on?'

Georgie bloomed and blushed, 'What do you think?

He was thrilled for her, 'I'm glad.'

'Here.'

She wiped the sweat off her breasts and handed him her wad of tissues, to his surprise,

'What am I meant to do with these?' he asked.

Georgie pulled up her panties, 'Keep them, as a memento of my love.'

'I *will* keep them, always.'

He sounded deadly serious. He treasured her, dreading the pain of losing her. The clutch of congealed mess in his palm, her intimate keepsake, would remind him of her scent, her sweat, her strange taste, in his dark, lonely nights; recalling the time they first made love.

Mildly amused by his reaction, she pulled on her t-shirt and scoffed, 'I was only joking!'

He changed the subject, 'Where are you from?'

'I grew up on a farm just outside Adelaide. Dad owned a million sheep. I used to help him dip them, watch them being sheared, feed the baby lambs, help Mummy in the farmhouse.'

'A million! That's a lot of sheep. How did you manage?'

'Daddy hired a load of casual farmhands for shearing, and during the lambing season.'

He grinned. Coming from a council estate, he couldn't begin to imagine what life must be like living on a farm out in the wild. He loved the twang in her voice, could listen to her talk all night. She hitched n zipped her jeans in front of him,

'When Dad died, four years ago, Mum sold the farm. We moved to a large house on the outskirts of Adelaide. I suppose you could say we're well off: we have a maid, gardener, someone to do the cleaning. You'd love Australia, the bush, the Outback, the white sandy beaches, wildlife. We had a veranda when we lived on the farm. I used to sit and watch the kangaroos play as the sun went down.'

He could tell by her sad, dreamy expression, the faraway look in her eyes, that Georgie missed home. He felt a knot form in his chest, a rising stab of panic, fearing he might lose her. He wanted to keep her, safe and well, happy in his loving embrace, always; he could never let her go. The drug-fazed mask of the girl's distress kept flashing through his mind,

'That sounds incredible. Were there any spiders or poisonous snakes where you lived?'

Georgie slipped on her pumps,

'Sure! Spiders, Funnel Webs, Red Backs - Black Widows. I checked for them before I got into bed, or if I sat on the toilet. You get used to it. A bite from one of those beauties can maim you. Dad's arm swelled to three times its normal size when the Red Back bit him.'

'Your Dad was bitten by a Black Widow?' he was intrigued, fascinated by the poisoning.

'The bite killed him. Dad's lungs gave out before we could save him with the antivenin.'

Georgie stared at her feet. He turned to face her, propping himself on one elbow. He felt gutted for her but needed to know the gory details. If he could just push her a little farther,

'Did he hurt when he died?'

She bristled with anger, 'How can you say that?! You're talking about my Dad!'

'I was only asking.'

'If you *must* know, Dad had terrible chest pains, stomach cramps, was sick, sweated with fever, had a seizure which killed him. There, is *that* enough for you?'

Flushed with temper, she ran for the door. He leaped out of bed and caught her, gripping her slender forearm tightly as she went to turn the key. She screamed at him: blue murder,

'Let go of me! You're hurting me!'

Worried she might be overheard, he spun her round to face him, holding her thrashing body against his torso until she calmed down,

'I'm sorry I said that Georgie, really sorry.'

'It's okay,' she exhaled, 'You gave me the creeps, that's all.'

He held her damp head in his hands and kissed her softly on the lips, feeling her relax, an easing of her tension. She giggled, his naughty little girl-child,

'Careful! You're all sticky!'

'Can I see you again?' he pleaded, letting her go.

One last time, she wanted to make love to him one last time. She played mind games with him, running her fingertips seductively along his lower lip,

'Maybe, where do you live?'

'15, Brierley Road, Ifield, Crawley,' he recited, 'Off the main drive from the station. You can't miss it.'

He felt her soften, emotionally exhausted. Felt her body slump against his, as she gave in,

'Say again. I haven't got a pen and paper.'

'15, Brierley Road, Ifield, Crawley.'

'I'll find it…'

He crushed her to his bare chest. Breathless, blushing, sweating profusely, she memorized his address, kissing him on the lips, then freed herself, opening the door. The landing was deserted. Georgie heard the others, leaving. It was time for her to go home,

'Tomorrow night,' she whispered to him, 'I'll see you tomorrow night. I love you.'

'I love you, too.'

He locked the door after her, annoyed that she hadn't mentioned the copperheads or death adders commonly found in Southern Central Australia.

* * * * *

JANIS WAS RELIEVED TO HEAR the pounding strains of *Brown Sugar* ascending through the floorboards from the cherub's grotto downstairs. The music helped her stay composed as she fought to quell her rising state of alarm. She stared down at Lindsey, lying naked, flat on her back on the bed, clutching her breasts, pressing the flats of her palms to her chest in a vain bid to control the bizarre tremors undulating through her body. Janis had never seen her twin in this state. She crouched beside her on the bed, scared of what she found. Lindsey ground her teeth, her eyelids flickering involuntarily, her pupils dilated. Janis felt her heartbeat. It was racing - wildly. She was pouring with thick sweat. Running a fever,

'What did he give you, Sis?'

Lindsey felt her mind drift upwards out of her head, her soul flit and float above her body, loving the forbidden, star-spangled red-dwarf universe she existed in, the exploding suns, flash-by comets, pulsing quasar stars, kaleidoscopic shards of red, orange, yellow, indigo, spinning incessantly in her mind. Her heart tried to beat out of her chest, she fitted, feeling her muscles spasm, wonderful orgasmic, shuddering, juddering, palpitations coursing like hot wires sewn in-and-out, in-and-out of her flesh, vaguely hearing an alien-girl roaring in her ears,

'What did he give you?'

Close to tears, Janis brushed the soaking wet hair off her deconstructed sister's face and kissed her forehead. She rolled Lindsey onto her side in case she felt like being sick, then left the bedroom, quietly closing the door behind her.

Georgie collided with her. She recognized her pen pal at once from the photo: short, stocky, blushing cheeks, bronze suntan. Only her hair was different. She had dyed it, cupric red,

'Lindsey?'

Janis was stopped in her tracks by the accent; the girl sounded Australian,

'No, I'm Janis. We're twins. People get us confused,' she sighed, her head still in a daze, 'You must be?'

'Georgie. I'm Lindsey's pen pal. From Adelaide?'

Janis turned to face her. Her eyes were red. She looked as if she'd been crying.

'I've read your letters to Lindsey. We keep no secrets.'

Georgie was shocked. Their letters were private and confidential. They contained intimate revelations of the two of them growing up becoming women, their love-lives, the dreams.

What else did she know?

'I saw you playing in the garden, on the swing,' Janis revealed, in a hushed voice, 'Saw you take your top off, saw your breasts. You're a beautiful girl, a naughty girl. I saw you playing, with him. Looks like you were enjoying yourself.'

It suddenly occurred to Georgie, how she must look: her straggly damp hair, dragged thru a clinch backwards, his wet patch on the front of her jeans. Janis edged towards her, tired, strained, seeking relief, in her clingy pink summer dress: no bra or knickers, just the dress,

'Did he fuck you?'

'No, I straddled him.'

Georgie cringed, couldn't believe she just said that.

Janis was blocking her way out. There was no escape. She didn't want to go. Janis needed release. Georgie found her intriguing. She let her kiss her… throatily. They stumbled into the end room. Janis locked the door, told her to take off her top, pull down her jeans, drop her pants. There was a chest of drawers. By the open window. Janis made her stand with her legs apart, palms flat on the chest, staring out at the night sky while she took off her dress. Georgie felt her squashed breasts, pressing onto her shoulder blades, her belly rubbing over her rear. The twin caressed her, gently, exploring her

~ 56 ~

splayed lips with her fingertips, the back of her fist massaging Georgie's clenched buttocks - while she relieved herself,

'That feels lovely, girl, so lovely.'

Georgie sagged to her knees, nerves tingling, in ecstasy, 'Don't stop, please, don't stop.'

After they'd made love, the young women kissed and embraced then quickly got dressed.

Georgie asked after Lindsey.

'She's not well, not feeling her usual self. I've put her to bed,' Janis explained, motherly, caring, intensely fond of her twin, 'Lindsey's had a bad trip. She's really suffering. Think I should call a doctor?'

'A bad trip?'

'Yes, she takes drugs to get high. I've never seen her this bad, tho'. Someone fed her dirt.'

* * * * *

HE LAY DREAMING ON THE bed next door. Happy, content, he surveyed the aftermath of his lovemaking with Georgie. Some of her hairs had moulted over the pillow. He picked them off individually, savouring the sweet smell of her scent. Wearily, he slid off the sheet and eyed their stain on the duvet. He dreaded to think what the twins' parents would say when they returned home. At least they hadn't smoked. His heart sank when he saw their traces embedded in the carpet from when he reached for her, having frightened her. He would have to watch how he spoke to Georgie in future - *if* he wanted to keep her for his own.

His thoughts returned to the mess. The duvet cover, sheet, and pillowcases would have to be laundered. Perhaps Janis would put a wash on in the morning? His seed would need to be scrubbed off. He took a hot sudsy bath, soaking off the snail's trail Georgie smeared on his itchy left thigh, then washed her sweet body scent off his face and neck, his chest. Once he had dried himself, scoured the bath, brush-cleaned the toilet, and hung the towels to dry on the hot rail, he moved on to the bedroom. After crawling over the carpet on all fours dabbing at his specks with a wet flannel, he made the bed as best he could, dressed, switched off the light, and went downstairs.

When he left the house, close on midnight, there was no sign of Janis, or the girl. Everyone was soberly bunched on the pavement. Sensing something terrible might have happened, he broke into their silence.

'There's been an accident,' an Indian boy explained, 'A girl OD'd. She's been rushed to hospital in an ambulance. Let's hope she makes it through the night. She's in an awfully bad way, unconscious, in severe spasm, bleeding from her nose.'

An awfully bad way.

He hung his head in shame, wanting to be sick, 'Yes, let's hope she does.'

By the time he arrived at Reigate Station, his pink day return ticket to Ifield was invalid. The ticket office was closed. He decided to chance his luck, catch the last train to Redhill, then wait for a train to Brighton. He alighted on Platform 3 at Three Bridges an hour later. The walk took him thirty minutes. He didn't crash out on his bed till three in the morning.

He slept on until early afternoon, then lay still, calm, reflecting on his unforgettable night. How the girl imbibed the small phial of concoction which he brewed for her in a saucepan at home. The spectacle she'd made of herself, dancing for him. He hoped she pulled thru. It was never his intention to hurt her. He tried to imagine how she felt, having her stomach pumped out in A&E.

Then he'd met Georgie and fallen in love with her. He recalled how she played with him, on the swing. How tenderly she made love to him. Her kindness and understanding when his immaturity brought their lovemaking to an abrupt end. He'd listened to her afterwards, making noises through the thin wall: her muted cries of passion.

He realised he was inadequate as a lover. Moreover, he felt overwhelmed by his failure to satisfy her, to consummate his love, for her. He couldn't believe she wanted to see him again,

'Tomorrow night,' she'd whispered, 'I'll see you tomorrow night. I love you.'

His hand groped around under the hospital-frame bed for his cheap plastic alarm clock. He checked the time: 1pm. He was meant to be in work by three! His soiled pants lay on the rug from last night. He pulled them on and flew downstairs to the kitchen. There were two large aluminium saucepans filled with water sitting on the fat-caked gas cooker. He brought them to the boil then carefully carried them upstairs to the bathroom. The first pan he used for a cat's lick, washing himself from head to toe with a flannel, the other he used to shave. Soon as he was dry, he sprayed the great smell of *Brut* on his armpits, tore into his room, threw on a t-shirt, shorts, dirty plimsolls, grabbed his wallet, a key, skipped past the living room, kitchen, and scullery, and went outside.

His back door faced the Munt's back door. He hated Munt with a vengeance. Denis Munt was a boastful show-off who'd relished the opportunity to tear off butterfly wings in front of him when he was prepubescent. His brother Bruce had thwacked a cricket ball through the window four years ago. He couldn't afford to have the glass replaced. It was covered with cardboard and heavy-duty tape. Thankfully, *their* door was closed.

He crossed the crazy-paved patio his father laid when he was little, sadly overgrown with weeds, and passed the raised front lawn, striding to the pavement. Cassie, a girl he played hopscotch with as a child, always told him never to step on the cracks. Stepping on the cracks was bad luck. He wondered how she was enjoying life in Australia. His thoughts returned to Georgie, his need to satisfy her on his mother's bed, spend the night wrapped in her arms, her surprise when she woke up in the morning.

First though, he had to excuse himself from work.

The nearest telephone box was ten minutes-walk away in Farndon Close. He wasn't at all surprised to discover that it was vandalized. Telephone boxes were always being smashed up on the Ifield council estate. The next kiosk was in Trenton Road by the local shopping parade, a ten-minute walk. Fifteen minutes later, he slotted one of the new decimal coins into the coin slot and was put through to the airport grill.

He was relieved when the call was answered by Katie Kaltman, the German floorwalker, whose job it was to greet diners, show them to their tables, and present the menu, ensuring they were comfortable. Katie was tall, elegant, refined, with high cheeks, pursed lips, fine auburn hair, and ink-blue eyes. The married woman had seduced him in the Chef's Office. His coming-of-age moment endeared him to her; they'd remained close friends ever since. She spoke eloquently, in a crisp, stilted, halting, stuttering voice,

'Hallo, Air Grill, how may I help you?'

'Katie, it's me.'

She brightened for him, 'Ah, how lovely to hear from you. Will I feel you later?'

Lies came easily to the weekend waiter, 'I'm really sorry, I can't come in to work today.'

Katie dropped the bonhomie, 'Ach, is that so? What is it this time? Headache? Have you overslept?'

'I've been up sick all night with vomiting and diarrhoea. I'm sorry.'

The floorwalker checked her gold wristwatch, 'The time is two o'clock. Your shift starts at three. Why have you left it late to call me? Your unfortunate,' she stammered, 'illness causes me great difficulty today. You know, I have delayed flight in little under two hours for two hundred passengers.'

He cringed with guilt at his latest deception. First, the desecration of the girl. Now this. His time was nearly up. He thought of the chaos that his absence would create. The Grill seated 256 customers: 128 in black leather booths, 128 on round tables of four. Eight staff were needed to service four tables with four customers on each. Delayed flight passengers were invariably rude, stroppy, and unappreciative. They complained about the menu: boil-in-the-bag chicken with mushroom sauce, peas, and chips, followed by vanilla briquette. And they never tipped. Thanks to him, Katie would have to serve them.

The phone made a bleeping noise. He didn't have any more change. He bleated, like one of Georgie's sheep,

'I'm *really* sorry.'

Katie lost her Bavarian mountain cool, 'Please!'

'Yes?'

'Janis called in sick also. Lindsey is in hospital.'

His heart fell into his stomach. The line went dead. He thought of the sachets of fungi lying in the fridge's tiny freezer compartment at home.

* * * * *

FRIDAY NIGHT WAS ONE OF those hot, clammy, sticky July nights when they couldn't sleep, not even with just a sheet over their bodies. Restless, tossing, turning in their attempts to relax, Kayleigh and Matt kicked off the cotton. Still, they perspired: wetting, crumpling the crisp-fresh sheet like incontinent children, until it was hard for them to find a dry strip of bed to lie on. Eventually, they rolled off each other, clinging to the edge of the mattress, and drifted into a fitful sleep.

Matt dreamed of Kayleigh on the sandy beach in Oz dressed for volleyball in her stringy bikini, holding hands as they waded into the warm surf. While she dreamed of him, manly and muscled, embracing her, kissing her, on the crumpled rucks, lifting her petite body off the bed in triumph, his trophy, as she pleaded with him to love her, to give her a child.

She rolled over to face him, her twisted beak brushing his lips. He ran his fingers thru her wet hazel hair. A frisson of need scintillated her soft body, pulsing inside her spinal cord, electrifying her. He ran his thumb over her pouting lips. She felt between his hairy legs…

He gasped in frustration, 'I can't, not *again*. Kayleigh. I'm too knackered.'

'Please, Matt! I want to try for our baby!'

The au pair appeared, bearing a tray laden with egg white omelettes, grilled mushrooms, vine tomatoes, thick-cut slices of toast, churned butter, coarsely shredded Seville orange marmalade, strawberry jam, Marmite, and a large pot of freshly brewed Brazilian coffee,

'I made you some breakfast,' she said.

Kayleigh twisted herself under Matt, craning her neck to see the girl, 'Put it on the side.'

'Sure!' the au pair did as she was told, 'Kayleigh?'

'Mm?'

'I've cleaned the kitchen floor, dusted, hoovered, hung out all the laundry, emptied the dishwasher, prepared you a buffet lunch, rolled your towels for your trip to the pool. As it's my day off today, I thought I might go into Town, meet a few friends, stay the night?'

Kayleigh hesitated, 'Okay...'

'See you tomorrow morning then?' the au pair pretended to leave.

Suddenly, Kayleigh yelled at her, 'Wait!'

The girl paused in the doorway, 'Yes?'

'Come and join us on the bed.'

Georgie casually slipped off her baby negligee and joined Kayleigh and Matt on the bed,

'What would you like me to do?' she murmured.

* * * * *

HE WAS STARTING TO THINK that testing the concoction on the girl might have been a bad idea. If she died in hospital, and her twin squealed, there was every chance that he would be convicted of her manslaughter and see out his life in prison. He dreamed of making love to Georgie on the funeral pyre where he was created, sleeping with her, loving her until sunrise. His sacred surprise. Her eternal dream. He was so preoccupied, preparing for her arrival, that he failed to notice O'Brien bearing down on him.

O'Brien lived across the road at no.12, a childless widow and close friend of his mother. She blocked his passage, politely interfering, as she invariably did,

'Oh, it's you! Would there be any news of your dear mother, sweetheart?'

He cringed: *sweetheart.*

'No news I'm afraid. She never changes.'

O'Brien explained, 'It's just, I was fond of your mum when we worked at the mushroom farm. I thought I might send her some flowers, a nice box of chocolates?'

He studied the ground, lost for words. The world needed more kind souls like O'Brien. When he lifted his head, he was close to tears, choked by the incredible stress he endured,

'That's so kind, but inmates aren't allowed flowers or gifts, in case they cut themselves.'

O'Brien recognized the strain, his grief, their mutual loneliness. She reached out for him,

'I'm sorry. I understand, believe me. Been lonely since Phil died. Give me a hug.'

She took him in her arms. They hugged in the middle of the road. For one lovely moment, he was with Georgie, she was reunited with her husband, and neither of them had a worry in the world. After a while, they found themselves standing on the pavement by her gate. O'Brien wanted him, badly. She hadn't enjoyed the *feeling* of a man since Phil passed. To hell with what the neighbours said. She was only thirty-two, young enough to love again. Her eyes shone with hope: *no harm in asking after all,*

'Would you like to join me for a cup of tea and a slice of my homemade chocolate cake?'

He moved close to her, smelling her, 'I can't, not today. Perhaps another day?'

She smiled, 'Of course, another day. I'm sorry, I got carried away. I *am* nearly old enough to be your mother, after all.'

He comforted her, brushing her cheek with his hand, 'No, you felt good. You were great.'

'Thank you,' she said, sadly, 'You don't know how much that means to me.'

'Be seeing you, then?'

'Yes, be seeing you. Take care of yourself.'

The sun burnt his face. He watched O'Brien walk the shady alleyway, back to loneliness.

* * * * *

THE LIGHTS FLICKERED, THEN CAME on, the train entered a tunnel. Georgie was struggling to keep her eyes open. She felt totally shagged if she was honest. She'd enjoyed herself pleasuring him. His lack of maturity only made her want him more. He intrigued her, gave her the impression he was lonely, struggling to cope with life. In need of love. Like her. Georgie felt sorry for him, she cared about him, missing him, already. And she couldn't wait for nightfall.'

Georgie smiled fondly to herself.

Her brief encounter with Janis had induced exhilarating sensations in her body. It hurt her to think that she might never see her again or meet Lindsey. She'd prayed for Lindsey in bed last night, prayed she survived. Then there was this morning's little episode, playing with Matt on the bed while Kayleigh, desperate to have a baby, watched. Georgie hoped she fell pregnant. They'd *tried* hard enough, *that's* for sure!

No wonder she felt so tired and dreamy. Georgie caught her reflection in the window. With any luck, she hoped, she might just grab forty winks.

* * * * *

HE PREPARED THE HOUSE METICULOUSLY for her arrival. She'd impressed him with her attention to personal hygiene, the way she prepared herself for him in the bathroom, her subtle dab of scent, her oral cleansing routine. Georgie would want to prepare herself again tonight, bathing in the morning, after their never-ending night of love. He turned on the transistor radio on the kitchen windowsill, made himself a lemon squash, then sat at the kitchen table making lists of things to do on the back of old envelopes.

I Am Woman played intermittently on the wireless. Feeling himself stir with eager anticipation, he stopped writing, shut his eyes, and pictured her:

Georgie - my woman.

There were seven sachets of fungi in the freezer compartment: toadstools, wild and magic mushrooms, all hand-picked on his bike rides to fields and forests, leafy glades, deadly-secret retreats. He'd seen a couple in the woods, lying, spreadeagled on a blanket, making love under the hot sun, surrounded by toadstools. That was when his fetish started. When he was fourteen.

After quaffing his squash, he opened the fridge door. Fortunately, there was enough food left for him to cook her breakfast in the morning. When he gave Georgie her surprise: eggs, bacon, mushrooms, spread, stale bread toasted under the grill. The butter was rock hard. He took it out to soften, extracting two fungal sachets from the iced-up freezer box to defrost before he stewed their contents.

Georgie would break his family tradition when she came tonight, arriving at the front door. He found a key in the wooden bowl of knickknacks, he kept it in the knife drawer, went to the hall, and checked the meter. Having used all his change on the call to Katie, he hoped the power lasted all night, imagining the lights going out just as Georgie climbed onto the bed,

She'll need hot water for when she prepares herself for me, for our aftermath, when we bathe together, when I soap her breasts.

He couldn't shake the image of her lying naked, still, and cold, in the bath out of his mind.

He plodded off to the scullery to fetch some coal.

The coalman always knocked twice before entering the back door in case he was still in bed. He'd stand and watch him lean forward, pouring out his dirty cargo like a human chute into the dingy coal hole, choking on clouds of dust, coughing, shouting,

'Coalman!'

He charged 60p a sack for anthracite, the hard jet-black coal that burned slowly in the stove, giving out intense heat.

The anthracite was stored behind three splintery wooden boards. He never tried to move them for fear of creating an almighty avalanche of coal and dust. He loaded a heap of fuel into its scuttle, carried it to the stove, lifted the cast iron lid, and poured it in. Next, he lit the gas wand with a taper, and thrust the flaming poker into a hole at the base of the stove. It took hours to heat up sufficient water for a bath. If the water weren't hot in time, he would boil a saucepan of water for her, if she fancied a cat's lick before she came to bed. His hands, face and nostrils were tarred with coal dust. He ran upstairs to wash, stripping off his soiled clothing in the bathroom, rinsing the heat from his flushed face, shivering as the chill of cold water spilt down his chest.

* * * * *

GEORGIE FELT THE NEED FOR her to find love grow inside her heart like hunger gnawing the belly of a starving war-child. It didn't help that her life had no sense of purpose, no pre-conceived plan, or career. She was a farm girl, pure, and simple. At least, she *used* to be pure when she lived in Adelaide.

Georgie recalled her sheltered life in Rose House, a short walk from the girls' church school she attended from the age of four. The beautiful Church of St Mary the Virgin.

Adelaide is famous for its beautiful churches.

Her thoughts reverted to her controlling mother, the birch-strict upbringing she imposed on her daughter,

Prayers before and after meals. Prayers at bedtime. Prayers of thanks for the sun, soil, wind, rain. Prayers for my daddy. How I miss frolicking in the hayloft with him. Even prayers for his dearly departed sheep!

Since his death, her mother had exerted a fanatical control over her. With that control came the punishments:

Smacking my bare arse if I didn't eat my greens, washing my mouth out with soap and water if her 'little girl' blasphemed. Rachael even used Dad's leather strap to lash me when I feigned illness in my vain attempts not to go to school.

The prohibitive mental and physical abuse Georgie endured behind closed doors as a child left her emotionally scarred. At the age of sixteen, once she had grown into a young woman, she dared to answer back, to fight, to question,

Rachael diminished and shrank, frightened of losing her authority over me, of her daughter's recriminations, the risk of being exposed as my child abuser. She threatened to send me to a convent where I could repent of my sins in silence. I told her to go to Hell. Unless she wanted to read about her sins in the local paper, hear them aired on radio, or have them raised, my red hate-flags, in front of our friendly churchgoing neighbours, Rachael would set me free. The die was cast, our umbilical cord cut, no going back. Rachael paid for me to travel to Europe. She never expected to see or hear from me again. In return, I vowed to stay silent.

She left the crowd of tourists at the Victoria Memorial, wandering into Green Park to find a shady tree, grassy patch, time, and space, to think. Checked her wristwatch. It was noon. The sun was at its zenith. There wasn't a cloud in sight. She felt hot, flustered,

Why do I have to sweat so much?

The scorched grass was littered with sunseekers, office workers using lunch hour to top up their already-brown suntans. Several women stripped off to their bras and briefs, basking on towels, creating spectacles for their hordes of shirtless male admirers. Georgie wished she could join them. There wasn't time, not if she wanted to enjoy her last night of passion. Surprised by her own daring, she came up with a plan for the night, a possible way for her to start a new life.

She unzipped her overnight bag, ruffling through the carefully folded shirts, jeans, panties. Her gold open-toed sandals were inside, along with her make-up bag, toiletries, favourite scent, a soft padded pouch. She unzipped the pouch. They were still in there. Her intimate precautions,

'Tonight,' she told herself, 'I'll make love naturally, flesh-in-flesh, without the cumbersome feel of a sheath.'

This daunting prospect left her giddy with excitement. Butterflies flitted inside her stomach. For the first time since the party, Georgie felt her appetite return.

She crossed the crowded park, found a sandwich bar off Piccadilly, bought a cheese and onion bap, banana, Penguin, and a can of Tab, then sat outside watching the world go by. The street was packed with sightseers, double-decker buses, taxis queuing at a red light opposite the hotel. Georgie bit into her bap, dreaming of how romantic it would be for her to enjoy posh afternoon tea, dancing herself dizzy with him at The Ritz.

Revitalized by lunch, Georgie walked the length of Piccadilly until she reached the statue of Eros, its fountain, splashing her hot face with water. Then she shopped in earnest, buying sexy lingerie at Ann Summers in Wardour Street, a stunning pair of scarlet satin hot pants, matching singlet, from a trendy boutique in Carnaby Street.

Satisfied that she had made the purchases necessary for an unforgettable night, Georgie spent the rest of the afternoon sightseeing, dozing on the Tube between stops, hatching out her secret plan.

Before her train was announced, she tried ringing Janis from a booth at Victoria Station. There was no reply.

Georgie caught the Horsham train as the light began to fade, hiding inside a toilet cubicle, its latch hard down. There, she underwent her final metamorphosis, emerging as a beautiful imago for her unsuspecting lover after dusk.

* * * * *

BY SUPPERTIME, HE HAD DAMP dusted, dusted, and brushed the whole house, paying attention to the cleanliness of his mum's bedroom and bathroom. He fluffed the pillows on her side of the bed, electing that Georgie should lie there, checked beneath the stack of dad's men's magazines he kept hidden from view on the tallboy shelf. There were three sheaths. He supposed three was enough. He quickly stowed them under his pillow.

Once he'd made the bed, it was time for exercises. He lifted his Bullworker, kneeling in front of the mirror, pulling the stiff cables, compressing its unyielding piston barrel until the muscles in his arms, legs, neck, chest, and abdomen ached, tensed, and toned. Admiring his v-shaped torso, he adopted a few super-man poses, amused by the sight of myself, a sweaty Mr Universe. He threw the device in the tallboy, then he went to the kitchen.

The coals were burning brightly in the stove,

Great news! There'll be plenty of hot water for Georgie, with a second bath-full for when we soak off in the morning.

He removed the gas wand, turning off the gas. The last thing he needed was an explosion! The radio played *Let's Stay Together*, the seven o'clock news came on. He opened a can of beans, grilled two slices of toast, then sat at the table scoffing his meagre dinner, listening to the latest headlines. The Vietnam War was over. The last US combat troops would leave in a month. But the Troubles in Northern Ireland persisted. He wondered if the world would ever find peace. At least there were The Olympic Games to look forward to - and his school exam results.

He switched off the radio, covering his worn-out face with his hands: one of life's failures. Instinctively, he knew that he had failed his Chemistry, Zoology, and Botany A Levels - even with his superior knowledge of fungi. Since his mother's hospitalisation, he had lost all hope, finding it impossible to concentrate at school and study at home. He struggled to deal with his gnawing obsession. Then there was the weekend and holiday job at the airport that he couldn't afford to lose; he must return to work, full of

~ 68 ~

apologies to Katie, next weekend. And the sixteen-pounds-a-week widow's pension he drew from the Post Office on the strength of a letter signed by Mary four years ago.

The sachet of fungi had defrosted, the butter on the ledge was soft. He took out a non-stick saucepan and sweated the mushrooms until they were coloured, adding a little water, stirring his cauldron attentively, seasoning to taste. Following the girl's overdose, it was important to dilute the broth to exactly the right concentration if he didn't want to endanger Georgie's life. He planned to administer the drug ti her orally, in bed, over breakfast. When the mushrooms were fully cooked, beige, and tender, he strained off the jus, placing it in a stoppered sloe gin phial to cool in the larder, saving the wildest, magic, toadstools in case she fancied an omelette.

Once he'd washed up and dried, he went upstairs to shave, brush his teeth, change into his best striped, white shirt, navy flares, stacked shoes. He hung his favourite stainless-steel medallion, St Christopher, patron saint of travel, round his neck. It made him feel manly. Increasingly nervous, edgy, incredibly excited, he sat on the edge of my bed and waited.

* * * * *

THERE WAS A LOUD, PERSISTENT rapping on the front door. It could only be Georgie. He leapt off the bed and bounded down the stairs like a greyhound chasing a hare, a hound smelling the scent of a vixen, *her* scent. Threw open the door. And she was there for him. Beautiful. Adorable. The first change he noticed in her was she was wearing a bright red rouge that complemented her scarlet singlet and tiny hot pants. Her chest, arms, legs, and feet were bare, pale, in spite of her time sunning herself on the beaches of Europe. She was wearing open-toed sandals, a post box red nail varnish on her toes. Her smile lit her face from ear to ear. She stepped over the mantel to be with him, the compulsion in her heart enriching the syrupy-smooth lure congealing within her enchanting voice,

'Well, how do I look?'

'You look sensational.'

'Thank you.'

He quickly shut the door, so the neighbour wouldn't see her. It would hurt O'Brien if she saw her like this. Georgie dropped her bag on the slate-tiled floor, reached, and took him by the scruff of the neck, stroking his wavy hair, rubbing his earlobes in the way he loved. He drew her soft body to him, loving the warm sensation of her breasts pressing against his chest, the inscribed medallion. They kissed, a deep, longing kiss, fully-open-mouthed, in the style of lovers who want sex: they ate each other's palates. She panted for him, his starving lioness,

'Been thinking about you all day. Don't know what's got into me. Need you.'

Her reassuring words filled him with affection for her, satiating his lust, heartening him,

'I *really* love you, Georgie.'

She took in all the flaking lead paint, the mould on the window, faded rose wallpaper, his threadbare carpet running up the staircase.

So, this is how the poor live, she decided, tinkering with the chain on his medallion. He felt different to her tonight, more masculine. Georgie asked him directly,

'Can we go to bed, please?'

He struggled to contain himself, to control his pent-up emotions,

'If you insist.'

She burst out laughing, loving his dry Sussex humour, the feeling of just *being* with him? She let him carry her bag for her, following him up the creaking staircase. Unlike home, there were no trinkets on the windowsills, paintings, or photographs, only bare walls. This place felt dull, bleak, unloved: a house, not a home. They reached the landing. Two of the ivory lace doors were shut.

What lies behind the doors? Who lives here? What are their lives like?

He hadn't discussed *his* life. It occurred to Georgie that she barely knew him. She only knew she needed him more than ever to fulfil her secret dream. A third door led to the bedroom where they would make love. There was a wardrobe in the corner, a patterned quilt on the bed. She asked for the toilet, her bath,

'Have to wash and prepare myself. Will you wait for me on the bed?'

He flushed puce, her candid statement, her enticing question, set his loins on fire,

'I put the boiler on, Georgie. There's plenty of hot water, towels, flannels, bath salts too if you need them,' he said, handing her the overnight bag.

Her puffy lips brushed his ear, 'Thank you, see you on the bed.'

Georgie entered the small room on her left and shut the door, bolting the latch firmly behind her, opening the frosted glass window to let in some air. She stripped off her singlet, hot pants, thong, hung them on a cheap plastic hook on the back of the door, and ran herself a bath.

* * * * *

NIGHT CREPT IN FROM OUTSIDE, cooling the hot air. He shut the window, drawing the curtain so that O'Brien wouldn't see them making love. Georgie had expressed a preference for lying on top of the bed. He wondered if she fancied a walk in the woods in the morning, a naked dip in the stream, drying off on his tartan fishing blanket? He could make up a picnic for her before she left him to return home. Life without Georgie would be unimaginable. She lit his whole existence, a shining beacon of hope in his dark, uncertain world.

There was a spare sheet on the top shelf of the wardrobe. He took it down, spreading it over the bed to protect Mary's quilt. He supposed he would have to visit her soon, at her reinforced sanctuary in the forest, the hideous mental asylum that reeked of used *Dettol*, to explain about Georgie moving in. The thought of seeing her: sedated, trussed in a straitjacket, dosed to the eyeballs, drooling, spitting, spluttering, as she tried to speak without her false teeth; filled him with dread - let alone attempting to have an intelligible conversation with her.

His mind filled with Georgie's face:

Would she want to see him again after he had administered her bizarre morning surprise? Would she partake? Suppose she didn't like mushrooms?

He slid his hand into his flare pocket, extracting the sheaths, tearing off the wrappers, removing each one in turn, arranging them tidily at her bedside. To use at her pleasure through the short summer night.

He removed his shirt, flares, pants, and socks, lying in the middle of the bed where she expected him to lay. Proudly, he fingered his sexy medallion. There was nothing else left to do but wait for his beautiful imago to emerge from her chrysalis. And spread her wings.

* * * * *

MEANWHILE, IN THE BATHROOM, GEORGIE swished the water in the bath with the blade of her hand to make sure it was lukewarm, tepid to her touch, anxious not to trigger yet another rash of embarrassing sweating before she made love. She turned off the taps, singing lightly to herself, reaching for the pile of towels her lover left for her, neatly stacked on their pedestal. The pink face flannel and matching towels were good as new.

Who are these were intended for. His mother? Sister?

Intrigued, she scanned the windowsill: a cannister of *Brut* spray-on deodorant, a dead upturned bluebottle, *Johnson's* baby powder, nothing unusual, bottle of *Silvikrin* anti-dandruff shampoo at one end of the bath, used bar of *Wright's* coal tar soap. An unlucky green toothbrush, rolled-up tube of *Colgate* on the wash basin. No other signs of male or female activity.

In her experience, homes gave up their secrets in the shadiest of places: in cupboards, drawers, wardrobes, tallboys, bureaux, desks, dressers, medicine cabinets. The sparkling cabinet hung on the wall over the toilet. She smiled in the mirror, opening the door with its fake brass knob. Other than a spool of sticking plaster, tube of muscle rub, and tub of *Germolene*, the cupboard was bare. Except for the small smoked brown glass bottle on the top shelf. Georgie removed it and examined the faded-yellow paper label: Tincture of Quinine.

Who does this belong to?

Her daddy fought in the jungles of Burma during the War, telling her stories of leech-infested swamps, crawling termite mounds, the endless plagues of bloodthirsty mozzies. Quinine was the antidote for recurrent malaria.

So where is <u>his</u> dad, his mum for that matter?

Her thoughts were rudely interrupted by a squabble of swifts jousting in the eaves. It was almost dark. Any questions could wait until sunrise.

Georgie placed the towels and flannel on the carpet within easy reach and clambered into the bath. She sat with her legs outstretched, contemplating her toes. The warm water came up to her hips, soothing her. She closed her eyes and relaxed, dreaming of how far she had come since leaving home.

Her journey had been an erotic carnival, a cavalcade of one-night stands, intimate liaisons, close shaves. Perilous near misses that stretched from Amalfi to Rome, Venice, Grimaud, Rochelongue, Tarragona, Cascais, and Reigate. Her acts of rebellion, she called them, reprisals. Retaliatory actions, full of contempt, reproach, imputing blame on her mother for the revolting way that Georgie was physically and mentally abused as a child.

She wondered if she could ever forgive Rachael for how she mistreated her, the ridiculous non-disclosure agreement she signed in return for financial security. Under the terms of the pact, she was bound to a lifetime of silence about Rachael, in return for a guaranteed monthly income until her death, when Georgie would inherit her entire estate. Unless Rachael met with an unfortunate accident: snake bite, car crash, encounter with a venomous spider, she was unlikely to die for years. The devout was healthy, an active fifty-something who avoided the temptations of sex, alcohol, meat, fish, and cigarettes; preferring to place her faith in an ever-forgiving god.

With Georgie's adventure into sexual proficiency came romance, heartbreak, her trail of broken hearts. Janis had succumbed to her deadly charms, joining her at the epicentre of a complicated web of deceit. Then there were the calculated risks she took: her chance meeting with Pasquale in the red-light district, a sordid backstreet in Marseilles. Pasquale, who invited his friends, 'mes amis', to join in the fun. They'd drawn out their flick-knives. Georgie fled their squalid apartment to save her life.

Now, she was about to entrap *him*. She soaked her crotch before climbing out of the bath, dried herself, reached for the *Johnson's* talc, and patted it on, tenderly, as if she still had her baby's bottom.

Georgie knew full well her promiscuity made her vulnerable to predators but she couldn't help herself. Couldn't control the surges of emotion in her mind - lowering her defences. She trusted him, inside her at least. His unfeeling comment, asking if her dad hurt when he died, had stung her heart. Did he genuinely care for her as much as she cared for him? Or were his cries of love just impulses? She had no desire to have his baby. Or did she? Georgie wasn't sure what she wanted anymore, other than certainty.

The daring lingerie by Ann Summers suited Georgie's needs perfectly, freeing the siren in her. Thrilled by her sensual transformation, she dabbed scent behind her ears, left the bathroom, and padded to the open door. He was waiting for her on the bed, a puma about to pounce, staring at the spider's webs on the ceiling. He heard her whisper, softly,

'Close your eyes.'

Feeling her presence, he shut his eyes, his heart pumping wildly for her. She set him free,

'You can open them now.'

He gazed at Georgie in awe of her: his Aphrodite, goddess of love, an angel come to save his lonely soul. She stood at the foot of the bed, beaming at him, dressed in just a g-string. He didn't know what to do with her at first. Her behaviour was daring. Her love, her tactile touch, intoxicated him, suffocating him, making it hard for him to breathe, smell, touch, taste. He climbed off the bed, his senses returning, smelling the animal scent on her. They lost all self-control,

'Georgie…'

'Kiss me, touch me, love me.'

He seized her, pushing the soft hair off her face, forcing her head back, hard, so that he could kiss her deeply, feeling no resistance. She spat out his tongue, freeing her mouth from his love-leech, his overt oral intrusion, imploring him to explore her body. He indulged her, leaving a trail of molten kiss down her neck and chest, alighting on her swollen breasts, cupping them in his hands, kneading them as he sucked her shiny nipples erect, a bloodthirsty vampire, ravenous for her love. She purred, her cat's paws clawing at the hairy small of his back, slashing his skin, loving the lick-spit she felt trickle down her stomach, probing her deep navel, the wet slop of her man's tongue slathering over her belly, as he ambled ever downwards,

'Pull off my g-string!'

Not: please, would you take off my g-string? Or: would you mind taking off my g-string? But pull it off! She thrilled as he tore off her string, unbinding her, untying her scorched lust. Felt his coarse fingers grip her soft buttocks. Felt him lick her wet cleft. Went all weak at the knees,

'Lie down!'

'Georgie, I...!'

Before he could finish, she shoved him in the chest, forcing him to fall back onto the bed. He lay momentarily winded, stupefied by Georgie's sexual bravado, happy for her to take control. His proud flesh reared, straining for her as she squatted over him, facing the other way, back to his, astounding him with her salacious, sexy, daring, her loving practicality,

'Keep still while I slip you inside me.'

'Georgie!'

She felt his hands caress her hips. Felt highly aroused if truth be told!

'Mm?'

'I'm not wearing a ...'

'Don't need to.'

'Why not?'

'I'm safe.'

He shook his head. She mounted him, reclining, her buttocks pressing into his hairy belly, her slender back hugging his chest. His face was smothered in sweat. She sealed his mouth with a kiss. Their lips parted. He felt her breath warm his cheek,

'Hold me!' she pleaded.

He fondled her heaving breasts, then gently slid his palm over her tummy, massaging her soft, hairy mound with his fingertips. She arched her body upwards...

After, Georgie lay on her side facing him, loving his tenderness, the feeling of being held in his burly arms, her deep calm: the aftermath of their lovemaking. She was crying. He kissed away her tears. She read his thoughts, softly kissing him back, saying in a whisper,

'I'm crying because you make me so happy.'

At first, he was lost for words. When he did speak, his voice was choked with emotion,

'You're all I have, Georgie. I love you.'

He burst into tears, crying on her shoulder. She held him to her breasts, stroking his damp cheeks, consoling him, conscious of the colossal risk she had taken: the cap, lying, unused in the hand basin, her endless quest for certainty in life.

'That's right, sweetest,' she soothed, 'Let it all out. Tell me. Why are you so unhappy?'

He remembered the toadstools, the deadly concoction in his fridge, and stopped crying.

His earliest memory, he recalled, was lying on a hospital bed in a darkened room being put to sleep with gas. He remembered a suffocating sensation, having a rubber mask fitted to his face, a strange-funny odour, feeling himself smile, laughing, drifting into contented, dreamless sleep. Except, he was conscious when the surgeon made the incision.

Georgie was horrified, 'They cut you *there* while you were wide awake?' she felt his head rub her breast, 'That must've hurt. What did you do?'

'There wasn't much I *could* do,' he said, feeling awkward, 'My lips were numb, my face was covered with a mask, my limbs were like lead, I couldn't speak.'

She ruffled his hair affectionately, giving his hand a friendly squeeze, 'You poor thing!'

'I was in agony. Ever since then I've had dark dreams.'

'You mean nightmares?'

'No, these are dreams, and they come true.'

Georgie felt as if a Funnel Web just crawled down her back, 'Don't! I don't like it.'

'Would you like me to tell you about them?'

'No, I wouldn't,' she insisted, changing subject, 'I've never fallen in love before. We just made love, didn't we? I love you but I feel as if I hardly know you.'

He snuggled up to her warm body,

'I've had a hard life,' he began, 'I was never told why the doctors operated on me that night. I grew up in a family without love. My dad was a cold-hearted man who seldom spoke to me. I wasn't allowed to speak to him, unless spoken to first. He loved his beer, golf, fishing. Dad used to take me fishing in the rain and make me sit outside the umbrella.'

Georgie felt the tufts of hair in his armpit, lightly stroking his hairy chest, 'He let you get wet? Didn't you catch cold?'

'I did catch cold. I was soaked by the time he packed up. He didn't want to get his gentles wet.'

'His gentles?' she giggled, enjoying the feel of her man's damp groin pressed to her thigh.

'Maggots.'

'Ugh!'

He continued, 'I used to go to the mudhills when I was little, to chase butterflies. I never hurt them…'

'I should hope not!'

'…just chased them. One day I caught a lizard, brought it home. It escaped, hid under the carpet. It's still here somewhere. Anyway, Dad wasn't amused. He kept a scratching stick for his back, so that Mum could scratch him if he itched. When she told him about the lizard, he swore at us. Damn! he said. It was the only time I ever heard him swear. He made me take off my t-shirt, then he smacked me with his stick until I bruised and bled.'

Georgie recalled the terrible abuse her mother subjected her to while her daddy was out, tending the sheep: *sheep may safely graze?* She found herself being drawn closer to him as his story unfurled. His life was nearly as strange as hers,

'How awful for you. Didn't your mum try and stop him?'

'Mum didn't dare say a word. She worshipped Dad as if her life depended, which it did. You see, Mary was seriously ill, paranoid schizophrenic, the doctor said, falling apart, creeping into the dark. I saw her descend into mental hell. Dad tried to manage her. In the end he couldn't cope. He used to send me on errands to the Parade.'

Georgie screwed up her face, 'The Parade?'

'The Shopping Parade. To buy cigarettes. He used to smoke sixty a day. Smoking helped him live with Mum's highs and lows. In the end he called our GP, Dr Reynard, round. He arrived in the middle of the night with a colleague. Mum was sitting in her armchair, watching the little girl on the tv test screen. It was horrid, Georgie. She chewed her lips until they bled, kept mumbling, 'I'll be fine.' But she was sick in the mind. When the doctors walked in, Dad warned them to be careful in case she turned violent. They found her in the kitchen with scissors, a biro, inking the eyes in her wedding photo, cutting out my dad's face. Dad was in tears. He asked Mum to calm down, hand him the scissors. She tried to stab him. I stood there wetting myself, screaming at her to leave him alone. Dr Reynard gave her two injections to put her to sleep. An ambulance turned up with its blue lights flashing, waking all the neighbours. I went outside in my pyjamas to wave her goodbye. The neighbours were all watching us behind their curtains. They didn't expect to see an ambulance in our road at three in the morning. Then a police car arrived - someone reported a disturbance. By then I was a bag of nerves. I just wanted everyone to leave so that I could be alone. Dad told me to go to bed. No: 'I love you, son.' Or: Don't worry they'll make Mum well.' Just: 'Go to bed'. I crawled upstairs and hid under the covers in case she came back.'

He broke down. Georgie comforted him, stroking his hair, kissing his forehead, holding him tight until the terror subsided,

There's more sadness, gloom, and despair to come, she thought, *more black, black, black, yet to pour from his tear-well of heartaches, his sorry lips. How can I leave him like this? Should I break my vow of silence?*

She disentangled herself from him, rolled off the bed, and stood up,

'I'm sorry,' she said, 'I have to go.'

Panic!

'Go?! Go where?'

'Don't worry so much. Nature calls! I *am* coming back!'

He sniffed a sigh of relief, 'I thought you were leaving me.'

She left the room without looking over her shoulder, her mind in a turmoil, her heart torn.

Georgie hobbled into the bathroom, leaving the door open. There was no need for privacy anymore. She had given her body to him twice in the space of a day but had yet to divulge the secrets in her mind. The cap was in the basin, upturned like the cap on a brown toadstool. It served no purpose. She'd made her decision. There was no going back. She just needed to be sure.

Sighing to herself, she rinsed it in soapy water, returning it to its pouch. Her clothes were littered on the floor. She folded them neatly, put them on her bag with her sandals, then went off to explore the house.

Georgie opened the box room door, shocked by the glare from the bare bulb. There was a smell of fresh paint. The window had no curtains. Instinctively, she covered her breasts and crotch to protect her modesty. If she expected to find signs of human habitation, she was disappointed. The box covered a recess over the staircase taking up a third of the room. Its wooden top was daubed in gloss. She dabbed it with her finger: tacky. The magnolia walls, ceiling and window frames were sparkling fresh with paint. There was a folded z-bed in the corner.

Was he expecting a guest, a lodger - or me to stay?

She tiptoed over the bare floorboards to the window. Save for a white minivan the street was empty, the streetlights switched off. Georgie hazarded a guess that it was close to midnight. There was no real night here in July. In three hours, it would start to get light. By five o'clock the sun would rise. She thought of her mother: sipping her mid-morning coffee on the veranda, watching the rain fall, wrapped up snug and warm, weathering the winter. What would Rachael make of her little darling now? She opened the window, needing some fresh air. The stars were out, filling the night sky with twinkles. There was a crescent moon. Everything was still, calm, and silent. Georgie felt a little insignificant.

A light came on in the house opposite. Someone else was finding it hard to sleep. Scared she might be seen, she backed out of the room, and shut the door. Georgie suspected he was asleep, judging by the snuffles coming from their bed. No need to wake him, not just yet. She entered his room.

His bed was in the far corner. Spread over the quilt was a copy of *The Sun,* opened to reveal a topless model. Georgie shrugged her shoulders: no surprises there then. What *did* surprise her was the poster on the wall; a psychedelic band playing amidst a fuzzy haze of flashing lights, fog, dancers, strobes. An orange notebook lay on the floor. She picked it up, flicking the pages. The book was full of scrawl, numerals. She had no idea what they meant. There was a collapsed chest of drawers. Georgie checked each drawer: socks, pants, shorts, t-shirts, a sweet smell of mothballs, nothing out of the ordinary. A clean rug. No dust or cobwebs. She was impressed with how well he coped, living on his own. Seemingly…

The last thing she expected to find was a fully made-up wooden cot, toy bell, baby's rattle, and, lying on the floor, a pink teddy bear.

Her mind flashed back to Kayleigh pinned to the bed by Matt while she cradled her crying head, assuring her that, this time, she would fall pregnant. Kayleigh and Matt had tried for a baby for years. Georgie suspected he was infertile.

She wanted a little baby of her own, a child she could suckle, cherish, nurture, love, treasure for the rest of her life. Seeing the cot, sitting empty, waiting for an infant to arrive, confirmed her aspirations. Georgie thought of the date circled in red felt pen in her pocket diary, the egg lain within her, ripe, ready for his sperm. She had 'kind of felt him' inside her but she had to be sure. This might be her last chance.

She crept up to the bed and lay beside him. He was asleep, flat on his back, lips rippling, away with the faeries. Silent as a prowling leopard, Georgie stalked her prey, running her soft hand over his flaccid organ until he was turgid, erect. He woke up craving her, her wanton words,

'Wake up, sleepy head. Want you.'

Georgie lay spreadeagled on the bed, irresistible to him,

'Lie on top of me,' she murmured.

He loved her with incredible ferocity, mounting her, pinning her arms and legs to the bed, as if she were his butterfly. Hungry for him, she licked his shoulder, savouring his skin. He felt her press her lips to his neck, opening her mouth, setting her jaws, biting, bruising him, piercing his skin, drawing off his blood, as they ascended her final pinnacle of love.

'I love you,' she whispered sweetly, afterwards, 'You can sleep inside me if you like?'

She rolled on her side. He snuggled up to her, gently shifting her slender leg, sheathing himself in her intimate warmth. The twilight sky lightened. They slept, deeply entwined, deeply in love.

* * * * *

DAWN BROKE WITH A GLORIOUS chant of birdsong, sunshine burst into the room. She stirred briefly in his arms, then they went back to sleep.

He awoke with a dead arm from sleeping on one side. Wearily, he peeled his body off of hers, careful not to wake her, straightening his legs, flexing his numb hand. The church bells were pealing in the distance at St Margaret's ready for *matins*. He checked his wristwatch: it was nine o'clock on a peaceful Sunday morning.

He climbed off the bed and admired her. Georgie looked beautiful asleep, bathed in sunlight. Vulnerable. He couldn't believe his luck.

His initial sexual longing for her had turned into a dangerous obsession: an infatuation. The air was stale, suffocating, stagnated by the heat of their lovemaking. He stood in front of the mirror, taking a good look at himself. His hair was bedraggled, ruffled by her touch. His eyes, sore and red. He stroked his bristled chin: needing a damn good shave. His chest was matted with sweat, his abdomen, slick with her secretions. He stank to high heaven. He bolted the bathroom door. Her bag was perched on the toilet. He slung it on the floor, flipped the lid, and urinated.

He ran himself a much-needed bath, enraged to find the water was lukewarm. Tasting her sour tang in his mouth, he brushed his teeth, rinsed, and spat her out. His neck was still tender from where she bit him. He suffered a cautious shave then climbed into the bath. Sinking underwater, breathing rafts of bubbles, he imagined all the fascinating things he would do to Georgie - when she woke up.

* * * * *

WHEN HE RETURNED TO THE bedroom, she was lying on the bed haphazardly: one knee jutting over the edge of the bed, her arm dangling loose, fingers brushing the carpet. Sensing his presence, she opened her eyes, wiped away the mascara crusts, and grinned, appreciating the bulge in his stone-ground shorts. The time for intimacy was over. Today, she would break his heart. Maybe tell him at the end? First though, she had to deal with life's little practicalities,

'Could you pass me a tissue?' she said, her pale cheeks coloured by a healthy blush.

He couldn't stop looking at her. She looked radiant, bathed in the morning sun. In the space of thirty-six hours, his love for her had turned into an addiction. He was dependent.

For a moment, she was at sixes and sevens as to what to say; he looked so pensive. She reached for his medallion, drawing him in to her, as if he were her puppy-dog on a lead,

'Come here,' she said, running her soft fingertips down his face, 'You're lovely and soft.'

He looked manly dressed in his tight-fitting shorts, medallion strung down his hairy chest. His face was smooth, velvet. She held his face in her hands and kissed him.

He broke into a broad smile. He loved her when she behaved like this. She was his paradise,

'I shaved for you,' he said.

'Like I shaved for you, last night.'

They burst out laughing, the ice had been broken.

'Yes! Like that!'

'You smell great.'

'It's the smell of Brut,' he declared, 'I made you breakfast. Think you should eat before it gets cold?'

'Oh, how lovely! What a treat!'

'Now let's sit you up, shall we?'

He pulled her body forward, fluffing the pillows behind her, sitting her up straight, his floppy rag doll. She loved being fussed over, breakfast in bed on a sunny Sunday morning. What a wonderful surprise. He drew back the curtains. There were no nets. The whole street could see them.

Let them see us, he told himself, *let the world see our love, let the world see my woman.*

A tiny voice:

'Hello?'

'Yes?'

'You were going to fetch me breakfast?'

'Oh, yes.'

He scurried off to the landing while Georgie made herself comfortable, returning seconds later with what looked like, to her, a giant beanbag with a board on top. She asked him,

'What's *that*?'

'It's a lap-tray.'

He set the tray down on her lap. There was bacon, omelette, buttered toast cut in quarters, a knife, fork, salt pot, pepper pot, tissue to wipe her mouth with, no drink. Still, the whole array looked most appetizing, even professional. Georgie was famished. She tucked in,

'This tastes delicious,' she observed, chomping away at the omelette, 'What is it?'

'It's wild mushroom. I pick them in the local woods. I'll take you there if you like. I've left the bath for you. I thought we could go for a walk to Ifield Mill. It's beautiful at this time of the year. Then we could follow the river as far as the woods. I could show you where I pick mushrooms. I thought you might like to see the church, share a ploughman's lunch in the White Hart. You'll love the pub, it's got white-washed walls, old men playing darts, we can sit outside, if you'd rather…'

He studied her face which had started to soften like warm pulled plasticine. To be on the safe side, he had decided to soak the mushrooms in his special concoction. The liquor would, he was certain, have been diluted during the cooking process. There was no point in harming her. He didn't want to *hurt* her in any way. He loved her, unlike the girl - he didn't love *her*. He noticed she had finished her omelette already, and started on the toast,

That's right! Eat it all up! There's a good girl!

Georgie was having difficulty chewing the toast, difficulty speaking for that matter. She felt her mouth swell, had to chew hard to masticate, to digest the toast, struggled to talk,

'Had enough now, thank you. Enough now.'

She had trouble focusing. Even his face was blurred. Nice blur though, dreamy, blur…

He watched her slump onto the bed, her face flushed and bloated. He took the lap-tray off her. No point in spilling toast crumbs on his parent's bed.

Georgie felt her brain fill and swell like a sodden sponge,

'Will it hurt?' she mumbled.

'No,' he promised, 'It won't hurt.'

She wasn't frightened. Even as her lips swelled up, she trusted him, believed in him. After all he loved her with all his heart, didn't he? Surely, he wouldn't let her come to any harm. An aura of subdued light formed around his head, a halo effect. She felt confused. Felt his body join hers on the bed, a strong arm round her midriff pulling her into him, supporting her. The tender grip of strong fingers in her hair, holding her by the nape, pressing her face to his shoulder. Georgie felt safe, secure. Her mind exploded into natural colour. She closed her eyes, the hallucinations began.

She was lying naked, spread-eagled on a woollen blanket under him, staring at the midday sun through gaps in the gently swaying trees. The trees undulated, moving in a lime green swathe on a sweet summer breeze, the tranquil, soothing lull of birdsong. Her mood went to perceived formality: mind full, white background noise, staff serving, blurred images, tables. She focused her mind's eye on a feast set before her: strawberries, cream, fizzing saucers, champagne, a mother, presiding over her tastes. Except, this mum wasn't cruel, dowdy, heartless. This mum loved her child. Georgie felt herself reach out and touch her hand, almost felt the diamond on her ring finger.

Then she was with him, laughing, happier beyond words, rolling in hay, helping her daddy dip endless fluffy droves of sheep. His muffled voice,

'That'll put hairs on your chest, Georgie, swimming in the dip!'

The dream went surreal: swimming wild in woodland, carpets of red and white toadstools. Dewponds, interspersed by hazels, birch, weeping willows, far as she could see, far as her bedraggled brain could take. Standing on a grassy bank, holding hands with god-knows-who, deciding when to take a leap of faith. Psychedelic dewponds, crazy artists' palettes, pastel shades: pear, avocado, kiwi, lemon, mango, peach.

Georgie jolted.

He felt her jolt, holding her hand tightly, she leapt...

Into dark olive waters. From which she surmised there could be no return. She heard her inner self, felt her body, suspend, float, in water, tiny, nude, foetal, baby, tethered by her umbilical cord. Her baby turned, inverted in womb, head down, eyes shut, shoulders back,

Brace yourself, Georgie, brace yourself, girl!

One, mighty push! She shot out of the womb, a rocket in a bottle set free, body, mind, soul reborn. She felt herself, slop out of her mummy's tummy, a slimy, bloodied mess of a kid, suckling on her mother's nipple. Her sticky eyelids peered open for the first time. She found herself in the real world, a survivor, cradled by her rescuer's arms, breathless, speechless, a child once more.

He held her in his arms, rubbing her back, stroking her thin hair, while the swelling in her throat, mouth, lips subsided. These were the moments he enjoyed most: the tender, loving, intimate moments when she needed him to care for *her*. He felt her hands wander over his hips, lips kiss his shoulder, as she came back to life. When he lay her to rest, he noticed her cheeks were damp from crying, she was blushing, her eyes were all shiny, and bright,

'That was the most wonderful time of my life,' she said in a small child's voice.

He brushed a wet wisp of hair off her face, kissing her forehead, relieved: she hadn't gone into coma,

'I'm thrilled for you,' he said, 'Do you remember how you felt?'

She couldn't wait to tell him, 'I felt as if I was floating in a dreamy land.'

He looked at her, puzzled, 'Dreamy land?'

'Mm, the Land of the Nod!' she laughed, impishly, 'I dreamed I was lying on a blanket in a wood staring at a cloudless blue sky through gaps in the treetops. You were inside my body,' she lowered her voice, not wanting anyone else to hear, 'My mind. The ground was *all* covered in toadstools.'

He recalled the time he saw the couple on the blanket in Ifield Woods; they were shrouded in toadstools, too,

'What happened next?'

'I found myself having tea with a woman in a hotel or restaurant. Can't be sure which.'

'Somewhere like The Ritz, you mean?'

'Yes!' she said brightly, 'That's right. Strange thing is, she was so kind, loving towards me. Wasn't like that in real life. If I tell you, what she did to me, will you promise not to tell?'

'I promise not to tell anyone,' he assured her.

Georgie started to cry,

'She abused me, brutally, if I did any wrong, or spoke out of turn. My mother believed I should live a chaste life. Rachael used her punishments to keep me under control, always when dad was busy: shearing, dipping the sheep. Things got worse after he died. She beat me for no reason, locked me in a cupboard under the stairs, washed my mouth with soap and water. Once, she even fed me dirt.'

The blood drained out of his face, 'How could she be so cruel to you, her own daughter? What did you do?'

'When I was sixteen, I mustered up the courage to fight back, confronted her, told her I'd report her to our church, police, a local rag, anyone to stop her hurting me. She changed, threatened to send me to a convent to keep me quiet. I told her where to go. We made an agreement. Can you believe that? She made me sign a legal document forbidding me from revealing the truth. In return I receive a monthly allowance.'

'She pays you to keep your mouth shut?'

'You could say that.'

Neither of them spoke.

They lay in each other's arms consoling each other.

Two lost souls.

'I dreamed I was a child again,' Georgie whispered, her voice laced with wonder, 'dreamt my daddy was alive, frolicking in the hay with me, the baby lambs. He gave me one as a pet, y'know. I called her Brenda.'

He burst out laughing, 'Brenda?! You *are* joking, aren't you?'

She giggled, 'Course I'm not. I named her after my aunt in Brisbane if you don't mind!'

'Ah, course you did.'

'Stop it!'

'Sorry, just teasing.'

It was late morning, Georgie was still in bed, unwashed. It occurred to him that the water in the bath would have gone cold which meant all the fuss of running up and down stairs with saucepans of hot water, so that she could have her cat's lick. Her hair was in a state, parted the wrong way, wet with perspiration at the tips. She'd started to sweat. Her skin was clammy from their body heat, adhering to his as they clung to each other on the bed. He was keen to show her the mill-pool, river walk, the woods where the couple lay among the toadstools. She breathed in his face. Her breath smelt of stale omelette,

'After all that I must've hallucinated.'

'What makes you say that?'

'Everything was weird, multi-coloured, psychedelic, flashing lights, flickering strobes, as if I were at a rock concert.'

He thought of his amazing trip to the benefit gig, The Greasy Trucker's Party in Camden, to watch Hawkwind perform live. Their incredible light show. The band epitomised his values - free drugs and free love. Only last week, their dancer, Stacia, had stood on stage before him in her short starry night sky frock blowing bubbles as they played *Silver Machine* at Guildford Civic Hall. Perhaps Georgie would dance with him in the aisles next time they went on tour.

'I found myself in a wood,' she said mysteriously, 'a strange, enchanted wood.'

The mention of the word wood roused him, 'How did you know it was enchanted?'

Georgie pinched his nipple, it hurt, 'If you stop interrupting me and listen, I'll tell you.'

'Sorry.'

'Stop saying sorry!'

She resumed, 'I was standing by a green pool. The wood was full of pools, each a different colour: red, yellow, green, blue, purple, rainbow. They stretched into the distance as far as I could see. I had no idea what it meant. I jumped into the nearest pool. Strange, I don't remember getting wet.'

'You jumped?'

'Mmmn,' her voice had taken on a dreamy quality, far, far away, fading...

'Like Polly and Digory!'

Georgie shook the fuzz out of her head and tried to concentrate, 'Yep...Like who?!'

'Have you read The Magician's Nephew by C S Lewis?'

'Can't say I have,' she shrugged, 'Why?'

'It was my favourite book when I was a boy. My only book. I still read it today. In the story, two children: Digory, the magician's nephew, and Polly, his only friend, travel to other places using magic rings. But to reach the other places they must first pass through a wood, a wood between the worlds.'

Georgie rubbed her eyes. She'd had a late night, an even longer morning,

'What's all this got to do with me?'

He cut her off, 'Let me finish. The wood was full of pools. To reach the other worlds, they had to jump into a pool. Each pool led to a different world! Can't you see? That's where you went, Georgie. In your dream. Where *did* you go? Where did *your* pool take you to?'

He would never forget what she told him next for the rest of his days. She spoke, hazily, as if she were in a trance,

'I floated in her waters, inside my mother's womb. I felt safe and warm inside her, happier than I've ever been, ever will be, tethered by my mum's umbilical cord. Her baby. I felt myself turn, invert inside her, head down, eyes shut, shoulders back then...'

She was weeping now, gently, onto his face,

'Brace yourself, Georgie, brace yourself, girl', I told myself. I felt her give me an almighty push, then I shot out of her.'

Happy, content, contemplating her deceit, Georgie lay on the bed cradling his head to her chest, ruffling his hair. He told her about the time his father died of a coronary away from home. The time his mother went to pieces and tried to commit suicide with sleeping tablets. The day she was admitted to the mental hospital nestled among the sweet chestnut trees, never to come out. The warm afternoon sun, when he watched the couple make love on a blanket in the woods, surrounded by fungi. His obsession with toadstools, magic mushrooms. The time he administered his deadly concoction to the girl, in pursuit of her all-time high,

Georgie interrupted him, 'We all make mistakes, me more than most. I'm sure she'll pull through.'

'I tried to call her...'

'She'll be fine,' Georgie insisted, sounding impatient, 'What time is it?'

He checked his watch, 'Coming up to one o'clock.'

'One o'clock! I must go! I'm meeting a friend in Reigate at four.'

More panic!

'Go? Go, why? Why can't you stay here with me?'

'She's in trouble. She needs my help.'

'What kind of help?'

'Stop badgering me, will you? It's none of your business.'

Georgie rolled out of bed, picking up her g-string as she skipped out of the room,

'I need the loo. You can run me a bath if you like.'

'There isn't any hot water left, he said hurriedly, 'I'll heat some saucepans. You'll have to have a cat's lick.'

Georgie had forgotten how poor he was. Her heart sank at the thought of what she was about to do to him. She loved this man, wanted his child, just needed to sort her head out.

'Come here,' she said, hugging him, 'I love you, but I really must go. What's a cat's lick?'

He sighed deeply, relieved beyond words: she still loved him, after all that he'd confessed,

'It's a head-to-toe wash with a flannel,' he grinned, 'You'll love it, Georgie. Promise!'

'*What* am I going to do with you?!' she mocked, disappearing into the bathroom.

He scampered off to the kitchen. Half an hour later, they bid each other a fond farewell on the doorstep. She turned away from him, unable to tell the unbearable truth to his face.

Georgie reached as far as the garden gate, stopped, and glanced at him, over her shoulder,

'I have to return to Oz. I'm flying out tonight. I'll write.'

She left his life, fading into the distance, her head down, not once daring to look back.

He slammed the door shut and slumped to the cold-tiled floor:

An empty shell of a man.

* * * * *

HE FOUND THE AIRMAIL LYING on the front doormat seven weeks later. The envelope bore a red stamp featuring a grey kangaroo. Beside himself with excitement, he slit it open, took out the sheet of blue paper, and read:

Sweetest,

I wanted to let you know I'm okay. I'll be okay. I enjoyed myself. I had fun.
I'll always love you,

Georgie

He felt as if she had just stabbed him in the chest, crying like a wounded animal, searching for her face, her heart, her love, in the darkest recesses of his mind: a lair, in which to die. He had failed his A Levels, lost his job, and lost her. He no longer had anyone to live for.

* * * * *

Aftertaste:

April Fool's Day 1973:

GEORGIE WAS HEAVY WITH CHILD. Her breasts were swollen with milk. Her abdomen, fully distended. She slumped on the wicker chair feeling her baby prod her stomach. Her fiancé marvelled at how she pushed herself to the limits of her endurance to birth her miracle. Tom treasured her, cherished her, every pounding heartbeat, each sublime kiss. He lay his head in her lap.

They'd found their way upstairs to the pink bedroom: her wedding cake bed with its nest of soft cuddly toys, the snow-white cot, the rocking horse, a cradle bedecked in pink. As soon as she fell pregnant, Georgie instinctively knew her baby would be a girl.

They enjoyed a perfect love, a love that was all-consuming, unselfish, and respectful. She was happy at last. Tom was all she wanted in a man: passionate, caring, considerate. Her eyes misted with tears. She took his hand, wrapping her fingers around his palm, and held him to her swollen belly. Georgie was enormous. The skin on her bulge was stretched. A brown line ran the full length of her belly from her protruding navel to her swathe of teak hair. Proudly, she rubbed his fingers over the round of her belly so that he could feel her baby kicking inside her.

Tom beamed with pride as he felt the baby reach for its father. Its tiny fists, pummelling the lining of its mother's womb, wanting to touch the man who seeded her with his sperm.

He felt her lightly stroke the hair on the back of his hand, seeking his intimacy. Exhausted, Georgie closed her eyes, savouring the smell of his skin as he moved closer. She felt his lips kissing her eyes, the welts of tiredness that dwelt beneath, her hollow cheeks. The subtle brush of his mouth over her pursed lips. His hot breath on her face. The tip of his tongue licking her neck.

Georgie stirred, feeling a delicious tingle inside her, a glorious hardening she hadn't felt for months. His tongue left a line of saliva down her chest, licking the salt from the moist fjord that separated her heaving breasts. She became aroused, pushing his hand inside her pants, guiding his fingers through her matted hair to feel her, alarmed by her own daring, knowing how she might gratify herself through his tender touch.

Tom brushed the shock of hair off her face, kissing her fully on the lips. She felt his eager tongue enter her wet red mouth; his tip tickling the back of her throat. He rubbed her. She gasped, struggling to control the thrill of her arousal,

'Strip for me.'

She admired her man's muscular physique: the hairy chest when he unbuttoned his shirt, his pert bum when he dropped his trousers, the rigid, rearing flesh that stood so proudly for her. Still wearing her bra and briefs, she stood up, a little dizzied by her rampant lust,

'Think we should lie on the bed, don't you?'

Stretched with torsion, he hobbled to her tidy bed and lay down at the centre, watching expectantly as she slipped the bra straps off her shoulders, uncupping each breast, leaving her bra hanging loose to tease him. She pushed her heavy breast up to her mouth for him, tickling her complected nipple with the tip of her tongue. He fought to contain himself,

'God, you're beautiful!' he cried, waiting for the moment of her intimate revelation with bated breath.

Georgie slipped out of her briefs, her explicit act of reveal exposing the beauty of her twitching bulge, the impressive contour of her breasts, the divine arch of her back, her fleshy buttocks. She was breathless, panting for him. A naughty expression crept over her face,

'Would you like to play with me?'

His heart nearly jumped out of his chest. Flustering, flushing scarlet, he nodded, 'Yes.'

'Lie back then.'

Tom lay back in awe of her as she clambered on top of him, sinking her belly comfortably onto his chest. She was run down. He saw her furuncle, a nasty boil, festering on the cusp of her left buttock. He caressed her gently, deftly, parting her soft flesh with his fingertips.

They heard footsteps on the staircase. Voices. The door swung open to reveal Kayleigh,

'We're here!' she yelled, 'Promised we'd stay in touch!'

The couple, lying inverted on the bed, didn't answer.

'Oh, is this a bad time?' her voice dropped to a whisper, 'Think we should wait downstairs until they've finished, don't you Matt?'

'I think we should,' he agreed quietly, smirking, stifling himself from laughing aloud.

That was the moment Georgie's waters broke.

* * * * *

TOM DIDN'T KNOW WHAT TO do with her at first. He gazed down at the ruddy face of their new-born and kissed her forehead. She was beautiful, like Georgie. She bawled, wailed, kicked and screamed, clearing her little lungs.

'I think she wants to be fed,' Kayleigh said, wiping clean her bloodied hands, 'Shall we pass her back to mum?'

Proudly, he handed the tiny bundle of joy back to her mother so that she could breastfeed her baby. Kayleigh assured them the midwife would be there soon. The kind lady living in the house across the road had let Matt use her phone to ring the hospital.

He appeared with a washing-up bowl full of warm soapy water and clean towels. Kayleigh washed the blood and slime off Georgie as the father looked on, thrilled for her, astounded by her. Tom mopped her sweaty forehead. She smiled weakly at him, shattered, her heavy head sunk deep in pillows. Georgie shut her eyes and rested, whispering as she fell asleep,

'Ellie, I'd like to call her Ellie… my bright shining one.'

* * * * *

Epilogue:

Valentine's Day 2021:

L. D. CHART F.C.A, F.C.C.A BECAME Managing Partner of the firm of accountants she set up with her husband in 1985. Lindsey and Richard have five grown-up children and live in a large country house near Ascot. Neither of them indulge in illegal drugs - anymore.

Janis married Chantal in Church on 5th April 2014. Having left Bristol University with a 2.1 in Human Biology, she retired early, after a distinguished career as a dentist in a major London practice. She now writes children's stories at their tumbledown cottage in Dorset.

Kayleigh gave birth to a 7lb6oz baby boy, Patrick. She and her partner Matt returned to Australia in early 1973 to live in Brisbane where they teach autistic children.

Rosalie O'Brien re-married, Phil, in 1982. He died of prostate cancer a year ago. They had no children. Rosalie, now 80, still lives at 12, Brierley Road. She has just had her first *Astra Zeneca* jab.

Mary died in hospital of a heart attack, aged 49, in the summer of 1972.

Georgie and Tom were married at All Saints Church Brisbane on Saturday 19th June 1976. A week before their wedding day, they received a letter from Rachael, saying she felt too frail to attend. The Bride was given away by Matt. Kayleigh, Lindsey, and Janis were her Maids of Honour.

Following her outstanding academic achievements at Brisbane State High School, Ellie graduated from The University of Queensland with an Honours Degree in Biochemistry. Still single, she is a member of a research team specializing in the development of young children's antiviral vaccines.

Georgie manages a charity shop for a society that helps children to cope with life's hardest challenges and face the future with confidence.

For a good friend, who was taken from us at such a young age, having truly fallen in love.

Intimate Exchange

SHE WAS SITTING IN THE restaurant when Keir saw her, noticeably different in appearance from the other students. Smartly dressed in a creamy-beige blouse, her top three buttons undone, a dark brown corduroy skirt worn above the knee. Her tights were flesh-tone. She had shoulder-length greasy brown hair. Keir tried to concentrate on what Quill was saying: his welcome to the college, daily timetable, lectures: cookery class, food, and beverage service, but couldn't take his eyes off her. She looked somehow different. Her face...

Quill: '...nutrition, management, accounts, law and housekeeping. Please do ensure you arrive punctually in the kitchen for Mr Stall and Mr Speller's classes: knives sharp, wearing pristine whites. I expect you all to dress in clean white shirts, black bow ties, black trousers and cummerbunds when working in the restaurant. Remember, you will be serving the Public, and we must constantly strive to give of our best. Are there any questions?'

Her face was strange, painted...

Quill, looking terribly formal in his stiff white shirt, silver tie, waistcoat, jacket, and pin-stripe trousers, nodded at one of the boys,

'Yes, Michael.'

Her face was an inverted triangle...

Michael was overweight, chubby-cheeked with a ruddy complexion and shock of bushy-blonde hair. For the first day, he'd chosen to wear flared brown trousers, a psychedelic-pattern purple shirt, kipper tie, and clown's chequered jacket. An eccentric: Chichester, Worthing, Brighton? Well-to-do, upper middle, unlike Keir. He probably attended college for the fun of it, in the absence of a career plan or need to work. His posh accent came as no surprise,

'Mr Quill, Sir.'

Keir cringed.

'Please, call me Peter.'

An audible sigh of relief passed round the room. Quill was human after all. Michael recovered,

'Peter, what is a cummerbund?'

They all fell silent. You could hear a pin drop. For a moment, Keir thought Quill was going to explode. Their welcome packs contained explicit instructions on formal dress code for students working in the restaurant. Cummerbunds were an essential requirement.

He glanced at her. She smiled at him. Appreciating his thick, curly teak hair, steel-blue eyes, lean smooth tanned face, slim physique. Her smile lit the *canvas* of her face. He smiled at her, excited by her. She was hypnotized by him. Quill noticed, grinned, then answered Michael's question,

'A cummerbund,' he explained to muted tittering from the girls, 'is the wide black sash I expect students to wear around their waists when they serve in the restaurant. You were issued with a list of what to wear when working in the kitchen and restaurant as part of your welcome pack. Did you receive it?'

The beau flushed, 'Yes, Peter.'

'But did you read it?'

Several students burst out laughing. She laughed. Keir loved to hear her laugh. He fancied her. Her face was delicately painted, a lovely masque: beige crème foundation, teak eyeliner, black mascara, dark cherry red lipstick. He was struck by her alien beauty, her intimate make-up.

Keir was rather scruffy, unkempt, in need of her care and attention. He needed her to cherish him, hoped she felt a powerful sense of attraction towards him, that she'd never felt this way about a boy before, and wanted to make him happy, too. He hadn't shaved. A hot flush spread through her body, scintillating her. She felt herself liquify in his presence. She raised an arm to speak.

~ 95 ~

'Yes, Gail?'

Her name was Gail! She had an allure about her. It was clear from how she spoke, she wasn't from those parts, wasn't a Sussex girl. Her voice rose, lilting sweetly, ending on a divine high, a personal question mark,

'Peter?'

Gail had their undivided attention. All eyes fell on her. Quill rubbed his chin, wondering what on earth was the matter with her,

'Yes?'

'I think I need to go to the toilet. Can you tell me where the toilet is, please?'

Keir felt his jaw drop. Gail stood bolt upright, clearly under stress. He felt for her.

Quill sputtered, 'Down the corridor, first door on the right.'

Keir watched astounded as she ran out of the room. His life would never be the same again.

* * * * *

THEIR FIRST LECTURE WAS FOOD Hygiene in the lab with Dr Goodlier, an overweight woman with a dense brown perm flecked with grey, an unsightly chocolate birthmark on her right cheek. No wedding ring that Keir could see. Feeling for her, blemished, tarnished like that, he took an instant like to her. She wished them all a bright cheerful, 'Good Morning Students!' then taught them how to wash their hands, using soap, water, and a stiff nail brush. They took it in turns to wash their hands.

Jill Aylett, a slim, tall, elegant girl with shoulder-length auburn hair, face of an angel, a future air hostess, stood at the basin, gently washing her hands. Keir noticed she was wearing glossy pink nail varnish which isn't allowed when handling food. She shook her hands, reached for a paper towel, and wiped her perfectly manicured fingertips.

Standing aside for him, she spoke in a curly-wurly foxy accent which had a deliciously soothing effect on him: warm molten milk chocolate stuck onto his palate. Swindon, Salisbury, Devizes? Keir found himself haunted by her emerald eyes, her soft dulcet tones,

'I saw you fancy the strangeling. Gail, isn't it?'

Strangeling?

He tried in vain to suppress his irritation at her condescending attitude,

'Yes, her name's Gail, and no, I don't fancy her.'

'You could've fooled me. You couldn't take your eyes off her. Word of advice if I may.'

'Go on.'

'Where I come from in The New Forest, we have a saying, 'You can never tame a wild horse.'

Keir stared at her, perplexed, 'And what's that supposed to mean?'

'It means,' she lectured, 'The girl's trouble. Don't go anywhere near her.'

His West Sussex sarcasm got the better of him, 'Thanks for that gem.'

'Don't mention it.'

He felt a kidney punch to the small of his back: Pat Huntley, a short, squat, dumpy blonde in a floppy black t-shirt and Levi's, goading him,

'Get a move on, nipper.'

Her accent was unmistakably Yorkshire Moors. He apologized.

She gave him a knowing look, 'That's okay, skip. No worries.'

Keir watched Jill strut back to her seat, tossing stray hairs off her face, turning her nose up at him, showing off as if she owned him. It was only then that he realised Gail was missing.

You can never tame a wild horse.

* * * * *

NICK WAS SITTING AT THE bench furthest from Dr Goodlier. Keir was disconcerted, alarmed to see him again, astonished by the coincidence. He sat next to Jill, Gail's seat, and Pat, enjoying the company of attractive young women. They fawned over him, reaching over to stroke the thick matt of ginger hair sprouting from the backs of his hands.

And why not? His rugged good looks attracted girls like moths to the lamplight when they were in the 6th form at Ifield. If anything, his face, and body had matured, hardened, like a ripening sex-cheese, over the summer holiday. He had a mean sallow face full of freckles, light beard, ginger hair, cruel thin lips. His body was lean, muscular, sinewy, without an inch of fat in sight. He wore a shiny russet leather bomber jacket that made him look hip, over a shocking tangerine vest: an invitation to Jill and Pat to stroke his manly mass of chest hair - which they did, eagerly.

Keir recalled how Nick ignored him when they boarded the 7.45 to Portsmouth Harbour that morning. Nick loathed him. He sat at the back, glowering with contempt, hatred. Keir took a seat at the front, trying to put him out of his mind.

Goodlier circulated with a box of sealed petri dishes, telling the students what to do with them as she doled them out,

'I want you to *carefully* remove the lid of the dish, then *carefully* press your right index fingertip into the agar jelly in the dish,' she paused, 'Now, *carefully* replace the lid and write your name *clearly* on the label. Next week we will review the growth of bacteria under the microscope. Find out how well you *really* washed your hands!'

Her voice was shrill with childish excitement, her tone filled with emphasis. She spoke down at them, treating them like children. Children, Keir suspected, she yearned for but could never have. He had a bizarre notion, an insightful vision of Gail, wondering if she wanted to have his babies.

The rest of Food Hygiene was taken up by an open forum discussion about the essentials of hygienic food handling. Keir established that Gail should have washed her hands after visiting the toilet. He thought of her dramatic exit. Where was she hiding?

'No nail varnish, make-up, or jewellery to be worn,' instructed Goodlier.

Jill's strawberry nails came to mind. Keir smiled as he dreamed of Pat's chunky gold necklace. Gail's thick make-up, plastered-on like war paint…

What would her face look like nude?

She intrigued him. He wanted her. He felt a soft hand shaking his shoulder accompanied by the unmistakable twang of Pat,

'Wake up, sleepy head.'

He opened his eyes, shaking his bleary head awake, 'What?'

'It's lunch-time. Going outside for a fag. Like to join me? Get to know me better? Well?'

She smoked. Keir imagined how she'd taste if he kissed her. Choking on her smoke. His mind drifted back to Sally at the 6th Form disco. Her sequinned top, blood-red hot pants, ruddy-rouge lips. Opening her mouth fully for him to taste her. The disturbing flow of smoky ectoplasm seeping from her mouth. Sally, seer at their private séance, spewing forth fug like a possessed medium hunched over a Ouija board. Summoning him like her dead. He craned his head at Pat, declining,

'Thanks, I skipped breakfast this morning. Need to eat.'

'Suit yourself,' she huffed, stalking off down the corridor to be with Jill and Nick.

Goodlier was collecting petri dishes. Keir made a point of thanking her for an interesting lesson. She flushed. Her flush made the ugly birthmark blight her face in scarlet. He felt sorry for her, understanding her anguish, the never-ending loneliness she endured, he heard her talking,

'Thank you, Keir, for understanding me.'

He gathered up his notes, slipping the thin sheaf into his plastic portfolio case, and left the lab without even looking at her, his mind preoccupied with the enigma that was Gail.

* * * * *

THE REFECTORY WAS LOCATED AT the rear of a prefabricated, late-sixties, concrete monolith. A clean rectangular room, light, airy, warmed by the unseasonal noon sun. To the left was a mishmash of round and oblong tables, and a line of square tables for two near the full-length plate glass windows. The fire doors were open, halfway down, leading to a paved courtyard. Beyond, stretched a grass field, bordered by a line of trees: oak, chestnut changing colours, beech, the hazy outline of downs in the distance. The courtyard was a hive of activity. Keir stood by the window and took a closer look.

Some of the girls, dressed in white nylon coats, were beautiful: not a smudge in their lipsticks, blemish on their faces, or hairs out of place. He surmised that these were Beauticians. Other girls were wearing smart formal charcoal jackets, skirts, crisp-white blouses. Receptionists? They seemed relaxed enough, chatty, at ease with each other. None of them smoked.

In contrast, the Catering students huddled along the window, sunning themselves. Pat and Jill were prone, flat-on-the-pavement, jeans rolled up to their knees, drawing heavily on cigarettes. Coughing, wheezing their guts out, between snatches of chat with an obese girl with frizzy hair and puffy cheeks who Keir didn't recognize. He caught a glimpse of Nick on the grass with his back to him, staring at the blue sky as if he were ship's boy in a crow's nest searching for some distant land. Relieved not to see his scowling face, Keir surveyed the refectory. The place was deserted.

His stomach rumbled. Time to eat. He joined the queue of one. A slim serving lady with saggy jowls, a lined face, and a pinned-on paper forage hat advised him that chips and beans were on the way. There was a choice of gammon steak and pineapple, chicken and mushroom pie, or fish fingers and peas. He scanned the cold display: stacks of cheese sandwiches, filled rolls, frozen gateaux, eclairs, Tab, boxed apple pies, jellies, Golden Wonder, Penguins, Snacks. Keir survived on a grant, a tight budget. He decided on fish fingers, chips, baked beans, and Penguin for dessert.

Emilia Unger: a shortish girl with mousy hair, round cheeks, and a shapely figure, turned to face him. She was wearing a flimsy see-through blouse. Keir could see her spotty breasts. Her face was covered in open sores festering in her lips, nostrils, chin, neck, and cheeks. She kept touching, scratching, itching herself. He found her distressing to watch. She spoke rapidly: coarse Sussex, a common girl: Bognor, Portsmouth, Hove?

'Great here, isn't it?' she said.

Keir nodded, surprised at how cheerful she was, given her constant discomfort. A chef appeared at the hot counter to top up the chips and beans. The dinner lady held out a plate in her serving cloth, dishing up gammon steak for Emilia while she scratched crusts off her spots, and asked,

'Pineapple, darling?'

'Please.'

'Chips?'

'Please.'

'Beans or peas?'

'Beans, please.'

'There you go, sweetheart. Lift your tray. Mind the plate. It's hot.'

'Thankyou.'

Emilia stopped scratching herself. Keir watched her face glow as she received her meal: as if she were receiving alms, manna from heaven; wondering at the conviction in her, the fortitude that made her carry on. How could she possibly handle food in her condition? Perhaps she wore mitts in the kitchen to stop herself scratching. Her pus was full of salmonella, poor girl. She cried,

'Sit with me.'

Keir shook his head, looking over her, desperate not to share her burden, to get involved,

'Sorry, I can't.'

'Why not?'

He spotted Gail at the far end of the refectory, her bowed head in her hands, her face covered, shoulders slumped, heard Emilia's tremulous voice, interfering, in the background,

'Don't you like me?'

'It isn't that.'

Keir wanted to tell her he admired her, to be her friend. But the sight of Gail clouded his mind. Instead, he focused on her rejection. Rejection was never his strongest point. His feelings for Emilia were not dissimilar to those he felt for Paula three years ago: initial fascination, intrigue, followed by repulsion at the rippling folds of flab she revealed to him on their last night, her vain enticement to make love to her. He'd blanched, fled the bedroom, told her he never wanted to see her again. Paula clung on in hope, a lovelorn limpet, craving his slim body. It took him six months to prise her off. His heart sank when Emilia persisted in fighting for her lost cause,

'What is it then?'

He shrugged.

She set down her tray, itching badly, scratching herself incessantly, a bleeding heart,

'Is it my spots?'

Keir couldn't bear to answer her, ignoring her, directing his attention at Maggie who'd pinned on a name badge during the kerfuffle. Emilia gave up all hope, storming off in a bate.

'Fish fingers, chips and beans, please Maggie,' he said cockily, watching her lift his plate, 'Do you have ketchup?'

She flashed him a lovely smile that lit up her whole face, made her look twenty years younger,

'In the bottle on the table, darling. Can I get you anything else?'

She looked sensational for her age,

'No thanks, Maggie. I think that's all for now.'

'There you go, sweetheart. Lift your tray. Mind the plate. It's hot.'

Careful not to tilt the tray, he walked towards Gail, content to study her feet, her bandy calves. She visibly relaxed, easing her legs apart for him under the table. The shin of her left calf had grazed, presumably during her rush to the toilet, laddering her tights, shaving layers of dermis off her skin. She'd bled, a flesh wound: her blood running in a scarlet rivulet down the front of her calf, over the bridge of her foot, under the vamp of her open-toed shoe, drying in a scab.

Keir was always grazing himself as a boy. He'd sit on a tree stump for hours picking off scabs. Still, he couldn't believe that she'd fled from Quill's room in open-toed sandals,

'Gail?'

At the sound of his voice, she uncovered her face, put her hands palms-down on the table, and stared at him. He could tell she'd been crying. Her eyes were sored red. Four streaks of mascara ran down her cheeks, smudging her perfect foundation with tear trails. Her delightfully snub nose was running. She sniffed,

'Yeah?'

'I saw you crying.'

'So? Girls can cry, can't they?'

'I was worried about you, the way you ran out of Quill's class.'

'Worried? Why'd you worry about me? Don't even know me.'

The soothing words flowed from his mouth unhindered,

'Gail, I *care* for you.'

'Sit with me,' she said, cheering up, 'Must look a mess. Don't have a tissue, do you?'

Keir pulled up a chair and sat opposite, pushing his tray aside to create space for her. On the table lay a half-eaten egg mayo cress roll. He noticed she'd picked out the cress, leaving it lying in a neat heap next to her can of Tab. She reached across and held his hand. Her hand felt soft, pudgy, warm. Keir lost his appetite. Fishing in his jean pocket, he found a Kleenex, offering her his tissue. She declined. Instead, Gail waved her hand and broke into an endearing childish, baby voice. A voice, he would learn, that she could put on at will when she needed his attention,

'Dab my eyes.'

Without a moment's hesitation, he dabbed her eyes dry, smudging his tissue black.

'Wipe my dose.'

Keir hesitated, worried by the intimacy of their exchange,

'I don't think I should.'

She insisted, raising her voice so that Emilia and Maggie could hear her,

'Wipe my dose!'

He wiped the runny snot from her cute nose, pressing the tissue into her nostrils to collect her mucous, squeezing her with his fingertips, wiping the gunge off her lip, her feint moustache. By the time he finished, his tissue was stained, deep cherry red. Gail regarded him, wild-eyed, a clown-girl without her make-up,

'Thanks.'

He stuffed the dirty hankie in his pocket for later, beguiled, mesmerized by her naked face. Gail felt the cream leather handbag sitting on her lap, took out a face mirror and embroidered gold make-up bag, unscrewed a silver tube, and applied deep cherry red to her flaking lip. In a smooth sweeping motion. Keir marvelled at her technique, letting her finish her mouth before breaking her silence,

'Why were you crying, Gail?'

She was baby-faced, with a well-rounded chin. The difference in size between her nostrils was remarkable. Her left nostril was three times the size of her right, which was miniscule. He delighted in the subtly creased divide under her nose, the childish purse of her lips. Gail opened her small mouth to reveal her off-white teeth. Her hand shook as she applied her lipstick to her thick lower lip. She was left-handed. She supported herself. With her right.

Keir enjoyed the flex of her bony fingers, noticing the chipped nail varnish. The simple gold band on her ring finger. Why did she wear a ring? Was she a child bride? Unanswered questions flowed through his tormented mind like mental syrup.

The intimate act of smoothing cherry red on her lips brought her out in a blush, a pink blossom filled her face. He witnessed her faint blemishes, the spots garnishing her chin. Keir glanced at Emilia, covered in sores. She looked up from sawing her tough gammon steak, scowling, hating him for discarding her in favour of a lesser-spotted adversary.

Keir studied Gail in intimate detail. Her spots were blunt dormant volcanoes, yet to erupt stress moles. Her blush ended abruptly in the soft puffy flesh under her chin, aligned with her beige foundation. The contrast between her face, neck, and chest was arresting. She had pale natural skin, a light dappling of freckles on her chest, from where she'd been kissed by the sun in the summer holidays. The fourth button on her blouse was undone. He thrilled at the shallow indent dividing her little breasts, dumbstruck by her sex appeal. Gail wasn't pretty, beautiful, even attractive, in the conventional sense. She was plain without make-up, plain sexy.

Keir asked her repeatedly why she'd been crying. She put away her make-up bag, squeezed his hand, and explained,

'Come from Wickleigh, Essex. Dad owns an engineering business. Spends his time working in the shed. Carol tends his every need, cooks his meals, washes his dirty pants, does the ironing, cleans the house, mows the lawn. They play table tennis in the garage at weekends. Sometimes, she *even* lets *me* play him. Never lets me play *her*. Oh no! She knows I'll *beat* her!'

There was no mistaking the sarcasm in her voice, the acid tone. Keir found himself immersed in her story, absorbed by the unfurling drama. He felt for the fork, lunch, his free hand, feeding himself cold beans, chips, and fish fingers, as the tension swelled up in her throat,

'I love Dad. Warn him every day about what she's doing to him, taking him from us, his real family.'

Keir gulped down a soggy fish finger before interrupting, 'His real family?'

'Yeah. I've an older sister, Bebe, twenty-one. She's beautiful made-up.

We've plain faces. We paint our faces. For you men!' Gail snorted, 'Bebe's a Beauty Queen. She's engaged to Pete, he's an engineer, like Dad.'

'A Beauty Queen? I've never met a Beauty Queen.'

Gail smiled, caressing his hand tenderly with hers, reassuring him,

'P'rhaps, one day, you will.'

He squeezed her hand, rubbing her mound of Venus with his thumb, in response to hers,

'I'd like that, Gail. Like that very much. What does it feel like, being a Beauty Queen?'

'Oh, it feels wonderful! Bebe competes in pageants all over the county. We go in Pete's car. He drives a Robin Reliant, y' know, a three-wheeler?'

Gail beamed from ear-to-ear. Her lips cracked into the loveliest smile. He was thrilled for her, seeing her this happy. Tears welled in her eyes. He wanted to take her in his arms and hold her, but couldn't, not in front of the other two,

'A Robin Reliant? How do you all fit into a Robin Reliant?'

'Oh, we manage,' she stared at her hand, holding his, 'Least we used to, before I moved to Eaglesham to be with Dad. Used to have fun, the three of us.'

'Three of you?'

'Yeah, I have a younger sister, Leanne; she's sixteen. Pete used to take us to TOTS.'

'Sorry, TOTS?'

'Yeah, TOTS. Talk of the South. It's a club in Southend. We used to row the boat, conga to Nellie the Elephant, dance the night away till the early hours, smooch boys. Lea was naughty. We had fun! Smooching the boys. Getting pissed.'

'You said Leanne's only sixteen. How did she get into a nightclub if she was under-age?'

Gail took a sip of her Tab, belching loudly,

'Oh, she *looks* older than that. Leanne looks beautiful made-up. S'pose that makes me her ugly sister.'

'Well, I don't think so,' Keir said graciously, 'I think you're gorgeous.'

He made her go all weak at the knees,

'Thank you, you *are* kind!'

He changed the subject, 'Why did you move to Eaglesham. When you were so happy?'

'Carol convinced me moving South was the right thing to do if I wanted to go to college. I was never any good at school. Couldn't concentrate.'

Gail looked out of the window. Her almond eyes searched the courtyard. She refocused.

'I can cook,' she continued, 'Nothing fancy, basic food. I can clean, do housework, wash, do laundry, make beds. I wanted to train to be a chef. But Carol wants me to go into management. She forced me to take the course. I didn't want to. I made a mistake coming here. Should never have left home. Bebe and Leanne: I miss them. Then there's the way *she* treats Dad. The way *she* behaves when I'm in *her* house…'

Keir felt her tense, her hand stiffen, gripping his fingers. She released him, staring at the ceiling, trembling with rage, struggling to assert herself.

He persisted, 'How does she behave, Gail?'

'She controls him,' she moaned, 'I listen to her, fucking him, through the bedroom wall. Carol isn't my real mum. My mum's dead. Killed herself when Dad walked out of our lives for *her*.'

Keir was shocked by her filthy language. She wilted in front of him, put on her baby voice,

'I can't live with her no more. I've run away from home, nowhere to live. Can you help me? I'll cook for you, clean, do the housework, wash up, do the laundry, make our bed?'

Our bed?

He was besotted with her. She had him wrapped around her face, her body. Her hand gripped his. There was nothing, in that insane moment, he wouldn't do for her. He pictured the two of them in love. The words fell out of his mouth,

'I'm sure I *can* help you, Gail…'

She *felt* how much he cared for her, loved her. She felt in love with him, her eyes sparkled,

'Well, if we're gonna sleep together, I fink you should tell me your name, don't you?'

Sleep together?

'but…'

He lied to her, told her his name was Rick, suddenly remembering,

'I can't be sure Mum and Dad will let me. Is there somewhere else you can stay at night?'

Cheese and Shin

Summer 1977, off Regent Street:

IT WAS AVRIL WHO ALERTED me to the deficiency in cheese. Not just any cheese. Not a blue-veined. Even tho' I was partial to blue: gorgon, stilton, even dana blue on occasion, served with a glass of finest crusty port; a blue that brought my lips out in an itchy red blooming rash. Those copper rods they insert to infuse the mould, infusing mould into my lips as the cheese enters my mouth. My pungent *allergenic* rash. Avril asserted that this deficiency was: hard not soft, mature not mild, cows' not ewes', or goats', smooth not creamy, nude not shrouded in crust or rind. Hard.

Still seated working in shirtsleeves, I averted my gaze from the dull green computer screen and swivelled my chair, leaning back to face her, clenching my hands in my lap - her nodding dog. I ventured a joke, a good craic, laughing at her, as she stood in our doorway,

'Hard cheese, eh, Avril?'

'This isn't a joke, Declan!' she hissed.

'I'm sorry, I...'

Too late, she slumped against our door jamb and started to cry. Avril looked beautiful that day: the sunlight shining on her flyaway, draught-swept teak hair, worn long enough to kiss her bare shoulders. Her face was a painting, a masterpiece of art: from the thick daubed-on eyebrows to her tiny turned-up nose, heavy rouge, pearls on her earlobes, the pearl choker, she wore on a thin gold necklace, around her gilded neck. In view of the heatwave, I'd relaxed the dress code for Avril. Today, she was wearing a tight white vest, barely held together by tennis pump laces threaded through copper eyelets, topped with a formal satin bow; a pleated oak brown corduroy skirt, tied at the front. Avril sported a subtle purring pussy cat tattoo above her ample left breast.

'Shut the door and lock it,' I said, kindly, 'Then pull down the blind.'

Avril stepped into our office, shut the door behind her, locked it, and pulled the bamboo blind,

'You'll get lippy on your collar,' she warned, sniffing tears, cheering up, 'then what'll you do?'

'I don't care if I do, Avril,' I cried, 'I only care about you, the way he treats you in front of the brigade, the porterage, the cleaners, waitresses, our suppliers...'

'Shush, Declan! You'll wake Baja next door!'

(Dermot Baja, our antiquated, septuagenarian cashier control clerk, inventor of bizarre devices: automatic fishing rod strikers, parsnip-pickers, boot-washers; occasional part-time accountant)

She sealed my lips, with hers.

We opened our mouths and kissed.

We all taste or smell of cheese: under our skins, between our toes, in our body folds, our glands. Avril tastes of sweaty dana blue. Once we'd finished kissing, I held her in my arms,

'What did he do to you this time, Avril?'

She stammered when upset, 'G-Gary swore at me in front of the other chefs, used the f-word.'

I was horrified, 'The f-word?'

'Mm, the f-word.'

'Why would he use the f-word, on you of all people, Avril?'

She stared over my shoulder, into the window, Carnaby Street was out there, five floors below,

'He accused me of forgetting to order the mature cheddar cheese for today's Lasagne Verdi.'

'And did you?'

'Yes.'

'Well then...'

I knew Avril so well.

Gary, the consummate professional, never swore at work, in front of staff, let alone at a woman.

She'd made herself cry.

For me.

* * * * *

IT WAS AVRIL WHO DREW my attention to the shin. Not just any shin. Her right shin. I was a rump man myself, an afficionado of rare T-bone, a connoisseur of prime filet, lover of buttock steak. It was the warm blood I enjoyed, warm blood, oozing out of red flesh. Not that I was a vampire, just a gourmet: of red meats. Even tho' I *was* partial to blue: sirloin, porterhouse, fillet served in blue stilton sauce, dana blue on occasion, served with a glass of fine claret, the elixir of life that brought my cheeks out in puffy red blushes; I preferred rare. The slithering of strips down my throat, the barely warm meat stuck in my incisors, bloodying my sore cracked lips and chin as the steak entered my mouth. My spotty, itchy, *allergic* rash - accentuated by the blue cheese.

Unfortunately, this particular avenue of pleasure had been cut off by Procurement. Following a tough purchasing negotiation with our nominated butcher, Gary was only permitted to feature shin on the menu. Avril asserted that *her* shin injury was mild not severe, bruised not bleeding, and nude, not shrouded in her usual flesh-tone tights or charred black woollen stockings. Mild.

Still seated, working in my shirtsleeves, I averted my gaze from the dull green computer screen and swivelled my chair, leaning forwards to face her, clenching my fists in my lap, concerned for her,

'Hurt yourself, Avril?'

'I tripped myself up, running up the stairs.'

'I'm sorry, I...'

'It's nothing really, only a graze.'

I ruffled through my in-tray, reaching up to my bookshelf, trying to find the Accident Book.

Too late, she slumped against our door jamb and started to cry. Avril looked beautiful that day. She'd made herself cry,

'I'm sorry, Declan. I know how busy you are.'

'Like me to rub it better for you?'

'Would you?'

'Shut the door and lock it,' I said, kindly, 'Then pull down the blind.'

Avril entered our office, shut the door behind her, locked it, pulled the bamboo blind, removed her skirt, and squatted between my thighs. I rubbed her grazed shin, her slender calves, the soft flesh on the insides of her thighs,

'How does that feel, better?'

'Mm, much.'

'You'll get yourself into trouble, rubbing me there,' she warned, smiling, cheering up, 'then what'll you do?'

'I don't care if I get the sack from Toby or if Coxie demands my removal,' I cried, 'I love you!'

'Shush, Declan! You'll wake Baja next door!'

She sealed my lips with hers.

We opened our mouths and kissed...

We all taste or smell of blood: under our skins, inside our mouths, in our body folds, our glands. Avril tastes of sweaty dana blue. Once we'd finished kissing, I held her in my arms,

'What did he do to you this time, Avril?'

She stammered when upset, 'G-Gary served fermenting shin in onion gravy to the Directors.'

I was horrified, 'Fermenting shin? How do you know it was fermenting?'

'Coxie summoned me to the Directors dining room to silver serve the shin to the Main Board.'

I broke out in a cold sweat, 'And?'

'I held my flat as close to Mr McTavish...'

'McTavish, the Chairman?!'

'Yes, Mr McTavish.'

I slapped my forehead in alarm, 'Oh, my God!'

Avril put on her skirt, straightened her vest, tidied her hair, and applied fresh rouge to her lips,

'Mmmn, someone like that.'

'I held my flat as close to Mr McTavish as I could. I didn't want to spill gravy in his lap...'

'Of course not,' I agreed, interrupting her flow.

'... so, I leaned forward, selected the three thickest slices of shin on the flat, gripped them with my spoon and fork, lifted them off, went to serve the dish, and the meat started to bubble...'

I couldn't believe my ears, 'Bubble?!'

'Yes, bubble and froth, and let off clouds of gas, a smell of rotten eggs. The gas filled the room. I think Mr McTavish was overwhelmed, he passed out, turned unconscious, his face blued like dana blue cheese mould. Coxie went apeshit at me. She made me cry. I felt so, so helpless. You weren't there for me. You were here, in the office, on your computer. Where you **always** are!'

Coxie! I dreaded Coxie when she went apeshit at us, 'Coxie! Oh, my God, Avril! Coxie! What did you do?'

'I helped Coxie bring round Mr McTavish, apologized for the poor quality of meat, promised a thorough investigation into the incident, then evacuated the room. What else could I do? Oh, and I covered my nose with a clean napkin, and returned the flat of shin in gravy to the kitchen.'

Pleased as I was with her, I braced myself for Gary's response, 'What did he say to you, Avril?'

She stared over my shoulder, into the window, Carnaby Street was out there, five floors below,

'G-Gary tasted the meat and told me there was nothing wrong with it. He accused me of lying.'

I *knew* Avril! Gary, the consummate professional, *knew* his shin from his rump, 'And did you?'

'No, not this time.'

Snowdrops

"Being deeply loved by someone gives you strength, while loving someone deeply gives you courage" – Lao Tzu

Paris, 1983:

HE WAS FEEDING HER SOUP from a silver spoon, and she loved him. Feeding her like that! The soup was thick and warm, coating her gums and teeth, teasing her glands into salivation, frothing before she swallowed her mouthful. She opened her mouth, licking her raspberry-red lips with the tip of her tongue, craning her head for him, then dropped her jaw so that he could feed her again. She dribbled some, felt the tiniest trickle run down her dimpled chin, but he dabbed her clean with a soft mouchoir, so the soup never reached her neck. She blushed. Her cheeks bloomed with roses.

He stopped feeding her.

She felt his hand brush her wavy teak hair behind her elfin ear. His fingertips pressed into the line of her parting. Her hair was parted on the left. He ran his hand down her smiling face and felt her straining neck, her vein. She pursed and puckered her lips to kiss him. Their lips touched, lightly at first. Then they kissed. She ran her fingers through his hair. She loved him. They kissed and kissed, as if their lives, their loves, depended.

His hand pressed on her, stroking her chunky gold necklace. He slid his fingertips under her flimsy satin top and caressed her neck and shoulder. She felt his hand grip her tightly, insistently, then heard a voice: vague, distant, coming close, closer. It wasn't his voice. Their lips no longer kissed. He released her. He drifted away. Her mind pleaded for him to stay.

There was birdsong: a dawn chorus. The hum of distant traffic, a car approaching, a bus. Children's laughter, muffled, in a nearby room. A shard of daylight filtered through the tangerine curtains, warming her face. She smiled as she felt the soft hand resting on her shoulder, shaking her awake, the sound of her mother's voice,

'It is time to wake up, Marie. Did you sleep well?'

Marie blinked at the sunlight as Maman walked across the threadbare carpet, went to the window, and drew back the gaudy orange curtains - sending up a fine mist of dust motes. The window was grubby, soiled with grime off the street, dashed with pigeon droppings. Maman looked down at the statue of Andre Gill, the noted cartoonist, standing formally in the middle of the small grey square, then she turned to face her daughter,

'I had the loveliest dream, Maman,' Marie said, pushing herself into an upright seated position with her strong legs, 'I dreamed I fell in love with a man.'

'Ah, but that *is* a lovely dream, Cheri!'

Maman was incredibly beautiful. Her stunning looks belied her age of fifty. She had soft, round, smiling cheeks. Her blonde hair had been cut into a bob, blow-waved off her face, giving her a youthful, boyish appearance. She was up, dressed in a shabby grey cardigan over a crisp, open-neck white blouse and navy jeans. Her sleeves were rolled up to the elbows in readiness for the chores to come. Maman could easily have passed for a woman in her late twenties were it not for the worry-lines etched into her face, the dark blotches under her eyes. She stuffed a hand into her jean pocket, flashed a radiant smile at her daughter, and sagged against the wall, propping up her spirits with her outstretched arm. Marie caught the sadness in her eyes, and challenged her,

'But I will never fall in love, will I Maman?'

Her mother, looking downcast, fixed her stare on a fat pigeon, squatting on the window ledge. She didn't reply. Marie felt like strangling her when she acted like this, shying from the truth: her terrible imperfections.

She persisted, 'Will I Maman?'

'No, Cheri,' her mother conceded, 'You will never fall in love.'

'But I still have you?'

'Yes, you still have me.'

They lived in a pauper's room, a homage to their poverty, which was sparsely furnished with a chest of drawers, wardrobe, table and chair, a sturdy three-legged stool, and a hand basin. But the walls were daubed with colour, delicate paintings: bright red tulips, yellow chicks, white blossom, azure blue seas, golden sandy beaches, shady harbours, a blood-orange sunset, and smattered here and there on a partially painted canvas, snowdrops.

Marie pushed the duvet off the bed with her feet, swung her legs off the bed, and stood,

'I have to go to the toilet, Maman.'

'Call me when you have finished. Oh, and run a bath for yourself, Cheri.'

Marie nodded and padded across the worn-out carpet to their bathroom while her mother busied herself making their bed. Mother and child had slept entwined in the bed since the fateful day that she gave birth there in front of her beloved husband, Georges. She recalled the look of shock on his face, on the midwife's face, when Marie slid too easily from her womb. How Georges burst into tears and stormed out of the room never to be seen again. The midwife staring sorrowfully into her eyes as she cut their cord and passed over her bloodied bundle of joy to Maman for her to hold and suckle, making her apologies, and leaving her to cradle the disfigured baby. That was all in 1960. Today was her daughter's twenty-third birthday. Maman pressed the creases out of the sheet, fluffed up the pillows, and drew up the duvet, admiring the unfinished painting hanging overhead. Her mind was clouded with guilt. Her throat was choked with shame. But her eyes were filled with tears of pride. She sank to her knees and wept for her tarnished child.

Marie closed the bathroom door with her bottom, then pulled at the light cord with her mouth. The place was a dingy hole with thick black mould growing on the window fan and around the bath. She hurried to the window, pulled at the fan cord with her mouth, reached for the bath plug with her left foot, gripping its chain between her toes, and pressed it into the plughole with the sole of her foot. Next, she turned on the hot and cold taps with her toes and went to the toilet. The lavatory was a dark hole in the floor with a wooden seat flush to the ground. Marie squatted over the abyss, sighing with relief as she freed her heavy bowel and emptied her swollen bladder. Then she called out to Maman,

'I have finished!'

Quickly, she stood up, reached for the cistern handle with her right foot, and flushed the toilet. Her mother strode in, brown mascara running down her cheeks, tore off a thick wad of soft tissue, gently eased her legs apart, and wiped her bottom, front to back, as if Marie were still her baby. After disposing of the mess, she splashed a little bath foam into the warm water and gestured for her daughter to clamber into the bathtub. Marie knew why her mother had been crying but didn't say a word.

Once Maman had bathed and towel-dried her child they went to the bedroom, which was bright, warm, and sunny, lit by dusty sunbeams. She fetched the sturdy three-legged stool and placed it in front of the hand basin. Marie sat on the stool, reached up for the loaded toothbrush with her right foot, turned on the cold water tap with her left foot, then cleaned her teeth. Maman stood at her side. She never ceased to marvel at the sheer flexibility in the young woman's toes: her *'fingers'*, the supple legs and feet: her *'arms and hands.'* As Marie dabbed her mouth dry, she swivelled on the stool to face her mother, delighted, and surprised, to see a smiling, happy, Maman cradling three parcels tied up with pink ribbons in her arms,

'Happy Birthday, Cheri!' she cried, stemming back her tears, 'Shall I put them on the bed for you to open?'

'Oh, Maman! I love you! Thank you! Thank you!'

Maman placed the two flimsy packages on the middle of the bed. Marie hesitated at first,

'Go on then, open them!'

She watched avidly as her daughter squatted on the duvet and tore apart the loose ribbons, pulling off the shiny red wrapping paper with her toes,

'I wonder what they are?' Marie said, grinning from ear-to-ear.

'You'll see! You'll see!'

Marie, who was born partly limb-deficient, well used to wearing old sweaters, knotted at the elbows, and Levi's, stared despondently at the beautiful royal blue satin sleeveless top and pleated white skirt, lying between her feet. Her mother had dreaded this moment. Had feared her attempt to celebrate Marie's womanhood, her stunning natural beauty, would cause this upset. Ashamed of the actions that she took, in all innocence, when *she* was a young woman herself: actions that directly resulted in her daughter's horrid deformities. Wishing the floor would open up and swallow her whole, she braced herself,

'What is it, Cheri?'

Marie lowered her head, so that her chin rested on her chest. Her wavy teak hair fell in a flop over her face. She cried gently. She didn't want to upset her mother by letting her see her cry on her birthday. Marie hated her body, hated her physical aberrations, hated herself, the human abnormality that she was. Why couldn't she be normal, like the other artists?

'I cannot wear these clothes, Maman!' she blurted, suddenly, 'You know I can't! Why have you offended me so?'

Marie's harsh words cut into her mother's heart like a bitter sword of hatred. Swallowing her pride, she begged her daughter's forgiveness, explaining to her beloved that she was only trying to make amends. For the mistake she made during her pregnancy. For the drug she took when she lived in England with her husband George (his real name): the Distval, otherwise known as thalidomide. Maman opened her final present, the small parcel, and withdrew a hard, black jewellery box. She took out the chunky gold necklace and hung it round her crying daughter's neck,

'This was Grand Mere's,' she wept, 'I want you to have it, to wear for me, always, because you are beautiful, Cheri, because you have nothing to be ashamed of. It is me who should be ashamed.'

She slumped on the bed and held her baby in her tender motherly embrace. Marie cried,

'Oh, I am so sorry. I love you, my dear, sweet, sad Maman.'

They cried, as one. They shed teardrops.

Snowdrops, Marie painted snowdrops - with her mouth.

Marion Filbert

2015:

MARION BEHAVES STRANGELY, SHELTERING ONLY weeks after her mother died. At nightfall, she leaves her bedsit over the baker's shop in the high street, walks to the rectory, and sleeps rough on the grass, using leaves for blankets, earth for pillows. Come dawn, come sunrise, she dusts herself down, shakes herself off, and starts all over again.

Marion is thirty-five and single. She is vigorous and healthy with a buxom figure, which young men find attractive, sweeping-long hazel hair, and a disarmingly beautiful smile: a pure, honest, convincing smile. She works the early shift at the local supermarket. Pleased for the company since her mother died. Her mother controlled her as a little girl. Beating her senseless for being young. Sending her to the cubby hole under the staircase for being forward. Offing her to bed without supper for asking questions.

How she misses her mother since she slipped the dose of sleeping tablets into her tea. How she needs to shelter the poor young, the needy filth, the starving youths. As repentance for her Sins.

One night, Marion goes to the park, finds herself a young tramp, takes him into her little hovel, and tells him to be quiet. Lest *the Devil*, Breda, her landlord, should find him. Lying on her sofa bed, undressed...

Marion is insane. She slayed her mother. Cut her into tiny pieces. Kneaded clumps of her hairy flesh into the flower border. And set her on fire at sunset. Marion Filbert still hears her voice.

She rents a bedsit with a grimy kitchenette, greasy stove, mouldy shower cubicle, single bed, sofa and collapsed chest of drawers. And in those drawers, she keeps her mother's ashes before their disposal sealed in a black urn gilded with red roses, her mother's chunky diamond rings, her five pairs of big pants, and two old bras by Damara mail.

And so, it comes to pass that she finds him sleeping rough in carrier bags on the village green, on a rainy Saturday night in March. And Marion, who deceives her victims into thinking she is a Good Samaritan, takes pity on him. Takes him into her bedsit. And onto her sofa bed where he sleeps soundly, opposite her, fully dressed, in his black sweater, drainpipe blue jeans, and olive ankle socks.

And, at midnight, when the bedsit is coal-dark, Marion stands over the dirty vagrant in her tatty grey petticoat, clasping a bloody great kitchen knife. Preparing to sacrifice him to her perverse, imaginary gods. He, nineteen, homeless and unemployed, stretches, yawns, aches, stares into her dark face and...

'I made you coffee,' she says.

He slouches on the sofa, gesturing for her to hand him the red mug. Its inscription reads:

STAY CALM! SOMEONE UP THERE LOVES YOU!

He grins, a smug grin, 'Oh, yeah, thanks.'

Marion has no shame. She pulls her petticoat over her head. Showing off her fanfare of dark chocolate moles, the spattered human pebbledash on her creamy skin. And reaches for her pure comfort summer highlights maxi briefs, sliding them up her lean legs.

He sips his coffee, watching her dress - never having seen a naked woman before last night. Marion blushes as she sees him ogling her. To think, she actually let him fornicate with her. She should have killed him. When she had the chance. Now, she feels dirtied, unclean, nervous as to what to do next,

'Did you sleep okay?'

'Yeah, best night's sleep I've had in ages, thanks.'

'Tell me something.'

'Yeah.'

Marion cups her ample breasts into her tea rose bra,

'Tell me last night meant something to you.'

'Last night meant something to me.'

'Don't be a child. You know what I mean. Why, I'll wash your mouth out with soap and water!'

She hangs her lucky silver charm around her neck. Straps on her silver wristwatch, her mother's copper bracelet. Callously, he brushes her soft body aside with a feint flick of his limp wrist,

'Go on then, try me!'

Marion blanches, shocked by his blatant disregard for her feelings,

'Do you really mean it?'

'Yeah, course I do!' he slurps his coffee, 'Mm that tastes good. Pass me my fags, will you?'

She pulls on her smartest, dry-cleaned, figure-hugging, grey-flecked-wool dress,

'No, you'll set the place on fire.'

'Pretty please?'

'No!'

He watches Marion intently as she stoops to slip on her sandals,

'You look nice.'

Her face lights up,

'Thank you.'

'Where are you off to then at this time of the morning?'

She flushes, stammering a little, 'Church, I go to Church every Sunday.'

'Cool,' he lies, 'What are you doing in Church?'

'Reading.'

'What does that mean, reading?'

'I'm giving today's reading to the congregation,' she says.

'Oh, yeah, what's that about?'

'It's about the temptation of Christ. The Lord moves in mysterious ways, doesn't he?'

He reaches for her. Puts his hand behind her head. Strokes her wavy hair. Pulls her towards him. They kiss, throatily. Gasping, panting, she pushes him off of her,

'I have to go. Be late for Church. There's bacon, sausages, eggs. In the fridge. Help yourself. To breakfast. Before you go…'

'…will I ever see you again?'

'Probably not.'

'Here. Take this. For your lunch.'

She offers him a £10 note.

'I couldn't possibly…'

£50 maybe, not £10!

'Well then. Take good care of yourself. Stay out of mischief. Thanks, then. For last night?'

'Yeah, thanks. You're a star.'

'You take care, you hear?'

'I will.'

She turns to face him as she reaches the door, and gives him a little wave, 'Bye then.'

He smirks, 'Bye bye…'

She enters the parish church of St Agnes in Aigburth and joins the congregation in the sacred holding of hands. Her god-fearing best friends, Mark, and Kimberley, arise from a pew at the back of the church to greet her. Secretly, she refers to them as her disciples, such is the intensity of their fawning over her.

'Peace be with you, Marion,' Mark says, his eyes sparkling with tears of joy.

She places her soft hands around his hands to comfort him, 'And with you, Mark'

'Peace be with you, Marion!' Kimberley bawls.

'Oh, and with you, Kimberley!' she calls, 'And with you!'

'We are so looking forward to your reading today,' they chime.

Feeling overwhelmed, Marion quickly turns away and strides down the aisle to the pulpit.

'Peace be with you,' says a strange girl with freckles, in a red leather mini skirt and white vest.

'And with you, Mary.'

She makes her way as far as the front pew. He is waiting for her. The man with the odd beaver haircut, and crazy eyes. He reaches out and squeezes her hand, tight, long enough to cause her discomfort.

'Peace be with You, Marion!'

He leers, a mouthful of rotting, black teeth.

Oh, my God! she stresses. He knows my name!

'And with you, Ha-Ha-Hannibal,' she stutters, wrenching her hand free.

Marion is relieved to feel the warm hands of Reverend Iain Smyth embrace hers. He reads her face, the quizzical look, speaks too quickly,

'Peace be with You, Child,' he says, his face glowing, all puce.

She announces to the whole congregation: 'Child? I am not your Child?'

'Ah, Mrs Mulgrew!' Smyth cries, hastily turning away from Marion, 'Peace be with You!'

'And with you Vicar!' retorts Mulgrew.

Marion stares down at the little boy slumped in the wheelchair at the far end of the front pew. His sad head lolls to one side. Drool and spittle ooze from his cracked lips. His thick, purple, tongue hangs out of the right side of his mouth.

Why is he still alive? What is the point?

The point is his mum loves him with all her heart, unlike Marion's cow who was cruel to her,

'Peace be with you, Sam,' she whispers.

The boy's mother speaks, looks exhausted, close to tears,

'Thank you so much, Marion.'

Marion looks up at The Cross on the altar, genuflects, bows her head, then makes her way to the pulpit where she sets down a sheaf of typed A4 sheets of paper for the reading. She goes and sits next to the strange girl in the third pew.

Excluding the Vicar, and Baxter the Organist there are nine worshippers in the congregation, she counts. Only nine!

The rest of the parish worship the new material gods: social media, flash hybrid cars, holiday homes, exotic erotic breaks, online shopping, football...

Marion lays down a tussock, kneels, clasps her hands together, closes her eyes and prays:

'Please Lord, give me the strength to carry on my good work till I meet you in Heaven. Amen.'

She glances sideways at the strange girl, kneeling in prayer. Her mini skirt has ridden up her legs, exposing her bare freckled thighs.

Some people have no sense of dignity or respect!

The Vicar reads the Notices, then everyone, except the little boy, stand up and sing the first hymn: To Be A Pilgrim.

'Please be seated!' Smyth cries afterwards, nodding at Marion.

The church falls silent as she steps up into the pulpit, and reads:

'Luke, Chapter 4: the temptation of Christ.'

She pauses for effect, then:

'And Jesus being full of the Holy Ghost returned from Jordan and was led by the Spirit into the wilderness. Being forty days tempted of the devil. And in those days, he did eat nothing; and when they were ended, he afterward hungered.

And the devil said unto him: If thou be the Son of God, command this stone that it be made into bread.'

Marion pauses while someone in the congregation coughs loudly,

'And Jesus answered him saying: It is written: That man shall not live by every word of God.

And the devil, taking him up high into a high mountain, shewed unto him all the kingdoms of the world in a moment of time. And the devil said unto him: All this power will I give thee, and the glory of them; for that is delivered unto me; and to whomsoever I shall give it. If thou therefore wilt worship me, all will be thine.

And Jesus answered and said unto him: Get thee behind me Satan; for it is written: Thou shalt worship the Lord thy God, and him only shalt thou serve... And Jesus answering said unto him: It is said: Thou shalt not tempt the Lord thy God. And when the devil had ended all the temptation, he departed from him...'

And so, it came to pass that, even as Marion was reading the parable of the temptation of Christ to the tiny parish congregation, the boy ransacked her bedsit until he found her mother's chunky diamond rings. A petty thief, he knew a thing or two about jewellery. Each ring was crusted with diamonds. The rings could easily be lost on the black jewellery market, for £5,000 each.

He took the rings in his fist, went to the kitchenette, and treated himself to a fine breakfast of fried eggs, grilled rashers of back bacon, and prime pork sausages, served up with lashings of HP sauce. Smiled ironically at the bloody great kitchen knife that she held over his throat in the dark last night before she sinned with him. Then, he placed his dirty plate in her dishwasher - and left her life forever.

When Marion returned to her bedsit, lying on the Formica kitchen work surface, she found a note:

GET YOURSELF A CHEAP SAFE, YEAH? BEFORE SOME CLOWN NICKS THEM?... LUKE xxx

And two diamonds rings.

You

2017:

IN HER MOST REVEALING INTERVIEW since her divorce from husband Jayson Louys Red-Ball tells you the real reason why she walked away from her marriage.

Red-Ball barely wears a shiny black leather jacket halfway down her back revealing an alluring, if tasteful, glimpse of her breasts. She stands in front of the off-white background in perfect contrast to her buoyant mood, a mood that tells you she is free to love again. You stand well out of camera-shot and begin the interview with an easy question,

'How are your children?'

'I don't intend to discuss my children. Our split was painful, heart-rending enough with those screams in the shower, the blood-tipped knife, plates smashing against the kitchen wall. Jayson and I remain good friends.'

'Do you really, Lou? It is alright if I call you Lou, isn't it?'

'Don't suck up to me!'

'I wasn't sucking up to you. I was asking a question. Are you still on good terms with Jayson?'

'Officially.'

'What's that supposed to mean?'

'For the children's sake.'

Red-Ball lets her leather slip down her shoulders and raises her chin, lifting her head to show you her bare, drainpipe neck. Her *gilded* neck. Complete with three, tiny love moles. She holds straight, firm, in the face of your interrogation. If Red-Ball doesn't want to answer you, then she won't. She'll just raise her head and stare at the ceiling. Let's take a closer look at the real reason why she walked away from her marriage:

Red-Ball, 45, has a divine chin, pink lips, a snub nose, false eyelashes, tell-tale studs in her left earlobe, and a shock of voluminous curled caramel hair that falls down her back.

She is content. She is free. She wants you,

'Listen! I'm excited. I forgot what excited feels like?'

'What kind of answer is that?'

'The right answer.'

'Can I ask you something personal?'

'Go on, everyone else does.'

'Do you love your kids?'

'How dare you ask me that! Of course, I love them! Dieter rang me only the other day from boarding school to ask me how my video was going.'

'What video is that?'

'The video for my new single, Crotch. It's out now.'

'Thanks for that. Carry on.'

'Where was I?'

'You were telling me about Dieter? The video?'

'Oh, yes! Dieter, I said, I err, uh, um, am currently wearing my leotard.'

'What did he say?

'He said: I'm not going to look at you, Louys.'

'Your son calls you Louys?'

'Mm.'

'What did you say?'

'I said, Diet, you have to understand, this is a crap world for attracting men unless you wander around in a leotard? It is quite sexy. Not, you know, boobs out, but real, empowering for women of my age. People expect me to sing the heartbroken song. I don't want to be that predictable. So, I've gone sexy and funky for the first man I find. I want him to say: Oh, you're not what I expected.'

'Thank you. We'll take a break now for the advertorial. Give you a chance to change into your next outfit.'

'You're welcome! Tasty shirt!'

Red-Ball rubs her hand up and down your hairy arm in a tactile way, slipping three slim fingers underneath your turned-up cuff,

'What is it, M&S?'

* * * * *

IN HER MOST REVEALING OUTFIT since her divorce, Red-Ball tells you why she walked away from her marriage.

She is wearing a trench coat undone at the front to reveal a lacy bra, sheer fishnet tights. Sadly, the outfit makes her look old, tired, jaded. Red-Ball puts on a weary smile. Her lips are cracked and chewed. Her snub nose is running. She wipes her nostrils dry with the back of her crinkled hand. Her skin is pale and flaky. Her hair has split ends. There are tears in her eyes. She opens her coat and bares her breasts for you which makes you feel queasy and embarrassed. A fading star about to be extinguished. Her big round green eyes well up with tears. She rubs your hairy arm in a tactile way, making you flinch. Then she bares her soul about the marriage split,

'I don't blame *him*. It was down to me to say something isn't right.'

'Why?'

'Well, I did go out more than I'd ever gone out.'

'What about your kids?'

'They board?'

'Silly me, of course they do.'

'I found a spark. I was enjoying myself. I guess I always was the perfectly behaved wife. Then I got married, had children. It kept me away from playing the game.'

'The game?'

'Yes, are you saying I was wrong to play the game?'

'No, just intrigued.'

'Why intrigued? Are you saying what I did was wrong?'

'No. I didn't take you to be that kind of a person.'

'Are you saying I acted indecently, is that what you're saying?'

'It's just that I remember the sordid headline.'

'What sordid headline?'

'Red-Ball Is Out on The Town Drunk Again.'

'That's untrue! I was home by 1130. Sitting with my husband having a bowl of Frosties.'

'Shall we move on?'

'I think we ought to, don't you?'

'I understand you're seeing a therapist.'

'Once.'

'Only once?'

'Yes, once. I saw a therapist once. When I told him I wouldn't be back, my therapist's bullying tone was hard to believe.'

Red-Ball bursts into tears.

'Kleenex?'

'Thanks.'

She wipes her eyes. Tears keep rolling roll down her cheeks. You feel for her: over 45, wealthy, a fading star, money can't buy her love, husband's dating a 21-year-old model, kids at boarding school. You feel sorry for her. Want to button her black trench coat, take her in your arms, give her a hug. But you can't. Hugging celebrities isn't allowed. She might sue you. Instead, you wind up the interview, passing her the box of tissues,

'Louys Red-Ball, after all you've been through the divorce, the battle to retain your kids, your breakdown, your sex video, a new single, the fashion shoot; describe your feelings at this time.'

Louys Red-Ball, 45, fading star, divorcee, alcoholic, drug addict, chokes back her tears, looks you straight in the eye and says:

'I'm happy. Scared. Stronger than I thought…

How about you?'

Ana's Orbs

Thursday Night:

THE DISCO ON THE VERANDA bar was in full swing, the dancefloor awash with flashing lights: lime, turquoise, strawberry, tangerine, orange, lemon strobes. DJ Lenox dimmed the lights down low and played his first slow number. I sank deep into a tufted black leather sofa in the shadows and watched the short, stocky, auburn blonde smooch a young olive-skinned man with a Balbo beard. Ana had changed into a sexy, full-length, black evening dress, split as high as her waist. Her partner caressed her hips. She drew him in and kissed him deeply. They seemed to be well acquainted.

Feeling lonely, I walked to the rocky beach and watched the lighthouse, its moving lantern, changing colours, and listened to the siren's sad song of the sea.

Friday:

My hotel was strictly adults only, lonely hearts in search of new love. I attended the welcome meeting at 11am. There were newly-weds, young couples, freed parents, middle and old-aged couples, singles looking for fun, and widows. I was approached by a nosy, interfering, old man,

'Wife not joining you?'

I grimaced, 'Afraid not. Moira was killed in a car crash four weeks ago.'

'Sorry for your loss.' he lied, looking away, 'Never mind, here comes our glass of bubbly.'

We were introduced to our holiday representatives: Tam, Elicia, Burt and Ana. Then I went on holiday. The hotel had no beach, just craggy rocks, sea swells. I lay on the lounger sunbathing most of the day, watching the heavily pregnant mums burst out of their bikinis, their virile husbands crouched at their sides, sadly surveying the other women - in search of bared breasts.

At noon I took lunch in the straw-thatched beach bar: an ice-cold cola and chicken wrap. I was served by the olive-skinned man with the Balbo beard, who caressed Ana's hips last night.

After a short nap, a siesta out of the sun, I wrapped my lean torso in a fluffy bathrobe, pulled on my tight red trunks and padded to the spa. A girl with a bushy moustache offered me a full body massage. I declined, protesting that I had a weak spinal column. She told me she cured bad backs, performed extras, too. I told her to back off. In my view, girls shouldn't offer men extras.

Instead, I worked my muscles on the sparse gym equipment. The shoulder press was the wrong way round and there were no mats for press-ups. I was entertained by the young, olive-skinned man with Balbo beard who caressed Ana's hips last night, pulling 112kg. Feeling puny in my cheap trunks, I quit the gym and dived into the heated swimming pool, crawling, and sputtering ten lengths breaststroke before I ran out of breath.

I towelled myself dry and sat in the sauna. A slim auburn girl in a skimpy bikini with a port wine stain covering her face walked in and sat down on the seat below me. I cupped water onto the glowing red coals with the ladle, steam rose. I made a polite comment to the slim girl about her burgundy face. She walked out.

At 3pm I took a rest in my room to escape the blazing sun.

At 4pm I attended Step Aerobics on the Fitness Terrace with Ana:

'Gut job! Give your toes a holiday! Feel your butt! Deep inhale, deep exhale! Very gut job! Feel your toes, feet, calves, thighs, hips, chest, neck, nose, mouth, head, roll your eyes back, drift away!'

I did everything she told me to do, thanking her for brightening my life, went back to my room and dreamed of her after I fell asleep. I couldn't get her out of my mind. Those stiff navy shorts, the busty olive-green top, her sturdy tanned thighs. I prayed that Ana would host the Quiz in the Bar.

At 5pm I sat on my own in the Beach Bar and took a Quiz. The other tables were full of Scots.

At 6pm I worked out in the indoor gym, swam the pool, and took a sauna. The fat girl with the beard was massaging a fat German on a large lounger. He had a broad smile on his red, blushing face and sweated like a pig. I couldn't see her hands, so I left.

At 7pm, I attended the Gala Dinner in the Restaurant. It was a self-service buffet. All the veg had feta cheese topping, baked with a crust. The head chef wore blacks, which struck me as unusual, a black baker's hat which flopped to the left. I asked the head chef why the dinner was described as gala. He told me every night was gala night at the Palacio del Mare, asking if I had an issue. I told him I had no issue with him or his craft, but that it might make a nice change to see broccoli, carrots, peas, squash, swede, and green beans served without the brown crust of feta. He told me to try the Beach Bar: they served pizza and Caesar salad with chips. I pointed out that both dishes contained cheese. The head chef bid me Bon Appetit and scarpered off to the kitchen.

At 8pm DJ Rot played obscure house music in the Lobby Bar. The dancefloor was awash with flashing lights: turquoise, strawberry, tangerine, lemon, lime green strobes. DJ Rot dimmed the lights down low and played his first slow number. I sank into my tufted black leather sofa, in the shadows, watching the short, stocky, auburn blonde smooch the young, olive-skinned man with a Balbo beard. Ana had changed into her sexy, full-length black evening dress, split right up to her waist. Her partner caressed her hips. She drew him in and kissed him deeply, for minutes on end. I think the in phrase at adult hotels is she ate his tongue and tried to suck his tonsils out.

We were interrupted at 9pm for a Gala Presentation by The Team, Tam, Elicia, Burt, and Ana.

At 9.30pm Rot appeared as Elvis. I went to bed but didn't sleep until the noise stopped at 11pm.

Saturday:

I was woken at dawn by the siren's lilting song of love.

At 8.30am I enjoyed a breakfast of fruit, nuts, and feta cheese on the poolside echelon. The coffee was too strong so I tipped it into the pool, enjoying its putrid discolouration. One of the goldfish floated on its back, poisoned by my coffee. The fat waitress told me, in a poor Texan accent, to have a nice day and asked if I was celebrating my birthday. I told her my wife was dead.

At 9am I walked to Eluder to search for socks and underpants. I was told Cretans don't wear underpants or socks as the weather is too clement. The nearest men's underwear shop was in Knauss, twenty kilometres away. I reverted to my trunks, hoping no-one had noticed my bulge.

I returned to the hotel at 10.30am just in time to change into my red trunks - and participate in Aqua Fitness in the Pool with Ana:

'Gut job! Give toes a holiday! Feel your butt! Deep inhale, deep exhale! Very gut job! Feel your toes, feet, calves, thighs, hips, chest, neck, nose, mouth, head, roll your eyes back and drift away. Marching! Swing those arms. Let your buddy roll like a porpoise in brine!'

There was a Couples Race. I was forced to swim with Ana. Gripping her shoulders, I lay against her back, feeling her taut muscles, the cleft buttocks, as she swam with me attached to her body, her willing limpet. We reversed roles. I was hopeless. I thanked Ana for helping me find my way to the edge of the three-tier swimming pool. She laughed heartily, told me to learn to swim.

After noon, I went sunbathing. The sun was intense. One of the heavily pregnant women was topless. I had to stare out to sea to calm myself. The sea was empty apart from three oil tankers on the horizon.

I waited until 1pm to take lunch in my red trunks in the Beach Bar. I spilled some hot chips in my lap, burnt my stomach. I was served by the young olive-skinned man with the Balbo beard who caressed Ana's hips.

At 2pm I took a restful siesta in my room, dreaming intermittently of Ana in her navy swimsuit.

At 4pm, feeling refreshed, I stood under the shady bamboo canopy in the Fitness Suite and enjoyed a Full Body Workout with Ana. Afterwards, I thanked her for changing my life.

She smiled and said, in stilted German,

'Thank you, I am so glad that you enjoyed my buddy.'

At 5pm I came last in the Quiz in the Beach Bar.

At 6pm I worked-out in the gym, pool, and sauna. The spa was like a morgue, corpse-white, the occasional vase.

At 7pm I attended the International Dinner in the Restaurant. I was forced to wear trousers and a hot cotton shirt. The International Dinner was the same as the Gala Dinner, except that the starter course, the so-called Vital Menu, was served with feta. I chose seafood pasta baked in a feta crust, followed by feta omelette.

At 7.30pm I returned to my room to change into a white tuxedo, black tie and 'Frank Sinatra' lined black trousers. I sat admiring Moira's photos, tears streaming down my face, until 9pm.

The Casino Night consisted of a Poker Table and a Roulette Table. Ana, wearing an odd dress with vents down the side, revealing the full extent of her tanned hips, span the roulette wheel.

'Rein de la plus!' she cried, incorrectly.

At 930pm, disappointed by Ana's embarrassing terminology, and out of chips, I went to bed.

Sunday:

I was woken at dawn by the siren's lilting song of love.

At 8.30pm I had Breakfast: greasy streaky bacon, frankfurters and eggs scrambled in ewe's milk, served with a feta crust.

At 9pm I joined The Walk to Colocynth Causeway with Burt as far as the Eluder Peninsula. Half-way across the spit, I stopped to watch a man and a woman hold hands at a café table. The woman was crying. A speedboat went past. I went to speak. The film producer told me to shut up.

At 1pm I had lunch in the Beach Bar: Caesar salad made with feta, followed by a clean shave, shower, and a strange dream about Ana, naked in a glass ball. I blamed the illusion on the feta.

Then, at 4pm I enjoyed Circuit Training with Ana, wearing my tight red trunks. She laughed! I thanked her very much. She said I should try her yoga class if I wanted to experience instant karma in my buddy.

At 5pm I came last in the Quiz.

At 6pm I returned to the gym, where I lifted two 1kg dumbbells, doggy-paddled in the heated pool, and took a sauna. I was joined by an attractive girl from Minsk called Luba who wore a turban of towelling around her head and ten-inch-thick sticking plaster around her midriff. She explained that she'd just had an operation for hole-in-the heart, that I mustn't say or do anything to excite her. I thanked Luba for her honesty, pulled up my trunks, and returned to my room.

At 7pm I attended the Seafood Buffet (the Gala Dinner - with fish and feta).

At 9pm I watched three sensational Russian acrobats hold each other in the Lobby Bar and pondered over the future of free speech.

Monday:

At 10am I attended Back Fit with Ana. I thanked her for curing my back pain.

She lightly touched my shoulder, and said, 'Take care of your buddy.'

At 11am I attended Aqua Fit with Ana. During the Couples Race, I had to swim with Ana, holding her shoulders, lying against her back, loving the feeling of her strong muscles, the cleft buttocks. I thanked her for carrying me to the rim of the three-tier swimming pool. She just smiled and turned away.

I went to the sea.

At 2.45pm I enjoyed a free full body massage with the bearded lady.

At 4pm I attended Dumbbell Fit alone with Ana. I mentioned to her that I wrote short stories.

'I would like to read one of your stories,' she laughed, 'Would you write a story about me?'

I said that I would love to write a love story about her, and she taught me how to lift dumbbells.

At 5pm I attended Stretch and Relax with Ana.

At the International Dinner, I was personally greeted by Ana, wearing an odd dress with vents which highlighted the perfect shape of her bare tanned hips. I wondered about Balbo Beard's hands, whether Ana would give of herself to him tonight on the dancefloor. I heard a siren sing of the sea. I heard my siren sing!

At 7.30pm I took an evening stroll by the beach and stared at the reflections of the Beach Bar lights, cast on the water.

At 8.30pm I went to bed. I was kept awake until 11pm by DJ Rot.

Tuesday:

Ana's day off:

I sat in my room and sulked all day. The Naturals Trio kept me awake until 11pm. I played 13-card patience until midnight but struggled to find the ace of hearts.

Wednesday:

I was woken at dawn by the siren's lilting song of love.

At 9pm, I attended Night Yoga with Ana:

'Very gut job! Feel your toes, feet, calves, thighs, hips, chest, neck, nose, mouth, head, roll your eyes back und drift away!'

She sent me to sleep under the stars. When I awoke, I found that Ana had made me a tiny cup of ginger tea. I thanked her politely. She lay down on the floor beside me. She looked beautiful.

Behind her buddy were two huge opaque illuminated orbs which changed colour from mauve to pink, strawberry, tangerine, lemon, lime.

Afterwards, I helped Ana clear up all her spent candles and washed up and towel-dried our two teacups and saucers in my bedroom.

'Meet me on the beach in fifteen minutes,' she whispered excitedly, as I presented her china.

I met Ana on the beach. A warm breeze of romance blew through our hearts. Waves of love crashed onto our souls. She made me feel young again. Ana's huge, opaque, illuminated orbs changed colour: turquoise, strawberry, tangerine, lemon, lime green…

They lay bobbing on the surf. One of the orbs slid open. Ana climbed inside.

She called to me, 'I must leave now.'

The orb closed.

I stared at her naked figure, hunched inside the orb, crying out vibrantly to me, crying with joy:

'Feel your body float! Enjoy the moment!'

She floated off across the sea into the dark night.

'What about me?' I cried. 'I love you, Ana, I always will. You can't just leave me here.'

She called me! My siren!

'Feel your body float! Enjoy the moment!'

The second orb slid open.

I climbed inside.

I bounced across the crashing waves to be with my love.

'Oh, Ana!' I cried, 'Oh, my siren of the sea!'

The siren sang her lilting song of love!

The Hide

WE WERE LOST. WE MISSED the village twice. Once when I drove us as far as Goldhangar, turned the Yaris round, and headed back to historic Maldon, unsure if we were on the right road. And when we passed through Tolleshunt D'Arcy, the brown tourist sign indicating a marina, ending up on the outskirts of Colchester. I pulled over, blocking a farmyard track. Darcy consulted the atlas spread across her bare knees,

'Ellsbury Wick must be here, somewhere, back there?'

She glided her ring finger along a yellow B-road half an inch as far as D'Arcy, after which my dear wife was christened. She made me laugh,

'Here, somewhere, back, there?'

I rubbed her forearm affectionately, loving her divine way with words, glancing at our eternity ring, the oath which said:

I'll always love you dearest, whatever our life may bring.

For some reason, her sweet sentiment invaded my larynx. I was struck dumb. The coughing fit descended upon me too early. Midday had yet to pass. Darcy held my hand tightly as I coughed and sputtered, bent over double with pain, my white knuckles clenching the steering wheel for dear life. Her face riddled with concern. And with good reason. I was too ill.

'Will you see the Hide?' she asked me, directly.

I wheezed like an asthmatic with emphysema, drew in lungsful of air, gasped, 'I'll see it.'

Darcy shook her head. She didn't believe a word. I turned the ignition, pulling over hard left to let a grass green tractor, a ruddy-faced farmer, haul a bumpy trailer of freshly baled hay past us.

Good day to you both, his gappy grin implied, *Welcome to the coastal marshlands!*

The day started badly. We set off early for our country rambles. On this occasion, I hurt too much. My muscle ached; joints ached. My heart ached - for a lost youth. Instead of helping Darcy pack our walking boots, russets, and blackberry waters in the Yaris, I pottered aimlessly about the garden fertilising her tomato plants in my fluffy gown. We eventually left at ten, only to be ensnarled in an endless traffic jam filing past Danbury on the A414 en route to a fuel fest. I watched an ambulance hurtle past, its blue lights flashing, siren wailing. Some unlucky soul…

Midday had yet to pass. Darcy brushed my cheek with the back of her warm hand, rousing me from my stupor. I turned right into a country lane and headed back towards Tolleshunt. She saw it first, a white wayfarer's sign, pointed left, the name shrouded by sweet chestnut leaves:

'Look, love!'

I glanced at the partial word: 'ick'. No wonder we missed it. We drove down a leafy lane until the landscape broadened, flattening into barren, sun-parched marshes, featureless monotonies, only brightened by occasional rows of holiday bungalows. Ten minutes later, I parked the Yaris in Church Street between the Nag's Head and the ancient market cross, and we clambered out.

A stern, swarthy man was standing outside the pub swearing into his mobile. He blushed and apologized when he saw Darcy. My beautiful wife has an arresting presence, an aura about her, guaranteed to make a countryman blush. I vaguely made out the shape of a young man throwing darts through the smoked-glass window of the bar. Other than that, the village was deserted. I heard my stomach tell my mouth it was time to eat.

Darcy was staring at a corner shop across the road. I stared into the cloudless blue heavens; the flaming yellow ball, riding high. My gut twisted, sending my torso into convulsions of pain. My face contorted with agony. Midday had passed. Darcy held my hand tightly as the searing heartburn subsided. Her ice-blue eyes shimmered with tears. The swarthy man cut his call and watched us. The youth stopped throwing darts. Darcy gazed at my face with her sad, blue eyes,

'Will you see the Hide?' she whispered.

I was unsure. I hesitated. I breathed deeply. I responded, 'I'll see it.'

Darcy was standing by the corner shop across the road. I noticed the Church. For the first time. The bunting from the Church fete. The freshly dug grave. Darcy was standing by the doorway. Then I was with her, inside the corner shop, selecting sandwiches. There was an odd girl with ruby hair. I asked her if she had a toilet. She shook her head sadly. Darcy was paying for her sandwich: double egg mayo on wholemeal. There were corn kernels in her palm, smoky bacon flavour. I felt the sandwich in my hand: roast chicken with sage and onion stuffing on malted white bread.

Darcy was standing outside the shop, wolfing kernels. I heard myself pay the ruby-haired girl. Her twin appeared. Her identical twin. I asked if she had a toilet. She said I should try the pub. Automated conveniences abounded beside the car park at Woodcliff Green about a mile away. Near the Marina. Where I proposed to Darcy. I thanked the twins, who were blanched white-faced with shock, for their courtesy, then went to find her, except that she was nowhere to be found.

I returned to the Yaris and wolfed kernels, nibbling crusts off my solid chicken treat. My gut hurt. I wasn't hungry. I felt her hot breath on my neck. Or was it the hot sea breeze on my face?

'I was on my toilet,' she murmured.

'On your toilet?'

'Mm!'

'And was it comfortable?'

'It had a warm wooden seat, darling. Will you see the Hide?'

'I'll see it.'

Darcy was standing by the market cross in her hiking boots. My legs felt leaden, heavy with ague. I stooped to tie my boots, lumbered across the road bearing her zebra-striped rucksack, a picnic, and we set off. The swarthy man resumed his call, the youth started throwing darts, the:

Automated Conveniences at Woodcliff Green are Closed for Repair Work

...the notice on the black door said. My heart sank, my bladder burst.

Darcy was standing with a sailing couple: deck shoes, matching khaki shorts, striped t-shirts, baseball caps with anchors, bronze tans, wrinkled walnut skins, crying,

'Try the disabled!'

'Thank you! Thank you SO much!' I sounded like a tweeter or online poster. They thank a lot!

When I left the toilet, as clean and flushed as I found it, I noticed Darcy had re-appeared farther up the road, just before the sail lofts. We mounted some concrete steps together to pick up the stony public footpath on the sea wall, the hot sun in our faces, our hair blowing stiff where we were exposed to the elements.

Presently, we arrived at a natural marina, a sea of greyish mud where the tide had washed out, leaving gaily coloured boats high and dry on mudbanks strewn with splintered boardwalks, an odd, discarded bicycle. I noticed that the newest yachts and motorboats were berthed closest to the sailing clubhouse. A swathe of wary faces looked down on us from their tiered beer garden: silent, frightened, masques of fear.

As we entered the nature reserve entrance beside Woodcliff Creek, I saw boats aged with grime, rusting hulks, skeletal frames sticking out of the mud. Nautical corpses lost in a no-man's land. Before us, the sea wall stretched for miles alongside the creek, enclosing the main body of the marsh. In the distance, the dark spectre of the nuclear power station and, on rising land behind a farm building, in stark contrast, a Second World War observation tower. I spotted an old red lighthouse ship, children playing, reflecting on the vanities of our past, the uncertainties of their polluted future.

If you have a dog then it must be kept under strict control because of the risk to the grazing North Ronaldsay sheep and suckler herd of Shetland cattle, your disturbance to wildlife. There wasn't another living soul as far as I could see, nor a dog, roaming the sea wall.

I saw Darcy standing further along the sea wall by the Leavings. There was fringing reed and scrub developing around the borrowdyke. Always worth a look and a listen in summer for reed warblers and buntings, as well as dragonflies. I joined her. We walked past the outflow sluice for the marsh, where precious water would gush out at low tide after the expected heavy

August rain. Just ahead of us was the new counter wall, the high grassy bank that wound its way across to Blockhouse Bay. A permissive footpath led us to the Hide, built into the counter-wall, from where we could watch the duck, geese, waders, and sheep, wandering across the grazing marsh.

Darcy stood at the entrance to the Hide. I felt my body twist and rack with agony. Felt my lungs heave, my heart pound.

'Will you see the Hide?' she whispered.

Frightened, I hesitated, breathed in, spurting out words like blood from an artery, 'I'll see it.'

I followed Darcy into the Hide. The Hide was empty. There were polished benches, one for each shuttered window, a wipe-board with smudged words 'sheep sighted' on it, and a handful of leaflets bearing the slogan: Join Us Today and Save Your Wildlife for Tomorrow. I sat down heavily on the bench and stared out of the window at the sheep grazing the dry riverbed. There were dozens of ghastly black flies crawling up the insides of the windows.

I found my final resting place.

Darcy was standing just inside the latched doorway. She mouthed her parting words,

'I'll always love you, darling.'

Then she turned to go.

Evie's Downfall

June 2019:

EVIE THREW HER TENNIS RACKET and tube of balls on the hall carpet, trudged upstairs - and cried. There was no-one to comfort her. As usual, her fiancé had slung on his faded boiler suit and scurried off to the garage. Evie decided to leave him to his own devices until she summoned him to dinner, his favourite: fish fingers daubed in baked beans, a jacket potato spattered with ketchup. After wolfing it down he invariably returned to his den until bedtime. Evie would be asleep by then.

Guilt-stricken, she reflected on the deceit she practised, how he might react if he ever found out. Scott was much too gentle to hurt her. She imagined he would hold his pudgy face in his hands, shake his head in disbelief, profess his undying love for her, then plod to the toilet, crying his heart out.

In a way, she was relieved, he wasn't there. At least, she wouldn't have to hide her lying eyes.

She reached the landing. There was a bookshelf under the window crammed with books she never found the time to read. A solid teak chest of drawers, a decorated Chinese punch bowl, a cracked globe. Evie sank to her knees and slid out the drawer stuffed with plastic folders: cherished photos: happier times, fleeting memories, holidays in Florida, Thailand, Italy, Mull.

Ashamed of herself, Evie bit her lip, made her way to the bath, and undressed. She rid herself of Nick in the shower, flossing her teeth, combing her wet hair, as if cleaning her teeth or combing tangled knots out of her beautiful flame-red hair might redeem her for their adultery. Then, she traipsed off to the bedroom.

Scott finished repairing his last plasma screen of the day. He checked his watch. Evie would be home from tennis, showered, naked, waiting for him to climb into bed with her. Perhaps she'd let him kiss her cheeks, give her a little hug. He shook his head. In his dreams. His love for her was superseded by his obsession. How did Evie feel about that? He clenched his fists in sheer frustration, impotent, unable to rekindle the flames of their long-lost love.

Evie stood in front of the mirror: head bowed, eyes closed, lips pursed, stony-faced. Cursing herself for what she'd done with Nick in the heat of the afternoon. Her pale freckled skin was sunburnt tell-tale blush pink, her lipstick kissed off by his hungry mouth, on the hottest day of the year. She folded her arms over her chest, afraid to look at herself in the mirror, fearing his memory, then raised her arms above her head.

No sign of an unusual rash, no prominent veins.

'I love you, Evie, I'll never leave you,' he promised her. She shook her head in disgust.

She placed her hands lightly on top of her head.

She wasn't bleeding, or weeping.

Evie lay on the bed and felt near her nipple keeping her other arm still by her side. She felt a slight twinge, a pull. Mildly concerned, she moved her fingers over her breast in a spiralling motion, feeling the underside of the breast. Placing her arm above her head, she repeated the examination for her other breast, the part of the breast which extended towards her armpit. When she was quite sure, Evie slipped on a comfortable, loose-fitting t-shirt and shorts, went downstairs, and put the jacket potatoes in the oven.

Scott was distracted by a whimpering sound coming from the doorway: Evie, mumbling,

'Supper's ready when you are, darling.'

Tears were streaming down her cheeks. His heart sank. She needed him more than he could imagine. They went inside. He took off his boiler suit, hurrying to the kitchen, to be with her.

Her shoulders heaved. Her nose dribbled. Black mascara ran down her puffy cheeks. A guilt lump caught in Scott's throat. Sad for her, worried about her, he pushed his food around the plate, heaping the dehydrated fish fingers in a sorry pile on top of the burnt baked beans, his cremated jacket potato. He'd completely lost his appetite.

Evie held her head in her hands and wept, her face concealed by a curtain of beautiful flame-red. Scott stood by her, cradling her head against his chest, stroking her rich mane. He loved her so much, feeling her pain, yet struggling to find the question, his dire sense of foreboding preventing the words from shaping in his dry mouth.

She buried her head in his chest. He held her tight, scrunching her up, hugging her like mad. Her breasts squashed against his chest, lips brushed his neck, kissing his skin, she murmured,

'I've got a lump in my left breast.'

He was shocked. He clutched at her. He tried to reassure her,

'It's probably just a cyst, Evie. I'll take you to see Dr Meredith in the morning, put your mind at rest.'

'Got a lump in my right breast as well.' Evie cried into his chest, bursting into floods of tears.

* * * * *

SUNDAY WAS THE DAY OF the charity flight in aid of the local hospice. Mia, the West Essex Air Cadets squadron leader, and Evie's sister received a text saying Scott had a summer bug and would have to pull out. Just as she was about to test the squad's knowledge of safety.

There goes my target of raising £500.

She put him out of her mind. Such men were sent to test her. She read the riot act to the team:

No flying without a helmet.

No flying within fifty metres of overhead power lines, communication cables, satellite tv aerials, transmitters, office rooftops, or cable cars.

No flying within 5 miles of civilian airports, over any political, military, medical, atomic, or scientific research establishment.

No snooping on neighbours at work, rest, or play.

No aerial horseplay, misleading gesticulations, or use of foul language.

All flyers to possess a current pilot's licence and membership card.

Before an airlift, flyers to declare all pre-existing medical conditions using the confidential online questionnaire and confirm that they had attended full bi-annual assessments of their general physical and mental health, eyesight, and hearing…

The cadets grew restless, shifting foot-to-foot under the weight of their cumbersome jetpacks. Raring to go.

'Shall we fly now, troops?' Mia teased.

'Can we just lift, girl?' Stella asked as Rick tightened her safety harness, unable to contain her excitement.

'Okay! Now, lift!' instructed Mia.

They selected lift and levitated, ascending into blue heaven. There was a crackling buzz in the cadets' helmets as their mikes kicked in.

'And stay right there! Now hover!'

Rick took the lead, pouring through the last-minute pre-flight checks: cautionary advice for less experienced cadets, while they hung, suspended in mid-air at a safe height of two metres.

Mia was the only flyer in the club who could afford the new AE-45 nuclear-powered jetpack. Rick was more interested in her tight-fitting, orange spandex jumpsuit, fly-in-your-face hair, her classic red satin lips. He watched intently as she donned her reflective ebon solar helmet fitted with its glare-proof sun visor.

He was her underling, the decoy, the aeronautical stool pigeon in the event they encountered operational difficulties. In other words, Mia delegated, in all but name, responsibility for the less experienced cadets to him. Under their joint leadership, WISC had never experienced an aerial fatality.

The learner flyers, who all rented their jetpacks, were Stella, Nina, Clyde, Rufus, and Nigel.

The flaming hot fireball hung high in the cloudless azure sky. Perfect weather for summer jet-packing, lazing around afterwards by the water's edge, liquid picnic lunch. The team flew in a tight v formation at an altitude of sixty metres. The triangular formation, flown responsibly, made it impossible for the four back-markers to overfly the three forward flyers.

Mia acted as forward scout to locate the idyllic lakeside setting for their picnic. Tired, thirsty, hot, irritable, without warning, she boosted. Boosted and climbed fifty metres. The immediate effect was to boost her fellow cadets into following her. Rick and Stella sat comfortably on her flanks. Nigel, Rufus, Clyde, and Nina held the back line. They jumped the narrow River Wid, hurtled over Swan Pond Plantation, skipped Causeway Cottages, and joined the route of the A414 trunk road to Ongar. All of them looked forward to letting their hair down. Creating a few mystifying crop-circles. Indulging in their picnic packs. Sunbathing. A discreet skinny dip: wild swimming in the lake, a power nap, before setting off for Mia's garden landing pad.

Thrilled, energised by her impromptu boost, Mia made out the field of golden barley by their sought-after acre or so of rippled water, sparkling in the distance. The cadets were now flying speeds of more than 90 mph, an exhilarating headwind gusting in their faces. They smiled at the gleaming windscreens of a head-to-tail traffic jam: impotent passengers clambering out of stalled vehicles, remonstrating with no-one, waving their arms in pointless piques, road rage. The jet-packers ignored them all, riding the skies: refreshed, revived.

Without a care in the world.

* * * * *

SCOTT WAITED IN THE CROWDED reception at The Elms Medical Centre, flicking through women's health magazines while Dr Liz Meredith examined his fiancée's breasts. When she emerged from her assessment, Evie's face was pale and drawn. She was shaking, frightened. The news scared him half to death. Evie told him she'd been referred to see a specialist, Mr Hill, at the general hospital. Said she'd like to go home. Spend the day talking with him. Just *being* with him? Asked if he could *be* there for her, help her come to terms with the shock.

Scott promised to support her always. Forget his hobby. He felt guilty for all the wasted hours he'd spent tinkering with his grown-up toys when he should have been enjoying *her* pursuits, sharing *her* interests. Evie took his arm, and they left. It was pouring rain when they stepped out into the car park. The sun had shone when they left home. They hadn't thought to bring a brolly.

Miserable, they walked along the forest road, the bright green leaves on the trees washed out, blurred, faded, like their hopes for the future. Evie felt her phone vibrate in the back pocket of her damp skinny jeans, drew it out, checked the screen. She had a new text:

Evie, sorry I left you in the lurch on Saturday. Had to collect Lucy and Poppy from a birthday party. Just wanted you to know I miss you. I'll support you. But I can't leave Alice, not with the twins starting school in September. Wanted to know if you're free for tennis next week?

Nick xx

Evie uttered a foul curse under her breath, her cheeks burned with anger.

Scott stopped walking, 'Something the matter?'

'Would you believe it?' she lied, 'It was Alice, asking if I wanted to play tennis on Tuesday?'

'What did you say?'

'What do you think I said?'

Evie was diagnosed with breast cancer at the age of 35.

Hill gave her two options: an intensive course of radiotherapy. or radical mastectomy. Scott squeezed her hand, staring over Hill's head as the rain drizzled down the window. Wishing, he could turn back time. Change the tragic course of events. Make Evie better with his own magic potion. Be her warlock, her wizard of love. But there was nothing he could do, except comfort her. He stared at her flushed face knowing that her mind would be working furiously. Evie's mother died of breast cancer.

Hill sat in his swivelled chair, hands clasped as if in prayer, waiting patiently, giving Evie all the time in the world to make the decision that could save her life. A bluebottle buzzed the window, an irritating distraction at such a testing time. Hill brushed the flakes of dandruff off his pin-striped suit.

Evie squeezed her man's hand, raised her head, took a deep breath, and thanked the specialist for explaining the choices available to her. Then, she requested the surgical removal of both of her breasts. After such a traumatic experience, Evie fervently hoped that her battle with the cancer manifesting inside her would be over.

In her words:

'Cancer drained the life out of me, made me feel like death, chewed me up until I ached deep inside, ate right into me.'

In the end, God bless her, Evie made the ultimate sacrifice, enduring the final cuts, had those stinking daughters of bitches cut out of her ulcerated breasts. Scott marvelled at her defiance, the contemptuous disrespect she showed for her bloody tumours. After she had left hospital, she tore the thick lint dressings off her lacerated chest in front of Scott in the bedroom. He consoled her.

God, but she was brave! How he loved and admired her. How he wanted to eat her all up, his woman sundae, there and then. How she screamed in anger, pain, raging as she ripped off her bloodied swaddling.

There was no sign of her hideous tumours. Nor of those beautiful breasts he first fell in love with deep in the bluebell woods, in the happiest years of their lives. Her lumps were cut out, sure, leaving her with just torn-out, tear-jerking wounds, stitches sewn-up by the surgeon who took her breasts away. At least, she was neatly stitched. She screamed,

'I hate you, cancer! Hate you!'

Evie broke down, reaching out for him. He held her close, stroking the wet hair off her scared face, cuddling her, kissing her inflamed cheeks. Anything to quell her shaking fury, her heart-wrenching soul-pain. He felt her, for the first time since God knows when. Felt the unfamiliar sensation of her bone pressing like plate armour against his manly chest. Felt helpless for her. Completely lost for words. What does a loving man say to a still-young woman when she has just realised, she will never suckle her baby?

Evie called the cancer her she-demon; it helped her to cope. With the cure she so dramatically requested of Hill. With the fact that. one day, her infernal curse might return to smite her, to plague her into an early grave.

So, what *does* a loving man say?

Scott started with what he considered to be a positive suggestion, 'Keep fighting, darling'.

Too late for that, surely. That battle was over, wasn't it?

He tried to assure her: 'Don't worry, my angel, we'll beat this curse together.'

'Beat what curse, baby?' she quizzed, all tired out, 'She-demon not coming back, is it?'

'No, course it's not. Never. Not ever.'

'You look well now,' he said, trying to flatter her.

'You really think so?' she sniped, 'Without my tits?'

He ran out of patience. Couldn't she see how hard he was trying, for her sake, to understand? He tried to answer. Evie interrupted, sparing him the angst, soothing his pent-up frustration:

'Please don't, darling. Just say you understand me and you'll always love me.'

'I understand. I'll always love you, Evie,' he repeated, sighing with relief.

'Well then, there's nothing left to worry about is there?'

She false smiled, kissed his cheeks, then turned to face the mirror, inspect her scars, lick her wounds. Evie vented out her full fury, swallowing hard, screaming herself hoarse, a woman possessed:

'You lost this time cancer! I won! Now fuck off out of my life and don't come back!'

Scott was shocked. He'd never heard his wife swear before. At least, he understood her now.

* * * * *

EVIE NEVER PLAYED TENNIS AGAIN. After a year in the clear, Hill confirmed the devastating news: the cancer had returned. Recurrent stage IV cancer now manifested itself in her scar tissue where growths were hardest to treat. A sentinel lymph node biopsy revealed, her cancer had spread quickly: in the form of painless swellings under Evie's armpits, inside her lymph nodes, leaving her with swollen dead woman's arms. Everything had been going well, all things considered, when the dreaded blight returned. Out of nowhere. Attacking her with a vengeance. Spreading its bloody mayhem up her spine, inside her lungs, her liver, threatening to invade her brain.

Hill explained to Evie that her condition could get worse. She should, therefore, embark on a course of treatment. Expediently. He and Martinson, the radiation oncologist, recommended chemotherapy.

Why didn't she go along with chemo? Was her hair *that* important to Evie?

Perhaps, Scott reasoned, *it was because she regarded her flame red hair as sacrosanct, her last stand so to speak, against cancer. Her final normality statement before she faded.*

Hill and Martinson suggested that she consider alternatives: herbal, holistic, stem cell, laser-invasive, invasive CRISPR-CAS9 cell, DNA mutation therapies. They advised her to attend clinical trials for radical new drugs: untested, controversial, Posi-interferons, equally lethal cell-busters.

Scott argued tearfully with her as they tried to come to terms with the enormous challenges facing them as a couple,

'Please, give it a try. What have you got to lose?'

Inexplicably, she refused further treatment. Other than sedatives, painkillers to help her cope with the excruciating pain. The somatic pain, a constant, dull ache which got worse whenever she moved. The visceral, deep-aching pain that cramped and twisted and tore at her insides. A pain so severe, unbearable, compounding her abject misery. Evie felt nauseous, she suffered bouts of diarrhoea, constipation, lost her appetite, lost weight, exhausted herself. Most of the time she spent bed-ridden or hobbling aimlessly around her bedroom.

She seemed hell-bent on dying with a heavy heart. Hill suggested she made plans. When Evie asked the toughest question, he regarded her compassionately, and replied:

'I'm deeply sorry. Without further treatment, I don't expect you to live another six months.'

She fell into a deep malaise, an inescapable pit of helplessness, withdrawing into a mystery-spiral of her innermost fears, entering the lair of the black dog through a shadowy doorway of despair. A door that led her to eternal damnation, impenetrable catatonic silence, struck dumb by her shocking prognosis.

They went to see a psychiatrist, Mr Mushtaq, who prescribed the most advanced medication available: hypnosis, electroconvulsive therapy, lithium, risperidone,

'Come in, please sit down, Evie. I see you brought your husband,' Mushtaq ventured politely.

A bony, angular soul of spritely disposition, Mushtaq smelled of Old Spice, Beef Madras. He reminded Evie of the Fay Maschler-recommended Indian restaurant in Brick Lane she used to frequent before she met Scott. The wiry waiters there told the most unbelievable children's jokes as they served her Chicken Balti with an ice-cold Cobra, she recalled.

'Evie?'

'Sorry, Mr Mushtaq, explained Scott, 'Evie has been a mute since she was re-diagnosed. And we're not married. I'm her fiancé.'

Mushtaq nodded graciously, taking notes on his tablet as they spoke, especially during the pregnant pauses in the conversation, not once taking his eyes off Evie. Scott saw him print off a prescription.

Bit early for that surely?

Evie stared blankly at Mushtaq, wincing with pain.

'Not well, are you Evie?' Scott said, flexing his sweaty fists. Psychiatrists made him nervous.

'Are *you* feeling alright?' Mushtaq asked him, 'You look tired. Perhaps a sedative might...'

'I'm fine, thank you.'

'That's good,' Mushtaq nodded furiously, sucking the leaky tip of his NHS biro, 'Go on.'

'Evie gets depressed these days, don't you? Can't sleep at night. Doesn't want sympathy, just understanding. Gets distressed. She's frightened of dying, naturally. Worries a lot about what will happen when she's gone? But she's not suicidal, are you Evie? I think we both thought, when Mr Hill operated on her, that would be the end of her ordeal. We were so wrong.'

Evie nodded, shook her head, nodded again, and burst into floods of tears. Mushtaq proffered his red polka dot silk handkerchief - which she gratefully accepted.

'Now, you must take these tablets, Evie,' he insisted, 'One in the morning, one at night. Please, to keep you on an even keel and help you sleep, you understand? You do understand, don't you?' Mr Mushtaq decreed over his hornrims, trying not to sound overly patronizing.

She nodded in the way velvety grey nodding dogs nod in car rear windows. He looked across the table.

'Scott?'

'I'll make sure she does. Thank you, Mr Mushtaq.'

Mushtaq glimpsed at his watch. Eleven o'clock, soon be home time. His spirits sagged as they stood to go. The woman looked soulless, emotionally deconstructed, ready for her death, her eyes: black holes of despair. He felt her loss bore into his heart. There was nothing more he could do. He blinked then turned his attention to the man: haggard, exhausted, struggling...

'No, thank *you*, Scott,' he said kindly, 'Please arrange an appointment for one months' time with my receptionist and take good care of Evie until next time. Mind how you go.'

Goodbye.

Electro-convulsive therapy and risperidone made no difference to Evie's state of mind. She needed professional palliative care, accepting she might have to go into a hospice. Scott saw the local hospice as a wonderful place. But, marvellous as the care nurses were, it was her last resort. Dare he say it? Evie's final resting place.

Throughout her fight with cancer, Evie maintained, Scott was amazing. Every day he cooked her meals, did the shopping, cleaned the house, washed up, laundered, ironed, took her to the clinic, pool, and gym complex where she adopted a punishing exercise regime. Until she was too ill to continue.

He wondered how she felt, having her independence taken away from her. He controlled her bowel motions, stool motions, mealtime, bath-time, bedtime. She tried hard to push herself, to cope without his help, but failed miserably. Because he never gave her an inch of space to succeed. At least, that's how Mia summarised the situation when they met on the back lawn.

'I don't know how you manage,' she moaned, 'I'm not letting you carry on like this a minute longer. You'll give yourself a nervous breakdown. Just look at the state of her. Can't you see she needs round-the-clock professional care? Evie should be in a hospice for goodness' sake.'

'She wants to spend her final days at home with me,' Scott shouted, 'Don't you care at all about how she feels?'

'I'm acting out of the kindness of my heart. Everything I do for her is in her best interest.'

'Is it now? Is it necessary to confine Evie to her bed, to ban her from leaving her room? What are you trying to do, Mia? Kill her off? You seem to forget she's your sister. Show her some damn respect, won't you?'

'You know what? I don't care anymore! I've had enough. I'm leaving!'

He told her to lower her voice, nodding imperceptibly towards the house, acutely aware that Evie was watching them from behind her shuttered bedroom window.

'Please, trust me, Mia,' he pandered, 'I'll work things out. She'll be fine.'

Truth be told, Scott found it impossible to cope, ground down by Evie's illness. His life had become increasingly intolerable as she turned: disturbed, unpredictable. She was driving him mad. He could no longer manage, realising, deep inside: he too was in desperate need of help.

His predicament came as no surprise to Mia. Was it any wonder when she considered all they'd been through? She stood in the garden, staring him out, hands on hips, business-like, tossing back her chestnut hair, trembling with frustration. Mia had heard it all before.

'Please, let me help, Scott,' she whispered, 'You know I love you.'

He sighed, 'Of course, I know!'

He glanced up at Evie, waved at her, blew a kiss at her inert mask. The face turned away.

'Well then, that's settled,' Mia was saying, 'I'll hire a Carer. Then, I'll find her a hospice, somewhere where she can see out her final days in peace.'

* * * * *

'EVER THOUGHT ABOUT FLYING FOR charity?' Mia asked one day, 'Think you should, don't you?'

Scott groaned, 'Charity? Which charity?'

'Any human, humane charity,' she stressed. Mia spent most of her time stressing these days, 'You know, hearts and minds, bodies and souls? That sort of thing. Look, Scott, if you must know I was thinking of poor Evie. How is she these days?'

Poor Evie? Scott fumed: *You don't give a damn about her, do you? Only care about yourself. Me too when it suits you.*

'Evie's bearing up well considering all she's been through,' he assured her, 'Some days are better than others. She's a fighter and I'm with her every step of the way. We're not going to let this beat us, Mia.'

'You love her to bits, don't you,' she stated, 'You worship the ground she walks on.'

He stared at his feet not wanting her to see his tormented face. He loved both women equally.

'Then why don't you <u>do</u> something that'll make her proud of you?' she continued, 'Give something back for once.'

Scott read her like a book. Mia, the schemer, deliverer of promises, the woman who made things happen. Truth be told, he admired her ballsy strength, and more. Mia Faith was the youngest Managing Partner in the history of Blossom, Prosper & Wynn - the prestigious City law firm.

'Sounds like you have something in mind,' he conceded.

She grinned, 'Haven't I always? Sunday 15th November. I'm flying Canary Wharf Circle in aid of Cancer Research. I want you up there, flying next to me, if you please.'

'November's months away. I'll check the diary.'

'I already did. I hacked your Outlook. You're free all day.'

'You hacked my Outlook! How dare you.'

'That's settled then, Scott,' she smirked.

* * * * *

EVIE AND SCOTT WERE MARRIED at Our Lady of Equality Cathedral, Chelmer Valley New City, on a sun-drenched, sweltering, September Saturday afternoon. Nigel, Scott's best man, took his side, dressed in top hat and tails, holding onto the two simple gold bands for dear life. Nina, adorably attired in an off-the-shoulder full length strapless silk pink number and an auburn wig, was the magnificent Maid of Honour, and Stella, the beautiful, bald, Bridesmaid.

Evie looked absolutely stunning in an arresting fairy-tale princess pink silk gown with a sweetheart neck, lace bodice, and layered train. The female vicar assembled choir-children, congregation, even the collection box persons, dabbed tears from their eyes as she walked, arm-in-arm, down the aisle with her proud father, Reginald, to the inevitable strains of Here Comes the Bride. Scott swooned at the sight of his bride and had to be revived with holy water from the chalice. Nigel carefully handed the vicar the wedding rings.

The exchange of vows was, in biblical parlance, a latter-day revelation, Stella and Nina made the vow together, on behalf of Evie:

'On this day, I give you my mind, heart, body and soul. I promise I will fly with you, hand in hand, wherever our journey leads us, together, living, dying, loving, forever and ever.'

Stella had organised a fabulous wedding breakfast for afterwards in the huge lemon-yellow striped garden marquee at the back of Rick's country manse in nearby Purling. The Bride and Groom, keen ballroom dancers, attempted to dance an Argentinian Tango. All too soon the wedding came to an end. The crowd gathered outside at dawn on the dewy lawn, chewing Parma ham and Emmental croissants, swigging bubbly from greasy magnum-necks. Then the beaming couple drove off in the direction of Aldeburgh, dressed as phantom jet-packers, to rapturous applause from their startled guests.

On the happiest day of their lives.

* * * * *

HE CLUTCHED HER TO HIS chest, her bony breastplate pressing on him, her lump swelling in his throat. Evie felt lumps, painful ulcers in her breasts, once. Her loving husband ran his hairy hand over her scalp to stay the cold wind. She looked up into those clear blue-sky eyes, glittering tears trickling down her cheeks, cascading diamonds of pride. Evie kissed him: a long, lazy, lingering kiss farewell. Scott was all she had. She didn't want to let him go. He soothed her, hugged her. Told her he wouldn't be long. Told her he'd soon be back in her loving arms.

He had to fly…

Scott rolled over and pulled the dog rose-decorated duvet behind him to keep himself warm. Savouring her decadent aroma as his face brushed her feather pillow. Eager to curl his manly body round her diminutive form. Dying to wrap her in an intimate bundle of passion: his soft, downy, human ball of fire. Any minute now she'd smile back at him, snug, cosy, in his burly arms, and slide her tender fingers up and down his tingling spine.

God, he loved Evie. And she loved him. She was his universe, his soulmate, in a sensuous solar system blended into one huge cosmos of never-ending love. He would be lost in a void, an eternal vacuum of cold empty space, without her. Space was too dark, too vast, for him to bear alone.

The strawberry lampshade centurions, mounted on shiny plinths of onyx, guardians to the galactic gateway to their private universe, shone in the night. Evie wasn't there. Just a lick of mouth-damp here, a lurid slash of lipstick there, and her moult: gossamer strands of flame red scattered on the pillow, her faint body imprint hidden in the hairline creases of their crumpled sheet.

What have you done today to make you feel proud?

The song played on his mind like sweet angel dust. He was so proud of her today. To think, he still had what it took: the right stuff.

'To boldly go where no jet-packer has ever gone before,' he dreamed, 'To fulfil my mission in inner space!'

Well, something like that. He lay awake, his head crammed with hopes, propped up on one vein-numb arm in Evie's boudoir, legs spread over their gigantic candyfloss-pink bed. Full of beans. Unable to contain the tremors of excitement that coursed through his mind.

It was early, still dark. Remnants of frost clung to the rust-dry crisps of dead leaves in the overgrown back garden, the sugar-frosted circular landing pad. Today, Scott would fly high over Canary Wharf in the OM-24 organic mega flow jetpack he'd assembled in his cluttered garage. Hidden under his figure-hugging jumpsuit, covering his undoubted heart of gold, lay a black tee-shirt with distinctive orange and white lettering:

WE WILL BEAT CANCER

He hoped to raise £400 towards Cancer Research, a gesture of his undying commitment to eradicating the blood red curse that blighted his woman's world.

Now, this 45-year-old kid was bulging at the midriff, bursting at the seams, greying at the temples. His face: set hard like tomb-granite. His nose: big, and boxer-flat, in deference to his advancing years. However, his hands and arms were strong: all the better to hug Evie with. The eyesight and hearing were good. He didn't need spectacles, hearing aids. But Scott's fat right leg was a veritable knot of bulbous blue varicose veins that forced the space warrior to wear thick-soled regulation army boots in case his ankles swelled, like hot air balloons, on landing.

He raised an appreciative cheer from the small crowd of spectators: dealers in futures, cyber-merchant bankers dressed down for Friday. Caught a few admiring glances from the girls in clootie-bobble hats, candy-stripe scarves, knee-length stiletto boots, as they sipped Pinot Grigio. Standing, clustered outside the trendy bar, glass in hand. Braving the biting autumn wind that blew chilly gusts off the open water. Cheering, waving wildly, but mainly laughing at him, as he turned and walked out wharf-side to South Dock:

'Go on, Old Man, show us how it's done!'

'Lost Robin, Batman?'

Scott prepared himself for take-off. They meant well. At least, he thought they did. Mocking him like that. Gloating. Mia felt embarrassed by their unfeeling barbs, heart-broken for him.

Why don't they understand? she asked herself. *He's a good man, a kind man. Show him some heart.*

But they offered him no respect, only juvenile contempt. Why? Because nobody likes a loser. Because every minute of their trumped-up, high-tech life was about outperforming the odds. They had no place in their hearts for charity.

'I'll show you,' Scott muttered miserably under his breath.

'Careful you don't do yourself a mischief in those tight trousers!' screamed one of the girls, a spotty brunette one, burping cheap plonk with her giggly cabal.

Scott smiled warmly, then raised his stiff middle finger. Bored, the group scuffled off, turning their backs on the human blackbird, meandering into the warmth of the bar.

'Ladies, Gentlemen, I am the Black Angel!' he cried, crazily, in a rasping, breathless voice - like Darth Vader.

Laughing hysterically, he climbed the steps to the platform, to a polite smattering of applause from an elderly couple out walking their toy poodle. He looked back, one last time, at Evie, smiling fondly at him, and waved. She coughed and turned to go.

Mia Faith hurtled past nodding her encouragement, 'Go on!'

Scott pulled the toggle. His chest screen flashed: jetpack engine ON! He took a deep breath. Held the jump key. And leaped! At first, he ascended slowly in hover mode, like an angel. He selected boost mode to increase horizontal flight speed. Then he was flying! Free! Awesome! Invincible! Black Angel! The titanium halo, floating, over his head, the twin-hydro jetpack, clinging to his back, his only lifelines. He soared through the sky at sixty miles an hour, like James Bond in Thunderball when he escaped from Colonel Jacques Bouvard's chateau. His enthusiasm: impossible to subdue. Scott gazed down proudly at the mere mortals scurrying around Canary Wharf, worker ants, hundreds of feet below, startling them as he buzzed past.

'I am master of all I survey,' he boasted grandly.

He shouldn't be doing this. He was fat, middle-aged, slowed down, out of shape. His GP said he had high blood pressure.

He said: 'I'm doing this for Evie. In Her Everlasting Memory.'

Had he gone raving mad? A jetpack only lasts for thirty minutes. He turned off hover mode, immediately losing altitude, falling like a stone.

Mia swooped by, 'Pull up! Pull up!

Evie looked up, spotting her birdman coming into view, zooming over Royal Victoria Docks, hurtling towards her. She could read his face now. His craggy, rugged looks. That frown of determination. His head, tiny in the reinforced ebon helmet. Vulnerable. Kind though. Warm. Loving. Generous.

His eyes twinkled with tears.

His ruddy cheeks squashed.

His nose bled.

He was coming her way.

'God, but I love you, Evie,' he screamed.

I love you too, babe...

'No! No! No! No!'

* * * * *

HE LAY STILL, UNDER INTENSIVE care, fully sedated, intubated, ventilated: a mess of tubes, wires, immovable, plaster casts. He looked dead, but his brain was active, dreaming, hallucinating. His mind, a sea of fragmented faces, haunting screams, flashing blue lights, crews in green, holding his head still, reassuring voices, then the descent into darkness.

Ruth, the ICU Doctor, looked down at him compassionately, checking the screen: undulating with peaks and troughs, flashing lights, for his vital signs of life. The signs were encouraging. Her patient was critically ill but off the danger list, making painfully slow, but sure, progress. He stirred, tried to move his head, couldn't.

Ruth gently placed a hand on her patient's neck, felt the needle, and very slowly inched it out. His eyes were closed. He felt no pain. She looked at the young Indian nurse, Hema, hair tied in a black ponytail, her brown hands: soft, caring. Hema peeled the sticky tape off his eyelids, brushed the hair off his face, felt the tension in his stubbly cheeks, mopped his brow. He was still dreaming.

The doctor gripped the thick corrugated feed protruding from his mouth and pulled it out of his throat. He awoke with a start and coughed. His breathing stilted, frightened. Hema stroked his brow, calming him. He looked frail, stretched out on the bed, arms and legs pointing at the sky like a dead fly on its back: unable to move or feel, paralysed from the neck down, his spine splintered, limbs stiff, swollen, shattered. Scott suffered severe head injuries. He could hardly speak.

'Where am I?' he croaked, his throat parched dry.

Ruth smiled, 'Hema, I think our patient would like a sip of water.'

The nurse raised a tube to his lips. He sucked on the tube, a baby sucking on a teat, felt a little better. His heavy head sank. His stubbled chin rested on his chest.

'This is the East London Hospital ICU,' Ruth explained, 'You have come out of an induced coma after four months. I'm afraid you suffered severe head injuries, bruising of the brain, multiple fractures of your neck, spinal column, pelvis, arms, legs. You're incredibly lucky to be alive. Your chances of survival were less than 50:50 when you were admitted.'

What did he think he was doing anyway, careering around Canary Wharf, Friday lunchtime, anytime for that matter? His careless, senseless, actions injured a disabled little boy, his mum, an Australian tourist, all of them disfigured for life when he collided with the cable car, and the window imploded, embedding shards of glass in their terrified faces.

Ruth remembered the detectives, waiting outside. Chris, pouring their third cup of syrupy tea, doling out chocolate bourbons, pink wafers. They'd have to wait a little longer to interview him.

Scott had a visitor.

She wondered how she'd break the news to him, her consoling words. He'd been through so much torment since their collision, their fleeting kiss. His zephyr on her frozen cheeks. Their final, endearing, enduring embrace.

The doctor appeared and asked if she would like to come through.

She sat by the bed, next to the man she loved with all her heart as he lay asleep, dreaming of her. Then, incredibly, she spoke:

'On this day, I give you my mind, heart, body and soul. I promise I will fly with you, hand in hand, wherever our journey leads us, together, living, dying, and loving, forever and ever.'

EVIE BEAT CANCER

Say Hello to Pearl

2019:

MIDNIGHT. THE RUTTING SEASON. WINTER came early to the pine forest of Tannochbrae. Snow fluttered down in heavy flakes, white poppy petals on an alien Remembrance Day. Cascading in swirls borne on the chill wind before settling on a blank canvas that stretched between her window and an electrified perimeter fence. Blanketing the flat rooftop of the institution in a shroud of secrecy.

Every so often, Toy would hear a loud crack as a bough bowed, bent, then snapped under the weight of it. Clumps of snow tumbling down, forming mounds, filled with the souls of those who lay so deep. There were eight mounds inside the fence, mounted with inconspicuous little red crosses like Christmas decorations. Testimonials to their earlier efforts. Failed experiments.

She thought of her parent's grey-stone cottage on the outskirts of Oban, the privet hedge, the clapped-out Cortina immobilized by snow. Janice and Peter waiting, snug in woolly waistcoats and tartan carpet slippers, sipping single malts in front of a roaring fireplace, wondering if they would ever see their missing daughter again.

Missing. That was the official explanation. Toy had gone missing from her studies at Edinburgh University. Her bedsit: left pristine, bed-made, laptop still on. Vanished without a trace. Except, her real name wasn't Toy. Her name by birth was Lauren Jane Smart, aged eighteen. An Oban girl, last seen boarding a Glasgow-bound Highland train. Never to be seen again. She cast her mind back to when she was a little girl, a lonely girl, an only child. God, how her Mammy and Daddy would be missing her.

What had possessed her to be Pearl's plaything? Money to pay for her crack addiction. The money *was* good: live-in, shared bed, free food, full board and lodgings, all expenses paid. Or was it the intrigue, the fascination of Pearl, the need for Lauren to be her dolly, their intimacy?

She recalled her childhood. Playing in the snow. Hard ice on a pavement. Ruts in the roadway. Skidding down the road with Mammy. Building a snowman. The other children, laughing at her, playing hide and seek behind closed brick walls. Jack Frost at her bedroom window. Cat's paws! Dripping icicles hanging off leaky gutters. Shards snapping off, falling. The back garden: yellow leaves sticking out of an imperfect blanket. Mam, sprinkling rock salt on the path. Snow, heaped against their garage, coating the wheelie bins. Tiny footprints: a robin redbreast. The elderly, struggling. The young, daring to break free.

And, in her solitary childhood, not a living soul to play with. Perhaps that was why she was here, as a toy, in a snow year. The full moon shone on her face: her figure, her body, silhouetted in dark relief against the vermillion sky, twinkling starlight, distant planets, far-off suns. Pearl,

'Come into the warm. Shake off your coat. Take off those gloves. Dust yourself down. Come and sit beside my fire. You must be freezing. Hot chocolate, warm minced pies, rich fruit cake!'

'Shtop teashing me,' Toy whistled with the lisp she'd endured: taunted and jeered at since birth, 'There ishn't a fire. Or a coat. Jusht me in thith thilly thlip.'

'Come to bed with me, Toy. I'm a big girl now!'

'I know that, do you think I don't know that?'

'Well then, come to bed.'

Toy was wearing a regulation institutional white slip. She pulled it off over her head and held it aloft like a white flag of surrender. Looked around in the half-light, at Pearl, lurking, half-under the sheet on her giant-sized bed. At the unblinking security cameras. At least Beattie, the Security Guard, had had the decency to switch them off at eleven. When they were intimate. Sensually intimate. In the way that only eighteen-year-old girls can be.

Beattie would be at his control desk, scanning the white-walled corridors for signs of suspicious activity. Not that there ever *was* suspicious activity. Tannochbrae was impregnable. Access and egress were controlled, limited to specific individuals by iris optical recognition. Beattie would be sprawled, half-asleep more like, over his unfinished ten-minute crossword in this week's edition of The Tulloch Herald.

Toy appraised the dark void behind the toughened glass window. There were no ghouls or deer, stags, or bucks, watching her. She went to take off her pale grey thong.

Pearl protested, 'Leave it on! I want to love you with it on.'

In the end, she left her thong on. After all, the weft accentuated her smooth buttocks. She went to lie in the bed with her mistress.

Pearl felt for the fluffy pillow, placing it in the centre of the bed, creating a soft plinth for her toy's head. She pushed back the duvet with her feet, admitting her lover to the centre, the heart of her bed. It was important that her plaything was relaxed before they were intimate. The toy had an unfortunate habit of squealing like a piglet when she came excited, a risk Pearl could not afford to take…

For fear of activating the noise sensors positioned around the bedroom door, attracting Beattie's unwanted attention. For fear of stirring McNiel and McCain in their adjacent bedrooms. For fear of reprisals. Punishment. She recalled the last time her toy squealed. Pearl's unpleasant leather restraints, buckles. Sleeping in a stiff straitjacket for twelve days. The constant threat of sedation. Solitary confinement in her room.

Worse still, McVie, the bitch, had taken away her toy, until she learned how to behave. Life without a toy was unimaginably hard, nothing to play with, no fantasies, no escapism, no-one left to love. Pearl had asked to be put down. No chance of that! She was unique, a valuable entity in her own right, a test tube creation by the eminent sperm donor Jack McGilvrae, her professorial namesake, and Dr Christine McVie, her surrogate mother: the conniving cow who birthed her, then treated her worse than a stray puppy.

Pearl set about relaxing her toy. Straddling her soft tummy. Gently stroking her locks of ruddy hair, her rosy freckled cheeks, with the back of her hand. Massaging her gilded neck, her narrow shoulders. Lifting off her own white shift so that her toy could play with her small breasts while she rubbed herself on her belly.

'Now what would you like to play, girl?' she whispered seductively, unusually for her.

In all fairness, she *was* about to grant the toy her dying wish. Pearl felt the strangest sensation, all tingly in her wingly.

Toy smiled at her, nervously. Felt like squealing. Felt like kissing. Felt most peculiar if she was truthful. And she was a truthful Oban girl.

Why had Pearl asked her what she wanted to play? She was toy here, not her. Girl? Why girl? And why now?

She lisped, more than she'd ever lisped, 'Kithes.'

'Kisses?'

'Mm, pleath say yeth?'

Pearl seemed mildly amused, 'Kisses! Do you love me, Lauren?'

Lauren! Pearl named her toy Lauren! She'd never named her toy before! Named her Lauren!

'Yeth,' Lauren lisped, 'I love you very much. You mean everything to me, Pearl.'

'Where would you like me to kiss you?'

'On the lipth.'

'What do you say?'

- *to your owner, your child-thing, your alien puppeteer,* Pearl reflected sadly.

'Pleath, kith me on my lipth.'

Pearl kissed Lauren Smart upon her wet pink lips, kissing her deeply, looking down at her. She, in turn, gazed up at her waxy complexion, the squashed-cherry lips, her dark, hollowed, eyes.

'What isth it Pearl? What ith it? No, pleath!'

Toy tried to squeal. Almost did. But for a fluffy pillow muffling her squealing mouth she might have. Pearl pressed the pillow hard into her girl's face. Felt her toy's blunt knees kicking her, bruising her firm buttocks. Felt her toy ripping, slashing, her pale cheeks, tearing out clumps of her rich chestnut hair, by the roots. Felt her love relax. Lauren was a fighter, a tough Scottish lass. Suffocation took a few minutes. She lost consciousness in seconds. She stopped breathing. Her body went limp. Pearl made her look decent: closing her legs, shutting her mouth, covering her toy's sad spent body with their doubled-up sheet.

* * * * *

THE CHEESE-WIRE WAS LOCATED IN the kitchen cupboard, down the corridor, past Beattie's control desk. Snow fell, a petal for the fallen dead-butterfly called Toy. Pearl showed her teak iris to a door. The frosted glass slid open. She padded barefoot, towards the kitchen.

Beattie looked up from the randy girlie magazine he kept well-hidden inside the pages of his free copy of the Herald and studied the beautiful young woman through the eye of the lens. If she was a woman. He couldn't be sure. McNiel once confided to him that Pearl was the natural outcome of McGilvrae inseminating the fat bitch McVie, with modifications. Post-conception, McGilvrae had surgically removed the foetus from McVie's womb and undertaken genetic reconfiguration and transplanted it back in again. The hybrid, Pearl, was birthed and breastfed by McVie, then placed in captivity for laboratory testing alongside cats, rats, dogs, birds, and human animals. Out of all the intellectual mammals, only Pearl survived the grossly invasive test regime.

Overall, scientific testing on live animals had fallen to its lowest level in the UK since 2007, with the exception of beagles (+16%). Until an urgent new imperative by NASA: preparation for human inhabitation of the Moon and Mars, demanded the introduction of designer foetuses, embryos, babies specifically grown for cloning and remodelling.

The research team at Tannochbrae under McGilvrae and McVie used Pearl's body to test for respirational difficulties in rarefied atmospheres, response to repeated doses of drugs, toxins, deadly viral strains, reaction of her musculoskeletal system to different atmospheric pressures. In more than two thousand tests, her body was used to determine whether continual intravenous injection of moon virus resulted in a higher resistance to infection.

Cats, rats, and dogs were used in 93% of invasive tests enacted since her sixteenth birthday, but there were still six-hundred-and-thirty-four additional experiments involving Pearl in this, her eighteenth year. Compared to five-hundred-and forty-one in her seventeenth year.

As recently as July 2019, the Director of Policy, Ethics & Governance at Genetic Research had insisted that the use of animals in medical testing remained essential for them to develop new and better treatments to understand the biology of diseases. If researchers applied for funding for studies involving animals, they were required to give clear reasons for using them and to explain why there were no realistic alternatives.

The head of the research animal department at RSPCA disagreed, inferring that, behind these numbers, were the lives of millions of individual animals. Each was sentient. Each was capable of experiencing pain, suffering and distress.

Responsibility for regulating animal experiments fell upon the Home Office. Since mammal-testing at Tannochbrae breached the terms of The International Medical Convention, only the Home Secretary and Prime Minister knew of the existence of Pearl McGilvrae. The scientists, cleaners and security men working on the project all signed highly confidential non-disclosure agreements with heavy financial penalties and a threat of solitary confinement for anyone found guilty of leaking information.

In 2014, the Home Office classified testing according to the level of suffering caused. A spokesman confirmed:

'Our legislation provides a rigorous regulatory system that ensures animal research and testing are carried out only where no practicable alternative exists, and under controls which keep suffering to an absolute minimum.'

Of the procedures carried out at Tannochbrae last year, 38.9% were rated mild, 14.7% moderate and 3.6% severe. Specifically, the majority of tests on Pearl were classified as severe.

Beattie, fifty-eight-year-old faithful husband to Annette, father to five girls, thrice grandfather, and Night Security Guard, watched attentively as she padded silently along the corridor from one security camera to the next. A uniformed guard of no great importance who obsessed over his own grandeur: he was used to seeing the tall, slim creature with pallid skin, straggly hair and a toffee-nose, prance about Tannochbrae naked, or with her modesty barely covered by her regulation institutional slip. But since she had grown breasts and hairs in her groin and armpits, he'd found her achingly beautiful to watch. He creased back the pages of his glossy rag, trying hard to concentrate on matters of internal security.

There were seven scientists based at Tannochbrae. McGilvrae and McVie shared a bedroom at the far end of the corridor, next to the laboratory, a rarely used entertaining suite, and kitchen. Beattie eyed the time on the blank camera screen. They'd be busy, rutting like the Monarch of the Glen and his doe deep in the forest. Dawn McNiel, behavioural psychiatrist, would still be writing up her latest report on the effects of toys on Pearl. Alastair McCain, the brilliant young biochemist responsible for concocting the potentially deadly toxins, fungi, viruses, and germs which he inoculated into his subject, would be sound asleep. A tormentor without a conscience. The three ghouls, the observational team: McLeish, McTaggart, and McPartland, all lived-out, in Oban.

Hot chocolate, warm minced pies and rich fruit cake were traditionally served to all those who were still awake after midnight in the run-up to Christmas. By Pearl. Beattie looked forward to receiving her generous offerings, exhausted by his long shift.

McVie, the cunning bitch, and power behind the throne, had condemned him to a variable hours' contract closely aligned to the hours of darkness. This meant that, in November, he had to live at Tannochbrae from 3pm until 8am the following morning. Add to that his one-hour trek by moped to and from Oban, breakfast, lunch, three hours sleep if he was lucky. He rarely saw his lovely daughters: Maira, Maisie, Maidie, Maribel, and Moira, who all attended local schools, during the dark months. Beattie had slept in a separate room from Annette since she lost interest in sex and started her stertorous snoring.

He searched for Pearl. She had disappeared from view. Into the kitchen.

No problem.

In ten minutes-time, his fine young beauty would appear before him, her slender arms laden with his tray of winter treats. He glanced up at the sprig of mistletoe that he hung earlier from the ceiling, far too early for Christmas, and strictly against the rules:

No Fraternization with the Animals.

Perhaps she'd oblige him with a seasonal kiss, a festive hug. A treat for a sad, lonely, old man?

The power failed. All the lights went out in the control room. The cameras blinked and switched off. He smiled as she ran her soft, slim fingers through his spiky, ginger hair, down his stubbled cheek, over his fat lips, round his flabby neck. His final thoughts, before the cheese wire cut his throat, were of holding hands with Annette. Kissing his beloved. Gazing out over the bay of Oban. Watching ferries cross to Mull. From the lofty heights of McCaig's Tower.

Immune to the cold, Pearl McGilvrae strutted out into the waiting world. Snow fluttered down in heavy flakes, white rose petals, cascading in swirls, settling on a blank canvas that stretched between her, an open gate, and the deactivated perimeter fence...

Say Hello to Pearl.

The Marital

THE RHYME 'SOMETHING OLD, SOMETHING new, something borrowed, something blue' refers to the things a bride is supposed to wear on her wedding day to have a successful marriage. And like most superstitions, it doesn't entirely make sense.

Monday 15th June 2020: The Bungalow, Lindsay Street:

I DRESS HIM FIRST IN his charcoal grey suit, white shirt, and tie, then let him watch me dress in my salmon wedding frock, making a grand show of rolling the blue garter up my thigh. I consider myself to be in fairly good shape for my age. Granted, my breasts have sagged. I developed jelly belly when my menopause set in. Oh, and I have thread veins, 'little spiders' webs' I call them, on my thighs. Otherwise, I think I keep myself very fit and healthy. He shows me no excitement, no physical or mental reaction, when I dress like this for him. He hasn't satisfied me sexually or emotionally for five years, since he suffered the severe stroke that left him partially paralysed from the face down. Now his body is being wasted by terminal prostate cancer there isn't much of him left for me to love.

Recreating our classic wedding (well, my blessing really, I have been married thrice) pose at The Marital was my idea. Prompted by a WhatsApp from Will, my son and insurance broker, confirming that my husband's life insurance policy had been successfully revalued by fifteen thousand pounds without an increase in payment premium.

Our excursion to The Marital will be the first time that Brian, being classed as vulnerable, has left our house for twelve weeks since Boris Johnson imposed the lockdown on March 23rd. Not that he has the faintest idea of what is going on around him. To be truthful, the lockdown could not have happened at a worse time. We had to cancel Brian's one-way flight to Dignitas.

I make him wait in the hall while I check the coast is clear. The keys to Will's off-cream Fiat Cinquecento are hidden under the doormat where he left them for me last night. I quickly stoop and scoop them up, then I survey the road. The street is empty. My neighbours are still asleep. A distinct advantage of us rising at dawn. I shiver slightly as a rush of cool air sends a chill up my arms and legs, making my soft downy hair rise on my bare arms, calves, and thighs, sending a swathe of goosebumps over my freckled chest. I freckle a lot when I sunbathe on our patio lounger with Bryce.

Granted, I have turkey neck and my laughter lines *have* started to stretch. Bryce doesn't seem to mind. He delivers my food packages to the back garden, through the side passageway, while Brian enjoys his afternoon siesta in cloud-cuckoo land in the bedroom at the front of the house. Isn't my young volunteer wonderful? I stand inside my porch and clap for him every Thursday.

I reach across Brian, who resembles a ventriloquist's dummy, and strap him firmly to the front passenger seat. Then I check my mirror, indicate, clutch down, select first, release handbrake, and we set off. The hot sun rises on a new day over the beautiful Essex countryside as we wend our way down the lane that leads to the wedding venue. My husband sits obediently at my side.

The Nuptial Gate, New Hall Lane:
GAIL, MY DAUGHTER FROM MY second marriage and wedding event organiser at The Marital, has left the gate unlocked so we can enter the grounds to the venue without interruptions from the security guard. I stare at the bank of CCTV cameras overseeing the entrance and pray that she bribed the guard to switch them off. The gate swings wide open as my son's car approaches. My thoughts turn to the new spade.

Did Gail manage to buy a spade without attracting the attention of the hardware store owner?

Dainty, demure Gail is the last woman you would expect to see queuing outside Home and House on a baking hot Sunday afternoon in search of a garden spade. My mobile rings. I drive through the gateway and pull up sharply on the gravel drive, making a rough crunching sound. Brian's head flops onto his chest. I smile to myself. My husband is asleep. He spends his life asleep these days. I swipe the phone and press it to my ear. The voice at the other end is shrill with excitement,

'Mum?'

'Gail?'

'Yes, who did you think it was, Gunga Din?'

Ignoring my daughter's trademark sarcasm, I say, 'The spade?'

'Is hidden behind the willow tree by the estate lake.'

I screw up my face in concentration, 'The estate lake?'

'Yes, by the beauty spot where you're recreating The Marital?'

I sigh with relief, 'I won't forget this, Gail.'

'Don't mention it. How's Dad?'

'He's fast asleep, Darling.'

'Can I say hello?'

'Of course, but he won't hear you.'

'Hello Dad. Love you, Mum.'

'Love you too, Petal.'

I cut her call, engage the gears, release the brake, and Will's car saunters slowly down the track, past a deserted golf course, in the direction of The Marital.

The Marital:

PRESENTLY, I COME TO A fork in the road. An immaculate white wayfarer's sign with gold lettering tells me to drive straight ahead for the wedding venue, conference centre and visitor's car park, or fork right for the scenic lakeside setting. As I turn right, I notice an unusual light glinting in the distance, the reflection of the sun on glass, or a mirror maybe? I put the optical illusion out of my mind and motor downhill, past the 15th hole, the 16th tee, and an overgrown grass tennis court, until I reach a bend in the road.

My heart skips a beat as I cruise round the bend and take in the view. I feel as if I have finally come home to where I consummated my marriage with my childhood sweetheart, thirty years ago. My eyes well with tears as I recall how we made love on the grassy bank beside the lake. I gave birth to my loving son, William, nine months later.

The Marital has changed since then. The estate lake is surrounded by trees: hazel, elm, beech, a solitary willow tree. The low stone wall where we posed for our wedding photos is still there, next to a short new tarmac path which runs down to a lover's platform at the water's edge. The scene is idyllic, the effect on me: highly romantic. I miss Bryce. I wish he were here with me, making sweet love to me in the long grass. I shake the notion out of my head and pull up on a hard standing a few feet away from the wall. My husband is still asleep, snorting like a warthog.

Carefully, I ease open the driver's door, swing my legs out of the car, stand up, and stretch my stiff limbs, inhaling, exhaling, relishing the fresh morning country air. The warm summer breeze kisses my cheeks. I listen to the sound of blackbirds, robins, titmice, twittering in the bushes. I swear, I hear a cuckoo,

Cuckoo! Cuckoo!

I smile happily to myself and follow the pathway down to the water's edge. The willow tree is overhanging the silent, rippling, gleaming water. I blink my bleary eyes as they adjust to the dappled sunlight reflecting off the lake which is crystal clear. I can see its muddy bottom, some clingy green algae, tiny fish fry spritzing near the surface. The shiny spade is lying in the couch grass that has sprouted up around the willow tree, where Gail said it would be. I scratch the sun-baked soil with the sole of one of my sandals, my heart sinking as I realize the ground is too hard to dig. My mind boggles at the daunting prospect of me standing in the shallows, attempting to bury his body underwater in the soft, yielding mud. I wonder if I'll be able to use the spade. I leave the spade where it is for now and make my way back to the car.

When I open the small boot, I see the spray of flowers, the single pink rose, that Will arranged for me. My son is meticulous. He leaves nothing to chance. There is a pink envelope attached to the stem of the rose. He is so thoughtful! I open it, take out the card, and read his message:

Happy Wedding Anniversary, Mum, with Lots of Love from Will xx

A lump of guilt, an Eve's Apple, forms in my throat at the thought of what I must do. I inspect my thick gold diamond eternity ring, the diamond bracelet gracing my wrist: tokens of happier times. Then I pick up the spray, close the tinny car boot, and pad round to the passenger door. I reach inside, shake my husband awake, unbuckle his seatbelt, and forcibly drag him from the car. He clings greedily to my waist for support as he shuffles the few metres to the stone wall.

We do our best to recreate The Marital:

MY SKIN FEELS CLAMMY IN the heat. My bare calves shine like buttercups in the sunlight. His face is flushed and sweaty. He starts to overheat in his dark suit. Expediently, I rip off his tie and unbutton his shirt, allowing some air to get to his hairy chest. The stone wall beckons us to join together in wild celebration, restate our wedding vows, to consummate our marriage vows. Somehow, I resist the temptation to make love to my husband, there and then, on the hot stone wall. Instead, I arrange him on the wall like a slovenly village idiot, with one limp leg slung over the wall, the other dangling loose at the front. I take his hairy hand, place it on his bony knee, and sit him up straight, as if he is staring into the eyes of the camera lens, heaven forbid. There is little more that I can do to recreate The Marital. He slumps on the wall like a sack of old spuds, unshaven, his eyes narrow, slanted, and weepy, his head hung low in its customary, hound-dog expression.

Waiting to die.

I do my best. I try to make the best of our sorry situation. I really do. I let my shoulder-length hair drape over his face, feel his hot cheek pressed against mine, crane my neck to prevent him from coming too close to me. He doesn't react, never reacts, doesn't even speak to me anymore. I lean into him so that he can feel my bare back, my perspiration, adhering to his exposed chest. He remains inert, incapable of feelings, sensuality, emotions, eruptions. My extinct, dormant, volcano-man. I hoick my frilly frock over my knees and flash my thighs, the searing sun their only companion. I clasp my spray in my lap, fold my arms, feel sad and lonely, my smile fades.

Our marital, our marriage, our life together, is over. It's time…

I tell him to sit still and wait for me on the hot wall. I have a pleasant surprise for him, I say. He doesn't move or speak. He lets go of me. Relieved to be freed of his deathly touch, I amble to the water's edge, see the wailing willow tree. And eye the spade. My sick mind conjures up possible connotations, potential hazards: the likely outcomes of several, repeated blows to the scalp and sides of his head: concussion, fractured skull, brain damage, internal haemorrhaging, severe bleeding, clear liquid weeping from his orifices. I know this. I found out on the internet.

An unsavoury thought flashes through my mind:

There will be blood, clear yellow fluid, lots of it. Then there is the disposal of his body, Brian's subterranean burial, to consider.

You might consider me selfish, but, staring out across the glistening water, full of beauty, and yes, life, I decide upon the only practical way to kill my husband, without leaving traces of his DNA all over me. I strip off my blessing dress, bra, knickers, and sandals and place them in a neatly folded pile behind a hazel bush, far away from the lover's platform. Then I pick up the spade and go to him. The sun warms my body, stilling my fraught nerves, as I sidle up to him. I stand before him. His eyes widen at the sight of me. He can't look at me, naked, like this. He bows his head in shame. I think he's crying. Crying for a long-lost love. I utter a few kind words, showing him my platinum wedding band,

'With this ring I thee wed. I love you, Brian. I always will, deep inside my heart. I'm sorry we have to end our marriage like this. I think it's for the best, don't you? You see, I'm having an affair with a male nurse, the volunteer who calls round with our food package? I'm sorry, love. I think I should end The Marital now, put you out of your misery, don't you?'

He raises his head. He looks me in the eye. I understand his sadness, his feeling of hopelessness. I raise the spade and prepare to swing it at his head with all my womanly might. He nods at me. I hear a voice behind me: Gail, recall the shining light, the optical illusion from the wedding venue, the car park, the mirror on Gail's moped, reflecting in the sunlight. Her voice screams:

'Mum! Stop it! What are you doing to Dad?!'

Instinctively, I throw down the spade, and seize my darling husband, loving him, shaking him by the shoulders,

'I was just about to give you your wedding anniversary present, wasn't I Brian?'

He fails to respond. He doesn't react. He never reacts.

Gail sobs, 'Mum, leave Dad alone! Leave him alone or I'll call the Police!'

I hold my husband's head in my hands, rubbing his tearful eyes dry, caressing his moist cheeks, and repeat,

'I was giving you your wedding anniversary present, wasn't I?' I shake him hard, 'Wasn't I?'

'Yus, Va-gin-ia,' he groans, like a pervert speaking through a sock.

I hug my husband. I love him dearly. I vow never to try to kill him again.

Gail's spiteful voice hisses in my ear,

'You can put your clothes on while you're at it, Mum. You look bloody ridiculous. Honestly, at your age…'

The rhyme 'something old (my husband), something new (the spade), something borrowed (my son's car), something blue (my garter)' referred to things I used on our wedding anniversary to try to end our unsuccessful marriage. Like most superstitions, it didn't entirely make sense.

The Potting Shed

SUNLIGHT STREAMED INTO HIS BEDROOM through a gap in the heavy plum drapes. Allen rolled onto his side and faced the warm Spring sun, clutching at her pillows. Ruth had been taken from him cruelly, at such a young age. His throat was sore. His head ached. He coughed, wondering if he had the virus. A tiny fireball hurtled across his weak right eye: the first sign of a migraine.

Tired, lonely, consumed by grief at losing the love of his life, he turned away, shutting his eyes, deep in thought. The bed was too big without Ruth. He'd have to buy himself a smaller bed. Their house was too big for a widower. He decided to sell her cherished antiques at auction and move into a flat. His spirits deflated. He felt sick. His hands shook. Allen fought back tears. How much longer could he carry on living like this. Without her?

Blearily, he reached for the phone-on-the-wall, pressed eleven buttons from memory, waited for voicemail, and left a message telling the office that he wasn't well. Might have the virus. Best work from home. He fell asleep. When he awoke, Allen felt the sun's rays burning the back of his neck. There was a copper silent-sweep clock on his side of the bed, by the kindle Ruth never found the time to read. He squinted at its vague yellow hands: it was seven o'clock.

Kean would be at work now on toilets, bathrooms, showers, cisterns, no call out charge, no job too small. Tall, bluff, big-hearted Kean, his friendly, reliable, local plumber. His *best* friend. Allen rang him on his mobile,

'Kean?'

'Yes?'

'It's Allen.'

'Hello, mate! How are you?' Kean's voice was rich, deep baritone. Warm and cheerful.

'Not good. I think I've caught the virus.'

'Sorry to hear that. There's a lot of it about.'

Allen mimicked him, 'There *is* a lot of it about.'

'How's Ruth?'

He didn't know what to say. How to break the news. His mouth dried, parched of saliva. He coughed, gulped, then blurted out the words,

'She's dead, Kean. Ruth died four weeks ago.'

He could feel his friend's face strain with disbelief at the other end of the line.

'Oh God! Tell me it isn't true.'

'It is true, I'm afraid. She was taken by the virus.'

'I'm sorry. Don't know what to say. If there's anything I can do to help?'

Allen cut the call and stared at their favourite photo: of Ruth dressed in antique white lace, her mother's wedding dress, gripping his hands in hers as they cut their wedding cake. The phone rang: Kean again, calm as ever,

'I lost you.'

'I need to meet up with you. I can't cope without her.'

The phone went dead. The sun blazed down. He poured with sweat, descending into panic,

'Kean? Kean!'

When the plumber spoke, his voice was flatter, dull monotone,

'I'm in Bulgaria.'

'You're where?'

'I'm at the villa with Celine. Don't get back till Sunday. Give me a ring on Monday.'

'But Kean…'

'What is it, mate? Tell me.'

'The cistern's gone in the bathroom.'

Allen climbed out of bed, drew the curtains, dressed in an old sweater, tracksuit bottoms, socks, trainers, and flew downstairs. The list, his keys and wallet were in the kitchen which he kept spotless for her. It was still early. If he hadn't caught the virus then with luck the supermarket might be empty. He could shop, come home, cook breakfast, have a bath, and go back to bed.

When he stepped outside, he was relieved to find the street deserted. Most of his neighbours self-isolated voluntarily. The supermarket was a five-minute walk away: past an Indian corner shop, Chinese takeaway, and a boutique NHS dentist: The Tooth Fairy. He noticed a sign on the door informing her clients that she had gone away until further notice. The surgery was closed. Another casualty of the virus.

It came as no surprise to him when he turned the corner and found the supermarket car park empty, other than a white van and a juggernaut bearing heavy hydraulic lifting equipment. The text hit his phone just as he was stooping to collect a shopping basket on the way in:

Come to The Tawney, we can marry and then we'll make love,

You can't ignore me, I'm the woman your dreams are made of.

Allen stared at the screen, momentarily transfixed, bemused. He had no idea what it meant. He saved the message, duly took the basket, and entered the store.

She was standing by the cut-price fruit selection, testing pears to see if they were ripe and ready to eat or not: Eat me? Keep me? A lithe figure with a short blonde-bob and a suntanned face, splendidly attired in her lightweight quilted beige jacket, a chequered beige and caramel scarf, skinny brown jeans, and trendy flat cap. A woman who promised warmth, finesse, the softest of touches. She dipped a thumb inside her pocket, pulling at her jeans, swaying her hips, and cooed brightly,

'Don't say hello then.'

She strode up to him, wrapping her slim fingers around his left wrist, holding him still as if he were a bad boy at school. She was tactile, *very* forward. He was horrified. Suppose she had the virus? She looked sensational. Her touch was tender, erotic. Allen hadn't felt a woman's touch since Ruth had lain asleep in her death bed, her pneumonia-riddled lungs rattling out their final breaths, her solitary last rites. He'd held her limp hand, felt her slip away. He shook his head out of her trance,

'Antonia?'

'That's me. How're you?'

'Sorry, I was miles away.'

'That's ok. I'll let you off this time. How're you keeping? Well, I hope? Not infected, are you? Wouldn't like to think I'm holding the hand of a man with plague. If you're unclean, you should be tucked up in bed, y'know.'

She had an uncanny effect on him: raising his spirits, lifting his heart, soothing his woes. It was impossible to feel low in the presence of such a lovely person. He bared his soul to her, gripping her hand. She felt soft and vulnerable, held like that, responding gently, squeezing his fingers,

'I started sweating last night, brought out a cough, felt a migraine come on, don't feel so good.'

To his surprise, Antonia tightened her grip on his hand. Why did she do that? Was she lonely?

She answered his prayers, 'So, that's why I'm here. To look after you. Make you feel better.'

Allen frowned, mopped his sweaty brow, acted kind of confused, 'I don't understand. How?'

She brushed his doubts aside with a sweep of her free hand,

'I'm immune, you see. One of 'the herd', lucky to be alive. I sweated the ague out of me, fought her off single-handed, battled her on my own, in solitary. She tested me, made my very bones hurt, filled my lungs with snot and mucus, till I could barely breathe. But I sweated her out, refused to give in. And now I'm here.'

He regarded her slim physique with fresh interest, astounded at her resilience, her drive,

'How much did she take out of you, Toni?'

'I lost two stone. I'm afraid there's not very much left of me,' she released his hand, touching her flat chest, 'Left me looking boyish, here, and here, if I'm honest. You can barely feel them.'

She lowered her head despondently. For a second, Allen thought she was going to cry. But she bounced back. Antonia was the living definition of strength. She lifted her face for him and smiled. Her eyes were gleaming with tears. He wanted to take her in his arms and comfort her.

He noticed Joe the supervisor, Stacey the cashier, Brian the assistant manager, staring blankly at them. Had best not hold her. Not here. In front of them. They might be reported to the Police. Cohabiting or touching another human was a notifiable offence, resulting in an instant fine and a criminal record.

Instead, he glanced around. The store was empty, like most shelves, stripped of every item by last night's panic-buying epidemic. Allen had seen the cars queuing past his house, the grimly determined faces of men, women, and children on their final family outing for months.

She intrigued him. He needed to know more. All of her suffering. Antonia, the first woman he had seen, touched, felt, since they took Ruth away from him to the temporary mortuary outside town: her interim resting place before her interment with the other ten bin-liner-bagged corpses.

He held her hand. Sod the consequences. He cared for her,

'How long did she plague you for?'

'Eight weeks.'

Allen was appalled, 'Eight weeks?!'

'Mm.'

Inside her chest, her little heartbeat wildly at the prospect of his company, his love, the ending of her abject loneliness. He made her feel safe, secure, made her lighten up within. She wanted to, needed to love him. Hell, her life needed purpose! Antonia bit her lip, ventured her question,

'I'm sorry for your sad news, Allen. The way she took Ruth from you was callous, heartless. You must be lonely. Me, I survive. For what, for who? I don't really know anymore.'

She gazed into his red-rimmed eyes, searching for signs of hope, filled with earnest expectation,

'Can we be friends again, please?'

He sighed, a deep sigh of relief, bordering on latent euphoria. Antonia's intent, her olive branch, thrilled him to the core. The chances of finding her, of even seeing her again today, in the store,

'I'd love that, Toni, I'd really love that.'

He glimpsed the three Store staff, pretending not to notice, going about their daily preparations for shoppers they might not serve again. Antonia reached for his swarthy face, took his cheeks in both hands, and kissed him firmly on the lips.

Delighted for her, Joe, Stacey, and Brian exchanged glances. Their smiles told her all she needed to know, made her day:

Don't worry, we promise not to tell the Police.

Allen felt all the stress, the tension from his devastating bereavement lift like mist burning off of a summer's lake at dawn. They stood there in the aisle by the bruised pears, embracing, at one with each other. Presently, he broke the silence, sharing the omen that had haunted him all these weeks. He stumbled over his tongue at first. She felt him tense, drew him close, held him tight: his pounding heart beating against her chest until he had calmed, and was able to speak,

'Ruth has been sending me messages,' he faltered, 'Messages from beyond the grave. I think she misses me. Think she can't cope with our parting. With how she was taken from me. By the ague. By her. By them.'

He broke down. She wiped the tears from his cheeks, let him cry, sharing the intimacy of his grief,

'They buried her in a pit of lime, Toni, lime!'

'I'll take care of you, Allen. Look after you, always. We'll make her proud of us. Help the sick, the vulnerable, the aged. Make her proud of you, darling, up there in Heaven, okay?'

He snivelled, she had this funny way, this incredibly positive aura about her, 'Yeah, thanks.'

'Don't mention it. You're welcome. All part of my customer service scheme!' she laughed.

He laughed back, couldn't help himself. She had that effect: filling him to the brim with joy, her joy. She buoyed him,

'Now, show me what Ruth said...'

Allen scrolled up the message on his phone and showed her:

Come to The Tawney, we can marry and then we'll make love,

You can't ignore me, I'm the woman your dreams are made of.

Antonia paled, tried to hide her true feelings for him - the secret. She kept her secret, for now,

'My goodness! That's some message. How d'you know it's her?'

'I can't explain it. I just know?'

She felt her shopping bag: its bulging contents between her calves. Felt the distinct urge to pee. Pressed her thin thighs together, kept it inside for later, when she got home. Made her decision, looking serious for once,

'I'll help you find her. We'll put Ruth's soul to rest. I know the Tawney. D'you ride?'

He beamed a little, showing off his manly pride, 'A little, I have a mountain bike. Why?'

Antonia lifted her limp wrist and checked her chunky bracelet watch: it was still only seven-thirty. She had all the time in the world, for him,

'Meet me at the railway bridge at eleven. I'll make us a picnic. It's a lovely ride. You'll love it! She'll love it! We can all love as one!'

It occurred to Allen that the ague might have rendered her loopy, fruitcake, nuts, raving mad. He rubbed his unshaven chin, took the wallet from his baggy tracksuit bottoms, frowning at her, watching him, the hope stamped all over her luscious face,

'Well?'

'Well, what?' he gasped, stifling a chesty cough.

'Are you game?'

He relaxed at last, grinning broadly for her, 'Game as I'll ever be.'

'See you at eleven then. Don't be late,' she bent down, delving inside her shopping bag, 'You'll need some of these. Here, take some.'

He reached out to her, touching hands, loving the feeling of their soft warmth, 'What are *they*?'

'Toilet rolls,' she said loudly, 'The *very* last ones, Allen,' she quietened, 'For an awfully long time.'

His saviour let go of him, stood up straight, took her bag, pecked his cheeks, span on her heels, and left.

His shoulders slumped. He felt all the energy drain from his body. His head ached; bones ached. The virus seized him with a vengeance, forcing droplets of thick sweat to ooze from every pore in his body, wetting his teak hair black, sheening his brow with perspiration. Shocked by his contagious transformation, Joe backed away from him, his hands raised high, mood altered,

'Stand well back!' he shouted, for the benefit of all and sundry.

A burly Indian security guard, face clad in eye goggles, a tough grey rubber mask, approached him, expediently. Joe appeared flustered,

'Please leave the store or I'll call the Police.'

Allen stared at the puffed-up millennial as if he were crazy,

'I need shaving foam, deodorant, sanitiser, brown sliced bread, kitchen roll, washing-up liquid.'

Joe, his cheeks flushed with anger, eyes burning with rage, finally lost all sense of self-control,

'They're out of stock, now get out!'

The middle-aged unhappy shopper felt the guard's iron fist grip his upper arm. He noticed that Ali Sadiq was wearing royal blue surgical gloves.

Why were the amazing doctors, nurses, and carers unable to obtain personal protective wear?

Allen was forcibly propelled towards the exit. He twisted his head, and took one last look at the supervisor,

'How dare you treat me like this. You haven't heard the last of me. I intend to complain to Customer Services.'

'Customer Services are all dead.'

Allen was horrified, 'They're what?!'

Ali Sadiq intervened, 'You heard what the man said.'

Allen was shoved outside onto the pavement. The automatic doors slid closed and locked, leaving Antonia's toilet rolls strewn across the tiled floor.

Antonia crossed the empty high street and walked past a restaurant in a state of reconstruction, a bistro, ladies' hairdressers, and a green café, wondering if they'd ever reopen. At the junction, by the fire station, she turned right into Simmel Street. The undertakers were open for business, busier than ever. Her council flat was a short trot past the closed sports centre, through a leafy cutting on the left.

There were four single-bedroom flats in the house known as 3, Hill Crescent. Antonia lived on the first floor. She saw the wilting daffodils in the overgrown front garden, suddenly feeling an immense sense of loss. Felt weak, listless, guilty. Ruth used to love daffodils. Spring was her favourite season.

The sun's warmth diminished as a cloud scudded across the sky. The slightest zephyr kissed the blonde hairs on the back of her neck, like soft lips, tentative touches, invisible fingertips, stroking her cheeks. She felt giddy. Her shopping bag slipped to the ground as she sought to steady herself, leaning against the porch. A presence gripped her, tightening around her chest. The sombre mood passed. The sun came out again.

Antonia saw a woman in the corner of her eye. She glanced over her shoulder. The garden was empty. Scared, she reached inside her zip-up jacket pocket, took out the key, unlocked the door, and quickly stepped inside.

Since Ruth's untimely death, Allen had become a recluse, constantly phoning the office with excuses for not going into work. Instead, he completed tax assessments in their three-bedroom terraced house in the high street, submitting the outcomes online.

Privately, his senior partner at the firm was relieved that Allen preferred to work remotely. Half of the office team had struggled into work on a crowded Underground train and succumbed to the virus. Seven had since died of respiratory failure in an overwhelmed hospital intensive care facility. There was talk of closing the firm at the end of the tax year and laying off all the staff.

No-one had an inkling of how long the pandemic would continue to proliferate: weeks, months, years? The mood of the nation changed to one of uncertainty and fear. Allen contemplated his fate: an indefinite period of self-isolation. *If* he survived the virus. He had few friends to speak of other than Kean, who could be stuck in Bulgaria for weeks, a handful of casual acquaintances at work.

Ruth *was* his life. They'd been trying for a child. It was all too much. He slumped against the supermarket wall coughing his rasping dry cough, out of breath, intensely fatigued, smiling inanely to himself at Antonia's ridiculous outpourings of false comfort:

'I'll help you find her. We'll put Ruth's soul to rest. I know the Tawney. Do you ride? I'll make a picnic. It's a lovely ride. You'll love it! She'll love it! We can all love as one!'

Ride? He could barely stand. Doubt crept into his mind about Antonia's true intentions. Was their meeting really a coincidence? Or had she planned it all along? Had she sent the ghoulish messages from Ruth? If so, how could she act in such a despicable, cruel, way towards him?

With the doubt came a growing sense of guilt at the way that he cheated on Antonia. His illicit trysts with Ruth in the cheap Airbnb in Gants Hill. Pretending to work late at the office while Toni cooked his favourite creamy turkey lasagne for supper. The hurt he inflicted on her when she returned to her flat to find him packing his bags. The way in which he left her, crying on the toilet. Wasn't *that* cruel? And through it all she'd never stopped loving him. A love-lump formed in his throat as he recalled her desperation, the hope in her sad eyes, her offer of a new life:

'Can we be friends again, please?'

Antonia scaled the concrete stairs to her flat. Everything was going well: her poetic messages to Allen, her surveillance of his house, their perfectly timed meeting in the supermarket. She breathed a sigh of relief, slammed the door behind her, dropped the bag on the floor, and rushed to the toilet. After she'd peed, she washed her hands for twenty seconds, dried them on a sheet of kitchen roll, then she stared at herself in the mirror.

She took off her cap. Her scalp was burning hot, her hair saturated with sweat. The sweat ran down her face, soring her eyes, making her wince. Its salt tainted her mouth, leaving a briny tang on her palate. Her head ached. Her muscles ached. She struggled to catch her breath.

Must've caught the virus from Allen, she decided, *So much for my herd immunity. I need him, want him. Can't stand this loneliness any longer, feel so lonely without my baby.*

She closed her eyes, picturing The Tawney in her mind's eye. The wonderful walled garden, she discovered on a cycle ride. Its broken walls, smothered with ivy. The overgrown vegetable plot strewn with dandelions and weeds. The disused potting shed. Her secret - which lay within.

I should get some rest, she resolved, *I'll feel better after some sleep, feel more like making love.*

Sensing a thrill inside her, Antonia brushed her teeth and went to her bed, forgetting to unpack the shopping which lay scattered on the bathroom floor.

Allen pulled himself together and trudged homewards. At the end of the lane, he turned right into the high street. At this time on a Monday morning there would normally be a queue of cars stretching from the mini roundabout, opposite the new home hub, to the traffic lights at the far end of Bell Common. Today, other than an ambulance which tore past him with its siren wailing and a white delivery van, the street was empty.

He stopped to read a hastily scrawled notice on the glass door of the first restaurant, an Indian, in a small parade of shops. The notice said that the owners had been forced to close indefinitely as a result of the virus. Allen inspected other signs: at the entrance to a Chinese restaurant, a trendy gift shop, Turkish barber's, a designer kiddie's clothes shop, the local estate agents, dry cleaners. All closed due to the virus. Why hadn't he noticed them before? The Indian corner shop was still open. He decided against going inside for fear of seeing the latest news headlines.

At last, he reached home. He crossed the crazy-paved garden, inserted a key in the lock, and paused to listen. The world fell silent. There was no constant drone of traffic from the nearby motorway. No workmen's bustle. Or children's laughter. Only birds, singing. He'd never felt so alone in his life.

Antonia stood in front of her bedroom mirror, unwound her scarf, removed her quilted jacket, then pulled her worn brown tee-shirt over her head. Topless, loving the tickle of the sun on her bare skin, she appraised the soft puffy protuberances jutting from her boyish chest, her exposed ribs, the cute stub of belly button protruding from her wasted stomach.

'Oh God, won't you look at me now,' she murmured, bursting into tears, 'Hope I please him. Hope he can love me like this.'

She forced herself to spit out the words, 'His sad little boy-girl.'

Crying, blinking out her stinging teardrops, Antonia undid her belt, pulled down her jeans, and climbed into bed. She lay on her back, shut her eyes, and dreamed of the potting shed, imagining the look of surprise on his face when she shut the shed door behind her, locked them inside, and stripped off in front of him: the divine explanation she rehearsed every night.

Allen closed the door behind him and walked through the small hallway. Past Ruth's treasured lounge diner. Her walnut writing desk, shelves crammed with books, embroideries, paintings, trinkets, cameos, knickknacks, the dusky pink chaise longue, her comfortable armchair,

'My little bird's nest, see sweetheart,' Ruth so lovingly used to call it in her soft, lilting Welsh.

He leaned against the jamb of the diner door, staring at her empty armchair, bathed in sunlight.

Then *she was there*, for him. Ruth, his beautiful bride. Her oaken hair flowing in flouncy curls, fluffy waves, into the small of her slender back, kissing the milky beige skin of her breasts. Her caramel peek-a-boo nipples clearly visible through the elaborated patterning of her white lace.

He sank to his knees, suppressed, compressed, confounded by her beauty, her virginal purity. Ruth had saved herself for him for their wedding night. She took his breath away. Her skimpy bodice accentuated her bare shoulders, her slender arms. He started to cough. Her slim fingers were buried within the lacy folds, the stiff furls, of her dress. He felt a sharp stab in his chest.

Antonia propped her faithful old bicycle against the mossy wall and stood at the railway bridge, gazing down at the deserted station platforms, their empty trains. There was a shrill whine, a brief announcement, and one of the trains moved off. She watched it fade into the distant heat-haze and wondered if life would ever return to normal. A sense of hopelessness possessed her. The virus plagued her mind and body, weakening her inner resolve to survive the onslaught of her second wave. Then there was the portent, the warning the woman mouthed when they met in the garden. Her deathly vision of their future. Were they destined to die of her virus? Was their mutual infection a punishment for falling in love again, so soon after her premature death?

A train rumbled into the platform. A blackbird sang. Antonia shook herself to her senses. Life without Allen, his love and care for her, would be unimaginable, her dire loneliness unbearable. She would despair, lose the will to live, end it all. She felt the rucksack between her legs, knelt down on the smooth tarmac and unzipped it, revealing the chilled cans of ginger beer and foil-wrapped low-fat cheese and vine tomato sandwiches: the best menu she could muster given the circumstances.

Anyway, it's too late to change my mind now, she decided, *I made us lunch.*

Antonia drew her phone out of her quilted jacket pocket and checked to see if she had any new messages or missed calls. Unsurprisingly, there were none. She checked the time on the screen:

10:30.

Her heart fluttered with excitement.

When Allen woke up on the carpet, Ruth had disappeared. Groggy, he felt the hard bulge inside his sagging tracksuit bottoms vibrate. He withdrew the phone from its velvet cover and looked. The orange circle next to the saffron message icon indicated that he had a new message, it read:

Come to The Tawney, we can marry and then we'll make love,

You can't ignore me, I'm the woman your dreams are made of.

His mind raced. He selected apps. WhatsApp was on a second screen, next to Skype, Assistant, and Play Music. The orange circle next to the green quote icon told him: he had a new message. His heartbeat like a funeral drum. His mind instructed him to leave the message well alone, avoid temptation, trust to fate. Against his better judgement, he opened it:

Come to The Tawney, where we married and then we made love,

You can't ignore me, I'm the woman your dreams were made of.

Allen collapsed in a pool of tears, gripping the phone. His battery was low. His device had fifteen percent power remaining wasting away - like him. A yellow sun shone on the screen. Vaguely remembering Toni's rendezvous with him on the bridge, he stared blankly at the time:

10:30

Distressed, Allen shook himself out of his stupor. He'd been asleep for two and a half hours. Deciding to forego breakfast and a bath, he flew upstairs, changed into his best pale grey t-shirt and matching chinos, threw on some sneakers, and visited the bathroom. He peed briskly before sanitizing his hands and brushing his teeth. His beard needed trimming. There wasn't time. He checked his face vainly in the mirror:

Hair looks good today. Shame about the shadows under my sexy brown eyes. Can't be helped.

Allen descended the stairs two-at-a-time, raced through the kitchen, crossed the artificial lawn, and hurled open the door to the garden shed. His hybrid mountain bike *still* had two flat tyres.

11:45

He isn't coming, I know it.

With a heavy heart, Antonia mounted her ladies' bicycle, adjusted the strap on her dayglo pink helmet, selected first, and slowly pedalled up the steep incline of Station Hill. She met Allen hurtling down the hill in sixth. Passing her by in a grey blur at great speed. He called out to her,

'Toni!'

Her heart leapt inside her chest: the thrill of him,

'Allen! What kept you? I thought you'd stood me up.'

He applied both brakes at the same time, so sharply that he left the saddle, almost flying over the handlebars in his bid to stop. He pulled up opposite her, near their local care home. She scootered across the road to be with him. His smile filled the width of his face. She had never seen him so happy. He warmed her heart. Toni was delighted. Allen had suffered so much grief since Ruth's death. She would make him happy, she vowed, always, for the rest of their lives. He was laughing, madly.

Love it when you laugh, she reflected,

'Well, why're you so late?'

'I had some punctures to repair. Do you believe that?'

She sounded surprised, 'Oh, *really?*'

Allen flushed and looked down at his pedals. Toni was used to his lies, inured by his deceitful past. He stopped lying to her,

'I'm sorry, I was ill. I went back to bed, and overslept.'

Antonia sighed with frustration, 'How're you feeling now?'

'Better, thanks.'

'You don't look better. You look awful.'

'I'll be fine.'

'Allen,' she said firmly, 'It's half hour ride downhill to The Tawney. There's a steep uphill climb all the way back. Are y'sure you can manage it?'

Barely concealing his irritation, he snapped, 'Sure, I can.'

Antonia shook her head at him. She made her mind up, 'Okay, let's go then, shall we?'

There were shattered terracotta tiles on its roof, allowing the sunshine in, covered with clinging moss. The windows were coated in thin green algae, creating privacy for her, the solid oak door bore a sturdy padlock.

The Potting Shed where she and Allen had first made love.

Antonia had cleared away the broken clay pots and left them piled in an untidy heap by the garden wall. The green and yellow mattresses, arranged neatly on the splintered wooden floor, were brand-new, bought at a local garden centre, which was closed except for collected orders.

The sun hid behind some thick black clouds. The air turned dense and muggy. There was a thunderstorm brewing. They removed each other's cycling helmets and strung them onto their handlebars. The bikes rested against the garden wall. Allen pushed his hand through his soaking wet hair. His t-shirt was drenched in sweat. His tight-fitting chinos clung to his red-sore crotch, abrading his groins with an inflamed rash. He felt weak, sick, uncomfortable in the stultifying heat. Antonia felt sorry for him. She took his hand in hers and led him to the potting shed door.

She mothered him, 'C'mon, let's get you inside out of the heat, shall we?' peering skyward, 'Looks like rain, doesn't it?' unhinging the padlock, 'I've a surprise for you,' opening the door.

Eagerly, she gestured for him to step into the half-light. There was a rumble of thunder. A flash of blanket lightning illuminated the dark skies overhead. The first spatters of heavy rain fell on their bare heads. Allen lingered, inhaling the freshly charged air. The clouds burst. Rain teemed down from the heavens, soaking them both to the skin. Invigorated by the cool refreshing rain, they entered the warm earthy dry of the potting shed. The air was stale: filled with must, dust, soil, an unfamiliar putrid smell. Antonia firmly shut the stable door behind her and set the lock.

Allen surveyed the shed: bare walls, cobwebs, bare floor, window daubed in grime, mattresses?

The rain drummed on the rooftiles. Deliriously happy and content, Antonia recited her poetry,

'Come to The Tawney, we can marry and then we'll make love,

You can't ignore me, I'm the woman your dreams are made of.'

Allen slumped to his knees, crawled onto a mattress, and lay with his hands behind his head, exhausted, overwhelmed by his mixed emotions,

'It was you all along, wasn't it? The text, the message, our chance meeting in the supermarket.'

'Course it was me. Who did y'think it was, Ruth?'

She felt inside her pocket, drew out her white-gold wedding ring, and slid it onto her ring finger,

'I still love you, Allen. D'you still love me?'

He was lost for words. Ruth had been dead for only four weeks. He had rediscovered love with his ex-wife. Dare he commit his heart, mind, and body to Antonia, so soon after Ruth's decease? The rain splashed down on the potting shed roof. But they were safe: snug and warm, inside. Her longing, yearning face implored him to love her. He wanted her. He pushed himself up off the mattress, went and clung to her. Felt her slim fingers clawing his damp hair. Her lips kissing his earlobe, whispering gently in his ear,

'Let's get you out of your wet clothes, shall we? Might as well make the best of the situation.'

He stood perfectly still as she peeled off his tee-shirt, pulling it over his head. She smudged his cheeks with nude lipstick, thumbing his tightly closed lips, prising them apart, savouring his hungry mouth, swallowing his saliva, loving his acrid taste on her palate. He felt her lips trailing down his bristled neck, through his fuzz of hair, her lambent tongue flickering like a snake's lick, teasing his nipples. Voraciously, she tore out the copper stud holding up his chinos, pulled his fly, unfurling him, exposing his classic charcoal grey men's briefs, the bulge which grew within. Antonia pulled his trousers down as far as his knobbly knees, wishing she had a cane,

'They're stuck!' she remarked, giggling.

Allen sat on the mattress, removed his sneakers and sports socks, then shed his cloying chinos. Straining, rearing, for her, he wanted to take down his briefs. She raised an admonishing hand,

'No, leave them on. Sit still and wait for me.'

He sat on the floor with his legs crossed like a child at a school assembly, watching her undress. When she was wearing just her soft panties, Toni lay on the mattress beside him. They listened to the downpour, strumming, sheeting, over their heads. The sun came out shining thru the rain. She turned to face the window, childish in her excitement, boyish in her physical appearance,

'There'll be a rainbow.'

She lay back for him, ready, willing to make love. He teased her nipples with his lips, plucking at her tender growths, pleasuring, arousing her, sucking, pulling, even twisting them. His mouth released her tiny breast. He asked her his vital question. She gave him her determined response,

'Want to have your baby, Allen.'

His hand slid over her exposed rib cage, pausing to caress her cute stud of navel, her divine belly. She rasped, struggling to breathe, sweating profusely. He felt inside her panties, parting her mound of lush, soft, moist hair, gently caressing her. She thrilled to his touch, running her fingertips through his damp hair, pausing to rub his earlobes, venturing down his neck, his taut spine, until she reached the fuzz of hair in the small of his back, sighing, pleading for him,

'Make love to me.'

Struggling to restrain his burning desire for her, he pulled her panties down, lifting each of her legs in turn to unravel the tangle around her ankles, thrilled by her denouement. He lay on her, crushing her fragile body with his physique, groaning as she slid her soft hands inside his briefs and peeled them off, exposing his clenched hairy buttocks to the warmth of the breaking sun,

'I love you, Toni.'

She gazed into his weary eyes, imploring him, demanding of him, 'Love me, baby, won't you?'

His forbidden fruit. They kissed...

He thrust himself deep inside her, gasping as she wrapped her slender calves around his thighs, loving the thrill, the joyride of her impalement, seeding her, her rash of disappointment, his sad voice,

'I'm sorry, I...'

'That's okay, honey, I love you. Anyways, it's the thought that counts, isn't it? The sentiment?'

She caught her breath and fell asleep, emotionally fulfilled, their bodies intimately entwined.

He turned his head and saw her, watching them through the grimy window. She looked sad, wistful. Her bushy brows were raised in pity for him. Her eyes: teary, sorrowful, mournful. His mouth dried, he couldn't speak. Her lovely face. The sublime contour of her chin, her sensuous high cheeks, her soft, snub nose. Tears ran down her blushing face, trickling as far as her mouth. She parted her thin lips. He felt her breath on him, her soft beige brushing his lips, her mouth enfolding his. He struggled for breath, suffocating. Demented thoughts pervaded his distrait mind.

Ruth changed: she wore a soot-black fascinator. A wide-meshed veil covered her face as far as her crude hair lip. Allen craned his head, worshipping his bridal queen, his adored wife on their wedding day, their sacred words. He felt her excruciating pain as she died, her love stabbing him deep inside his heart, as she opened her blood-red mouth to speak,

'Come to The Tawney, where we married and then we made love,

You can't escape me, I'm the woman your dreams are made of.'

Her face became indistinct. Ruth gradually faded away. He felt Antonia, stirring beneath him. He looked into her eyes. They were brimming with tears. Her face was lit by the happiest smile. He brushed her damp cheeks, brushed away her tears, stroked her hair. He loved her *so* much,

'You're crying, Toni.'

She found herself wanting him again, rubbing the hairy small of his back, clawing his buttocks,

'I always cry when I make love, y'know. How're you feeling?'

He relaxed onto her, sighing contentedly,

'I haven't felt so well in years. I love you, Antonia.'

She felt his weight, his manly body bearing down on hers, igniting his passion with her promise,

'It's over, Allen, I promise. She's gone. I can feel it. I can feel her, sweetheart, I can feel her...'

Allure

verb: to entice or tempt someone.

noun: attractiveness, appeal.

allure: the power a woman has over a man.

March 2020:

I WAS WORKING AS A server in Eva's eco-green café and bar when we met. Eva's was all-organic, the trendiest place in the high street. From the outside, it looked like a private house: white-washed walls, jet-black door, brass knocker, bay windows on either side. The café was dingy on the inside. A lurid pink neon sign screamed *Eva!* at the rear wall, painted-white tables, and chairs. The menu was a wall-sized blackboard. Straight ahead was a ladies' toilet and the small kitchen where Eva toiled to make her living. Eva smoked a lot, in the tiny brick-walled back garden. I manned the bar, served food, cleared tables. In the summer, we had stackable tables and chairs outside on the pavement.

But it wasn't summer. It was early spring. The sky was overcast with patchy rain. I watched the absent sunset through the drizzled window, then walked past all the empty tables to the bar.

Other than Friday and Saturday evenings, when we were packed to the rafters, Eva's wasn't busy. We were busier in the mornings and lunchtimes when we offered our discerning female clientele hand-made smoothie bowls, invigorating herbal cocktails, wholesome vegan tapas on boards, delicious home-baked vegan cakes, organic coffee. Thursday evenings were dead. We didn't serve food. I manned the bar, served drinks, cleared tables. Eva caught up with her admin.

It was Thursday evening, last light, when she walked in out of the rain. Her hair was streaked with wet. She removed her dripping hooded mocha puffer jacket, shook it off, and scooted past me to the toilet, without giving me so much as a glance. I couldn't help but notice that she was wearing a revealing pink floral print open-backed wrap bodysuit, tight high-waisted light blue riot mom jeans, and white trainers. Shaken, but unstirred, I turned around to polish the glasses.

We offered our customers a choice of exotic cocktails, select organic beers, or vegan wine.

I heard her voice: soft, syrupy, sensuous, prompting me to serve her. Suppressed my cough.

I turned to face her, asked her what she wanted to drink. She told me she wanted Sex on the Beach.

I smiled, *Don't we all?*

She had that rare allure of a woman who knows she is beautiful, sexy, gorgeous. I pulled down bottles of vodka, peach schnapps, cranberry, orange juice, and set them on the counter before her with a jug and glass.

She raised her brows a smidgeon, pursing her lips in the most divine pout, brushing the thick mane of damp auburn hair off her face. I was beguiled by her. So mesmerized, I knocked over her glass. It rolled towards her doughy hand. Strange, that she had such old hands for a young woman. She stood the tall glass up on its base and laughed at me,

'I think you need another one, don't you?'

Hungrily, I prised the glass out of her hand. My fingertips felt her softness,

'I'm sorry.'

'Don't be,' she soothed.

'Sorry?'

'I said, don't be. I want you to share a drink with me. I'm celebrating tonight.'

'I can't, staff aren't allowed to…'

She stared at me intently with her clear almond eyes. Her eyelashes were perfectly stiffened: spiked hairs with mascara. She fluttered her eyelids innocently at me. I felt myself go weak at the knees. She placed her hand on mine, rubbing my mound of Venus with her wrinkled thumb,

'Save it for later, eh?' she murmured.

I nodded my appreciation, filling her glass with cracked ice, mixing her drink in a frenzy,

'What are we celebrating?' I asked inquisitively.

'My first modelling assignment.'

I divided the blend between our glasses, stirring gently, probing her avidly, my pulse racing,

'Your first modelling assignment?'

She smiled a delectable, knowing smile. She giggled at me childishly,

'I'm going to model: topless, lingerie, sportswear, swimsuits.'

Her wrap had come undone at the front. My jaw dropped. My heart raced. I gibbered,

'Topless?'

'Yes.'

I gushed in stupid admiration, 'Oh, well done you!'

She blushed, staring at her hands resting like kitten's paws on the polished wooden counter,

'Thank you.'

I garnished her drink with orange slices, unscrewed a jar of red maraschino cocktail cherries,

'Would you like one, or two, cherries?'

'Oh, two I think, don't you?'

I dispensed two cherries and handed her the glass. I charged her. She paid in cash. I marvelled as she took her plastic skewer, fished in her glass, spiked each cherry, and sucked them off one at a time. Then she ate the flesh of the orange, passing me her rind, and swallowed her whole Sex on the Beach in one. She gasped for breath. I covered my mouth and coughed,

'I'm sorry,' I said, pouring myself a tumbler of water, sipping, 'I've had this ticklish cough.'

Her mood changed. Her face clouded with concern. She moved away from me,

'How long have you had it for?'

'About a week. It comes and goes. Why?'

She didn't answer. Instead, she felt inside her jeans, drew out a scrappy card, and left it on the counter. On the card was her number and motif. She pulled on her puffer jacket, zipped it up, went to leave,

'Call me when your cough has gone,' she said, 'Take care of yourself, and stay safe.'

I watched her go. Didn't think straight. In my state of bewilderment, I forgot to ask her name.

Eva's eco-green café and bar closed on Friday evening and hasn't reopened. I lost my job. The cough got worse. By Saturday morning, I couldn't breathe. I rang 111, was admitted to hospital. My condition worsened. I was sedated, connected to a respirator. I didn't regain consciousness until Thursday evening on the last day of April. The doctors and nurses were incredible. Had it not been for their intervention I would have died. They restarted my heart five times.

My heart...

I was discharged from hospital last week. Self-isolation feels very lonely when you're frail and weak. I can't leave my bedsit. Don't want to. I'm frightened to go out. The weather reflects my mood: dull and overcast with patchy rain.

This isn't summer, is it? I sit and watch the absent sunset through the drizzled window, then stare at the A4 buff envelope that waited for me on the doormat when I arrived home. I can't bring myself to open it. It's from her. I know it is. Instead, I take her calling card out of my pyjama pocket, find my phone - and dial her number.

'Call me when the cough has gone,' she said, 'Take care of yourself, and stay safe.'

The number is disconnected. My heart sinks.

Carefully, I open the buff envelope, sliding out the glossy colour photos. The first pose shows her wearing a skimpy turquoise swimsuit slashed as high as her waist. She pulls down the front of her swimsuit to give me a tantalising glimpse of her breasts. She looks sensational. I force myself to stare at her other pose. She watches me intently with her clear almond eyes.

She is topless, wearing black lingerie. Her breasts are stunning, breath-taking, perfectly rounded, with flat almond nipples. I weaken. My heart nearly dies in my chest. I drop the card, her motif:

Save me for later.

There is a soft knock at the door. I can't bring myself to open it. It's her, I know it is.

My destiny.

The Bristling

April 2020:

THE BRISTLING INVADED HER SCALP like itchy dandruff, infuriating her, forcing her to push her wavy blonde hair behind her ears, and scratch her crown. It spread like wildfire, tainting her face, her swan-thin neck, with an invisible rash, fanning out over her shallow chest, her little breasts. Irritating her nipples, scratchily, until they stood proud in silent protest at its invasion. The bristling nestled in her armpits, creeping down her knobbly spine to the small of her back into the crevice dividing her firm buttocks, kissing her thighs - teasing her to the point of madness.

She stood before the mirror, naked, writhing, squirming, her face, and body red, sore with cruel blush, and asked herself how much more of this intrusion she could take.

He stood outside the station entrance and watched her step out onto the silent street. A youthful man who found himself, conquered his condition, and wanted to help others. He felt immensely sorry for her. She was really suffering, enduring constant physical and emotional discomfort, at her wits end. He wanted to help her but couldn't pluck up the courage to approach her. Such behaviour was frowned upon in the current climate of social distancing, self-imposed isolation.

She crossed the road and saw him, eyeing her up. Her heart lifted. He looked relaxed. Content to lean against the dirty station wall in pristine, soft white slacks. Soft. The word struck a chord. He was wearing a soft blue shirt. His sleeves were rolled up to the elbows, his arms covered in soft brown hair.

Soft. He had three buttons undone, revealing a gingery, hairy chest. She flashed him a lovely broad smile that lit up her face from ear to ear and dimpled her cheeks. He smiled back, a warm smile, an 'I care about you' smile. She loved his face, the soft swarth on his pock-marked cheeks. She wanted to stroke them. Run her fingers through his thin auburn hair. Kiss his dry lips. Her eyes twinkled. He grinned at her kindly. She felt her blush, the bristling, spread over her face, her body, felt uncomfortable, embarrassed. Her heart sank.

He turned away and entered the station. She followed him through the ticket barrier, up some stairs to Platform 2 for the next train to Romford, Stratford, and Liverpool Street. He was two metres from her. They were alone on the platform. He wanted to reach out to her. She wanted to explain. Their mouths were dry. They couldn't speak. There was a train coming. A fast train. Rapidly approaching them. Accelerating on the curve.

'Ah, this is my train,' she gasped, just loud enough for him to hear her.

His head turned. The train indicator was blank. The station was empty, apart from them. He moved closer to her. She distanced herself from him. There was an automated announcement,

'The next train does not stop here! Stand back behind the yellow line on Platform 2!'

'Here's my train,' she cried, smiling: a haunted, hopeless, desperate smile, edging ever forward.

'Fast train approaching!'

He saw her smile. It was a still, bright, warm, sunny, glorious, morning. He saw her despairing.

She padded up to the platform edge and stood there testing, gripping the edge of the platform, with her toes. She had bare feet. Why hadn't he seen that? He had been too busy studying her blushing face. He heard her cry as the train sped along the platform,

'Hello, train!'

'Stand back! Stand back! Look out!'

He pulled her back at the last minute. The train sped past.

'You could have got yourself killed!' he yelled angrily.

She fell into his open arms. Instinctively, he pushed her away from him.

~ 200 ~

She toppled over like a falling statue, and landed heavily on the tarmac, bumping her forehead. For a moment, she lay still, crumpled on the ground, in the recovery position. He looked around, at the other four platforms. No-one was looking. No-one ever looked, these days. She groaned, and complained,

'Don't just stand there. Help me get up.'

He backed off from her. She calmed. He noticed the nasty gash on her forehead, a piece of grit. Blood trickled down the left side of her face into her hazel eye giving it a bloodshot appearance, down her dimpled cheek, into the corner of her mouth, ending in a single trail down her graceful neck. She wiped her head with the back of her slim hand, smearing blood into her hair. He felt guilty, stupid. She looked a mess. The wound was deep, probably needed stitching. No chance! The hospitals and doctors' surgeries were bursting at the seams with Covid-19 patients. He took out the wad of paper hankies, he kept for his sneezing emergencies. She had succeeded in dislodging the grit. Her blood was flowing freely. He noticed the tear in her skinny blue jeans, two tears – one red, one clear – rolling down her cheeks,

'It's alright,' she sniffed, 'I'm clean.'

He knelt beside her, soiling the knees of his pristine slacks. The tarmac felt smooth, warm. She searched his face, his open mouth and nostrils, felt him breathing on her bare neck. He took the wad and…

'Are you clean?' she interrupted.

'Yes, well, err, I've not been tested.'

She smiled at him, through all her blood and gore, so glad that he saved her life, when she went to jump under the train…

'Neither have I,' she laughed.

He couldn't help laughing at her; she looked in such a sorry state. He stared at her intently. She was lovely, fresh-faced, beautiful, in a natural kind of way. She nodded, craving his attention,

'It's alright,' she repeated, beaming, 'I *am* clean.'

Tentatively, he stemmed her flow of blood.

Her skin was pale. Her blush had faded. There was no sign of her bristling at all. Yet...

'I suppose I should thank you for saving my life,' she said in a tremulous voice, clearly upset still, weeping gently.

His heart went out to her. To think that such a beautiful young woman should be driven to end her life by jumping under a train. The thought of her body, cut to shreds by the spinning wheels, devastated him.

He'd been there himself once, had the ague. The bristling felt every bit as bad as Covid-19, except that it occupied the sufferer's *whole* body: permeating the skin through each pore and orifice, entering the viscera via the bloodstream, attacking the heart and brain. It might kill her today, tomorrow, next week, next month...

Death was a welcome release from her cruel blush. She knew that when she tried to commit suicide. Her wound stopped bleeding. She looked up at him, for his helping hand, his support, an act of kindness.

He could save her.

'I suppose so,' he said.

She rolled over onto her back and propped herself up on her elbows. The thin brown and beige, short-sleeved sweater she was wearing accentuated her remarkable swan-neck, the bare sloping shoulders. Her arms and legs were unusually long and slender, he noted. In a past life, she might have lived as a giraffe.

'Well, are you going to leave me lying here all day?'

She was forceful, strong-willed, fighting back, against the bristling. He liked that. Strength of mind and self-belief would be essential if she were to win the battle for her life. She recovered, sat up, stretched her arms out in front of her. He took her hands in his and pulled her to her feet. She breathed a long sigh of relief, let go of his hands, and brushed herself down,

'Thank you.'

'Don't mention it.'

He shrugged his shoulders, turned away, and paced up and down the platform, pondering what to say next. Couldn't bring himself to ask her the question: 'Why did you try to kill yourself?', didn't need to, he already knew the answer. He had stood on the pavement, watching her draw the curtains, open the curtains, leave for work, through the door, next to the beauty parlour: the home of perfect skin.

She read his thoughts, gathered up her jute bag: the spilt, womanly odds and sods, ran up behind him and went to speak. Her meek voice was drowned out by a station announcement. An empty train glided into the platform and came to a halt. Its doors slid open,

'The train on Platform 2 is the 8.15 service to Liverpool Street, calling at Romford, Stratford, and Liverpool Street.'

He turned to face her. Had to think quickly. *Say something, man!* An empty carriage beckoned. He edged towards the open doors. Frustrated by his silence, she pleaded to him, her eyes, sad,

'Look, I'm sorry, okay? I saw you, watching me, every day. I have the bristling?'

'Stand clear of the closing doors.'

He stopped dead in his tracks and asked where she was travelling to. She said she was going to work. There was a shrill, peeping sound, a warning. The doors were about to close. He took a step nearer the train. She drew a railcard out of her tight jean pocket, held it up for him to see, her season ticket,

'Except,' she raced, 'I don't work. I lost my job. Because of the lockdown? The virus? I travel. Something to do. I'm lonely. I pretend to go to work...'

The doors closed. She missed her train.

Thank goodness.

He drew a long sigh of relief, spoke, at last,

'And that's when you contracted the bristling, is it?

He managed nine words! She smiled, slowly nodding her head.

'I can cure you. Would you like to be cured?'

'Yes! Yes! Please!'

Her whole face lit up in a bright pink blush. She started to bristle. He shook his head sadly at her vain attempt to control the spread,

'Do you trust me?'

She felt the bristling raise the hairs on the back of her neck. This man saved her life. If she couldn't trust him, who could she trust? The bristling spread over her narrow shoulder blades, down her back, her front. She started to squirm inside, hating the bristling for its callous assault,

'Yes! I trust you! Can you help me, please? Can't take much more of this. Please, help me?'

He held her hand. She let him hold her hand. He offered comfort. More than that. He gave her hope.

Together they left the station.

The ticket hall was empty, the booking office closed. Shutters concealed the kiosk where she used to stop and buy a paper. She wondered if it would ever re-open, worried for the livelihoods of the charming Indian couple who ran the shop. Her thoughts were permeated by the bristling, the ravaging nettle rash that bloomed on her torso, upper arms, and thighs. Soon it would infest the creases in her elbows, the damp behind her knees, her forearms, calves, festering athlete's feet, the blotched webs between her fingers. She tightened her grip on his hand. He felt for her,

'How long before you start to sting?' he asked, as they stepped out onto the station forecourt.

She stared him in the face, 'Five, ten minutes. How far is it to your... clinic? Is it near here?'

He hesitated, avoiding her question. Instead, he looked up and down the high street. Her flat was over the road, between the beauty parlour and local Co-op minimarket. Nearer the railway bridge was the town's only chemist. Two queues of blank-faced shoppers, standing equidistant from one another, stretched hundreds of yards in opposite directions. There were no other signs of activity.

The station forecourt, usually packed with commuters and shoppers, was devoid of people, the cab rank empty. He let go of her hand, so that he could shield his eyes from the glaring early Spring sun. She went and stood in front of him, jabbing him hard in the chest,

'Is it near here?' she persisted, shoving him backwards, 'Tell me!'

He threw up his arms in mock alarm, laughing at her, 'Hey! Easy! Easy!'

Oh, he made her blood boil!

'Have you any idea?' she shrieked, 'What it feels like to itch and sting and hurt all over? Idiot!'

Aware that she had aroused the interest of all the bored, unhappy shoppers standing opposite, he grabbed her by the arms and drew her in, close to him. She loved the feeling of him, holding her tight, easing her discomfort, smiled to herself, spoke in an even voice. She knew his pain, how he must have suffered, by the pensive expression on his face, wanted to hear him admit it,

'Well?'

'Of course, I do!' he hissed at her, 'How do you think I discovered the cure?'

She felt the invisible wasps crawling over her flesh, felt them sting her flesh, 'How far? Please!'

He was a good six inches taller than her. He let go of her, looked down forlornly at her beautiful, imploring face, 'I live in Thrift Wood.'

Her spirits sagged. She withered visibly. Her chin dropped. His words stung her. She gave up,

'Thrift Wood's twenty minutes' walk away!'

He took her in his arms and rocked her gently, consoling her, stroking her damp hair,

'I'm sorry,' he groaned, 'So sorry.'

She wriggled herself free. Her whole body stung. The swelling began. Her lips were swollen by the time she spoke,

'It's too late,' she mumbled, 'Too late for sorry,'

She stung all over. The stinging, the most intense bristling she had ever endured, flourished on her head, limbs, and torso. A penetrative body-mould, rafts of jellyfish stings, agglomerating in her crotch, crevice, armpits, scourging her, scurrying thru her scalp like raving mosquitoes on a hot summer's night. She looked up at him for her epitaph, his carefully chosen words of admiration, dare she say: respect. Instead, he gripped her shoulders and shook her to her senses,

'You must fight it, understand?'

She shook her head sadly, her face sagging with resignation, like a woman with Bell's palsy in both cheeks, then blew the words, her zephyr, in his face,

'Can't. Don't want to.'

He held her lovely head in his hands, forcing his fingers through her wet hair, stretching her flushed cheeks with his palms, making her listen to him, caring about her, sharing his hidden emotions, shouting at her,

'You must! I can cure you! I've been there! Suffered the bristling, the rash of stings! Trust me!'

He felt her relax, let go of her jaw. She could just about murmur,

'How?'

He caught sight of the line of shoppers across the road, ogling her like vultures over prey. He let them have their moment. After all, there was little enough entertainment in their lives: the telly, a good book, a video workout, some remote-distance learning with the kids, a singsong, clapping with the neighbours every Thursday night, the fortnightly walk to the supermarket. A fed-up-looking woman dressed in a red t-shirt with an NHS motif, fleece, and trousers, let two customers into the chemist's shop. He turned to her, told her exactly what he wanted her to do:

'Don't let the stinging inside you. If it gets inside you, it will make its way in your bloodstream to your lungs, heart, and brain. And kill you.'

She nodded, grimacing nervously. He had her undivided attention,

'Try to stay calm.'

Calm!?

She raised her bushy eyebrows. She was listening to him, though. He continued,

'Don't let it in. Breathe out forcibly, force it out. Keep your mouth shut. Clench your buttocks,' he blushed slightly, his first sign of weakness, 'Close your legs.'

She burst out laughing, 'You should be so lucky!'

He laughed with her, couldn't help it. Her sense of humour, her means of coping with adversity, infected him. His feelings for her stretched far beyond admiration; something akin to fondness, love. He pulled himself together and apologized,

'I'm sorry, I think it's best you keep your mouth firmly shut.'

She gave him her last beaming smile, dimpling her cheeks, parting her lips, baring her gleaming white teeth, then set her jaw, and looked down: really glum.

Her thoughts were interrupted by a loud chattering noise. They stared at the vehicle, emerging rapidly from under the railway bridge. It swayed from side to side, veered sharp left, slammed on its brakes, and screeched to a halt in front of them. The last thing they expected to see that morning in Shenfield high street was a black taxicab. The window slid down on the passenger side, revealing the young driver. He had dark ebony skin, huge brown eyes, thick rubbery lips, and his shaven head was crowned with a tuft of wiry black hair. He was naked from the waist up, lean, sinewy, and fit…

My, now that's hot! she thought, grinning at him…

…and he couldn't have been a day over eighteen,

'What you smiling at, lady?' he said, laughing.

She didn't reply. Her lips were sealed, her face hot, flushed, and swollen. The driver turned his attention to her travelling companion. The time for polite pleasantries was long over. The virus saw to that. The taxi driver didn't mince his words, just pointed at her beetroot face,

'What's the matter with her?'

He squeezed her hand, worried for her, reassuring her,

'She's suffering from acute anaphylactic shock. If I don't get her to my clinic in ten minutes, she'll die.'

The driver blanched, taken aback, 'I'm sorry, I have to ask...'

'Yes, we're both clean.'

'Get in.'

She was shivering in the warm sunshine, working up a fever. Beads of perspiration formed on her widow's peak. She slumped against him, exhausted by the collapse of her body's immune system in the face of the brutal bristling. Her body stung all over, leaving her feeling wretched, miserable: her condition only worsened by her tight-fitting skinny jeans and coarse-woven top. Resisting the urge to strip, she allowed him to bundle her into the taxi. He slammed the door behind him and let her rest her weary head on his shoulder as they slid around on the polished leather seat.

The black cab was perfectly-suited for transporting infected victims to hospital – a glass screen protected the driver from the herd. Payment was by contactless. The passenger windows were securely locked. They heard the door-locks click. The taxi inched forward. A mesh voice spoke,

'Where to?'

'The Martlets, Thrift Wood.'

'Nice! I know a short-cut through the woods. It's pretty this time of year.'

'Please, hurry.'

He felt her limp body sag against his as the taxi lurched forward. Held her close, protective of her. Her skin smelled fresh, natural, a slight hint of face cream. She wasn't wearing any make-up or perfume, didn't need to. She fell asleep in his arms. He was pleased. Proud of her. He struggled to keep his emotions in check.

The taxi turned right into the high street, accelerated, and shot past the watching shoppers. At the busy garage, beyond the railway bridge, they turned right, then left into a leafy avenue. The driver unlocked the windows so that his passengers could get some air. The young man in the back breathed in the fresh morning air, savouring the sound of birdsong, the warm sun on his face, as the taxi swayed from side to side, gliding past the estates of the wealthy. He envied them their peace and solitude, imagining them swimming in their private pools, sunbathing on terraces, playing tennis on secluded courts, behind their tall cypress hedges.

How many of them would escape the virus?

The taxi braked suddenly as a black cat darted out into the road. Her head slid down his hairy chest and rested in his lap. He stroked her hair as she slept, loving the feeling of her head on him. The taxi driver interrupted his thoughts, explaining that he'd taken the cab over from his father when he succumbed to the dreadful plague,

'I haven't passed my driving test,' he admitted, in a dulled voice, 'I only work locally. London's a no-go zone anyway. The Police have set up roadblocks along the forest road.'

'I didn't know that. Look, I'm sorry about your father. Did they let you see him?'

'Thanks. He died in hospital on a ventilator. I wasn't allowed to visit. There won't be a funeral.'

They continued the journey in silence. The sun went behind some clouds. He felt cold, tried to reach the window switches, but couldn't. The windows slid up automatically. He saw the brown eyes watching him in the driving mirror and nodded in appreciation. The taxi came out of the shadows, turned right into a winding lane, past an empty playing field, a vacant farm, rows of silent council houses. They reached The Martlet's, a development of luxury apartments on the boundary of Thrift Wood. His wallet was in his back pocket. He reached back. She stirred. The driver spoke, his voice choked with emotion,

'There's no need to pay. This one's on me. Look after her, won't you? She's a beautiful lady.'

She looked over his shoulder at the driver as he helped her out of the car.

He looked so young.

'I will. Thank you. You're kind. Take care.'

'Don't mention it. Stay safe.'

He stood and watched the taxi trundle off down the lane in the direction of Brentwood. She slumped against him, barely able to stand. He slipped a hand under her armpit to support her, feeling the soft mound of her little breast. She let him hold her there, loving his tender touch, hoping he would save her life. He felt her tense and bristle, her heat spreading on his fingertips, then told her of the cure,

'When we enter the apartment, undress in the second bedroom, and go to the bathroom. Your treatment involves full body suspension in a hot foam bath, scented with a natural herb remedy. When you have bathed and dried yourself, return to the bedroom. On the bed you'll see I've laid out the only clothes you will be able to wear going forward. Get dressed, come to the lounge, and I'll call a cab to take you home. The treatment takes three months to work. After that, if all goes to plan, you'll never suffer the bristling again. I know you haven't got any money. Don't worry, I won't be charging you. This is for free.'

She stared up at his face. His nose was too big like a hooter. His button ears were well set back. He reminded her of a friendly gnome, she used to see in her neighbour's garden when she was a little girl living in the Suffolk countryside. But his eyes were full of love and kindness.

His apartment was on the second floor. He slipped his free hand into his trouser pocket and dug out a key fob, pressing it against Flat 7. She managed a tiny smirk: seven was her lucky number. He pushed the glass door open with his rear and manoeuvred her into the lobby. There was a colourful montage covering the length of the wall: a rocky beach, sluggish olive sea, set against a cloudless azure sky. He vowed to find the location, and take her there one day, if she pulled through. He pressed 2. The lift door slid open.

Flat 7 was half-way down a silent corridor, its walls were drab, grubby fawn. Her body slumped against his. He wrapped an arm around her waist, unlocked the door, stepped inside. She began to hyperventilate. Quickly, he showed her the bathroom, guided her past the plate-glass window of his bedroom to the spare room.

She vaguely took in her surroundings. The place reeked of wealth, his masculinity. Save for a double bed with black sheets, pillows, grey duvet, floor-to-wall mirror, white built-in cupboard, a photo of a young girl with wavy blonde hair (her?) on the bedside table, and a stack of GQ magazines, the room was empty. There was an open sliding glass partition to a small balcony overlooking a deserted playing field. She sat on the bed, started to undress. He couldn't bear to watch her. He turned away,

'I'll go and run your bath,' he said sheepishly, 'Soak yourself until the water is cold. Dry off with the soft white bath towels on the bath rail. Then put these on, only these, no underwear.'

He slid the fitted wardrobe open and produced a soft white jacket top with a wraparound sash at the waist, and a pair of soft white slacks, not dissimilar to those that he was wearing. He held them up for her to see,

'Softened by the monsoon dew.'

She smiled appreciatively: he was lovely, such a lovely man.

I know! she mused, *and the moon is made of cheese!*

That word again: soft. He left the clothing on the bed for her and went to the bathroom,

'When you're decent,' he called, 'come through to the lounge and I'll make us some brunch.'

Her heart seemed to swell in her chest. He made her feel content, secure, needed. She had never felt so happy:

I'm falling in love with him, she dreamed, pressing her palms to her chest, *I can feel him, here, in my heart. Hope he feels the same way about me.*

With a deep sigh of relief, she pulled her coarse woollen top off over her head, unbuttoned her skinny jeans, peeling them off her legs. She reached behind her back, undid a clasp, and slipped off her black bra. The sun's warmth permeated her skin, lifting her spirits even higher. She sat on the edge of the bed in her black panties, relishing the moment, wishing it would never end.

Her face blushed.

The bristling returned with a vengeance, penetrating every pore, entering her body, her mouth. She felt her flesh creep from her scalp to her toes. Felt the rash, blooming in her throat, caught up in her breath. She struggled to breathe as the itching, stinging, searing pain surged like neat acid into her lungs.

This is it, she decided, *I'm going to die.*

He was foaming her bath, emptying the contents of a 250ml brown glass bottle of the cure into the water, splashing her water for her with his hand, imagining her naked body, soaked in suds. When her scream came, it was a hoarse, dry scream, a guttural death rattle, filling up her throat. It chilled him to the core. He turned off the bath taps, stood up, dried his hands, then walked to her bedroom door, dreading to think what he might find.

She was sitting on the bed, facing away from him, the sun illuminating her shiny hair. Her head was craned upwards. Her beautiful swan-neck stretched taut. Veins stood out of her: varicose, purpled. One of her arms was crooked and bent, the other she managed to stretch, straining her slender bicep, clutching a pillow. Her knobbly vertebrae poked out, like healing stones, along the length of her crippled spine. The muscles in her back went stiff, stone-rigid with tension. She was frozen. A morbid statue of herself. Unable to move. Paralysed with fear.

He stood in front of her, studying her petrified face: her eyes had nearly popped out of her head. Her nostrils were flared and runny, the corners of her mouth were drawn back in a hard grimace, a sardonic grin: her dreadful gape. She clamped her legs closed in one last, desperate attempt to stave off the bristling. Her body poured with sweat. Her black panties were soaked, saturated.

Carefully, he slid his hands under her armpits and lifted her to her feet. She felt like a tree in his hands. He was her gardener, come to plant her, give her new life. Overwhelmed with pity for her, he crushed her in his arms. Slowly, the bristling subsided. He felt her body stiffen. She clung to him. Fondly, he brushed the thin strands of hair out of her eyes, seeking to reassure her,

'It's over. The bristling's gone away. How do you feel? Better?'

'Mm, much,' she sighed, 'Thank you.'

'Don't mention it. Let's get you to the bath, shall we?'

She was deeply touched by his kindness, the affection in his voice, his tenderness towards her. *He might just love me*, she hoped. She slipped out of his arms, following him to the bathroom.

He sat on the toilet pedestal and watched her pull down her panties. She took his breath away. He yearned for her. Wanted to feel her little breasts pressed against his hairy chest. Wanted to slide his hands down her slender back and grip her soft buttocks. As he pressed his proud flesh into hers. But couldn't.

She looked at him enquiringly as she raised one slender leg and dipped her toes into the warm, sudsy water,

'What's the matter? Haven't you seen a naked woman before?'

He shook his head sadly, 'No, I only treat male patients.'

Never mind, she smiled, climbing into the bath. She let her body sink into the foam, exhaling pleasurably as the soothing sensation permeated her skin. The 250ml bottle was perched on the rim of the bath. It was empty. She picked it up and read the handwritten label:

Natural Remedy

Content, happy at last, she ducked her head under the water, flashed a wide, subterranean smile, and blew bubbles...

* * * * *

Softly:

ONE YEAR LATER, THEY MADE their way through the ravine, down the sandy path, until they reached the lonely rocky beach, washed by a sluggish olive sea, set against a cloudless azure sky. They found an empty patch of sand, unrolled their beach towels, and spread them on the ground. She turned to face him, her cheeks full of health and colour. She put her hands on her hips, looked up into his shiny eyes, and flashed him a lovely broad smile that lit up her face from ear to ear, dimpling her cheeks. He smiled back at her, an 'I love you' smile.

He was wearing a soft blue shirt. His sleeves were rolled up to the elbows, his arms covered in soft brown hair. He had his buttons undone, revealing his gingery, hairy chest. She loved his face, the swarth on his pock-marked cheeks. She stroked them, ran her fingers through his thin auburn hair. Softly, she kissed his dry lips. Her eyes twinkled. He grinned at her, lovingly. She felt her blush spread over her face, her body, felt wonderful,

'Fancy a swim?' she said.

He felt shy, awkward, didn't want to make the first move, 'I'm sorry, I can't swim.'

She loved him so much, craved his touch. His shyness made her want him more. She giggled,

'Just as well. Neither can I!'

She reached up and drew his head close to hers, smelling his natural aroma, rubbing noses. She kissed him softly on the lips, then deeply, prising his willing mouth open with her tongue. He stood still while she undressed him, pushing his shirt off over his shoulders, unzipping his soft white slacks, pulling them apart. He sprang out for her. Nervously, he fumbled with her soft jacket top. She helped him: untying the wraparound sash around her waist, slipping out of her soft white slacks, clinging to him. He felt her little breasts press against his hairy chest. He slid his hands down her slender back, gripping her soft buttocks, he pressed his hard flesh into hers.

After they had made love, she lay with her head resting on his shoulder, running her fingers through the hair on his chest, making him blush,

'Love you,' she murmured, dreamily.

His face flushed scarlet, he stroked her damp blonde hair, 'I love you, too. Will you marry me?'

'I might! If you're kind to me.'

She kissed his shoulder, felt snug, warm, and loved in his arms,

'David?' she asked, presently.

He gave her slim hips a tender squeeze, 'Mm?'

'You never told me what was in the bottle.'

He held her tight, whispering softly in her ear, 'Water.'

'Water! You cured me with water?'

'Yes, that. And a little drop of love.'

Selected, Really?

2020:

MARLENE AND I SNUGGLE UP together, lying on top of the bed, mid-afternoon. When the sun feels fiercest on our skins and our stomachs have had time for lunch to go down. Very carefully, she climbs off of me. Her breasts still heave from her exertions. Her soft, peachy cheeks blush like scorching-hot wildfires. She lies with me, her head resting lightly on my sweaty chest, listening to my pounding heart. Tenderly, I stroke her damp ringlets of shocking, white-blonde hair with the pads of my fingers: proud of her, loving her, admiring her. My wife is so lucky to be alive,

'I love you so much, Marlene, my heart could burst for you.'

'I love you, too, darling. You *are* my life.'

She whispers her affection for me in short, stilted gasps, sniffing. Crying for the baby she can never bear. I had 'the snip' for her. Had myself sterilized. Knowing that the act of childbirth would kill her. Gently, I brush the tears from her cheeks, and hug her body close to mine, as if she were my fragile doll, careful not to bruise her, or scratch her. One tiny bruise or blemish, the smallest of nicks or cuts – that's all it would take to kill her. She shifts her body up the bed, inspecting my face with her tired red walnut eyes, Marlene, the shielded, at her most vulnerable,

'Callum, promise me you'll never leave me alone.'

I promise her. I can live with her. I haven't left her side since she started shielding seven months ago. She has seen whole seasons pass. Watched daffodils, bluebells, tulips, wilt in our borders. Salmon roses, climb the garden wall in full bloom. Pears and apples, ripen and fall. Tomatoes, yellowing, reddening. The first mists of autumn. Watched me through her small glass bubble,

'Promise me, you'll die after me, Callum,' she says mournfully.

I solemnly promise. My sole purpose in life is to protect her from harm, to sustain her tenuous grip on life for as long as possible, until the inevitable slip, the tiniest blip in her concentration, takes Marlene from me. I do everything I can to prevent her from bruising, contusing, bleeding to death. I prepare her food, taking care to remove the sharp edges – bones, burnt titbits, pips, stones, even gristle. I dress her in soft clothing without zips or buttons. I bathe her, wash her, dry her, launder her clothes, wash up, hoover, clean the house, make the bed, open the mail, go online, and order the shopping, switch on the TV, charge her phone, take her calls, switch on her kindle, love and cherish her,

'How long must I go on living like this, indoors, Callum?'

For the first time this afternoon, I struggle to answer her. Mark e-mailed me yesterday on my private address. Mark, my best friend, in Louisiana. We grew up side-by-side in council houses. He prospered: went to a Roman Catholic school, grammar school, Oxford, achieved a DPhil in Biochemistry, emigrated to Philadelphia, moved to Louisiana, specialized in Virology. I left school without any real qualifications, struggled to find a job, reason to live, a sense of purpose. Until I saw the bizarre card in the corner shop window:

Full-Time Live-In Companion Required to Care for Haemophiliac.
Generous Salary and Comfortable Accommodation Provided.
Apply in Writing in Strictest Confidence to:
PO Box 54, Forest Avenue, Aigburth, Essex.

I recall how I took down the details, returned to my tiny bedsit, and flicked through my late mother's Collins Dictionary:

haemophilia – *n* an inheritable disease, usually affecting only males but transmitted by women to their male children, characterized by loss or impairment of the normal clotting ability of the blood so that a minor wound may result in fatal bleeding.

usually affecting only males…

I remember writing to PO Box 54, never expecting in a million years that the haemophiliac might be a woman. I received a reply three days later. To my amazement, Marlene invited me to her late parent's terraced house for an interview. We gelled at once, had the same likes and dislikes: music, reading, health, wellbeing, organic food, a love of Nature, flowers, and gardens. To misquote Mark: we had the same biochemistry. Marlene relaxed in my presence, confiding in me. Her late father was a haemophiliac. Her mother transmitted the disease to her baby. She had been damned for the rest of her life due to her mother's selfishness, for which they made allowances – in the form of a bestowed inheritance. I realized, then, that if my application was successful, I might never have to work again. We were attracted to each other. Marlene's heart ruled her head. I became her companion, her live-in carer, her lover. I will never leave her side. I vaguely hear her voice, insistent, raised, fizzing in my ear,

'Callum? How long must I go on living like this?'

I apologize to her, then I tell her the awful truth,

'Mark thinks the virus has mutated, become more virulent. There's no known treatment for Covid-21, little chance of discovering a new vaccine this, even next year, when we don't have an effective vaccine for Covid-19. He thinks you'll have to shield for seven months until the second wave has receded.'

I feel her hot breath on my cheek as she finally explodes,

'Seven months! I can't survive another seven months cooped up here, sealed inside this place. I'll go insane, mad. I'd rather be dead!'

Marlene's soft body sags onto mine, as if she is physically drained of all hope. Her purgatory could last forever if the 'man in the street' continues to act irresponsibly, spreading the deadly virus at raves, parties, gatherings. I decide not to mention Mark's concern that air conditioning in restaurants, shops and garages actually circulates contaminated air and distributes the virus. She can't take much more isolation, not even with me, unless…

The doorbell chimes downstairs.

'I'll get it.'

I watch Marlene turn away from me, roll onto her side, and swing her short legs off the bed. She sits still while she carefully puts on her soft hand mitts, stands up, and slips into her soft red satin Chinese dragon gown, tying the sash firmly at her waist. Then she skips around our king-size bed like an excited child, pads across the landing, and goes to the bathroom window. I hear her calling,

'Who is it, please?'

Seconds later, Marlene appears in the doorway looking mildly deflated, somehow hopeful.

'There was no answer. It might have been the Postie; he rings the doorbell. I'll go and see.'

I sit up, resting my aching back against the headboard, perch my silver Ray-Ban reading glasses (a present from Marlene) on my nose, and squint at my digital wristwatch: 15:46, blinking the sunlight out of my eyes. The Postie has arrived later than ever since the outbreak of the plague, never this late. So, who rang the bell? False alarm? Wrong house? A child's prank. Or a cruel hoax? I climb off the bed, throw on a t-shirt and shorts, and go downstairs.

Marlene is waiting for me in the hallway, clutching a plain white envelope. She holds it up for me to see, puts on her silly-child voice, and innocent baby-face. I love her when she acts happy!

'Look, Callum, it's a plain white envelope!'

'What does it say on the front?'

'It says: Strictly Private & Confidential, FAO Marlene Carlton,' she laughs, 'Would you open it for me?'

Despite her mitts, we are not taking any chances – the *slightest* nick. Marlene is an extreme rarity, a woman with haemophilia, one of fewer than twenty thousand cases each year in the UK. I am so proud of her. I love her, admire her. My wife is so lucky to be alive. Considering all that she has endured: the blood in her urine and stools, her large deep bruises, her frequent nosebleeds, and bleeding gums. The emergency infusions of plasma to stop her bleeds. I help her manage her condition, help her live as normal a life as possible. She is being treated with antifibrinolytics to prevent her blood clots from breaking down, fibrin sealant to promote clotting. But there is no known cure, unless…

I slit the envelope open and take out a single sheet of A4 folded three-ways, unfold it without looking. I hand it to her,

'What does it say, Marl?'

'It says: I've been selected.'

'Selected, really?'

'Yes,' she says, without a trace of emotion.

'Well, go on, tell me! Selected for what?'

Marlene casually shrugs her shoulders and smiles at me. Her smile lights her face like a radiant beacon of hope. She bursts into tears of happiness. I take her in my arms. She whispers to me,

'I've been selected for gene therapy, Callum!'

Gene therapy – taking normal genes (the ones that tell the body to make the clotting factor) and putting them into Marlene's body. The new genes *should* make the clotting factor in her blood rise, and greatly reduce her bleeding.

I feel as if all of our Christmases have come at once.

Marlene couldn't take much more isolation, not even with me, unless there was hope.

Now she lives, in hope, that one day…

Basque

Friday Night 19th March 2021:

HE WASN'T COMING. SHE COULD feel it in her veins. Lizzie picked at her last few, stone cold greasy bacon and cheese loaded fries, rubbing her bare legs to keep warm. An unpleasant fluid flowed from her nostrils into her mouth. She wiped her nose with the back of her hand. How could she forget to bring a hankie with her on a night like this? She checked the time: ten past eight. He was an hour late. Perhaps she should give him up, go home?

The kindly man in the snack wagon trailer sitting in the corner of the empty car park asked her if she would be alright? If she felt safe? A woman, alone on a damp bench after dark, miles from home. Lizzie thanked him from the bottom of her heart for caring about her – when thousands of men didn't.

'I'll be fine,' she assured him, 'I can take care of myself.'

If she was attacked, alone at night, she always had her phone. Lizzie was sitting near the bus stop opposite a row of dingy cottages lining the main road. If all else failed, she would hurdle the chain-link fence, leap into the middle of the road, waving her arms, and stop a passing car. Wouldn't she? Suppose he was stronger than her? Supposing, he fooled her?

Her bottom froze at the thought beneath her thin candy-striped dress. She wriggled on the bench to restore her blood circulation, rubbing her blueing hands, shrugging into her navy woollen coat to keep warm. Lizzie checked her phone: no texts or messages. His entreaty to her and, she suspected, millions of other lonely hearts on the dating app, had taken her breath away, being sexist, arrogant, self-centred - and intriguing. She scrolled his grinning face up on the screen and read his plea to women, for the tenth time that day:

I am looking for a beautiful woman, early 30's, to love, cherish, worship and adore. A woman seeking attention to herself. A Boudicca or a Helen of Troy to stand on my glass pedestal for all the world to see and fill the empty space in my heart.

Her heart sank. He wasn't coming. Lizzie stood up, brushed herself off, threw the greasy chip box into the convenient green bin and began her long trudge home. Her sullen mood was interrupted by the crunch of tyres on gravel. She stared in disbelief at the silver-grey Porsche 911 Carrera S glinting under the streetlight. The car interior lit up. The passenger window slid down. Lizzie recognized his warm-friendly, smiling, handsome, boyish face at once. He spoke to her calmly, eloquently in a sophisticated tone: clear, refined, and hot.

'Sorry I'm late. You must be frozen, Lizzie. Jump in. Let's get you home, shall we?'

She held back, nervous, frightened yet exhilarated, unsure of what to do next, 'Simon?'

He pushed at the car door, 'Yes, Simon. Are you coming with me or not?'

She had missed her last bus home. The forest walk was dark, cold, and lonely. His car offered her warmth. Without hesitation, Lizzie climbed inside, and firmly closed the door.

The car heater was on. Lizzie could feel its warmth heating up her bare legs, constrained, hemmed-in, unable to move through lack of room. Her legs were too long for the footwell. He regarded her slim bare legs. Perfect. Her legs were perfect in length and shape, aside from the pale beige skin imposed by the recent chill. He suspected they'd tan well enough, as would her arms, chest, back, neck, and soft face. Lizzie's dress was hitched high. Her thighs were on full view. She felt his eyes fall on her legs, felt vulnerable, alone with him,

'You're staring at my legs.'

He pulled his head away to face the windscreen, the dark void constituting her escape,

'Your legs are cramped,' he said, twisting in his sunken seat to face her, 'Open your legs.'

Lizzie was terrified, looking at him, horrified. Her stomach heaved, she felt a strong desire to purge out all her fatty, smoky, half-chewed, BBQ chicken morsels, fat-soaked twice-fried chips, sickly caramel apple slice. An even stronger urge to purge him out of her. But she couldn't resist her desire,

'What did you just say?'

'I said, open your legs. So that I can adjust your seat?'

Lizzie exhaled, 'Switch off the light.'

He dimmed the light. She opened her legs. He rolled the sleeve of his angora sweater as far as his elbow and felt her. She felt his forearm, resting on her thigh, the subtle flick of his wrist, anticipating Simon's next command,

'Push back with your legs.'

Lizzie pushed, hard. The seat jarred back. His hand slid up her thigh. She felt his warmth, opening her mouth for him. They kissed. The kiss of the starving, the lonely, the unloved. It had been months since she last enjoyed a man's touch. She offered him no resistance.

Simon slipped the clutch, released the handbrake, the car edged forward. Their way ahead was filled with promise, the road behind dark and foreboding. Lizzie relaxed in the leather seat, thrilled by her new-found luxury, watching the man's white knuckles grip the wheel. His eyes were fixed on the gloom ahead. She buttoned up her dress, clumsily, dreamily - in the dark.

'Look out for the deer, Simon,' she said, searching the forest verge for signs of life.

He glanced appreciatively at the umber silhouette of her beautiful face, 'The who...?'

'The deer. They've a nasty habit of running out in front of your car on this road. A driver hit one last week. It smashed his windscreen, flew through the shattered glass, and pulped his head and chest. The poor man didn't stand a chance.'

Simon eased his foot off the accelerator, 'Neither did the deer, innocent creature.'

Lizzie warmed to him, wanting to touch his face, feel his smile, his heartbeat. So, he loved animals? Could she love him one day? The intimacy of his caress just now wasn't lost on her; she'd liquified under his touch. At the age of thirty-two might she finally have found love? She studied his facial features fading in the shade: serious, noble, intent. Could he fall in love with her maybe one day? She hoped so very much being lonely, soothing him,

'I suppose not, but I wouldn't want that to happen to you. Would you come home with me, Simon?'

* * * * *

'I'M SORRY I TOUCHED YOU like that,' he said, climbing the concrete stairs to her flat, 'It was forward of me.'

She brightened, 'Don't be! I enjoyed it.'

He'd broken the rules, touching her there. They broke the rules. Supposing rules are there to be broken? Lizzie prepared to break another one. Her hands were shaking. She felt gut sick with nerves. She stood outside the door fumbling with her keys, then turned the lock, flicking a switch, holding his hand,

'Shall we go inside?'

Lizzie led. Simon hesitated. At the bus stop, in his car: Lizzie had projected the grace and dignity he was looking for: an intimate, sensual charm. He hadn't expected to find himself in this shit hole. The room was an absolute dump, a sordid stain on her refined personality.

On the left-hand side stood a broken flat-pack cabinet, torn-up Formica work surface over grubby pine cupboards, a fridge, microwave oven, and a bronze aluminium chair. Next to the microwave squatted a plate of half-digested mozzarella pizza. Simon estimated, from the dried sauce crust covering its rim, the dish must be at least two days old. He grimaced in disgust. Lizzie read his mind, and confessed,

'I live in a mess, Simon.'

'You live here?'

'It's all I can afford.'

He refused to comment.

At the lighter end of her abyss hung a woeful net curtain, full of soot from the trunk road outside. Lizzie's unmade single bed occupied the far right: the sad bed of a single woman. There was no art on display, pleasing ornaments or cameos, no book to read, evidence of learning, or culture. Just filth. Even the air smelt stale, a sickly-sweet odour of curry from the Indian takeaway downstairs mixed with an acrid stench of vomit. A thick brown drape cordoned off whatever lay behind.

Her sanitary facilities?

Hanging off the wall, opposite her bed, was a plasma tv screen, her only contact with the cruel world. He took in the threadbare crimson rug, the remote lying by the kettle, shaking his head with sadness, pitying her for living in such dire straits. If only he could help her change her life somehow. Frustrated by her mess, he made up his mind to leave,

'I think I should go.'

She begged him to stay, 'Please don't, Simon.'

He left her wringing her hands, without so much as a goodbye.

After he had gone, Lizzie closed the door behind her, took off her coat, and hung it on the back of the door. The room felt cold and lifeless without him. The emotional strain he put her under, excitement, anticipation, drained her energy. Reverting to her ugly stereotype, she withdrew into her protective shell, a hermit crab's solitary confinement, drawing back the curtain on her real self to reveal her unsavoury innards.

The box of tissues sat waiting for her on the cistern. The mustard-yellow lid and seat were flipped back, primed for her. She untied her lemon satin waist sash, unbuttoned the amber studs on her dress as high as her chest, then took it off. Lizzie knelt before the toilet as if in prayer, purging herself. Once she had sloughed out the entire contents of her stomach, she dry-retched, pulled the handle, closed the lid, and stood up. Wiping clean the corners of her mouth with a moist tissue, she appraised herself in the mirror: gaunt, tired, and lost to love. Lizzie brushed her teeth, found her phone, put on a nightie, then she went to bed.

For the last time, she scrolled his face up on the screen:

I am looking for a beautiful woman, early 30's, to love, cherish, worship and adore. A woman seeking attention to herself. A Boudicca or a Helen of Troy to stand on my glass pedestal for all the world to see and fill the empty space in my heart.

He wasn't there for her anymore.

She cried herself to sleep.

* * * * *

SIMON COULDN'T STOP THINKING ABOUT her. He returned to his apartment on the village green, made himself mint tea, which usually worked, then stayed awake, tossing, turning, trying to remember her face: her short, wispy, quiff of black hair, teak eyes, unusual skin, thin lips, glamourous high-set cheek bones.

The next day was a blur of fading memories, a vain attempt to put her out of his mind, to move on. Conquering his mourning for her took a monumental effort of will. He spring-cleaned the hall, bathroom, bedrooms, lounge, kitchen, and veranda to a state of hygienic perfection, sterilizing his Porsche in the residents only car park.

After a light salad lunch, he went online and reviewed the hundreds of options on offer. None of them compared to Lizzie. For all her squalor, filth and neglect, Lizzie the woman was naturally beautiful. Her stench had made him nauseous. He couldn't wait to leave the flat. In Simon's pristine world the slightest blemish, stain or smear made the difference between impression and distaste, excitement and disappointment, sensation, and disgrace. That was how his world was - in glass.

In the end he wiped her from his mind with a gruelling seven-mile run through the forest as the light began to fade. Only for Lizzie's face to return to haunt him at night, as he lay in bed trying to pluck up the courage to say sorry to her.

Next morning felt different. The clouds parted overhead, the sun came out, his spirits rose with the sublime warmth of spring sunshine through his windscreen. Shielding his eyes from the glare, Simon pulled into the deserted church car park, killed the engine, and felt for his phone. He imagined she'd be standing legs akimbo on her mat in her grey tracksuit, laptop open, tuned in to You Tube, waiting for Body Crew to start issuing her instructions. He wasn't wrong. The phone rang eight times before she answered in her rich, plummy, breathless voice,

'Hello?'

'5-4-3-2-1.'

'Mum?'

'And shake it off.'

'Just a minute, darling.'

He waited while his mother signed off. The video stopped playing in the background. She gave him her full, undivided, attention,

'Simon, how lovely to hear from you!'

'How's it going?'

'I've lost two pounds already! Two pounds! Oh, and I had my first jab on Friday.'

'Well done, Mum!' he enthused, 'Keep going!'

'I will! I will keep going. How are you, dear?'

'Busy as ever.'

Diana tutted, 'You're always busy. What are you busy with now?'

'I'm planning the re-opening,' he informed her, appreciating her vested financial interest.

'What is it this time, shark, newts, frogs, jellyfish, snakes, not those dreadful eels I hope?'

Simon laughed, 'No, no, no, not the eels! I'm going for something different this time.'

'I'm all ears, dear,' she keened.

'I can't tell you, it's a secret.'

'Ah! But I love secrets!'

'Sorry Mum, you'll have to wait until the opening.'

'Will I be invited?'

'Naturally.'

Her voice cheered up, 'Good! Then I shall wear my new dress!'

There was a brief pause. Simon pushed the car door open and listened to a cackle of crows cawing in some nearby pine trees. He took a deep breath of the sweet fresh country air, preparing to break the news.

'Simon?'

'I'm still here. Mum?'

'Yes?'

'I think I've just fallen in love. Think I've found the woman of my dreams.'

His mother's voice broke, 'Oh, darling, I've gone all teary. Your father would have been so pleased. What is her name.'

'Her name's Lizzie,' he said proudly.

'Lizzie! How delightful! And is she pretty?'

'Very pretty.'

'And is she like us?'

'No, I'm afraid she's not like us, not OCD.'

'Then if you really love her, you must help her, dear, and learn to accept your differences.'

Simon cut the call and climbed out. His stout walking shoes and rucksack were in the car boot. Once changed, he set off on his solitary walk, leaving a bunch of fresh daffodils in the car. The public footpath took him over a metal stile into a bumpy field full of horses. His spirits soared when he saw his faithful old friend, the piebald, grazing in a corner of the meadow away from the other horses. They stood out from the crowd, the two of them. The horse was black and white, unlike his future.

The lockdown almost put his gallery in the West End out of business. Almost. Had it not been for his mother's financial support his unique aesthetics would have been lost to the world forever. The animals were sent away to a private zoo in Kent while he decided what to do next. They were in safe hands, unlike him. Simon was lonely, emotionally insecure, a stifled flame of creativity waiting to flare, his glowing embers of suppressed passion freshly stoked by a red-hot poker called Lizzie.

He reached the muddiest stretch of the walk, a hoof-trodden bog of potholes by a brook, taking measured steps to avoid sinking in the quagmire. Simon lost his footing, wobbling, nearly falling over. Steadying himself at the last moment, he focused on the path that lay ahead.

The re-launch of the gallery, tentatively scheduled for Friday 25th June to coincide with the anticipated lifting of all restrictions four days earlier would be a private viewing, the likes of which had not been seen since 1991 and, he hoped, just as shocking. His attempts at emulating his idol's stunning art using live animals had paid the bills, earning Simon considerable notoriety as proprietor of a novel arthouse zoo in Mayfair before dwindling into insignificance.

The Physical Impossibility of Death in the Mind of Someone Living is an artwork created by Damien Hirst. Consisting of a tiger shark preserved in formaldehyde, displayed in a vitrine, it was sold for an undisclosed amount estimated to be eight to twelve million dollars.

Simon crossed the second horse field in a daze, passing through a metal stile to a wildlife conservation area criss-crossed with badger setts, pitted with foxholes, erupting molehills. He remembered the illuminated skull, another Hirst masterpiece, that he first experienced inside a tiny blacked-out room at an ancient stone gallery off the main square in Florence.

For the Love of God is a sculpture. It consists of a platinum cast of an 18th century skull encrusted with 8,601 flawless diamonds including a pear-shaped pink diamond located in the forehead known as the Skull Star Diamond. The skull's teeth are original and were purchased by Hirst in London.

The bomb-hole was filled with crystal clear water - no-one knew its true depth - situated in a vast stubbled cornfield off the main footpath. Simon wouldn't be disturbed here. He could swim wild, swim free: unclothed, unshackled, uninhibited. He stood at the lakeside stripping off his clothes, then plunged into the icy water, his invigorated mind fermenting innovation, culturing thrills, cultivating adventures in contemporary art.

He struck out for the far bank, imagining Lizzie's face embedded in glass.

* * * * *

SHE SLIPPED OFF HER NIGHTIE and stood in front of the mirror, inspecting herself: tall, slim, graceful, as beautiful as ever,

'You're looking great today, Lizzie. Not a single hair out of place. Not a spot, mole, pimple, wart, birthmark, cut, bruise, sore, chafe, abrasion, weal, burn or graze. Beautiful!'

'Thank you.'

She smeared her armpits with deodorant: no pulls or lumps or ouch, twinges in her breasts,

'See, you haven't got breast cancer. In fact, you have the perfect body, a lovely skin, and a perfect complexion. Life could be worse, much worse. Not a good time to fall ill, is it?'

Lizzie pushed her right leg forward, bent at the knee, stretching upwards, trying to touch the ceiling as if she were reaching for the stars, repeating the lunges for forty-five seconds,

'Suppose you're right. Should count, myself lucky,' she breathed, switching to her other leg.

Conversations like these were not uncommon in Lizzie's lonely life. Ever since she was a little girl at the orphanage, she had kept a confidante, an invisible friend, on her shoulder. Who looked like her in the mirror. Who talked like her. Almost.

Same, same but different as Kim taught her in Vietnam. She closed her eyes, threw up her arms, and stood with her feet one hip-width apart. Remembering the Chinese lanterns swaying in the hot breeze over the river at Hoi Ann at night. The water puppet theatre in Ho Chi Minh City. The tunnels of Cu Chi. Their struggles. Kim taught her their struggles for freedom. How to carry on against impossible odds, when all seemed lost, and triumph over adversity. Lizzie side-lunged for forty-five seconds, then changed sides,

'I dreamed of him last night,' she admitted.

'Tell me about your dream.'

'I dreamed we fell in love, and he worshipped and adored me, his Venus de Milo with arms, standing there before him, on his glass plinth, in all my naked glory. I dreamed we made love on glass.'

Lizzie shut up while she got down on her hands and knees, working herself hard with two minutes-worth of burpees. She prepared to lateral deep squat,

'You should have been a writer, Lizzie,' she told herself, 'with an imagination like that!'

'Could have been a lot of things,' she pushed-up off the floor, raising and extending one long, bare leg at a time, 'a model, air hostess, actor, a celebrity. A shining star for all the world to admire…'

Her other self interrupted her, 'But you're a dental receptionist. Not much fun, is it? Being a dental receptionist. Why didn't you?'

Lizzie curtsied, ninety seconds of curtsy lunges, 'I suppose I lacked the confidence after what took place at the orphanage.'

Mountain climber. She became a mountain climber, pushing up, legs extended, bending at the knee, raising one leg, then the next,

'And now you're lonely.'

Push-up, jumping jacks, push-up, jumping jacks. Come on Lizzie, you can do this, you can change your life, come on, cross the t off can't, you can do this, change your life...

'Yes, now I'm lonely.'

Relax, lie on my back, knees bent, feet flat on the floor, shoulder-width apart.

Imagine I'm with him.

Push up my glutes and trunk as far as I can, engage my muscles.

Imagine I'm making love to him.

Her best friend, her only true friend, spoke up for her,

'You loved him, didn't you, Lizzie? Loved his touch.'

Push-up to plank.

Imagine I'm under him, all over him.

'I loved the way he challenged me. I want excitement, crave adventure, seek the struggle, demand the triumph only he can give me. I'm changing my ways for good. Goodbye to my sick, my bulimia, I can beat that, fight that. I want him back. I'll start by cleaning out this tip.'

Push-up to plank.

You can do this, Lizzie. You can do this.

She lay on her back, naked on the floor, raised her legs, arms, bent her knees: a dead fly.

The Crunch:

'But he left you, didn't he?'

She curled up in a ball and held herself, 'Yes.'

'Gone,' she wept gently, the tears of the lonely.

'Forever?'

Lizzie felt the acid bile rise in her gut – the mountain berry fruit and fage from breakfast.

'Yes,' she cried, crumpling on the floor, 'forever.'

SIMON LEFT THE DAFFODILS ON his father's grave, drove to his luxury apartment, and entered a period of self-imposed isolation which he was prone to do when planning his next move, or licking his wounds. Lizzie hadn't made contact. He didn't expect her to. She probably felt too hurt, wounded by his rudeness, moving on, ready to start another search for love.

His was the next move.

He spent the mornings creating a concept for his exhibition in June. Defining exhibits. Designing displays in terms of capacity, shape, form, colour, texture, size, environment, atmosphere, content. Then there was the frequency of openings to consider. How many guests to invite. The all-important admission fee for this 'fantastic never-to-be-forgotten experience'. His client's safety: face masks, hand sanitizers, sanitation, social distancing.

Simon planned on giving a brief personal welcome to no more than thirty clients (half the usual amount) in the foyer over a glass of Prosecco, peach Bellini, cranberry, melon juice. Or one of his famous traffic light cocktails: red cherry brandy on amber amaretto on green crème de menthe. That should set tongues wagging! Oh, and some dried, non-greasy eats: toasted naan-style flatbreads with brie and cranberry crusts, dry snacks: corn chips, salted macadamia, wasabi, the sort of thing he could knock up at home. He never used caterers, preferring to host the evenings himself, four evenings a week:

Thursday to Sunday: matinee 5.30pm for 6pm followed by a late-night display 7.30pm for 8pm kick-off.

After his introduction, guests would be invited to enter the blacked-out viewing suites in pairs to marvel at his creations, illuminated by ceiling mounted accent lights directed at the displays. Flash photography would be prohibited, as would eating, drinking, smoking, and touching exhibits. Autographed portraits of the displays would be made available for clients to buy in a choice of colourful frames, together with virtual reality tour CD-ROMs of the suites, the latest computer-generated digital montages of exhibits in different poses, and copies of his book, from the foyer. All that was missing were the displays themselves.

The afternoons, Simon spent working out with weights, intense floor exercises, keeping his magnificent body in shape for her, thinking of her, his beloved possession, his future. How to win her back? He decided to order her an unusual gift, a token of his affection for her, befitting her grace and style, an invitation that might yet change her life.

After his routine power naps, he listened to expressive music: Arcade Fire, his favourite creative group, cooked himself light healthy suppers, checked his social media messages, took early baths, then went to bed to read: the latest futuristic science fiction and fantasies.

Saturday nights were reserved for click-and-collect and pay-at-pump sessions at the local supermarket. Life in lockdown took a structure, a framework Simon used to stop himself going insane. His sense of loss, his grief for Lizzie, turned to heartache. Throwing caution to the wind, he went online and ordered her surprise.

On Sunday night, he watched his favourite film, Nocturnal Animals.

He didn't return to the bomb-hole until Monday, a beautiful, warm sunny day with a mild south-westerly wind, perfect for swimming. Alone with his thoughts, Simon plunged into the ice-cold water, crawling as far as the mass of tangled brambles, lichen-petrified trees, and bushes covering the far bank. Treading water, he swivelled his body, breast-stroking back to the solitary fishing swim where he left his clothes. He heard a foreign voice,

'Hi, I'm Joely. Mind if I swim here, too?'

She spoke in a Deep Southern drawl: Alabama, Louisiana, Mississippi? And had the most achingly beautiful face he'd ever seen clear blue eyes, a sexy snub nose, thick strawberry lips, a pronounced chin. Her face was surrounded with shade-upon-shade of fiery red hair: copper, chestnut, ginger, amber, an ocean of full and flirty waves that rolled over her chest and shoulders, ending in delightful oaken ringlets. Her skin was as pale as clotted cream. He worried that she might burn in the fierce afternoon sun.

Joely: my perfect redhead.

'You're American,' he said.

She dropped her jute bag on the ground and took off her ash grey t-shirt, running shoes, and tracksuit bottoms, revealing a striking magenta swimsuit.

Standing, hands-on-hips, her pretty head cocked to one side, she watched him tread the underwater current with his muscular legs,

'Is it that obvious?'

She sounded worried.

He reassured her, 'You have a lovely voice. Where are you from?'

Joely stooped and splashed her face and chest with water, it was freezing cold, it felt great,

'Mississippi originally. I live here in the village now. Share a house with six other girls.'

Simon recalled a house that he drove past on the way to the church: its high walls, locked gates, closed-circuit security cameras, the flag, fluttering limply in the mild spring breeze,

'The one with the Stars and Stripes?'

An American in Essex.

'That's right! Think I should swim now, don't you? Before I catch cold?'

There was a sunken bench, a relic of long-lost summer picnic outings, before the crater was formed by an enemy bomber shedding its payload after a midnight raid, then flooded, forming a natural lake. Simon swam over and stood on it. The water came up to his waist. He flexed his biceps, triceps, pecs, and abs in a valiant one-on-one attempt to impress her,

My Darcy, Joely imagined, flushing, *only hotter.*

She crouched on the bankside preparing to dive in. He admired the perfect musculature, her poise, her strength. Suspecting, she worked out in a closed private gym to keep herself slim and fit. Suspecting, Joely could hold a pose, control her breathing, hold herself rigid for him. She was nearly in his grasp, at touching distance. He thrust his pelvis at her. A naughty smile spread across her face as she sized the eel dangling between the man's legs.

He blushed, 'Sorry, I forgot my trunks.'

'That's okay. I've seen a man's cock before.'

I bet you have, he dreamed, 'I'm Simon.'

'Good to meet you, Simon. Let's swim, shall we?'

Joely dived into his life headfirst, powering off across the lake face down in the water, her strong arms cutting through the chill, throwing her head back every few strokes to suck in the tepid air.

Admiring her from afar, Simon turned in the water, then followed her, calm, preoccupied with her future. Joely's body was well-toned and perfectly proportioned. He imagined her head and torso mounted in glass.

She had different ideas. Men, particularly lean, mean, charming men were hard to find in a rural village during lockdown. Joely decided to take matters into her own hands.

After swimming fifty lengths past two disinterested geese, exhausting herself, she headed back to the bank. The water was deeper than her five-foot six height. There was an orange lifebelt suspended over her head on the bank, next to a sun-blanched sign which read:

DANGER DEEP WATER

With immense effort, she grasped the side and heaved herself out, falling flat on her face in the grass. Laughing, dripping wet, skin coated in goosebumps, Joely hauled herself up and tugged a beach towel out of her jute bag. Simon was swimming towards her, ten yards out. She dabbed the sun glare from her eyes. He reached the bank, watching avidly as she pulled the straps down on her swimsuit, exposing her bare creamy shoulders, her chest, a subtle invitation to him,

'Come in, Simon.'

You sound like my mother when I was young, he reflected, *Come in, Simon, it's teatime.*

He clambered out of the water, instinctively covering himself with the ridiculously small white hand towel, he stole from a luxury hotel in New York. Embarrassed, he reddened, looking away from her, drying himself as best he could. Other than some fine hair on his forearms, a line of fluff running down his belly, his body was bald, solid muscle. Simon shivered; the veins jutted out of his biceps. Joely was thrilled to bits. She encouraged him,

'No need to be shy. You've got a lovely body.'

'It's been so long since I met a woman.'

'I know how you feel,' she sighed, 'this lockdown's been tough for all of us. Look at me.'

He watched Joely peel off her swimsuit, leaving it slopped in a wet heap around her feet.

She handed him her towel,

'Dry me.'

Simon dried her roughly: her head, torso, arms, and legs.

'Let me hold you.'

She held him tenderly in her soft hands. They kissed and embraced. They lay on her towel.

After they'd heavy-petted, Simon escorted Joely to the main footpath, following a freshly excavated ditch bordered by piles of stricken branches, clumps of mud, a ridge overgrown with brambles, hawthorn bushes in bridal blossom.

Joely explained that she was single, an unemployed actress waiting for the theatres to re-open, barely surviving on furlough. Seeking excitement. She stared at the olive-green water in the ditch, a messy vinaigrette leading nowhere, like her life, and asked him,

'Can I see you again?'

'If you want to.'

'I do want to.'

They exchanged numbers as they reached three red fir trees where the path diverged: left for the church, right for the village. There was a crude wooden footbridge, planks over a muddy stream, steps leading to the primary school. They listened to the sound of children playing. Joely let go of his hand and kissed him on the lips,

'This is me, I'm afraid, Simon,' she said, 'This is *me*.'

* * * * *

Thursday 1st April:

THE DOOR BUZZER SOUNDED JUST as the phone started to ring. Lizzie answered the phone,

'Dentists, would you hold a moment, please?'

Quickly, she edged out from behind her desk, crossed the small reception area and opened the door. It was Montgomery, wearing a crooked black face mask, looking to all intents and purposes like a masked bandit, for his five o'clock with Ashkira. Lizzie adjusted her mask and checked,

'Mr Montgomery?'

'It is!'

'Would you like to come in and take a seat? The dentist will see you in a few minutes.'

'Thank you.'

Lizzie gave her patient a polite smile, shut the door, and returned to the desk,

'Sorry to keep you waiting. How may I help you?'

'I've got toothache,' a miserable voice complained at the other end of the line.

'Sorry to hear that. May I take your name, please?'

'Smith. Ned Smith.'

'One moment.'

She scrolled through the database on her screen,

'Ah, here we are, Mr Smith. Can I just check your date of birth?'

'29th April 1997.'

'Thank you. And what seems to be the problem?'

He sounded irritated, 'I told you, didn't I?'

She frowned, *an awkward customer. Never mind, going home in half an hour,* 'Sorry?'

'I've got toothache. I want to see a dentist.'

Very awkward.

Lizzie stayed calm, ever the professional,

'I'm sorry, Mr Smith, our appointments are all taken today. We close at five-thirty. If you're in pain I can see if I can fit you in on Tuesday.'

'Course I'm in pain. I can't wait till Tuesday. I want to see a dentist.'

Unpleasant callers like this patient were increasingly common during lockdown. Selfish, arrogant, rude. Montgomery gave out a worried look that asked if everything was alright. Lizzie returned him an appreciative, if false, smile, struggling to retain her composure,

'Tomorrow's Bank Holiday I'm afraid,' she explained, 'We're closed until Tuesday. I'm really sorry.'

Smith's acid retort shook her to the core, 'Fuck off, Bitch!'

The line went dead.

Ashkira appeared just as Lizzie burst into tears, her face barely distinguishable in the see-through visor and mask, eyebrows flagging, forehead wrinkled with concern, wishing she could console her friend,

'What is it? What's the matter?'

Montgomery intervened, 'I think some idiot just upset your young lady on the telephone.'

'Thank you,' Ashkira said, stony-faced, 'Lizzie, if a patient has abused or threatened you in any way you must tell me. I can have him or her struck off our list.'

'I'll be fine. I just need a good rest, that's all.'

Ashkira wasn't surprised by her reply. It had been a long, hard slog for both of them since the reception team was cut in half. Added to that, the practice manager was on long-term sick leave, so Lizzie had to work every Saturday with the hygienist. She was shattered, emotionally, physically exhausted. Ashkira suspected, there might be something else the matter: love hurts, loneliness, a lack of will to carry on?

She persisted, 'Would you like to have a chat over a mug of coffee when we finish? I'll pay.'

The receptionist wiped her eyes, 'I'll be fine.'

Montgomery was ready for his filling. He requested a pain-killing injection. The dentist beckoned him towards her sparkling, squeaky clean clinic. She turned to face her friend,

'Go home and have a lovely, restful Easter holiday. Spoil yourself. See you on Tuesday. Now take care of yourself, Lizzie, and stay safe.'

'Thank you, Ash, I will. You, too. Have a nice Bank Holiday.'

Lizzie donned a black face mask, walked into the Indian corner shop, and bought six large Quality Street Easter eggs for herself to enjoy. She planned to eat them when she was lonely, three on Friday, three Monday, vomiting them up afterwards to keep herself slim. She wondered if she could face going back to work again next week. What was the point?

The grey polythene package lay on the doormat outside her room. She slammed the door, knelt down, tore off the wrapping, and read the bizarre message typed inside:

If you would like to be that woman, come to my apartment wearing my gift under your dress: bare arms, bare legs, no make-up, at 7pm on Easter Saturday night.

Simon

Apartment 10, The View, Aigburth Green.

For the first time that day, Lizzie's face lit up in a genuine smile.

* * * * *

Saturday 3rd April:

LIZZIE COUGHED, BLEW HER NOSE, threw the tissue away, and washed her hands. Standing in front of the mirror, she took a swab and opened her mouth, running it over both tonsils, trying hard not to gag. Cautiously, she inserted the swab in each nostril, rotating it slowly, soaking it before leaving her deposit on the testing device.

Her gift was on the bed. Intrigued by his message, she slipped it on, put on her favourite candy-striped dress, some sensible shoes, buttoning on her mauve cardigan to keep warm.

Two weeks had passed since their intimate encounter in the car. Lizzie missed his touch, his fragrance, his kiss. Her heart leapt into her mouth, contemplating the night ahead. Would he take precautions? She assumed he hadn't been so careless as to expose himself to the virus while they were apart. Assumed she was the only woman in his life. She sat on the bed reading The Mail, crossing off the minutes until her result flashed up.

The coloured control line next to the C indicated a valid test result. There was no line next to the T. Breathing a sigh of relief, Lizzie put on her mask and coat, and left.

The downhill stretch to the station was bleak and empty. In happier, safer times she might have expected to meet a group of theatregoers, partygoers, heading for the West End. She wondered if those days would ever return. Desperation borne of loneliness made her risk her health to meet Simon. He could at least have offered to collect her in his car. But that wasn't his way. He was a dark horse who enjoyed exerting control over her, she relished that. It never occurred to her that she might be putting herself in danger. Until she reached the stone steps.

The road ended abruptly, narrowing to an unlit concrete footpath. There were ten flights of five steps (she'd counted them often enough), leading to a blind corner, the shortcut to the station. Lizzie glanced at the smashed streetlights, gave a little shiver, then descended the leafy stairs. She reached the bottom. Who was waiting for her on the corner? A masked abductor, a rapist, a murderer, a gang of teenage thugs with razors and slash-face knives?

These are the fears sent to test women on the streets, to test me, she thought, the Reclaim the Streets vigils still fresh in her mind. I won't be cowered into submission by a warped minority of pathetic men. I deserve my freedom as much as they do and intend to take it.

She took a deep breath and turned the corner: no boogie man, no man with steel claws, no bloodthirsty beast wearing a clay mask. The coast was clear, tonight. The old tarmac path skirting the carpark was illuminated with spotlights. She felt safer, but still hurried to the station. The booking hall was silent. There was a train. She swiped her card and boarded. Her carriage was empty. The doors slid closed, trapping her inside. The train rumbled off into the night, leaving the lights of the town, passing sombre fields, forbidden forests, until she reached her destination.

It was impossible to miss The Green lying at the heart of the village, surrounded by a parade of shops, a closed village hall, a derelict pub at the north end, private residential homes on either side. Lizzie found the modern apartment block by the hall. The entry gate was signposted:

THE VIEW – PRIVATE RESIDENCE – NO ENTRY WITHOUT AN APPOINTMENT.

By the gate was a panel: numbered buttons, a grille. Inhaling sharply, Lizzie pressed 10.

A bell chimed, a mesh voice said, 'Come in.'

The gate clicked open. As she crossed the car park, Lizzie saw his gleaming Porsche. She smiled to herself. He clearly treasured his privacy. A secure door. She pressed his button. Simon answered, immediately,

'Come to the first floor. I'll meet you by the lift.'

She ran up the fire stairs, taking him by surprise,

'I hate lifts,' she panted.

He opened his arms, 'I've missed you, Lizzie.'

Simon was wearing the same angora sweater as last time, faded chinos, loafers, no socks.

Pleased that he hadn't changed, Lizzie stepped up to him, 'Missed you too, Simon - lots.'

They embraced. He made her feel warm, loved, secure. Made her life worth living. Simon cherished her. She felt his heartbeat against her chest. Happy, warm, content, Lizzie held his hand, letting him take the lead. They left the lift lobby. His pad was the one with owls faces on the doormat, at the far end of the corridor,

'We shouldn't be doing this, should we?' he teased, opening the door for her, 'After you.'

'I want to. Rules are there to be broken, aren't they?'

He didn't reply, just removed his loafers. Lizzie brushed off her shoes and stepped inside. There was a built-in wardrobe on the left. She let him take off her coat, bent at the knees, took off her shoes. Barefoot. He stood on the parquet floor, beckoning her. His apartment was pristine. Lizzie wandered past a glass partition into a bedroom, which was dimly lit.

For romance?

Other than a giant-sized black bed, the room was unfurnished. Hanging over the bed was an illuminated photo of a neon green frog. It took her breath away. She felt him join her. Felt him put his arm around her waist, loving him, holding her tightly there, she smiled,

'It's beautiful. What is it?'

Simon gave her hips an affectionate squeeze,

'It's a treefrog. They spend their days sleeping under leaves in the rain forest. If they're disturbed, they bulge their red eyes at you, flashing their orange-webbed fingers, startling you while they leap to safety. At night, they ambush flies, moths, crickets, with their long sticky tongues. Like to see some more?'

Lizzie was entranced. 'I'd love to.'

Simon ushered her into a second bedroom with sliding glass partitions, leading outside to a small balcony, and a mirrored fitted wardrobe. There were men's magazines: GQ, Men's Health, scattered on the floor beside the bed. Lizzie assumed this was where he slept. Otherwise, the bed was identical to the first: jet black duvet, sheets, pillows. The image on the wall was even stranger, if more familiar, than the frog: a hedgehog with red eyes and lemon-yellow spines. Lizzie was amazed,

'Why…?'

Simon explained, 'It's an albino, they're extremely rare. Like it?'

'She's lovely.'

He laughed, 'It's a 'he' actually. I cooked us dinner. Hungry?'

Her tummy was rumbling, 'You cooked dinner? For me?'

'I wanted to make up for the way I treated you. It was wrong of me to leave you like that, after I led you on.'

She held his hand, 'Simon, you didn't lead me on. I loved the way you touched me in the car. This is my fault for living in such a mess.'

He turned to face her. She looked beautiful sad. He would change her life. If she let him,

'Lizzie, I suffer from OCD.'

She shook her head in surprise, 'OCD? How strange! That makes us complete opposites!'

'They say opposites attract.'

'Yes, they do say that.'

'Shall we eat?'

'Can we? I'm starving.'

Simon guided her to the lounge. Lizzie's jaw dropped: the lounge was in darkness, other than the moonlight shining on its glass door. There were photos scattered round the walls, starlets spotlighted by discreet accent lights,

'My goodness,' she gasped, 'What are they?'

Simon introduced his friends: an albino koala with pink eyes, ears, and a leathery nose, a purple salamander, a mandarin dragonet, a blue, poisonous, dart frog. Lizzie stood still, mesmerized by the creatures' beauty, their explicit colours. As a child, she hadn't owned so much as a cat or a guinea pig. Pets were not allowed at the orphanage. She found her voice,

'You seem to have quite a fascination with strange animals,'

He corrected her, 'Not strange. Rare, exotic species. I display them as art. At least, I used to.'

Lizzie was shocked, 'You killed them and put them on display? Simon, how could you?!'

'I didn't say they were dead. Have you ever heard of Damien Hirst?'

She rubbed her chin, 'Vaguely. Didn't he display a pickled shark in a cage or something?'

Simon gave her hand a squeeze, 'That's right. Hirst preserved a dead shark and displayed it in a vitrine. I used the same technique, displaying unusual creatures in glass cases except that mine were alive, preserved in warmth and colour, bathed in light.'

'Isn't that cruel?'

'On the contrary, all of my creatures were comfortable, well-fed, cared for and safe, which is more than you can say for most animals. Since we seem hell-bent on destroying their environments: the rain forests, savannah, tundra, grassy lowlands, we leave these species fighting for survival. Unless we change our ways quickly, thousands of animal and plant species will be lost to future generations.'

Lizzie thought of her humdrum existence, the room, exercising to stay trim, her dull job, feeling helpless, inconspicuous in the grand scheme known as Life on Earth. She never seemed to find time to consider other people's feelings let alone the future of wildlife, her planet. She resolved to do more. Separating her recyclable plastic, cardboard, paper, and food waste might be a good start. Meanwhile, her mind filled with images of the animals, lit up in glass cases, presumably for the pleasure of richer human beings, until they died,

'You said 'were', Simon,' she ventured, 'What happened to them?'

'I had to close the art gallery when the lockdown hit us. Don't worry, all of my creatures were donated to a private zoo. They're well looked-after. Unlike us. We forget sometimes, we're only animals. We need caring for too. Shall we eat?'

He seated her at a black glass-topped dining table set for two lit by a single candle. A dish of queen olives, an open bottle of organic Fiano on ice. No fuss or flowers, quite simply, romance. She loved that. He wore his heart on his sleeve, treating her like a woman, with surprising respect.

What did he want of her?

Before Lizzie could ask, he pulled down her napkin, filled her glass, pushed the olives in her direction, and started to question her,

'Tell me about yourself.'

Lizzie spiked an olive and sucked it off its stick,

'There's not a lot to tell. I was abandoned at a food bank, soon as I was born, grew up in an orphanage. I have no idea who my mother is.'

He sipped his wine appreciatively, 'I'm sorry. That must've been extremely hard for you.'

'It was hard. I was bullied by the other girls. They hated me for the way I looked.'

'How did you look?'

'Like a big fat dumpling? Soft, doughy, round?'

Lizzie stared sorrowfully into her glass, her eyes aflame with candlelight. Simon reached across the table and gripped her wrist, impaling olives with his free hand, easing them off with his teeth, swallowing them whole,

'I find that hard to believe, you're beautiful and slim.'

She blushed, 'I met a man who changed my life.'

He found her intriguing.

What was it she said? There's not a lot to tell.

We all find a story inside ourselves if we probe deeply enough,

'Are you still seeing him?'

'Of course, I'm not.'

'How did you cope with the girls bullying you?'

'What is this, Simon? An interrogation?'

He shook his head, 'I need to know.'

'Why?'

He didn't answer. She gestured with her hand, accidentally slopping wine over the table,

'I learned to live with it. Hid myself from them, when I could, with my invisible friend.'

'You had an invisible friend?'

She finished off her wine, mopping up the spillage with her napkin. He refilled her glass,

'What was her name?'

'Her name is Lizzie Two.'

'Is Lizzie, too?'

'Yes, is,' she giggled like the little girl she once was, spouting proudly 'I'm Lizzie One.'

'Why do you remind me of Thunderbirds? 5-4-3-2-1! Lizzie-birds are Go!'

She put on her happy face and burst out laughing. Simon sagged with relief. He preferred this childish Lizzie to the sad, dull, adult version, couldn't wait to find out more, but first,

'I think the salmon's ready. Would you excuse me?'

He stood abruptly and ambled over to the oven, part of the open plan kitchen that sat in a corner of the lounge. Lizzie blinked as the lights phased on, absorbing her environment, his chic, minimalist, unadulterated luxury: white modular sofa, state-of-the-art immersive home theatre and audio system, contemporary shaker kitchen, all modern, all new, and meticulously arranged on the spotless polished wooden floor. Lying, incongruously, in the centre of the living space was a soft touch, shaggy, dense pile, teal blue rug. She wondered who that belonged to. Not him, surely?

'Can I help?' she called.

'No, you're my guest tonight.'

Only tonight?

He was wearing mitts to remove the baked salmon steaks from the oven. The night was young. Lizzie helped herself to a third glass of wine while he served the meal.

She let the salmon melt in her mouth: moist, tender, succulent, cooked to perfection, no less than she expected of Simon. Everything about him, his home, his looks, lifestyle, was perfect. Except for the gallery. That wasn't perfect. That was a closed crab shell waiting to be occupied.

With what?

'This is delicious, Simon,' she said, masticating, 'What's in the glaze?'

'Oh, just honey and mustard. Do you cook?'

He cast his mind back to the snack wagon. Lizzie, freezing on the damp bench. The dried up, half-digested pizza in her room. No, she didn't cook, from fresh. How did she stay so slim? And her skin. Her skin was blemish free. He might have expected a few fat spots on her chin, the amount of junk food she poisoned her body with. He watched her wrestle with her asparagus. If anything, it was slightly under-cooked by his standards. Tough. She would have to manage. Lizzie raised her head and studied his face, his earnest face,

'I'm a terrible cook, I'm afraid. I survive on pizzas, burgers, fish and chips, takeaways...'

He interrupted her, forking new potatoes as he spoke,

'I can't understand how you manage to stay so slim. You have such a lovely complexion.'

She dreaded this moment, saw it coming, the moment she brought up food.

Brought up food: bad choice of words, Lizzie.

I know, do you think I should tell him?

I think you have to be honest, don't you? He cares about you. Can't you see it in his face?

Simon stopped eating, resting his knife and fork, waiting for her answer, real concern written in his eyes. The candle flickered between them. The air felt thick, sluggish, gloom-in-the-room, stifling her. For the first time that night, she needed to be sick. Instead, Lizzie took a mouthful of wine, refreshing her palate, gulped it down, and told him the truth,

'I purge myself.'

His face creased, 'Purge yourself? What's that supposed to mean?'

Lizzie stared at a blank space somewhere above the man's head,

'I throw up the bad food I eat, all the fat and muck, cleansing myself. I cleanse my body. Gastric detox. Keep myself looking young. For everyone to admire. For you, maybe.'

She fell quiet. The silence sat on them like a heavy beef meal stuffing full a vegan's gut.

'You binge eat to cope with being lonely?'

'Yes,' Lizzie lowered her head to face his.

He pitied her: the sight of those glistening tears, welling in the corners of her eyes, shining in the candlelight as they rolled down her cheeks, breaking his heart,

'You're bulimic?'

'Yes', she was crying freely.

'I can help you. Will you let me help you, Lizzie?'

'Yes, please help me,' she implored, 'I can't live like this any longer.'

They ate the rest of the meal in silence.

* * * * *

CHRIST! HE WAS DIFFICULT, EMOTIONAL, hard for her to manage. Sometimes he would behave, focus on the assignment, not stray into her mind, her feelings for him. Others, he'd bare his heart to her, his love, send his intimate cravings to her. Scenarios, he called them. And she, in need of the money, agreed to record them for him. Trouble was, she was starting to connect, to empathize with him. Starting to enjoy herself. And she didn't know where to stop.

Joely flicked up her e-mails and read his deranged love letter to her one more time:

Hi Joely,

So glad I met you at the lake. I think about you every waking hour. You're brilliant, know that? You capture his voice perfectly, English, middle-class, arty-farty type. Wasn't sure you could do that, being American. I love the vulnerability you impart to her. She's just like that: emotionally vulnerable, susceptible to his charms. I should add, Joely, that she's desperately lonely, seeking adventure, a way out, and bulimic; she spews out food to keep herself slim. Disgusting, isn't it? Think I should let him help her?

Sorry, a few changes this time:

Can you make her voice sound more Essex? Not common, Essex – maybe West Essex?

Forest: it's pronounced forest as in forage, not 'for rest'. She's not going to rest, not yet!

Thank you, Joely.

I love how you bring them to life. Can't wait to hear you again.

I miss you,

Simon x

Her reply:

Hi,

Sure! I'll do those for you. By Monday if that's okay? Ready for more. If you are!

Take Care of Yourself,

Joely x

Her phone pinged. She stared at the unusual present lying on the bed, hand-delivered, left deposited outside her door, smiling knowingly to herself as she opened his message,

Who can this be from, I wonder?

The invitation she was waiting for:

Meet me at the bomb-hole wearing my gift under your tracksuit, bare arms, bare legs, no make-up, 3pm Easter Sunday.

Simon x

* * * * *

FRESH STRAWBERRIES, FAGE, SAUTERNES, CHEESE, Port. Other than a moderate excess of alcohol, which left Lizzie feeling merry, the meal was healthy. For the first time in days, there was no queasy tickle at the back of her throat, no heaving stomach. She felt happy, loved, and well. Wondering how much out-of-season strawberries cost, Lizzie decided to visit the market early on Monday and begin a new regime of healthy eating: five fruits a day. Her mind strayed into unchartered territory: his bold invitation, Simon's unusual request. She wanted to ask him what it meant, but he hadn't finished with her yet. He leaned forward and blew out the candle. Lizzie caught the faint smell in her nostrils. Black smoke. Rising.

He pressed her, 'You were telling me about your life.'

Eager to move on, she related the few highlights of her life as Simon listened, attentively. Lizzie told him she was adopted at the age of ten by the loving Clements family, growing up in their thatched cottage, attending the village school, making few friends. Her teenage years: her shame at being fat, the fruitless weight loss diets, punishing exercise routines. College: training to be a receptionist. Her thankless search for love. The job at the dentist.

What it felt like to be lonely and unloved - the endless drudgery of it all. Her face lit up,

'I won the lottery.'

He was stunned, 'The Lottery? How much did you win?'

'The Postcode Lottery,' she grinned like the proverbial cat with the cream, 'I won £5,000! Not a lot. Still, it was enough to treat myself to a holiday.'

'Where did you go?'

Lizzie perked up, 'I went to Vietnam on a guided tour. Have you been there?'

'No, I never travel to the Far East.'

'You should. I had the time of my life. Everyone is so different. So friendly. Proud. I met our tour guide on our first night in Saigon. He took me to an all-night bar for a beer. We sat and talked into the early hours about the struggles of the Vietnamese People, The War, napalm bombs, the hideous deformities the children still suffer to this day. He taught me to have pride in myself, never to give up the fight, however hard life might be. Taught me to purge myself, cleanse my body of all the fat, oil, and grease. Cleanse my inner soul. I sat behind him on the coach to Cu Chi, followed him into the tunnels where his family hid from the enemy until they emerged, victorious. The tunnels stretch for miles, Simon. There were hospitals built underground.

We went out to a different restaurant every night. One day, we paddled in boats along the Mekong until we reached a floating restaurant. They served us fish baked in river mud. Can you imagine?! In Ho Chi Minh City they cooked us street food in the gutter. In Hue I drank an iced coffee. Never eat the ice cubes if you go there, Simon. They're made of dirty water. I was so ill, weak with the trots. In the end, Kim brought a huge bowl of rice stodge up to my bedroom and made me eat it all up. It tasted like cement, but he clogged me up inside.'

Simon raised an eyebrow, 'He did, Kim?'

'Yes, he was my guide.'

'Did you...?'

'What kind of woman do you take me for?' she licked her lips, teasing him unashamedly.

He held up his hands as if under arrest, her arrest, 'Sorry, Lizzie, I didn't mean to imply…'

'A nun?' she went on, 'Of course we did. Every night. On my bed.'

'Sounds like you had an incredible holiday.'

'I did, I'll never forget Vietnam,' she said, sounding wistful.

He returned to his first love, 'Did you see any wildlife: monkeys, water buffalo, snakes, lizards while you were out there?'

Lizzie cast her mind back to the creature that ran in front of the coach as they entered the grounds of a Buddhist temple, 'I think I might have seen a gibbon. I can't be sure.'

'A gibbon?'

'Yes,' her eyes sparkled, 'And Kim hung a live snake around my neck for a photo in the jungle. He told me it was a python?'

Simon perched on the edge of his seat, 'A python? Good grief, what did you do?'

'Would you believe, I stood very still?' she laughed at herself, 'Now I work for Sparkler's Dentists. That's me, I guess.'

There was nothing left for her to say. He was about to make coffee, stack dirties in the dishwasher, drive her home, kiss her goodnight, say goodbye, she suspected, - except that,

'You haven't told me why you asked me to wear this basque?'

Lizzie walked to the teal rug, untied her lemon waist sash, slowly unbuttoned each amber stud, and slipped out of her dress. She threw it on the floor, her gauntlet, turning to face him. He was shocked by her transformation. She looked sensational. He wiped sweat out of his eyes. The basque clung to her body like a comfortable sheath, begging the question,

'What do you want me to do?'

He sat on the modular sofa, brandishing a Galaxy S21, 'Pose for me while I video you.'

Lizzie felt her pulse hurtling round her bloodstream, 'How would you like me to pose?'

'Lie on the rug. Imagine you're cramped inside a box,' the artist said.

She lay on the rug, held her knees, and drew her legs up to her breasts, in a human ball,

What must I look like? He must be able to see my...

'Like this you mean?'

The artist stood over her, circling her like a mongoose about to bite a snake, videoing her, capturing her head, limbs, her torso, from every conceivable angle, aroused by her shape,

'Yes, like that,' he sank back into the sofa, 'Bend your right arm at an angle. Push your hand through your hair. Splay your fingers. Pretend you're pressing them against a wall.'

She interpreted his instructions, 'How does that look?'

'Great. Hold your left arm up straight, spread your fingers. Imagine you're touching the ceiling.'

As if I'm trapped inside a coffin trying to push off the lid.

This was easy; she performed stretches every day. Her heart pumped love into her mind.

'You've caught the sun,' he told her, 'Your limbs are tanned. You have a beautiful body.'

'Thanks, I try my hardest.'

Try my hardest for you, Simon.

'Look the other way. I don't want to see your face.'

'Why not? What's the matter with my face?'

'Nothing's the matter. I just don't want to see it, that's all. Now, do as your told.'

Loving this, aren't you?

She smiled, looking away. Simon pulled his angora sweater off over his head, shed his chinos, sitting on the sofa in his boxer shorts. Seeing her, posing for him, felt as if all his birthdays had all come at once,

'Push your body up with your left leg. Arch your body. Balance on your toes. Imagine you're in a cage. Press your knee against the side of the cage.'

The instructions flowed thick and fast as the artist became more excited. Lizzie thrilled.

I'm in his cage.

'Bend your knee. Rest your foot on your thigh. Knee to the ceiling. Toes to the wall.'

I'm his caged animal. I want him to set me free.

The artist stopped filming. He set the Galaxy to mute, left it on the sofa. He set her free,

'I love you, Lizzie. Lie on your front. Stretch your legs.'

She hyperventilated with excitement, obeying his commands, waiting to be released. He straddled her thighs and unlatched the five silver clasps that held her bodice together. She felt his lips brushing the nape of her neck. Felt his lips kissing their way down her spine, plucking at each vertebra until he reached her L12. She murmured through her clenched fingers,

'How will you help me?'

He unfurled her basque, peeling it off her back, pressing the furls neatly into the curve of her breasts, her slender waist,

'I'll care for you.'

He ran his hand over the fine black down on the small of her back,

'I'll create an environment for you to live in that's warm, comfortable, safe and secure, ensuring that you're well-fed. I'll make you happy. Make your wildest dreams come true.'

Warm? Comfortable? Secure? Well-fed?

'You make me sound like one of your animals.'

She wanted him.

Natural instinct took over.

They prepared to mate.

He pulled down his shorts.

She unfurled her basque as far as her hips, freeing her breasts, then got up on all fours.

Like an animal.

* * * * *

Sunday 4th April:

LIZZIE SAT UP IN BED, stretched her arms, and yawned - after the happiest night of her life. They had spent the night having sex but she wasn't ready to have his baby. There was too much uncertainty in her life: the job, Simon. Was he ready to commit to her? It occurred to her that they hadn't taken any precautions. Should she be worried? He wasn't there to ask. She checked her i-phone: 09:06. How she missed the peal of church bells on Sunday mornings.

She blinked away her sleeps and scanned the bedroom. Her basque lay in a bundle on the duvet: soiled, saturated. Perhaps she could wash it off before she left? If she left. The sun burnt her skin through the glass. Her basque would soon dry. Lizzie didn't think to bring her bra, briefs, suspender belt or stockings. His instruction had distracted her. His side of the bed was empty. Missing his body warmth, the musky smell of his skin, she got up.

It wasn't until she went for a pee that she found his second gift to her, an unexpected gel in a white spray-bottle labelled Nestorone ® / Testosterone. Lizzie had read about this in a newspaper: the male contraceptive. Simon must be on the trial. She felt deeply touched. To think, he took the gel to protect her while they made love.

She found him working on his laptop at the dining table - in his birthday suit. He took a good look at her, standing still, across the table. If anything, Lizzie looked more radiant than ever. She blushed, then she went to be with him,

'Hello Simon, did you sleep well?'

He rubbed his eyes, 'Hardly at all, precious. You?'

Lizzie wrapped her arm around his shoulder and gave him an affectionate hug, 'I barely slept a wink.'

She kissed his forehead, 'You look exhausted. Come back to bed.'

'Will in a minute,' he yawned, 'I'll just finish this.'

'What are you writing?'

'A story.'

She was fascinated, 'You write stories?'

'It's nothing really, just a bit of fun. I took up writing during lockdown to kill the time.'

Lizzie peeked over his shoulder: something about a neon green tree frog, 'Can I see it?'

He sounded irritated with her, 'I'll let you see it when it's finished. Let's go back to bed.'

She persisted, 'Does it have a name?'

'It's called Basque.'

'Basque? What a strange name for a story.'

Simon clicked 'Save', closed the laptop, and stood up. They embraced. She felt his hands slide down her back, grip her buttocks, feel between her thighs. Felt her legs turn to jelly,

'Lover,' she hissed.

He pressed his flesh into her belly, felt her soft breasts rubbing his chest, gasping, 'Yeah?'

'Write a story about me.'

* * * * *

JOELY FELT THE WIND CHILL slice into her cheeks and shivered. He was late. She checked his text again to make sure she had the right time:

Meet me at the bomb-hole wearing my gift under your tracksuit, bared arms, bare legs, no make-up 3pm on Easter Sunday.

Simon

A group of walkers approached the lake: a middle-aged man dressed in a white t-shirt and shorts, an auburn-haired woman in her early twenties wearing a red mini skirt, and an old man with long greasy hair and a black tracksuit, carrying a cane. Joely felt conspicuous. For some irrational reason, they unsettled her. She didn't want to be left alone with them.

She cursed under her breath, 'Where are you, Simon?'

The woman, who was baby-faced, screeched like a child, 'Teddy, can we sit by the lake?'

'Course we can, Carlie,' soothed the younger man, 'You can dip your toes in the water.'

The old man tapped his cane impatiently against his leg, as if he were in pain, and leered at her.

Joely climbed out of the grass and strode off across the field. He wasn't coming. Hadn't even bothered to call. She decided to go home, hurrying to the main footpath. The phone vibrated inside her tracksuit bottoms. She pulled it out: Simon,

Can't park. Church car park full. Meet me at The Hart.

Of course, you can't, moron, fumed Joely, today's Bank Holiday Sunday.

'Sometimes, Simon!' she shouted, at no-one in particular, 'Some-times!'

When she had calmed down, Joely ambled down the path, past the firs, over the planks, up three steps, past the empty school, out of a dark alley into The Hart's car park. He was sitting in his immaculate Porsche, his usual smug self. He opened the door to admit her,

'I couldn't park.'

'Don't give me that crap. I've been waiting for ages for you. I'm frozen. I'm going home.'

She was misbehaving herself, hoo-hooing like a crazed gibbon, embarrassing him in front of the silent crowd of onlookers that thronged the beer garden eating pudding. He cringed,

'I think you should get in the car, Joely.'

She stamped her foot in anger, 'Get lost!'

'Get in the car. Everyone's staring at you.'

'Don't tell me what to do,' she said, sullenly, 'Be nice to me, won't you?'

Simon apologized. Joely climbed into the car. He drove her out of the village, into the open countryside, past the horses, until they reached the church. Other than a dusty black Fiat, the car park was empty. Joely couldn't decide whether Simon had lied to her earlier, about the car park being full. They parked on the verge, a grassy slope that led up to the church. The grass around the weathered graves was freshly cut. Dotted around the bank were tiny memorials to dead children, Joely presumed, white wood crosses, metal baskets filled with dried flowers. The lawn was covered in tulips, daffodils, early bluebells, dying crocuses. She couldn't help but feel overwhelmed; the scene was so peaceful and tranquil. The sun broke through the clouds, lightening her mood. Joely, felt much happier, relaxed.

'I'm sorry I lost it with you, Simon,' she said, faintly.

He shook his head, 'I'm the one who should be sorry.'

There was a pleasant silence. The sun felt warm on their faces. He felt guilty, tired, worn out by Lizzie who he'd left, asleep, in his bed. Joely held a different fascination for him. Her poise, her posture, and shape captured his imagination.

They watched an old man in a wide brim hat sit in a deckchair by the church porch and paint. The scene was idyllic, the air soporific. Joely shut her eyes, content to sink into her snug leather seat and doze. But Simon broke her magic spell, gently nudging her to her senses,

'The weather's warm. How about a walk in the woods? I brought a rug for you to sit on.'

Joely rubbed her eyes, only half-awake, 'For me to sit on? I don't understand.'

'I've a surprise for you.'

She perked up, 'What kinda surprise?'

'I'll tell you when we get there. Shall we go?'

* * * * *

THE HORSE FIELD WAS EMPTY. They crossed the sundried bed of a brook and walked towards a metal stile beyond an electricity pylon in the corner of the second field. Joely heard the rumbling noise first. She looked back at the horses galloping in their direction, and yelled,

'Run Simon!'

'What?'

He froze when he saw the rag of colts stampeding towards him. Joely tugged at his arm,

'Quickly! Move!'

They fell through the stile just as the first of the horses reached the barbed wire fence. Simon stood, bent at the waist, gasping in lungsful of air,

'What, what, happened there?'

'I think they expected us to feed them,' Joely laughed, barely out of breath, affectionately ruffling her man's hair, 'Are you alright, lover?'

She called me her lover.

Simon felt an inexplicable thrill coarse through his veins. He pictured Joely stretched out on a towel by the lake naked drying off in the sunshine. He straightened. She took him in her arms, whispering naughtily in his ear,

'That's what we are, isn't it? Lovers. Haven't shown you my lovely gift. Like to see it?'

There was a sign, nailed to one of the trees:

They had reached the woods. He led her through the trees, past badger setts, swathes of bluebells, until they found a lonely, grassy space, bathed in sunlight. The air was vibrant, alive with birdsong. Simon thought of Lizzie, lying in his arms, after making love. Could he possibly love more than one woman? He shook her from his mind and spread the rug on the ground. Joely undressed, sitting unlacing her trainers, pulling them off. Barefoot. She pulled the grey tracksuit top over her head then wriggled out of her bottoms, leaving her clothes in a neatly folded pile in one corner of the rug. Simon marvelled at her creamy skin, her astonishing physique. She was wearing a patterned magenta basque with a black lace trim. She crossed her legs, stretched her arms, and sat bolt upright, staring up at him,

'How do I look?' she purred.

'You look incredible,' he commented, breathlessly, 'How does it feel, comfortable?'

'I hardly feel I'm wearing it. I'm really pleased with my basque. Thank you, Simon. What did I do to deserve this?'

He couldn't answer her, directly. He flushed and looked away. They heard a rustling noise in the undergrowth: fox, deer, rabbit, a hare? A hare had bolted across the field in front of them before the horses stampeded. The sun went in, the clouds rolled over, Joely felt the first specks of rain smack her bare shoulders,

What have I just done?

'Simon? What is it?'

It was raining, quite hard. Joely stood on the rug and dressed. She broke his heart. Joely broke men's hearts. He struggled to find words to describe how much he loved her, and Lizzie, he loved her just as much. Joely laced up her trainers, feeling empty, cold inside,

'I'd like to go home now,' she said with a heavy heart, 'Would you walk with me, please?'

Simon picked up the rug and shook it off. He wrapped it round Joely's shoulders, covering her head, choking back tears as he spoke,

'Here, keep you dry.'

The rain streamed down his face. His hair was soaking wet. He held her close, protecting her from the driving rain. They left the woods, reaching the sign. She reached up for him, the rain splashing her face, in her eyes, running down her neck. Joely kissed him, fully, on the lips, murmuring to him,

'I love you, Simon. Talk to me.'

They stood by the hawthorn hedge; its bridal blossom, blurred by the teeming rain. Joely clung to him, caressing him, stroking his firm face with her soft hand, until he confessed,

'The woman in the story, she really exists. Her name's Lizzie and I love her. We had sex.'

A fresh wind blew in Joely's face, the clouds rolled on, the sun came out, Joely laughed,

'You had sex? When?'

Simon, expecting a hefty slap round the face, was confused:

Why is she laughing at me? What's there to laugh about?

'Last night, this morning,' he admitted, in a feeble voice.

'This morning! No wonder you look so tired! Mind if I ask you a question?'

Her eyes sparkled like dewdrops glistening in the summer sun. Her face flared with joy. He was stunned, amazed by her. They rubbed noses like horses, dogs, rabbits, deer, tapirs, animals. Human animals, rubbing noses, expressing love for one another. He breathed on her face: pure, warm relief,

'No, go on.'

'Do you love me, too?'

Simon said, 'Yes, I love you, Joely. As much as I love her. But in a different way.'

'We can always be lovers,' she ventured.

They stood holding hands like first dates, by the metal stile, watching the horses. Some of the colts were frolicking, rolling on their backs, waggling their legs. Joely popped her question,

'You said you had a surprise?'

Simon turned to face her, gripping her hands, staring into her eyes, broaching her surprise,

'I'd like you to perform for me. That's what actors do for an audience, isn't it? Perform.'

Joely cast her mind back to the animals she saw lolling on the rocks at the top secret naval base south of San Diego when she was just a child, pictured herself, returning to his stage,

'Yes, we do,' she reflected warily. It had been six months since she last appeared onstage. Joely trod the boards - carefully, 'I'm not prepared to be your performing sealion, Simon.'

'I don't expect you to.'

'What do you want of me?'

He told her what he wanted.

Joely sounded relieved, excited, 'Really? Is that all?'

'That's all,' he confirmed.

'And what do I get in return?'

'I'll care for you,' said Simon, 'I'll create an environment for you to live in that's warm, comfortable, safe, secure, ensuring you're well-fed. Make you happy. Make your wildest dreams come true.'

* * * * *

BASQUE OPENED FOR PRIVATE VIEWINGS at an art gallery in Mayfair on Friday 25th June.

Described as an artistic interpretation of the effects of environmental destruction on the survival of rare animal species, the exhibition features two permanent displays:

An Intimate Intrusion into Animal Love is a living model resembling the sculpture of a woman in a patterned magenta basque. Her head, torso, and creamy skin are discreetly lit by accent lights, sealed in a transparent orb. She crosses her legs, stretches her arms, sits, bolt upright, then she studies your face, like a monkey at a zoo.

The Frustration of Captivity for Humanity is an artwork depicting woman wearing a black satin basque, fully illuminated, displayed inside a sealed, rectangular glass box. She lies on her back, holding her knees, her legs drawn up to her breasts, creating a human ball. Her arm bends at an angle, her fingers tear at her hair, her splayed digits feel the glass, trying to touch the ceiling. She pushes her body weight up with her leg, arching her torso upwards. Balancing upon her toes, she presses her knee against the side of the cage, desperately trying to break free. She is looking away from you. You cannot see her face. Slowly, she rotates her head. Beguiled by her, you stare at her beautiful, frightened face, mouthing at you,

'Let me out.'

Their polygamy continues.

Taylin Stuns

2021:

THEY TELL ME TALK IS cheap. Well, that appears to be the case. If you believe the news headlines accompanying the hot Instagram shots of beauties clogging up my feed. Crawling expositions, such as:

Michelle wows in figure-hugging outfit in candid new snap.

Cindy displays endless legs in thigh-split silk dress.

Sofia floors fans as she poses in white bikini and diamonds.

Amanda causes a stir in skinny jeans.

Rebel looks phenomenal in orange catsuit – and fans are obsessed.

Kelly showcases incredible figure in hot pink dress.

Zoey's abs must be seen to be believed.

Davina stuns in sheer dress and underwear.

Holly stuns in elegant black gown.

They clearly haven't met Taylin.

Taylin *really* knows how to stun.

Taylin stuns us all with her beautiful face. She's lost weight. She looks incredible. Her ash grey eyes are clear and shiny. Her tears have dried. The bruises have gone. Her skin complexion is perfect, her turned-up nose delightful. She turns to face us. I see she's wearing poppy red lip gloss, my favourite.

Briefly, she glances up at the video camera mounted on the far wall, watched by an impatient, expectant world. Her husband looks down on her, unable to let her rest in peace, even in death.

Annabel, one of the new breeds appointed by the clergy, graciously nods her head. Taylin opens her mouth.

I sit with the other 18 guests, socially distanced, in the intimate seclusion of the small woodland burial park chapel, waiting for her to speak. A blinding shard of sunlight cuts through the dewy firs, warming our grieving souls. Barney is there, fluffy-grey haired, dandruff on his mourning suit, a black tie strung loosely around his scraggy neck. We are wearing facemasks. I avert my eyes, pretending not to notice him, embarrassed by his presence, worried he might spread the word.

Scandal spreads like plague in our little hamlet.

Taylin carefully removes her fishnet mittens, picks a sheaf of papers off the lectern, and reads:

'I would like to begin by thanking you all for the kind and moving words of comfort and support you have given me since my husband's premature death. You've all paid such moving tributes to him from across the world, whether it be the world of business, where he excelled, the world of jogging, for his charitable commitments and undoubted acts of generosity, or from the Clubs. I thank each one of you from the bottom of my heart. I appreciate that, due to this ghastly bug that's going round, most of you can't be with me today to share my most intimate memories but I know that you're here with me in spirit. For that Zac and I will be eternally grateful.'

She averts her gaze to Zac, her stepson, who is shifting, uneasily, in his seat in the front row,

'Zac, you are like a son to me. I would like to thank you for your moving tribute to Dad, your stolid words of praise for him, the pride you expressed for him, until he changed. As you rightly pointed out: it was as if someone switched off the light in his mind. Thank you, darling, for all the love and kindness you've shown me as your stepmother. Like you, I'll never forgive him for the despicable way he treated me.'

A murmur of alarm spreads through the chapel as Zac tears off his mask, bursts into tears, and runs to the pulpit to embrace Taylin. The congregation, the worlds of business, charity, sports, and Clubs look on as they hug each other in full view of the camera,

'That's alright Mum,' he cries, 'I'm only sorry I didn't catch the bastard red-handed in the act.'

Annabel is dismayed, 'Thank you Zac, for your kindness and understanding. If you could return to your seat now, please (*before you infect me*), I am sure Taylin will still be able to feel your warmth and love for her from there.'

I smile proudly at Zac as he releases Taylin from his love-clinch, dons his mask, and sits down.

'Well done, Zac,' I exclaim, under my breath.

Taylin turns her attention to me. She wants my love and support. No, she *needs* my support,

'Garrett, would you like to come up and join me?'

The congregation, particularly Gerry's friends and relations, bay, and sway in silent protest.

Annabel fires a look of barely disguised irritation at me, then coos, like a dove of peace,

'It's alright, Garrett, you can go up to be with Taylin. Don't forget to put on your mask when you come back down.

I stand up, survey the fools around me, then stroll up to the rostrum to be with Taylin. We hold hands. Her hands feel gravestone cold. I reach behind her, out of view, and gently rub her back.

'Garrett,' she reads, 'You grew to love my husband like a brother, with your passion for motoring around the Norfolk Broads. Such happy memories: picnics on the riverbanks, liquid lunches in the local hostelries, boozy suppers at the Club, drinking in the hostel till midnight. My husband loved to drink. Then you discovered the barbaric way that he treated me and agreed never to speak to him again. Oh, maybe once, at the very end.'

Taylin grips my hand tightly, her lips quiver, and she bursts into tears. I take her in my arms to comfort her.

'Thank you, Garrett, 'she sniffs, 'Thank you for all your love and kindness in my darkest hour.'

I release Taylin from my tender embrace and put on my mask. To Annabel's relief, I return to my seat and listen to her read,

'My husband and I were married for seven years, too long in my opinion.'

The congregation gasps.

'I would love to be able to stand before you all and say that I'm devastated by my loss, but I'm not. You are all familiar with his public face: kind, generous, charitable, funny, professional, a true gentleman who was loved by all. But did you know he had a dark side?

Taylin stuns.

The congregation brays collectively as she removes her high-neck black frock coat. Other than a solid nickel necklace, black stilettoes, black silk stockings, a black suspender belt, and black lace gloves, she is naked. Her body is covered in bruises. I worry she'll catch cold. The doors to the chapel have been propped open to allow the air to circulate. Taylin is shivering. I feel for her. There is little I can do to help. I catch her eye, mouthing silently at her,

'Put on your clothes. You've made your point. At least, I think you have. Put on your clothes!'

She ignores me,

'Did you know he abused me?'

The funeral descends into uproar. Several mourners stand, shaking their fists in anger, strip off their disposable facemasks, and protest. Annabel throws her arms around like a race official trying to flag down a speeding Ferrari, desperate to establish calm, peace, order, respect, love,

'Please! Be seated!'

We all sit down.

Taylin hasn't finished yet,

'Did you know he came home drunk from his boozy bashes at the Club and beat me black and blue? Well?' she screams, performing for the camera, 'Did you know that?'

The sense of guilt and remorse in the Chapel is palpable. Several mourners bow their heads in shame, others hold their heads in their hands and weep. The horror at Taylin's treatment sweeps the internet. In seconds, her beautiful crying face, her bare shoulders, will appear on news feeds all over the world:

Taylin stuns mourners with semi-naked funeral protest.

'No, of course you didn't,' she cries, 'You were too busy fawning over him to care about me!'

My heart goes out to Taylin. She stoops and plucks her coat off the floor. She puts on her coat, a black satin facemask, her gorgeous fishnet-lacy mittens, collects her notes, then steps down from the rostrum. Annabel shakes her hand, wraps an arm round her shoulders, comforting her,

'Thank you, Taylin, for that moving tribute,' she says, 'That must have taken an *awful* lot of courage,' she turns to face us, 'Would you please stand, if you are able?'

We all stand in silence, saluting Taylin's bravery.

The undertakers take up positions around the coffin. The head undertaker, distinguishable by his top hat and veil, issues them with a measured order,

'Gentlemen, if you please…'

Taylin stuns.

Throwing her body over the coffin, she grants her husband one final blessing,

'Goodbye, Gerry…'

The whole world watches her, expectantly, impatiently.

'…and good riddance.'

Taylin stuns me with her beautiful face. She looks incredible. Her eyes are clear and shiny. Her tears have dried. The facial bruises have gone. Her skin complexion is perfect, her turned-up nose, delightful. She turns to face me. I see she's wearing poppy red lip gloss. My favourite.

If looks could kill…

I always knew I could kill for her.

And kill for her I did!

Occasionally

2021:

EVER SINCE I WAS A little girl I've been frightened of the dark, things that go bump in the night, faces at the window, black mirrors, that sort of thing. I write about them – dark, erotic, fantasies. Those of you who know me, and read me, will understand why.

You see, I'm an insomniac. I wake up in the middle of the night with a story idea, write it down, go downstairs to the kitchen, and make myself a midnight feast of milky mint tea and hot toast. I live on my own in Marriage House, a red-brick farmhouse with a black slate roof, encircled by a dense hedge of dark cypress, well-established ivy climbing its walls. She knows the place well. I unlock the door and breathe in the cool night air, so rich, with the aromatic scent of pine.

I let her in.

The intruder stands behind me. Her mouth, nostrils and chin are covered by a thick black mask. Her shaggy teak hair hangs over her face, scratching her crazed walnut eyes, accentuating her baggy-lined eyelids, her umber weals of tiredness. She looks exhausted. I feel the tip of a knife blade press into the side of my neck, hear her excited voice for the first time,

'Do what I say and you won't get hurt.'

I decide not to nod my head, standing quite still, while she puts on my blindfold. The blindfold is made of coarse black linen. She fluffs my hair out of the way, then ties the knot securely at the nape of my neck. I feel its torn edges tickling my skin. The blindfold covers the bridge of my nose and eyes, ending above my forehead, at my hairline, my grey-streaked widow's peak,

'Hold your hands behind your back.'

She arrests me. I obey her, clasping my hands to the small of my back while she ties my wrists. I feel her cord cut into my flesh. I'm dressed for bed in a loose black chemise and panties. My world is black tonight. My whole world is black. I feel her soft hands, slim fingers, grasp my shoulders and turn me round. I am her dummy. Her robot. Her wish is my command. The tiled floor feels cold under my bare feet. She propels me towards the kitchen door. I relish the warm tufts of carpet between my toes, as we cross the hallway. She pushes me upstairs. I am bat blind. I can't see her but I can feel her, sense her apprehension, smell her nervous sweat. At the top of the stairs, we turn left. My midriff brushes against the smooth bannister. I feel myself being guided. I am forced to take three steps forward. She shoves me face-down on the bed. I twist my head to the right to breathe, careful not to let her blindfold slip, then I plead for my life,

'I keep the key to my safe in the top right bedside drawer,' I explain. 'The safe is located under the pillows in the left-hand bedside cupboard. Insert the key and turn the dial to the right. Inside the safe you'll find my passport, my most expensive, precious jewellery, my purse, a key, and a red notebook. The key opens my jewellery box which I keep under the bed. In there, you'll find my diamond necklace, diamond earrings, diamond pendant, gold bangles, bracelets, pearls. The notebook contains all my passwords, details of my bank accounts. Take all of it, but please, don't hurt me.'

The effort of revealing my innermost secrets leaves me drained of energy. I want to sleep, to dream, fantasize. Make her go away. I exhale, shutting my weary eyes. I listen to her reassuring me,

'I'll hurt you if you misbehave. I don't want your money. I want us to play games. You will play games with me, won't you?'

She presses the tip of the knife blade firmly into the side of my neck. I agree to play her games. She unties my wrists as my reward, and asks,

'Do you wear stockings?'

'Occasionally, you'll find a pair of black stockings with a red suspender belt in the top drawer.'

She looks around. We're alone in the moonlight. She speaks to me as if I'm a ragdoll, a corpse,

'Don't want to see you like this.'

She rolls me onto my back, then dresses me, drawing my stockings up my taut calves, over my knees, up my thighs, carefully attaching them to my ruby red suspender belt. I feel exhilarated. Can't wait for our next game to begin.

She leans forward and kisses me, tasting my flavour with the tip of her tongue. I feel her hands idly wander up the soft insides of my thighs. For a moment, she stands perfectly still. Then she lifts off my chemise. Other than my panties, stockings, and suspender belt, I am naked. She unties my blindfold and lets me watch. She is wearing a red short-sleeved sweater, faded skinny jeans, a silver belt. I marvel as she applies my make-up. My stomach is daubed with a tattoo of a magnificent scarlet rose in full bloom, its petals dripping dew. At my rose's heart she lays a solid diamond charm, sparkling violet, indigo, amber, emerald shards of light. Her beautiful phenomenon takes my breath away. I sink into my bed transfixed. Slowly, my petals unfurl. My intimate charm protrudes. She extracts her surprise from my navel and lays the iridescent gem in the palm of my hand. I ask her if I can keep it. She tells me, I can wear it as her keepsake, and gently replaces it in my navel,

'Sit up straight for me.'

I sit up for her. She puts on my blindfold. I let her take off my panties, stockings, and suspender belt. I am nude for her now, ready, eager, to play her next game,

'Lie on the towel.'

I feel the coarse texture of my beach towel lying on the bed beside me. I lie on it. Safe. I feel safe. On my towel. Happy, content, warm, secure, and satisfied. She tells me to keep still,

'Play dead, relax for me, let your body go limp.'

I close my eyes under the blindfold. My arms flop to my sides. My legs go slack. I fall asleep, dreaming that I am lying on her beach. I perspire. She rakes the wet strands of hair off my face, affectionately brushing my cheeks. I feel her place a warm bottle of suntan oil near my body, sense her squeezing a blob of oil onto her palm,

'Lie on your front.'

I roll onto my front and lie with my chin resting comfortably on the backs of my hands. She ties back my hair with an elastic band. Excited, I grip the edge of the bed. Although her tender touch will caress the whole of my body, she lightly covers my buttocks with a soft towel. She will soon strip it off of me when my skin falls under her soothing magic spell. Delicately, she glides her hands over my shoulders and neck, up and down my arms, kneading warm oil into my flesh. She rubs my back using long, deep strokes, pressing herself against me, so that I can feel her breasts, her hot breath on my cheek, fleeting kisses on my ear lobes, jaw, neck, spine. Slowly, softly, her tongue licks my lower back. I quiver as she removes the towel and spreads my legs apart. Gently, she massages my inner thighs. I tense as her fingertips gently brush my outer lips,

'How does that feel?'

'Mmmn.'

I roll onto my back. Once I've settled, she lubricates my chest, pouring oil all over my breasts.

'Be gentle with them,' I plead, 'They're sensitive.'

She massages my shoulders, working up and down my arms, using the balm to lightly skim my breasts with the palms of her hands, pausing to tease my stiff teats, circling my aroused nipples. Sending blissful sensations tingling through my body. She removes the blindfold, so that I can watch her undress. Breathing heavily, taking in deep gasps, she slips out of her sweater, jeans, bra, and panties. My jaw falls at the sight of her, naked, uninhibited. Her beauty intoxicates me. She licks her lips salaciously. Her eyes are eyes half-shut.

We embrace. She holds me tight, enjoying my hand buried in her soft belly, pressing her mouth against mine, her dewy, rose lips. Our membranes adhere, bound in an infinitesimal moment of intimacy. We pause to catch our breaths. She is crying. Tears of joy moisten her fiery cheeks. Her smile illuminates her face. Her soft lips brush my ear. I lie back and arrange myself on the crumpled towel.

She licks my tummy, plucking out my charm, tasting the salt in my navel. With my leg hiked over her shoulder, she kisses my inner thigh, massaging my soft, outer lips. By now, I am all dreamy, dripping wet, and smothered in oil. She kneels between my legs. I gaze into her shiny eyes, the luckiest woman in the world. She covers my eyes with the blindfold. I feel her tongue. My face flushes. My breasts swell. My heart races. I grit my teeth, flex my hips, arch my body upwards,

'What're you waiting for?' I slur, 'Want you.'

She pours warm oil all over me and massages my cleft. My skin feels soft, smooth, scintillated, blushing, I'm on fire,

'Oh God!'

I thrill to petit mort. She grips my hand and combs my hair. A single tear trickles down my cheek, from under the blindfold. Gently, she removes the damp cloth and kisses my face dry. We lie in our passionate embrace, our bodies entwined, her head snuggled to my sweaty breasts.

'I love you,' I say dreamily, 'You're my world.'

She tells me, she loves me too. My heart races with excitement. Her eyes sparkle like stars on a clear summer night. She smirks mischievously, twirling a strand of her straggly teak hair, and murmurs, in my ear,

'What would you like me to do next?'

'Kiss me.'

She kisses me, a longing, loving kiss. She is all I have left in the world. A tingling sensation passes through my body. Her cheeks blush roses. She asks me,

'Do you know what it means when we kiss like that?'

I only know I love her more than life itself. I sit up for her. She ties on my blindfold and forces me to stand in front of the bed. She maims me gracefully, silently, drawing the garotte tight around my neck. I thrash my head from side to side. My brittle nails tear out my assailant's hair. My elbows pummel her ribs. I strain and stretch, kick and bite. She clings on, until my near-death. Calmed, I relax onto her chest. I fall asleep, dreaming of the time when she made love to me. My neck still entwined, my sad head flops forward, my dead eyes staring into her empty space.

She waits by my bedside for me to come to. I open my eyes. The blindfold has gone. She hasn't put on any make-up. Her beautiful teak hair is a bedraggled mess. Her eyes are bleary, blotched blood-red with tiredness.

Dawn breaks at last. Sunlight streams through our window. She climbs onto the bed to be with me. We kiss and embrace,

'Have you missed me, Jacqui?' she says.

'Have I!'

She gently strokes my cheeks, and kisses my breasts, 'What kept you?'

I roll my eyes in disbelief. We lie hand-in-hand on the bed, enjoying the hot sun on our bodies. I am content with her. She is naturally exceptionally beautiful. I want to spend the rest of my life with her. My thoughts turn to lockdown. I'm frail, sick, vulnerable, forced to stay indoors. I sunbathe with her, make sweet angelic love to her upon our crumpled bed, then whisper naughtily to her,

'I hope you packed my bikini.'

My girl glances at me, smiling, 'As if I'd forget. Honestly! What do you take me for?'

She takes me in her arms and holds me tight, stroking my hair, smothering my lips with kisses,

'My true love, girl,' I murmur, drawing her naked body, snug and close to mine, 'My true love.'

Ever since I was a little girl I have been frightened of the dark, things that go bump in the night, faces at the window, black mirrors, that sort of thing. I write about them – dark, erotic fantasies. Those of you who know me, and read me, will understand why. You see, I enact them with her. We live out my dreams. Fantasies are our life. Nightmares are my death…

IS IT TODAY?
SEXY CANDID PROVOCATIVE DISTURBING

HJ Furl subjects disarmingly vulnerable characters to distressing conflict in a world of isolation and controversy. A filthy glue-sniffing girl begs you for help at dusk. A racist mother and her young children face certain robotic annihilation. Chaos breaks out on a long-haul flight when a tourist is incapacitated by bugs. Unclad soldiers hunt down a ruthless insurgent. A widower wanders through the wilderness searching for his dead wife and little boy. A male and a female contestant fight a beast in the deadliest game of chance in the world. A schoolboy is challenged to a cruel dare by a bully. Thrill seekers are infected with a deadly virus in their remote jungle retreat. An airman is fated by a mysterious wartime dancer. A three-year-old girl goes missing presumed dead in a blazing inferno. A car crash victim stalks a gigolo hell-bent on revenge…

Is It Today? they meet their fate?

What will **you** do when the harsh realities of modern life become too much for you to bear?

Will fantasy be your only salvation?

Is It Today? is my first devastating anthology of short stories, available from Amazon.

About the Author

I LIVE IN A REMOTE lighthouse on the coast with my two Siamese cats, a robot, and live-in lover. When I am not busy dreaming, I comb the beach for unusual shells and your plastic waste, saving stranded marine mammals. Of indeterminate age, I love to swim in the ice-cold ocean to keep myself looking young.

HJ

May 2021

Twitter: @furlhj

Website: www.isitodayhjfurl.com

Blog: www.hjfurlswritersblog.com